THE
SONS
OF
THESTIAN

M.E. VAUGHAN

MAG MELL
PUBLISHING

First edition published 2015 by The Zharmae Publishing Press
This edition published 2016 by Mag Mell Publishing
Winchester, Hampshire.
Great Britain
www.magmellpublishing.com

ISBN 978-0-9956149-0-1

To find out more about The Harmatia Cycle world, visit:
www.harmatiacycle.com

Printed and bound in Great Britain by Clays Ltd, St Ives plc

In loving memory of my Maman,

I promised I'd write you a book without any blood, magic, or violence.

I'm sorry.

x

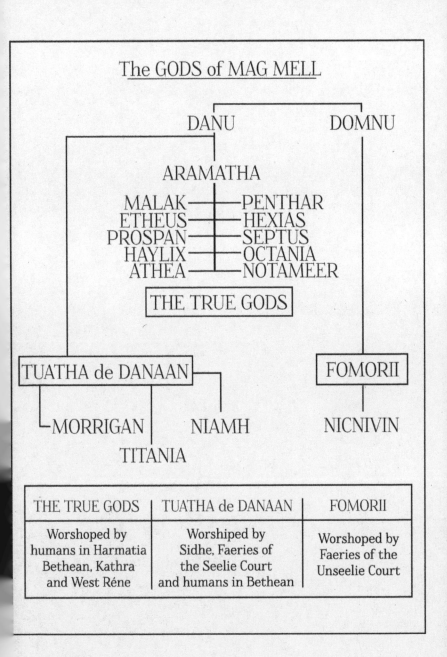

The GODS of MAG MELL

DANU — DOMNU

ARAMATHA

MALAK — PENTHAR
ETHEUS — HEXIAS
PROSPAN — SEPTUS
HAYLIX — OCTANIA
ATHEA — NOTAMEER

THE TRUE GODS

TUATHA de DANAAN — FOMORII

MORRIGAN — NIAMH — NICNIVIN

TITANIA

THE TRUE GODS	TUATHA de DANAAN	FOMORII
Worshoped by humans in Harmatia Bethean, Kathra and West Réne	Worshiped by Sidhe, Faeries of the Seelie Court and humans in Bethean	Worshoped by Faeries of the Unseelie Court

PROLOGUE

"For this, there will be blood."

"Run, damn you, run!"

The moon was a sickle in the sky, and darkness feasted. In the deserted streets, two figures stumbled through the night and ran, framed by the bolted doors and accusing shutters that loomed either side. Above them, the clouds reared like the shattered columns of a broken heaven, and there was a stillness in the air—a stillness like death.

Jionathan shot a quick look over his shoulder to the empty road behind. He was running out of time. It wouldn't be long now before hooded figures were flocked around them. Or worse, creatures of nightmare—the Night Patrol in all their terrible glory. Jionathan's companion stumbled and collapsed against the wall of a house, his breath curling in the cold air.

Along the cobbles, black tendrils reached out greedily, snapping at their heels, as if the shadows themselves wanted to engulf them. Jionathan darted back to his comrade and grabbed him by the arm. "Move, you fool," he urged desperately, his body lurching forward as the other's knees buckled. "Damn you, Rufus, no!" Jionathan seized him by the chest and heaved him up. Rufus shook his head meekly, eyes shut in resignation. "Get up—*get* up!" Jionathan's voice dipped with fear, the sound of footsteps echoing ever closer down the narrow streets. They wouldn't be alone for long. "You're going to get us killed! Get up! Rufus, get up, or by the gods I will leave you, I swear!"

Rufus gave a long moan as the first roar erupted into the night, sending tremors through Jionathan's body. The ground and the windows rattled, almost as if they, too, were fearful.

At the sound, Rufus found his feet, terror rekindling his waning strength. Hurriedly, he and Jionathan continued, feet catching clumsily on the stones of the slim pathway. The beast roared again, distant, but piercing.

Breaking into an open square in the Southern Quarters, the pair stood caught by the web of sound as the bells began to toll above them, marking the start of curfew.

Jionathan's gut jolted with urgency—he'd thought he had more time, but the night had crept up on them.

Rufus smothered his ears with the palms of his hands, as if trying to defy the menacing bells, and Jionathan searched desperately for shelter. No one would dare open their doors to them now, not for bribe or threat. It was too late.

Suddenly, from across the square, Jionathan spotted an open doorway to an empty guardhouse. The guardhouses were scattered all through the city, and were usually manned during the day. A few years ago, a sleepy set of guards would have been occupying the space at night too, watching out for drunks, thieves, and troublemakers, but since the introduction of the curfew, no other soul dared to be out after the bells had tolled. When curfew fell, the streets belonged to the Night Patrol.

Determined, Jionathan seized Rufus by the elbow, and pulled him across to the guard hut. He forced him through the stout door, and bundled him beneath the table. Rufus began to fight vainly, but the drug had made him delirious, and Jionathan had no trouble restraining him, pushing him against the wall. Rufus growled, and Jionathan shushed him, grey eyes darting in all directions as he listened for footsteps.

"Stay here," he said, as Rufus's head lolled back, the opium taking its toll. "Keep quiet or they'll find you...and the gods help you if they do." Jionathan stepped away and straightened. Rufus made one last valiant attempt to reach for him, but his arm fell short, and he slumped back defeated. Jionathan prayed he would keep still and silent.

Moving to the doorway of the hut, Jionathan listened out. He could hear the footsteps again, and for a moment he deliberated on what to do. If he hid with Rufus until morning, he stood a chance of slipping out of the city when curfew ended. But no, he knew better—there were too many hours until sunrise and the Night Patrol would follow his trail to the guard hut eventually. Zachary would sniff him out. And if they found Jionathan, they would find Rufus, who was in no state to defend either of them.

Jionathan cursed, the familiar, bitter taste of failure already on his tongue. This was the furthest he'd ever gotten, and he'd be damned if he let this opportunity get away from him now. He had to escape. He had to.

As he set off back into the city, another roar pierced the sky, catching Jionathan off guard. He turned and fled in the opposite direction, leaving Rufus in the safety of cover.

Breaking headfirst into the streets, Jionathan tore through the lower districts. He'd left his sword and provisions at the wall, but there was no time to fetch them now. If he was going to reach the gate, he had to forfeit unnecessary detours.

A sudden flash of red burst behind his eyes, and he ducked his head as a something sleek and black rushed through the air above him, swooping down. Zachary had found him.

Jionathan darted right, straight through a small opening in the wall, trying to cut through the city to the gate quicker. Squeezing his way between the buildings he broke out into the parallel street and sprinted away. He could hear the beat of Zachary's wings close by, and knew the monster was hovering above him, watching.

Jionathan didn't bother to look around. Zachary was almost impossible to see in the dark, and without any real moonlight to reflect against his black scales, he blended almost perfectly into the night.

A sudden rush of air on his back was the only warning Jionathan got when Zachary swooped in again. Jionathan threw himself to the ground, his body aching as he hit the stone. Zachary's talons grazed his shoulder.

"Argh!" Jionathan seized the severed skin, blood—hot and thick—swelling out between his fingers. From somewhere down another street, came a wolf-like howl, and then another from behind, the night coming alive with noise. The smell of blood was drawing them in.

Blocking the road ahead, Zachary hovered in-front of Jionathan, his wings beating up dust. His onyx eyes looked oily, and gleamed as he watched Jionathan stagger to his feet.

"Well done, you've caught me again, Zachary," Jionathan goaded, baring his teeth. "Shame you never extended the same effort for Sverrin's killer."

The comment earned him the reaction he'd hoped for. Zachary's anger was tangible in an instant, a cold fury illuminating his lightless eyes. He rose up into the air, and then he folded his wings and dove down toward Jionathan, preparing to scoop him up. Jionathan held his ground, brash and fearless until the last moment, where he dove suddenly to the side. Zachary, unable to pull back, collided with the ground, and Jionathan took his opportunity and ran.

From the castle far behind, another roar erupted, and Jionathan almost sobbed. The city's veins were alive with monsters, but it was the creature at its heart that he truly feared—a creature so vile, so alive with hatred and hunger that the mere thought of it made his blood run cold.

Up above the bells ceased their ringing, and Jionathan

4

knew he'd run out of time. Breaking out into the main street he sprinted hopelessly toward the looming gates, but they had long since closed. Reaching them he slumped, small against the vast structure that stood tall and proud, golden spires thrust into the heavens. With a sob, he slid to the floor, running his hands down the iron wall that separated him from his freedom. "No!" His voice broke, and he whimpered. "No…"

All around, he saw them approaching, but he was too exhausted by defeat to care. What was one boy against the Night Patrol?

Jionathan rested his head against the gate and watched from the corner of his eye as Zachary landed a few strides away, morphing from his dragon-like shape into a humanoid figure.

In the past Jionathan might have put up a fight, but his body seemed too heavy now to even perform that meagre task. Instead he watched as Zachary approached, his black Magi robes sweeping along the dusty road as he removed his hood with a familiar, merciless smile.

"Now then, Your Highness," Zachary greeted softly. "Shall we return to the castle?"

Jionathan dropped his head and closed his eyes in defeat.

CHAPTER 1

"You 'ear the chase las' night?"

The guards were talking again. From where he was still hiding under the table, Rufus drew his stiff legs in, cursing as one of the guards took a seat, muddy shoes a breath away from Rufus's own.

"The Night Patrol were howling something awful," the other guard muttered. Rufus gritted his teeth, bunching himself in tighter as the first slouched, leisurely, scratching his bulging belly. The pair seemed to be in no great hurry to begin their morning patrol and, for Rufus, who'd been trapped as he was for near an hour, the delay was becoming increasingly dangerous. "Who's dead, do you know?" the second guard persisted. "It's not always easy to tell when the Patrol are done."

Leave! Rufus thought, teeth gritted as his stomach gave an unruly gurgle, burning. It wouldn't be long now before he was discovered. And when he was, the guards would take one look at him, wretched with the careless stench of alcohol, and throw him straight in the stocks for drunken misconduct. Rufus's stomach rolled at the prospect, and he pressed his fist to his mouth as it gave another unhelpful gurgle, louder this time.

"N'one. Well…that I know of, 'least." The guard at the table—a

Corlavite by accent—didn't hear Rufus's discomfort, or if he did, accounted it to his comrade.

"*Oh*? You mean there were survivors?"

There are never survivors. Cease your chatter and leave, Rufus thought, angrily. All it would take was for the Corlavite to stretch his leg or drop something and Rufus would be at their mercy. Worse, he'd have no way of explaining himself, either. Try as he might, Rufus couldn't recall how he'd come to be in the guard hut in the first place, let alone under the table. He vaguely remembered running, and feeling sick, but nothing else. He touched a hand to the back of his head and winced, his skull thundering. His hair was matted with patches of dried blood. He'd been bottled, of that at least he could be sure.

"Survivors—hah!" The Corlavite laughed abruptly, making Rufus's ears ring. "None to date. No, i'was that lil' bugger Jionathan last night, fleein' the city."

"Again?" The second guard also took a seat. Rufus pushed his hand harder to his mouth, and bit his knuckle.

"Aye, was nearly out this time too."

"Malak's tits—what's he running from?" the second guard grumbled. "He's the Prince of Harmatia, he's fed off golden plates, sleeps in a bed warm and soft as a woman's touch, and has enough pretty handmaids in the castle to keep any man happy. What's he want out *there*?"

"It's all for attention, if y'ask me," the Corlavite replied. "You 'ear the eldest daughter of King Markus also ran off? Lost herself in the Myrithian Forest."

"These bloody nobles." The second guard stretched his leg out, his boot precariously close to Rufus's groin. Rufus winced, pushing himself back as far as he could go.

A sudden crash from the opposite wall caused the guard to jerk to his feet, almost kicking Rufus in the process. "What was that?"

"Came from outside." The Corlavite also stood and together

the pair approached the narrow window carefully, allowing Rufus to slip out from beneath the table and straighten his folded form.

He brushed himself down with relief, ironing out his clothes and, seeing that the guards still blocked the doorway, waited a moment for effect before making his presence known.

"Is it wise to be speaking of your future King in such a manner?" Rufus asked, with all the pomposity he could muster. If he played the lord they were more likely to overlook his tousled state. The guards whirled around, drawing their swords. Rufus didn't falter—he'd been threatened with worse, *by* worse. "After all, his agents might be anywhere at any time."

The men paled as they took in the sight of his robes, the uniform identifying him as a Magi of the King. Of course, neither of them knew that Rufus hadn't appeared before them by way of some dark art, but had been crouched surreptitiously beneath their table all morning. Tall and dark haired, Rufus was already an imposing figure, and he used that to his advantage now, looming over them as the tension rose.

"Milord." Both guards bowed, and he waved them off impatiently, taking a stiff step away from the accursed table.

"My good men, please—*please!*—straighten yourselves. Why, you look near frightened to death."

"Milord, forgive us our words. We meant no disrespect to the Prince," the first began, but Rufus silenced him with a single finger.

"Now, come, come—I tease, that is all. There is no need for such alarm. After all, as a Magi, it is not my duty, nor my sworn obligation to name and punish traitors of the realm..." Rufus drew off thoughtfully. "Wait," he reconsidered. "No, no I am mistook. It is the other way around, is it not? Apologies, my friends. Please—panic."

Both guards began to tremble, stammering excuses and pleas. The sentence for treachery was public execution, and on the wheel, no less. Rufus raised his hands in apology, giving the pair a guilty smile.

"Enough." He abandoned the aristocratic tone—it had served its diversional purpose. "I can only be so cruel. Your words weren't treacherous, or even dishonest. Take courage, you're no more traitors than I am. *Please*, I'm sorry, don't look so frightened. It was a dark jape, nothing more. I'm sorry."

At the change of his tone, both men exhaled, shooting each other nervous glances, relieved but still on edge. Rufus took the opportunity to seize a confiscated bottle of wine which was set on the table, and took a long, thirsty swig. He'd swallowed at least a third of the bottle before he remembered his audience.

"Apologies," he said dryly, wiping his mouth with the back of his hand. "It's been a very long night."

Neither of the men dared to object, and Rufus replaced the bottle, noticing that the Corlavite had begun to scrutinise him, as if trying to call back a memory.

He recognises me, Rufus realised. *No doubt from some childhood misadventure. Or perhaps some adulthood misadventure...*

It was time to go. Rufus had no intention of seeing the mood he'd so carefully crafted change from relief to suspicion.

"Well, I've taken up quite enough of your time, my friends. I bid you good day," he said, and sidling past the pair he stepped quickly out into open air, before they had a chance to question him.

Moving out into the square, Rufus spotted a group of mischievous children down the side of the street, playing with a rather crude toy catapult. They appeared to be preparing to propel a rather large, rotted looking cabbage toward the side of the guard hut. Rufus couldn't help but smile at them, even though the sunlight made his eyes water and the smell of rotting vegetables was enough to turn a healthy man's stomach. Not so very long ago, he might have been amongst those grubby children, though in truth he'd always preferred books to mischief making. Rufus probably owed his escape to these children, who'd no doubt caused the distraction that allowed him his freedom.

Of course, Rufus could have conjured his own means of getaway eventually, but time had been of the essence and his somewhat cloudy perspective of the world had left him with little more than a sarcastic temperament and desire for petty revenge. Thus he, a respectable Magi of high social standing, had regressed to being inadvertently rescued by a group of brats playing with rotten vegetables and a dubious-looking catapult. If Rufus had been anything like his fellow Magi, he might not have laughed at that, but he did, and lingered a minute longer to appreciate the truly putrid explosion as the cabbage collided with the guard hut.

Nodding to himself, Rufus turned and continued his journey, making his way down through the stone streets toward his home. Although the morning was in its full glory, the city's narrow network of roads were high walled, and blissfully shaded, much to the relief of Rufus's stinging head.

The city of Harmatia, capital of the country with which it shared its name, was the largest fortress in the whole continent of Mag Mell. Built on what was once rolling moors and marshland, it was fortified by two colossal walls that circled the entire city. Every hundred strides there was a lookout post, guards patrolling the inner and outer walls constantly throughout the day. Between these walls, the dregs of society lived in dusty, shadowy slums that saw very little sunlight.

Across to the west, at the head of the city, a colossal castle reached into the sky, parchment-yellow stone gleaming in the rising sun. The spectacular building connected with the inner wall and protruded out into the city, facing into an enormous courtyard and the royal gardens. Beyond this, separated by the Magi Towers, was the forum, the largest public space within the city, used for markets and executions. This spacious area aside, the city was tightly compact with pathways and side roads, which acted almost as a maze, should any enemies attack.

For Rufus however, the complex layout of the city was

as familiar to him as his own bedroom, and he made his way through the Southern Quarter with ease. Reaching his street, he stalked past several houses before stepping into a tall tailor's shop, hearing the familiar tinkle of a bell above his head as he opened the door. The darkness that greeted him soothed his aching head, and he sighed with relief, making his way through the shop past the bundles and stacks of clothes and linen.

"Who's there?" a voice called from up a narrow stairway behind the serving counter. Rufus slipped past it into the house beyond.

"Only me," he replied, his voice hoarse, and continued past the stairway into a small rectangular kitchen just beyond the shop. Up above he heard the groan of floorboards as he picked up a pot and filled it with water from the supply they had at hand.

The same male voice called out again. "Rufus?"

"In here," he replied without looking, as he hooked the pot above the fire and ran his hand, once more, through his filthy hair. He heard footsteps making their way down the staircase.

"We thought the Night Patrol got you."

"You sound *devastated*," Rufus said dryly.

"Where've you been all night?"

Rufus didn't respond and instead sank into one of the kitchen chairs just as his father appeared in the doorway.

"Rufus?"

Rufus peeked out from behind his fingers, his head in his hands, and slowly he raised his face. "Sleeping under a guards' table, apparently."

"Oh gods, boy, you're a mess." Torin clucked his tongue. "Here, let me see."

Rufus held still as his father leant in to examine him. Torin, like Rufus, was tall and slim in build, and had the same dark hair, angular cheekbones and a sharp jaw line which he kept unshaven. It was not uncommon for the pair to be mistaken for brothers, being only seventeen years apart, but Torin had a kinder face for

11

his warm, moss-green eyes. Rufus's own were too pale, the colour of winter—a cold and intense azure.

Gently Torin released Rufus's scalp. "You must've taken a bottle to the head, from the looks of you. Healing Septus, Rufus, it's lucky you've got that Magi healing of yours, or that might've really hurt."

"Hm, yes, lucky me," Rufus grunted.

His father ignored him. "Looks like you're going to have a few nice new scars to add to your collection, but it's all healed up otherwise. No need to call the physician, 'less you're feeling unwell?"

"No more unwell than I should do, with the Betheanian malady."

Torin barked a laugh, brushing a hand up to the stubble on his chin. "Aye, well that'll teach you for losing track of your bottle. You Magi may be able to drink a normal man dry, but you're not as immune as you'd have us all think. Now, we'd best wash those robes—can't have you going up-side looking so sullied, can we?"

"No," Rufus agreed, palming his eyes. They stung, his head spinning. "Would you close the shutters? It's too bright."

"It's a fine morning, Rufus-lad—young man such as yourself should be enjoying it," Torin chuckled.

"Oh Hexias give me strength."

"Call on the gods all you like, you little shite, the shutters are staying open." Torin gave him a tankard of water, and then offered him a swig of poitín to dull the pain. Rufus declined the alcohol. His father watched him curiously, arms folded.

"So, what kind of trouble did you run into this time then, huh? To get yourself in that state?"

"Etheus knows, I don't remember." Rufus massaged his temples. He longed for the feel of a pillow beneath his head— to lie suspended on a cotton mattress with a heavy quilt over his shoulders. But the hour of the day would offer him no such luxury.

"Rufus!" His father interrupted his daydreams with a clap of his hands, and Rufus realised he'd been dropping off to sleep where he stood. His father frowned in concern. "Maybe I *should* call for the physician?" he said, but Rufus shook his head sharply. Torin chuckled. "You're not still frightened of him, are you?"

Rufus glowered. "I'm not unwell, and I've *never* been frightened of him, I simply didn't like his method of diagnosis," he said, before—at his father's dubious expression—insisting, "it wasn't *fear*."

"Hah. My son, you used to squeal like a pig for the kill at the *sight* of him. We'd set you off to work with a face like sour milk," Torin cackled, and Rufus turned away sulkily. His youthful apprenticeship as a physician hadn't been a happy one, though far be it for him to complain—few achieved such honourable apprenticeships in the Southern Quarter. His master hadn't been a kind man, but Rufus had learnt a great deal. "Here, I'm sorry for laughing, no need to look so ashen," Torin said. "Let me heat you some water to wash with—you look like death."

Rufus forced his expression to brighten. "Thank you, but I've already seen to it." He motioned toward the pot he had set over the fire. Torin stared at Rufus with open disbelief.

"What," he began, exasperated, "by the power of Athea's arse, are you doing heating it like that, boy?"

"Excuse me?"

Torin motioned to the open window, where sunlight was still pouring merrily through. "It's just past the tenth hour, Hexias is now on the horizon, and Notameer above our heads."

"Yes," Rufus said. The sun god had certainly risen—Rufus's stinging eyes and thundering head could attest to that. Torin paced toward his son, and taking him by the chin, steered Rufus's eyes up to meet his gaze.

"How old were you?" he asked, "when you began to rifle through my books on magic? Five, was it? Even that?"

Rufus tore his head from his father's grip and stood, his arms tightly folded against his chest as he moved sullenly to a dark corner. "I was seven, father," he said softly.

"Seven my *arse*. At seven you'd read them all, and were demanding more. You'd barely found the tongue in your mouth, lad, and you understood those books better than I did—I who'd read and studied them over years." Torin threw his hands in the air. "Rufus," he fretted, "you have a *gift*. You're a Magi for Octania's sake! A base-born child, raised high on your sheer brilliance alone. The youngest man to ever be apprenticed, by the leader of the Magi no less, and the only one to've never undergone formal training. With a touch of your hand you could've filled that pot and boiled it instantly. And yet instead you took from our morning supply and placed it over the fire for several tedious minutes." Torin shook his head. "*Why*, Rufus? Why?"

Rufus shifted, dropping his gaze with discomfort. "I didn't think."

It was a feeble excuse. He'd hoped to delay this discussion, but his abstinence was becoming increasingly difficult to hide, especially from his parents. It wouldn't be long before Torin saw that Rufus had all but quitted magic entirely. It made Rufus want to laugh—a Magi abandoning the very art to which he sold himself.

Torin choked, "Was I cursed with a half-wit for a child?" he murmured to himself.

"If you were, the condition is entirely hereditary." Rufus crossed to the fire and checked the pot. The surface of the water was broken by furious bubbles and ripples. Rufus felt the heat on his face, and unable to resist, dipped a finger into the water. The temperature was comfortable on his reddening skin, and Rufus unhooked the pot and brought it to the table. His father winced as he watched Rufus pour the boiling water into a basin.

"One of these days that wash basin'll crack," Torin warned. "You always boil it too hot. These are made for us ordinary folk. You'll need to wash out of a stew dish."

Rufus looked apologetically down at the water, and dipping his hands into it, leant forward and splashed it across his face. Torin twitched as a droplet of water hit him on the arm, and he quickly covered the burn and rubbed it.

Rufus undressed quickly, removing his black, hooded robe first and throwing it over a chair. Beneath his outer robe, he wore a sturdy, high-collared jerkin, also black, though decorated down the front with brass buttons along the right folds where the cloth overlapped. Carefully, Rufus removed his shoes and dropped his trousers, fingering the buttons of the jerkin and undoing them, before slipping it off as well. This left him in only a plain white, cuffed chemise and his small clothes.

His chemise was the worst off, badly stained with drink and—Rufus grimaced—more blood. He tugged at the cuff of his sleeve, almost anxious to remove this final curtain to his abused body. He didn't like to think about what state he was in beneath it. Reluctantly, he pulled it over his head, and his father gave a long whistle.

"And I thought your *robes* were tarnished," he said, and Rufus observed the damage. As he'd suspected, his chest was dark and bruised, his wrists littered with scrapes and cuts, like he'd fallen numerous times and scrabbled away on his forearms. The worst was the pain in his back, and he showed it to his father, who smiled grimly.

"Looks like you took a fall, or maybe it was a chair to the back. How do your ribs feel?"

"Unbroken," Rufus assured.

"Small blessings. You'll hurt for some time, but it'll heal fine. Always does with you."

Rufus nodded and ran his hands through his hair, tugging gently at his fringe

His father frowned. "What is it?"

"Nothing," Rufus said, turning to his cleaning water.

Torin circled the table slowly, his eyes narrowed. "Rufus-lad," he warned, "the first thing you do when you're upset is toy with that hair of yours."

"I do no such thing." Rufus splashed the scalding water on his face, leaning over the basin. Torin took a seat at the table opposite Rufus and scrutinised him. Rufus rolled his eyes and, cupping a handful of water, he scrubbed it through his hair, washing it clean of blood and the smell of ale.

"Your mother won't be happy when she sees the state of you," Torin said absentmindedly, and Rufus winced. "Ah, that's what it was."

"I don't want her to fret."

"She'll fret regardless. We both will if you come home looking like that."

Rufus caught the towel his father threw to him and wiped himself down, scrubbing himself clean and dry. The water in the basin had turned a grimy yellow and made Rufus's stomach turn. He took it and, stepping out of the kitchen, emptied it out into the small garden at the back of the house. Returning, he made to pass through and go upstairs, but his father blocked his path. "Speak with me a while."

"I have to go, I've got duties. I'll be late as it is," Rufus said, but Torin stared him hard in the eyes, and Rufus sat down compliantly. Though Rufus was taller than his father now by three thumbs, he knew better than to defy him.

"Rufus, your mother and I are worried," Torin started, and Rufus grumbled, rocking back in his chair so it balanced precariously on two feet. "How old are you? Sit straight," his father ordered, and Rufus dropped forward again. "Staying out all night when you have duties in the morning, getting into fights, tempting the wrong side of the law—this isn't like you."

"Hexias give me strength," Rufus huffed. "You make me sound like a renegade. I don't know what happened last night, but I'm inclined to believe that it wasn't my fault."

"Whose was it then?"

"Jionat's," Rufus said, and his father's frown deepened.

"Prince Jionathan?"

"That's the bugger."

"Watch what you say," Torin scolded, and Rufus mounted to his feet, gathering his sullied robes in his arms.

"No I won't, it was probably him who bottled me—the little shit."

"You've no proof of that. And he'll rule one day, so mind your tongue."

"Aye, he'll rule," Rufus said. "And with the King—Aramathea bless him—in his current state, I can't imagine it'll be long in coming. And on that day, we're damned."

"You say things like that, and wonder why he doesn't like you Rufus." Torin sighed. "It's in his blood to rule, boy. Harmatia was promised to the Delphi many centuries ago, and his father married Éliane of the Delphi to see that promise fulfilled. Our great city's not what it was. This curfew's stifled more than a few livelihoods, and the Night Patrol've…well…"

Frightened half the city to death, Rufus wanted to say, but he held his tongue.

His father persisted. "Prince Jionathan may come as a salvation in these dark times. You can't argue with blood, my boy."

"Yes, blood's a powerful thing," Rufus agreed, moving toward the stairway. "But I meant that the Magi are damned, not the common folk. For all we've done to him, when Jionat ascends to the throne, he'll see to it we never practise magic again." He stopped at the base of the stairs and glanced back. "Oh, and father, Jionat doesn't *dislike* me," he said, catching his father's green eyes. "He *hates* me."

CHAPTER 2

Rufus had always found the great castle of Harmatia to be a building of quite indescribable beauty. Despite its magnificent size, there was such a dedicated perfection to the placing and carving of each stone that one couldn't help but admire it. Even Rufus, who'd known the castle intimately now for almost six years, found himself slowing his pace in order to appreciate the sights around him.

The details of the castle were precise, from the arches and pillars to the carved gargoyles and statues, which were so life-like that there were many stories of the figures coming to life in the dead of night. Of course, whilst such a momentous body might have taken centuries to build and perfect, much of the work owed itself to magic. The Magi, in their founding years, had helped to build the whole city, from the castle to the fortress walls, meaning that the work had taken a mere few decades to complete.

The castle itself was shaped almost in a square. The outermost wall fed out into the public forum, the ground level little more than an open corridor of pillars, guarded at all times. At each side was a 'Magi Tower', which connected beyond this to the

Academy, where young boys could acquire a formal education in magic. A handful of these trained candidates would then proceed to be apprenticed by existing Magi, who would continue their education and guide them into specialising. The criteria to become a Magi were very high—a minimum of eight years formal education by an approved association or teacher was the very least one usually needed to even be considered for apprenticeship. As such, many of the students wouldn't succeed in ascending to the formal role of Magi, but they'd still be recognised as having received one of the finest, if not most expensive educations in Harmatia.

Moving past the Academy, Rufus crossed a long courtyard toward the main castle entrance. Either side of him the castle's arms reached out, as if in a perpetual embrace. These wings housed many lords and ladies, who often kept smaller apartments in the city so as to remain close to the court. Rufus knew that several of the Magi lived amongst these walls.

Reaching the main body of the castle, Rufus ascended the stairs two at a time, passing the two Magi guards who stood to attention at the door.

He'd barely entered the bustling entrance hall when a voice called out to him, and he turned in time to spot a young man striding toward him. "Merle!" Emeric Fold waved, and Rufus started toward him. He was supposed to have helped Emeric that morning with a theoretical assignment for a presentation at the academy.

"Fold," he said, "I apologise, I—"

"No need," Emeric assured. "I saw to everything myself. You seem tired."

"I am," Rufus said, studying his companion. Emeric Fold was a Magi a few months older than Rufus, apprenticed to Marcel Hathely, Zachary's second-in-command. As with all Magi, Emeric's aging process had begun to slow with his increased use of magic and he, like Rufus looked closer to eighteen than twenty-three. Whilst Rufus hated it, Emeric wore his youthfulness well. He was a spry young man, with dark ash hair that gently curled atop his head and a pair of bright brown eyes. His slighter height and the natural curvature of his cheeks gave him an amiable appearance, and when he smiled he had dimples that any mother would be envious of. Despite his sweet appearance, he was one of the few that Rufus could name as a member of the Night Patrol. It felt strange to Rufus that a man with whom he was so readily acquainted could, at the bells of curfew, become such a creature of nightmare.

"Rufus, you really do look rather ill," Emeric noted with a gentle concern. "Are you sure you're well enough to be attending to your duties? If you wish to return home, I can make your excuses."

"No," Rufus said quickly. "You've done enough for me Emeric, thank you."

The smaller Magi pursed his lips in friendly disapproval, and then smiled. "If you're sure. The Queen's been asking for you."

Rufus was surprised. "Queen Reine has?"

Queen Reine DuBlanche was the King's first wife. The daughter of Bozidar La'Reina, King of Kathra, Reine had brought with her marriage an abundance of wealth to Harmatia, as well as furthering political stability within the two countries. Having been married and crowned Queen at Thestian's side during his coronation, she was now acting regent during his time of illness.

"What could she want with me?" Rufus asked.

Emeric winced. "The Prince," he replied, and Rufus sighed.

Thestian had taken a second wife several years after being crowned. Whilst the custom of having two wives was a rare one in Harmatia, being an old Kathrak tradition, it wasn't illegal. He'd married Éliane of the Delphi for love and had adored the son she gave him with all his heart. Jionathan of the Delphi had been named Prince only by formality, but following the sudden death of his older half-brother, Sverrin DuBlanche, the title of heir had fallen to Jionathan.

Needless to say, despite the fact that both Sverrin and Jionathan had been as close as any brothers might, Queen Reine held no fond feelings for the new-crowned Prince.

"Where is she?" Rufus asked, and Emeric directed him to the Queen's parlour, before excusing himself.

The door of the parlour was guarded when Rufus arrived, but even from outside Rufus could hear the sound of low grunts and hisses of pain. Rufus had a dark suspicion he knew what he'd find, and he approached wearily.

"Say it again," he heard the Queen command.

"I will not...run away...like a coward," a strained voice replied.

Rufus entered and was met by Queen Reine, who sat poised at a window seat, drinking tea from a delicate, porcelain cup. "Again," she said, sipping daintily, before glancing up to Rufus. Her face brightened at the sight of him, and he bowed, looking around the room to check his suspicions.

Sure enough, Jionathan was knelt upon the floor in the corner, his arms outstretched before him. Behind him, a guard held the Prince in place, whilst another held a cane. Jionathan caught Rufus's gaze and narrowed his already hooded eyes, his face tense. Without warning, the cane was brought down onto his wrists, and Jionathan clenched his jaw and exhaled forcefully.

"I said *again*, Jionathan," Reine repeated.

"I will not...run away...like a coward," Jionathan growled, his breath short and hard.

Rufus felt a flare of anger erupt in the pit of his stomach at this spectacle, but he caught his tongue before he said something foolish, and masked his expression. "Your Grace," he greeted, his voice cold and calm. Zachary had always told him that in the game of politics, your worst enemy was your emotions.

"Look at Hathely," Zachary had said. *"He has the monotony of a sleeping man, and speaks as much as one, too. No one suspects a sleeping man, Merle. Hold your tongue, check your temper, school*

21

your face, and then when you strike, it will be hard and without mercy."

The Queen's bronze eyes seemed to flash with an all-knowing mirth, and she curled a finger through her golden hair.

"Rufus Merle. You are late. I sent for you some time ago."

"I apologise, my Queen." Rufus bowed again. "Please allow me to make my amends."

Before Reine could answer, the crack of the cane cut across her, and Jionathan cried out sharply, and swore with such fervour that even Torin would have been impressed.

"Jionathan, such vulgar language is unacceptable in my presence. You are the Prince of Harmatia, not some Betheanian peasant," Reine chided sweetly, her voice even. Jionathan gritted his teeth, his arms shaking.

"When my father hears of this—" he began, but though his voice was strong, Rufus could hear how tired and beaten Jionathan was beneath his façade

"When the King hears of this, he will be wholesomely glad you received an appropriate punishment for yesterday's misbehaviours," Reine responded, taking a steady sip of her tea. Jionathan grew still, his face ashen, and suddenly Rufus found himself once more in the streets of Harmatia, the darkness looming above, the monsters at his heels.

"You're going to get us killed! Get up! Rufus, get up, or by the gods I will leave you, I swear!"

Rufus jolted as the memory dissipated. He put a hand to his forehead and released a shuddering breath, his body quivering under the sudden fear which had flooded, unbidden, over him. In an instant he remembered Jionathan's frightened eyes, the sound of bells, and the footsteps of the approaching enemy. And then the memory, as sly as a fish, slipped from his grasp, and his eyes focused once more on his feet.

What was that? he wondered, and tugged at his fringe. His stomach rolled, and he pressed his fingers to his lips, unsure of whether it was caused by the drink or his fear.

"Pray, tell me, Lord Merle. Have you heard about this?" The Queen turned to him with glee, and Rufus schooled his expression, swallowing down the bile in his throat.

"About what, Your Grace?"

"Why, the Prince's behaviour."

Rufus chose his words carefully. "It's my understanding the Prince tried to leave the city last night."

Reine laughed. "Delicately put. Yes, he did. Spent the evening hiding out in the slums with the dirt, like a common criminal— oh! But I apologise, Lord Merle." She put her hand to her mouth, covering her smile. "You hail from the slums, do you not? I meant no disrespect."

Rufus felt his throat tighten. "I was raised in the Southern Quarters, Your Grace," he corrected calmly.

"Ah, yes, of course. And remind me, what is it your parents do?"

"My father tailors, Your Grace. My mother is a midwife."

"Most respectable occupations." She nodded. "You are not the son of some common whore, then?"

"If I am," Rufus responded, before he could help himself, tongue hot in his mouth, "she was a very pretty whore."

Reine raised her eyebrows and gave him a sweet smile. Rufus mimicked it with one of his own. From the side, Jionathan squirmed against his captors, and Rufus addressed the Queen once more.

"Your Grace, if you might forgive me, the reason I was late is that I was speaking with Lady Éliane. She's requested that her son join her. It's my understanding she'd like to discipline him herself."

"Lady Éliane?" Reine feigned surprise. "I was not aware that she had left her chambers these last few weeks. The poor dear does suffer terribly with the baby, but having a child at her age is, well...brave, shall we say?"

23

Rufus saw Jionathan pale further, dropping his eyes down, and Rufus swallowed his anger at the unspoken instigation.

"*Show nothing, Merle,*" Zachary had said. "*Show nothing, and you lose nothing.*"

"She felt much stronger today," Rufus said, "and called me to her chambers. I was sent to fetch the Prince direct."

"So the Lady uses Belphegore Odin's little protégée as a messenger dog?"

"I do my duty as it's required of me."

The Queen considered him. "Well, far be it from me to deny a mother her son..." She gestured for Rufus to do as he would. "See him there, and then accompany him to his chambers. He is not to be left unattended."

Rufus nodded and stalked to the Prince, who dropped his arms in relief. The guard didn't release Jionathan's shoulders, and Rufus fixed him with his coldest stare.

"You'll excuse me, sir, if I ask that you release my charge," he said, and even the guards in the doorway shifted with discomfort. The Magi had always been highly regarded, and equally feared. Now with the presence of the Night Patrol, however, people never knew whether the Magi they slighted, would be the same Magi to corner them one black night, and eat them alive.

The guard released Jionathan rapidly, as if he'd been burnt, and stood back against the wall. The Prince straightened, rolling his shoulder. Rufus watched the movement carefully, drawing on his limited medical knowledge. Whilst the movement indicated there were no broken or dislocated bones, from a gap in the collar, the Magi spotted a bandage and frowned.

That'll have been Zachary, he thought sadly. Jionathan stood, and Rufus drew back.

"If you'd follow me," he gestured toward the door, but Jionathan had already stalked past him. Rufus ground his teeth and, bowing to the Queen, followed the boy.

It took him very little time to catch up with Jionathan, whose stride offered no challenge to Rufus's naturally long gait.

"I shan't expect any thanks from you, then," Rufus muttered as he came up alongside the Prince.

"I haven't heard any similar words from you, Rufus. Don't try me," Jionathan bit back, and attempted to stride ahead. Rufus lengthened his step with ease, and kept pace. Jionathan scowled, fixing his eyes ahead.

The Prince hadn't always had a temper. Once, he'd been a kind and compassionate boy, full of love, wonder, and empathy. But the years and trials had mutated Jionathan's passionate nature to something more aggressive and intense, and Rufus wasn't unaccustomed to being on the receiving end of a sudden, burning burst of anger.

Whilst deeply unpleasant, these heated turns never lasted long and often ended with the Prince looking exhausted and lost. It was those times that Rufus knew his presence was needed the most, even if it was unwanted.

Moving past a servant, who ducked her head and rushed out of the away, Jionathan began to slow, his clear, grey eyes, like tarnished silver, glazed in thought. Rufus checked his own stride accordingly, and watched the Prince with silent concern. There was sense of defeat in the slump of Jionathan's shoulders. His thick, curly mane of walnut hair hung limply around his face, and was dusted lightly in white chalk and dirt. Rufus had always found Jionathan to be a little wolf-like—lean and powerful. Yet now there was such a fatigue in his face, the look of a man weary with failure and weary with life. It might have alarmed him, but Rufus had seen this depression forming for some time now, like an icicle growing in winter. The years had changed the Prince, and not for the better.

"That's not the way to my mother's chambers."

Rufus faltered in his path as Jionathan stopped. "Excuse me?" he asked, and Jionathan's frown deepened.

"My mother," he said. "She sent for me."

For a moment Rufus was lost, and then he recalled his lie. "Oh. Yes, I see. No, I'm afraid she didn't. That was a cunning lie I told to get you out."

"A lie? You lied to the Queen?" Something close to a smile appeared on Jionathan's lips, rare and grateful.

"Of course, though perhaps if you had *some* powers of self-preservation..."

"I told you not to start." The smile disappeared, and Jionathan started once more, pacing ahead. Rufus persisted behind him. "Why are you following me?"

"Those were my orders," Rufus said, and once more Jionathan attempted to storm ahead. "Oh don't be so obstinate, Jionat."

"It's Jionathan," the Prince corrected tersely. Rufus ignored him.

"If you think refusing to be civil will deter me, then you seriously underestimate how stubborn I am."

"What do you *want* from me, Rufus?" Jionathan groaned.

"First, perhaps some gratitude."

Jionathan stopped short. "And you think you have earned that, do you?"

When Rufus didn't reply, Jionathan carried on ahead, Rufus trailing close behind. He'd never been one to give in easily. In fact, Rufus was famed amongst his peers for being notoriously relentless and 'unsociably stubborn' in his commitment. He'd once even thrown himself off the top of the Magi towers just to prove that—with the right manipulation of wind and air—he could. Rufus remembered the horror in his master's eyes and the way Lord Edwin, head of the Healing Sect, had clutched at his throat like he'd forgotten how to breathe. And Zachary, of course, laughing gleefully as Rufus landed and rolled awkwardly on cushioned impact. Rufus could still remember Zachary's words.

"I have gained a brother whose brilliance has made him stupid! Praise the gods, that madness will inherit Harmatia long before it descends to mediocrity."

Rufus might have smiled at the memory, but the liberal days of his magic use were gone, and thinking back to those happy times made it difficult to breathe.

"I thought I might find you together." A voice startled both Jionathan and Rufus from their thoughts. Éliane of the Delphi, the Lady of the Harmatian court, approached them slowly from an adjoining corridor to the right.

Éliane was a woman of exceptional beauty—tall, elegant and with long, sun-kissed hair, she was lovely in every way. Rufus had not seen her in some time. The late stages of a difficult pregnancy had limited her movements, but as she stepped slowly toward them now, it was with great poise and posture. Her long blue gown whispered along the floor. The colour matched her eyes—a pale, summer sky.

"Lady Éliane." Rufus bowed, and from his side Jionathan's face brightened with joy.

"Mother," he greeted and, moving to her, he embraced her carefully, mindful of her unborn child. "You should be resting."

"I had an audience with your father. He wants to see you."

"You should have had a page fetch me then, rather than come yourself," Jionathan scolded gently, as Éliane brushed a hand through her son's curls.

"I lie in bed all day waiting for nightfall so that I may repeat the process, my love. There's no sense to me being confined to my room, especially when I desired the walk." She kissed his forehead tenderly, before darting her eyes up to Rufus. As their eyes met, Rufus felt a shiver run through him. There was always such an intensity to Éliane's gaze that Rufus was never sure whether she simply distrusted him, or genuinely loathed him. Even Emeric, having witnessed one such exchange, had demanded *what* Rufus could have possibly done to make the Lady look at him like that.

"Like she's trying to set you on fire with her eyes alone," he'd jibed, and Rufus had agreed.

Despite her obvious and unwarranted contempt toward him,

Rufus had always been drawn to Éliane. He maintained a private fancy that one day she'd forgive him the unspoken wrong he'd committed, and that they'd take a walk in the gardens and speak until the skies grew dark. Looking back to her cold eyes now, Rufus resigned himself to the fact that if such a day ever came, it wouldn't be soon.

"Go ahead," Éliane said to Jionathan. "Your father is expecting you."

Jionathan grew still, a look of unease passing over him as he silently obeyed and turned, starting toward the King's private wing. His mother watched him with a soft sigh, resting her hands on her belly. Rufus moved to follow the Prince, but Éliane touched his arm with a stern look.

"I'm to accompany him—"

"He knows his own way," she said firmly. Rufus looked warily after the Prince and concluded that there was little risk of the boy disobeying a direct summons from his father. No doubt, the Prince would find himself with a new escort when their meeting was done.

"Does the King know?" Rufus asked.

Éliane bowed her head. "He may be sickly, but he's no fool." She started slowly toward her chambers, and Rufus fell into step with her.

"Then His Majesty is angry?"

"His son and only heir has once more attempted to flee the very city he is soon to rule. The news was unlikely to delight him."

Rufus gave a short, humourless laugh and folded his arms. "Did you go to lessen the blow?"

"That is a mother's duty, but the King is a fair man. He understands that Jionathan is troubled—ah!" Éliane drew to an abrupt halt, her hands clutched to her stomach.

Rufus ducked his head to examine her face. "Are you in pain?"

Éliane gave him a patient smile, her eyes squeezed closed with discomfort. "The child is active today," she eventually said, and

Rufus gently laid his palm on her belly. From beneath his fingers he could feel the baby kicking and moving, and he beamed as he felt a tiny hand press against his own.

"Calm, little one," he whispered. "Be calm." The hand gently retreated from his palm, and the baby grew comfortably still. A warmth filled Rufus like a gentle happiness, and then Éliane spoke.

"Thank you," she said.

He retracted his uninvited hand quickly. "I apologise."

"No, no. You calmed him," Éliane said, and Rufus watched her, his mouth dry. "I am sure you have many duties awaiting you. I shall not deter you from them, Lord Merle."

"I thank you, Your Ladyship." Rufus bowed his head, and turning he strode quickly back down the hall. He could feel her eyes trained to the back of his head all the way until he turned the corner.

⁓

The guards greeted Jionathan at the door and let him enter. Standing at the mouth of the chamber, he allowed his eyes to adjust to the stiff darkness of the room. He couldn't remember the last time the shutters or windows had been opened—it seemed years ago now that the physicians had bolted them closed and plunged the dying King into darkness.

For Jionathan, the room was suffocating. It was thick with sickness, uncomfortable heat, and worse, the ever lingering presence of death that made it difficult to breathe. He hated it.

"Jionathan." A voice came from the gloom, soft and yet somehow powerful. It was said that Thestian could command an army in a whisper if he wished, such was the naturally authoritative and charismatic tone of his voice.

Jionathan remained still a moment. He could see the huge, silhouetted form of the magnificent bed only a few strides away, and he bit his bottom lip.

"Come here," Thestian ordered serenely.

Jionathan did as he was told and quietly approached his father's bedside, seating himself in a provided chair.

"Jionathan?"

"Yes, Father?" His voice was barely a murmur, dampened by the muffled air.

"Jionathan, you are my only remaining son." The statement was simple, and to the point. Thestian was not one to divert conversations, or tiptoe around a topic.

Jionathan shivered. "Mother will have another child soon. The physicians say it will be a healthy baby. I won't be the only one."

"Your mother is not young anymore. She knows the dangers, as do I. Physicians often make mistakes."

"Mother's in perfect health and the child will have just as much right to rule as I do."

Thestian stared at his son, and in the darkness Jionathan was able to make out the details of his father's face. Thestian's beard had grown long and unattended, flecked with more white and grey that Jionathan remembered. His skin seemed to sag a little, like damp rolls of cloth drying on a breezeless day, and his stormy grey eyes were outlined with dark, hollowing circles. In the lightless room the King seemed to glow white, like a ghost, and Jionathan found that, staring at him now, his voice died quickly in his throat.

"Are you jealous of your unborn sibling?"

"No, Father."

"Then why do you attempt to flee your home like a wronged convict? Why do you hate this land? You are the future King."

"I don't hate this land, Father. I love Harmatia, it's as much a part of me as my very soul. I'm not trying to flee the people, nor you, nor my mother. I'm not trying to flee from responsibility either."

"Then what do you run from? What has caused this frenzy

30

of desperation, that you should need to be dragged back to your *own* home, kicking and screaming like a child in tantrum?"

Jionathan winced. His father hadn't shouted, or even raised his voice, but the intensity of his words had been cutting. Jionathan wasn't sure how to respond. "Father, I…" He broke away, and took a deep breath, lowering his face into his hands. It was hopeless—he couldn't force an apology. He exhaled, and felt a steady weight against his head, his father's fingers brushing down to his face. He caught the King's eye. There was no blame there, merely confusion. "Father, I'm afraid," he whispered.

"Of what?"

"I don't know. I—I have terrible dreams, dreams which haunt even my waking hours, yet I can never remember them." He swallowed. "Sometimes it's as if I fall into a trance, I feel… danger—like a deer trapped in a den of wolves. I don't understand it, I can't rationalise it. All I know is that during these moments, I'm overcome with a need to escape. It's as if my very life depends on it—as if I were about to be devoured whole." He took a deep breath, steadying himself. "It's the Magi, Father. Their corruption taints the land. This city has become a feeding ground for those monsters, all because of what they preach to their apprentices. By night they ring the bells for the curfew, so that the Magi can practise transforming into monsters, led by that half-man Arlen Zachary. And should anyone mistakably cross paths with a Magi of the Night Patrol…Father, they're torn to shreds! They close the gates of the city in darkness, as if it were a pig pen, and chase stragglers through the streets, cornering and killing them. The things which have happened since you fell ill, Father, since Sverrin died—I can't even describe them to you."

Thestian paused, considering all that'd been said. "You are very quick to criticise, my son."

"I've felt the fear of being chased first-hand."

"Yet you survived. Surely then, the Magi must have control of their actions."

31

"All the more reason to punish them—they're murderers! Killing innocents!"

"They kill only those who break the laws of curfew."

Jionathan threw his hands in the air, his temper flaring. "So you would rule the people's lives?"

"Do not raise your voice to me," Thestian said calmly, and Jionathan hung his head, his fists clenched. "I have no control in this city any longer, my boy. I can do very little from this bed."

"But you're the King!"

"In title, yes, but I am dying now, and my power is fading fast. You must understand, Jionathan, I cannot protect you for much longer."

"You're not dying," Jionathan replied fiercely, and his father laughed for the first time. It was a painful sound.

"You are so innocent, my boy—promise me you will never be corrupted. When you are King, you may lift the curfew which the Queen has placed on the city. You may do all that you wish. But remember not to be too stubborn, and to heed the advice and council of others—the ability to listen is a virtue."

"Father, I can't…"

"Jionathan, you are destined to rule." Thestian's grey eyes shone, and Jionathan bit his bottom lip again. "You may flee this city if you are in danger of your life, you may do as you wish to preserve yourself, but the day will come when you *will* be King. I have named you as my heir, and this kingdom will not sit right until you are upon the throne. The years or days that may take are of no concern. You will rule, my son, as the Delphi were promised to. The city has waited centuries for you, and it can wait longer if it must. Do you understand?"

Jionathan gazed into the face of his father, his eyes a mirror of the dying man's own, and he knew the true meaning of his words. Slowly he nodded. "Yes, Father, I understand."

CHAPTER 3

Rufus stared dully at the text before him, his tired eyes lagging across the words. He'd been reading the same sentence for the past quarter hour now, unable to progress any further down the page. His head ached.

"By concentrating the manipulated element upon the punctured wound, the user may stimulate the body's core elemental system into producing a natural blood bandage at a swifter and more efficient rate." He groaned and rested his head in his hand, grimacing at a sudden loud bang to his left. The candles around him flickered dramatically as the door to the archives opened, and sunlight poured down into the grim darkness.

"Rufus, you're still here?" an elderly voice called to him, and a tall, wiry figure descended down the stone stairs.

"Francis," Rufus greeted the white-haired librarian as he moved toward Rufus's table, depositing a selection of books. Francis peered down at the page Rufus was reading.

"What's wrong with you boy, you've been on the same chapter for the last hour. You should have finished by now," he said, and Rufus shut the book with a grunt, leaning back in his chair.

"The words are swimming. I can't read them right."

Francis's eyebrows rose to his wispy hairline. "That's odd. I've never seen you have trouble with a book before." Francis leant forward and examined Rufus's face closely. "You drink too much," he stated. "It's infecting your mind."

"This damnable sunlight is infecting my mind," Rufus retorted, standing abruptly as he dropped the book on the table. "Well, what is it? Or did you just come here just to survey my incompetence?"

Francis bristled at Rufus's tone. "I chanced upon Lord Edwin and Lord Belphegore a few minutes ago. They were anxious to see you."

Rufus paled. "Where are they?"

"Upstairs, in the inner garden. But be warned, Rufus—there is sunlight up there, too."

Rufus fetched his outer robe, which he'd thrown across the opposite chair, and dressed himself quickly. "I'm sorry," he said. "I was rude. I'm angry with myself, not you. Forgive me, Francis?"

Francis couldn't help but smile, though Rufus saw him try to fight it. "Forgive you?" he chuckled, handing Rufus the sash to tie his robes. "I remember you when you barely came up to my shoulder, curled down here like some criminal in the night, reading books that weren't meant for your eyes. Tell me, boy, what sort of bookkeeper would I be if I made an enemy of a man with such a love of knowledge?"

"An incarcerated bookkeeper, if they ever discovered it was *you* who let me down here." Rufus clapped his shoulders. "You're a good friend, Francis."

Francis shooed him away. "Go, you drunkard. Your master is waiting."

Rufus climbed the stairs and, squinting, stepped out into the sunlit expanse of the Great Library. Built over a century ago, the building was quite unlike any other in Harmatia, several storeys high, with towering shelves, and a colossal dome in the centre of the building. The dome, in particular, was a sight to behold, pieced together with a mosaic of painted glass that filled the room with a spectrum of light and colour. The library housed three open floors, each one lined with shelves containing more books, scriptures, and scrolls than any other library in Mag Mell.

In the middle of the floor, below the dome, stood a large statue, commemorating the founder of the library, Horatio of the Delphi, Belphegore Odin's predecessor as leader of the Magi, and his master.

In the far corner a square section of the library had been left unroofed, so that natural sunlight poured down over an inner garden of luscious trees and vegetation, nourished by a natural spring in the centre. Rufus had always liked this little inner-garden, not least because there was a humbling quality about having something so modestly simple and natural included in the heart of something so vast and innovative.

It was here that Rufus found the two Magi he sought, sat together on a stone bench beside an impressive apple tree.

Morgo Edwin, leader of the Healing Sect, was a lean man with flaxen hair and a long, strict face. Before they'd been formally introduced, Rufus had always been wary of the man, who seemed to hold an air of intolerability. In truth, Edwin was deeply compassionate, and totally devoted to the care of others, putting everyone before himself.

When Rufus had shown a leaning toward learning to heal, Edwin had seen to it that Rufus received the appropriate material and tutoring to understand the complexity of what he planned to undertake. After all, whilst in ten years a Magi could become a master of wielding magic in combat, Edwin was a century and a half old and continued to insist he was only at the foundation of his healing ability.

"*Until I can revive a man from the jaws of any death, I will consider myself nothing more than a novice,*" he'd said one day to Rufus, and Rufus hadn't been sure whether he was joking or not.

At Edwin's side, the leader of the Magi, Belphegore Odin, saw

Rufus first and greeted him kindly. "Rufus." He stood, his arms open in welcome. Rufus, who'd feared the pair would be angry with him for his absence that morning, relaxed at the warm tone of his master's voice.

Belphegore, like Edwin, was not a young man. At a hundred and seventy years, he had somehow maintained a youthfulness about him that shone through the charisma of his smile and the natural energy in his step. Even for a Magi, who were naturally capable of living well up to three-hundred years, Belphegore had aged remarkably well and looked no older than fifty. The only indication of his true age was the deceptive colour of his hair and beard which were both white, and had been for as long as anybody knew him. He was a timeless figure, kind but authoritative, and Rufus admired him more than any man in the Magi. "There you are, we were starting to get worried."

"I apologise." Rufus bowed to the pair. He was taller than both, but still felt small in their presence.

"How are your wounds?" Edwin asked, his forehead pinched.

"My...my wounds?" Rufus said.

"Yes, we received some disturbing reports from last night that Prince Jionathan started a brawl. You were sighted with him, so when you failed to attend to your duties this morning..."

"My absence was the fault of my own incompetence." Rufus bowed again, unwilling to divulge the truth of the bottle cuts across his head. "Forgive me, Master, Lord Edwin. I'm fine..." He paused. "Bruised, but fine."

"It relieves me to hear it." Belphegore gestured for Rufus to straighten, leading him to the bench. He invited Rufus to sit, and then stood above him, making Rufus feel even smaller. "Perhaps there were some inaccuracies in the report. Can tell us what happened?"

"Last night..." Rufus ran his hand through his hair, his mind going blank. He still couldn't remember what had happened, or how he'd ended up in the guard hut. He was almost certain that it was Jionathan's fault—a bar brawl would explain exactly how he'd been bottled, and why he was covered in bruises. And yet, when Rufus thought of Jionathan's tired eyes, and the defeated sound of his voice, his throat constricted. Even if it was the truth, Rufus couldn't condemn Jionathan. He swallowed. "I was accompanying the Prince through the city for a walk. At dusk we were separated in a large crowd. I failed to reach him before the hours of curfew began. That's all I know."

The two senior Magi looked between one another.

"You are an honourable friend," Edwin finally said. They knew he'd doctored the piece for Jionathan's sake. Rufus ducked his head in shame, avoiding both of their gazes.

"I fear, Morgo, that that is all we are going to get out of him," Belphegore said in an almost congratulatory tone.

"Indeed, old friend," Edwin agreed. "And there are other matters that require my attention." He excused himself, giving a shallow bow to the pair before exiting the garden.

Belphegore touched Rufus's shoulder briefly, and smiled. "Take care," he said, and then followed Edwin, striding back into the library. Rufus waited until both were out of sight, and then slumped. He didn't like to lie, especially to those he respected most, but what else could he have done?

Sighing, he turned back to the apple tree before him. It had actually been planted in the garden by him, many years ago, under Belphegore's insistence. Rufus had grown it from a seed in the palm of his hands, during his trial, and Belphegore had decided to keep and nurture the tree as a sort of reminder to anyone else who might question Rufus's place among the Magi.

The entire fiasco had begun when Rufus was fifteen. Lowborn, but desperate to learn, he'd procured a student uniform from the Academy, and stolen into the library. To begin with, his visits had been innocent enough, but as his hunger for knowledge grew, Rufus became bolder. Unsatisfied with the available material, and desperate for more, he'd broken into the forbidden Magi archives. For two years he went undetected, devouring and memorising complex magical theory, until finally he was caught by the guards At first they thought he was an over-zealous student and were prepared to be lenient, but when it come to light that he wasn't even enrolled at the Academy, the charge had become a great deal more serious.

He was put before a Magi court and accused of the theft of knowledge and of being a spy. Rufus had defended himself passionately, insisting he'd only read the forbidden scriptures to satisfy his own desire to learn, and nothing else.

The Magi had been surprised by how much Rufus had understood of what he'd read, and when he was asked to demonstrate his ability, Rufus had taken the opportunity to show the beauty of creation, using a technique of his own invention.

He remembered it vividly. Lady Éliane had been amongst the spectating audience, with the young Prince Jionathan. Rufus, seeing that Jionathan had finished a rather juicy-looking apple, had asked for the core. He'd then cradled it in his hands, and using himself as a medium for all four elements, had carefully adjusted their concentrations and willed the pip to take life. And it had, a tiny sapling growing from the core until the roots fell between Rufus's fingers, and the tree blossomed and took flower.

At this display, Belphegore had passed his sentence: Rufus was to remain within the Magi as his second apprentice. The statement had brought with it a chorus of astonishment and incredulity, topped by the sound of gleeful laughter. For, from his seat, Arlen Zachary had cackled at the disbelief and disapproval of the nobles around him. From what Rufus understood, Zachary himself had been an unobvious choice as Belphegore's first apprentice, and he'd reveled to see his master beguile the crowds again. Rufus remembered Zachary leaping down, throwing a welcoming arm around his shoulder and addressing the onlookers with a glee— there was nothing he liked more than provoking a response.

"*What can I say? I've always wanted a brother. This odd little one will do me well!"* he'd said.

"You're hiding something," a familiar voice, colder now than in his memory, spoke, breaking Rufus from his thoughts. Rufus tensed, his mouth drawing into a thin line.

"I'm always hiding something," he replied, turning to the figure beside him, leant against another tree, a book in his hands.

"Oh, aren't we secretive today?" Zachary turned the page, his sharp eyes catching Rufus's own, before dropping back to the book. There was a menace in his face—a skin-deep smugness—and Rufus folded his arms protectively, standing. "Why did you lie to our master?"

Rufus's gut tightened, but he kept his face impassive. Zachary had all the traits of a bloodhound—he could smell even the slightest fear. "Lie? About what?"

Zachary shook his head. He was a tall man, only a little shorter than Rufus himself, and although lean for his proven strength, was noticeably more muscular. Rufus, in contrast, despite a set of wide shoulders, was lithe and perhaps even a little scrawny beneath his height. Zachary always seemed to tower over him. Once, that'd been comforting. Now it was frightening. "I smelled you on him—the Prince. I know you were with him last night, for much longer than you claim. And I know you were close when we trapped him at the gate." Zachary's light eyes, the hazel green of early autumn leaves, were fixed on Rufus, unblinking. Rufus put his hands behind his back, to hide their trembling.

"If you know, then why are you asking me?" he asked, and Zachary snorted.

"Why, indeed?" He smoothed back his ash-brown hair. He'd always worn it short and swept back, leaving his forehead clear and emphasising the strict line of his brow and the natural severity of his face. Rufus had once thought him handsome, but Zachary's honest smile had since become malicious, too dangerous to be considered attractive.

"Perhaps I wanted to give you a chance to confess, before I

called you traitor?"

"Your compassion knows no bounds," Rufus said, and Zachary chuckled faintly, an expression of cruel delight coming naturally to him.

"Oh Merle, my compassion is to go for a man's throat, instead of his gut."

"And mine, Zachary, is to call that compassion at all."

Zachary laughed openly, but the sound was cheerless and empty. "Do I sense a note of disapproval?"

"Who am I to question your senses?"

"Come, come—speak plainly now, we're friends, aren't we?"

Rufus arched an eyebrow. "Friend is not the word I'd use."

"And once we were so close," Zachary lamented mockingly, but for a moment Rufus thought he saw a genuine glimmer of regret in the other's eyes.

Yes, Rufus wanted to say. *We were friends once. Brothers even. I admired you. I cared about you. And then you became an animal. Then you became a monster.*

Zachary paused, almost as if he'd heard Rufus's thoughts, and his expression grew stony. "The world changes, Merle. Everything changes, and you can't stop that. All you can do is change it back." He put his hand on Rufus's shoulder as he passed, squeezing it, his voice oddly solemn. "Remember I told you that, if nothing else. Remember I did that, at least." And with that he departed, Rufus staring after him.

Francis, who had been spying on them through the foliage, waited until Zachary was out of ear-shot, before stepping out toward Rufus. He scrutinised the young Magi.

"What in Octania's name was that about?" he asked. Rufus didn't respond, running a hand up through his hair and tugging his fringe. Frowning, concern filled Frances's face, and he leant in hesitantly. "Is everything alright?"

Rufus nodded.

Frances raised his eyebrows, and then asked in a whisper,

"What *did* happen last night?"

Rufus was silent for a minute, and then started off toward the stairs. "That's what *I* want to know."

It was happening again, Jionathan could feel it. For almost two years now, he'd tried to fight this strange sensation as it came over him, but to no avail—it always triumphed eventually, and he was powerless to stop it.

He twitched and pressed his palms hard into his eye-sockets. Bright colours burst behind his lids and danced madly in a sickening twirl. He groaned and trembled, his forehead beading with sweat as he kicked out with a growl. It was no use, the hot rushing feeling was overbearing, and he could feel it taking over as he slumped back against his pillow. His fingers tightened into fists, which shook as the shooting strains passed through his body, making him convulse, his eyes rolling madly.

Fear. It was the only emotion he could name in the multitude of sensations—pure fear. The room seemed to contract, until it was so hard to breathe Jionathan felt like he was being smothered. Like his bones were soft and bendable, his limbs woolly.

The dancing colours formed into sudden images, which flickered before him, too swift to grasp. He saw his mother caressing her swollen womb, a song on her lips, and then she was lying bloodied in a bed, wailing. He saw his father sitting upright, shadowed in darkness, his face turning to stone until he was the effigy above a tomb. Jionathan saw a city fortress crumbling in a terrible earthquake, a vast flaming figure rising above it. He saw Rufus Merle marching through Harmatia, a great horde in his wake, his face set and war-torn. Then he saw Reine, her eyes bearing down on him as if he were something to consume. And with that came the roar of a beast, so strong it filled his skull to cracking point. He opened his eyes with a start.

For a minute he was petrified, and then the rushing feeling

was pushing against him once more, and he groaned, closing his eyes. His body was limp, and ached as if he'd been tossed among giant waves in a stormy sea.

He could hear Rufus outside of his room, consulting with the guards—no doubt trying to barter entry—and Jionathan gripped the bedcovers. The images had shattered, and once more there were bright colours in their stead, twirling and spinning menacingly, taunting him with their knowledge. He began to gasp, struggling to breathe. From beside him he heard footsteps.

"Jionat?"

He could feel Rufus hovering over him, concern pinching his voice, but when Jionathan tried to open his eyes, the room twisted sickeningly. The very fabric of reality seemed to be slipping from his fingers, and in an instant he seemed to part from his physical body. He rose up, like a ghost, and looked down on the room. Rufus was leaning over him, a hand pressed urgently against his face.

"Jionat? Jionathan, can you hear me?" Rufus demanded, and Jionathan considered himself. He could see his eyes rolling in their sockets, the perspiration peppered across his forehead shining like he had a fever. Each breath came out laboured and hard. Rufus had every reason to worry—Jionathan looked like he'd been poisoned.

Maybe, Jionathan thought, *I have.*

Rufus left Jionathan's side, striding to the door and throwing it open. "Find Lord Edwin at once—the Prince is taken ill! Go, the pair of you!" he shouted, and at the Magi's panic-stricken voice, both guards fled in search of the physician.

And suddenly Jionathan's opportunity became clear. As if waking from a deep sleep, he slipped back into his body and rose from the bed. Taking a hold of the candelabrum on the bedside table, he was upon Rufus before the Magi could turn. The first strike was too dull, and only sent Rufus reeling into the wall. Jionathan brought the candelabrum around again harder, wincing as he caught sight of the confusion and pain in Rufus's glazed eyes.

"Sorry," he said, and bludgeoned Rufus across the side of the head again. This time, Rufus dropped, blood seeping from his temple, and Jionathan wasted no time pulling off Rufus's outer robes. Working quickly, he wrapped himself in the Magi cloak, and then knelt at Rufus's side, hoisting him upright against the wall. He touched the wound and winced again. If Rufus weren't a Magi, it might have killed him. "I'm sorry, Rufus," he repeated, and then turning, fled from the room. If the guards did their job, Edwin would be there in a few minutes and could heal Rufus fully. For now, Jionathan's window of opportunity was getting smaller.

With the Magi hood up, shrouding his face, Jionathan made his way through the castle and out into the afternoon sun. In a dreamlike state he reached the main courtyard, keeping his pace even so as not to draw attention to himself. Only when he made it out into the forum did he begin to run, darting through the people and the market stalls. He judged that he had, at most, another ten minutes before the order was out to search for him.

Dashing down a narrow street, he sprinted across the cobbles. He'd left his sword and hunting armour in a bag the night before, hidden beneath some loose stones on the northern side of the city. They'd been set there for yesterday's escape, but Jionathan hadn't managed to reach them before he'd been caught by Rufus. Today, however, something felt different. He knew he'd make it out of the city long before Rufus had time to recover and come after him. Once out, Jionathan doubted the Magi would dare follow him beyond the gates. Rufus was too much of a coward for that.

I must go south, he reminded himself. *They can't send more than a few armed soldiers into Bethean without express permission from King Markus, and that could take weeks. It's my only chance.*

With his direction set, Jionathan skidded to a halt and made his way down a slim alley between two houses. He'd spent his childhood running through the city, playing an endless game of chase with Sverrin. Jionathan remembered how Sverrin would always be scolded for allowing his little brother to run amok through the streets, unprotected from dangers such as thieves or assassins. But in truth, Sverrin was never more than two steps behind Jionathan, and woe betide any man who crossed blades with the Warrior Prince.

Jionathan stopped beside the wall and surveyed his surroundings. Shrouded figures huddled in the corners, scuttling like ragged spiders between the overhanging rock shelters and the houses. He knew he'd go unnoticed here, as he knelt down and lifted several dusty bricks away from the ground. Brushing dirt away from a russet bag which lay hidden, he pulled the satchel up and reached inside.

Six years ago, Sverrin had announced that his hunting armour no longer suited him, and that its duty now lay in protecting the next warrior of the family. It hadn't fitted Jionathan for several good years, but now suited him snugly. Jionathan knew he could have had new armour at any time, but whenever he wore Sverrin's, it felt as if a part of his brother was protecting him even now, from beyond the grave.

Quickly he ducked down, and pulled the Magi robes away, slipping the leather armour over his body, and tightened the straps so that it fit close to his chest, over his chemise. Then he put his bracers on, fastening them around his wrists and, fitting his holster around himself, set his dirk into the back of his leather belt and slid his sword into the sheath at his side.

He patted himself down to make sure everything was secure, and then wrapped himself in the Magi robes once more, throwing the satchel over his shoulder. It contained within it a water flask, bread, a blanket, fire flints, a coil of rope to set traps, and a small pouch of gold. He could hunt for food, and the Myrithian Forest wasn't short of fresh springs. He would use the stars for navigation.

Moving again, he stalked quickly back up to the streets, making sure to stay within the shadows or pass through groups of people. He went unnoticed in the heaving masses.

With a grim smile he pulled his hood down further over his face. He could feel his heart galloping in his ribcage—he'd never succeeded in getting so far.

Up ahead a patrol of guards suddenly appeared, and Jionathan watched them warily, before skilfully moving, unnoticed, into a parting between two houses. He stepped out into a much less crowded street parallel to the previous and continued his journey, head down.

Rounding a corner, he drew to a halt, his mouth going dry. After so many failed attempts, Jionathan had lost the illusion that the gods would ever help him escape the city, and yet it seemed at last they favoured his cause.

In front of him the blacksmith straightened, passing his hammer to an awkward-looking assistant, who fumbled with the heavy tool. The horse tossed its black mane irritably, its bay coat gleaming in the sunlight as it shifted, muscles rippling. Freshly shoed, and from the looks of it, recently cleaned, fed and watered too—the horse looked set for a long journey. What's more, Jionathan recognised the horse from the castle's stables. He'd never ridden it, but he'd seen it at work several times during hunts, moving powerfully and quickly across the moors, leaping over streams and ditches as if it were flying. If this was not a blessing from the goddess Malak, the patron of travellers and merchants, then Jionathan resigned himself to being faithless.

He watched as the blacksmith's apprentice appeared again and saddled the horse, securing the girth tightly around the belly and patting it down. Jionathan could have laughed.

"Is it done yet?" A tall stable boy with straw-coloured hair stepped out from where he'd been shading himself under a balcony. The assistant bobbed his head, and the stable boy moved toward the blacksmith's forge to pay the due. The moment they were in the forge, Jionathan struck, moving deftly toward the horse. The bay watched him, chewing on its bit with boredom. Jionathan patted it lightly on the neck before nimbly untethering the horse from the wall. The horse's ears pricked up as he whispered soothingly to it, pulling the reins over its head and then, seizing hold of the front of the saddle, leaping up onto the bay's back. The horse let out a loud whinny, startled by the sudden movement, but Jionathan patted it quickly, and with a single squeeze to the horse's ribs urged it into a canter. They sped away into the streets as the blacksmith came running out of his smithy, alerted by the sound of the horse's hooves on cobbles.

This time Jionathan did laugh. He'd never thought to try and take his own mount before, simply because stealing a horse from the stables was too costly with time, and much too risky.

Charging through the streets he traversed the city in three times the speed he might have on foot, until suddenly the gates were only a few strides away.

The patrolling guards spotted him as he approached and formed a wall with their bodies, shouting at him to halt. Jionathan urged the horse on faster—he had no intention of stopping. With barely two strides distance between them, the guards finally threw themselves out of his path, and Jionathan was free, galloping out into the wilderness.

The roar of the wind filled his ears, but it didn't drown out the bestial scream that echoed

CHAPTER 4

"Get up! Get up!" Jionathan's voice was shrill inside his head, and Rufus twitched, trying to shake it out. *"You're going to get us killed! Get up!"*

Rufus opened his eyes. Everything was blurry, and his head was aching. He didn't move, his eyes falling shut again. Almost as soon as they did, Jionathan's voice was back.

"Rufus, get up, or by the gods, I will leave you, I swear!"

Get up? That was a haughty order, considering it was probably Jionathan's fault Rufus was in this state. But that didn't matter, because there was something Rufus had to do—something very important. If only he could remember what it was…

He tried to force his eyes open again, but everything hurt too much, and he felt so heavy. Jionathan's voice was still shrill in mind—where was he speaking from? And why did he sound so frighetened.

Ah, Rufus realised, *they're my lost memories.*

That was right, that's what Rufus had been trying to do: he'd been trying to remember what had happened during Jionathan's failed escape attempt. Belphegore and Edwin had questioned him, and Rufus had needed answers.

Eager to see where that distant voice took him, Rufus submitted to it and fell back into the previous day, his body slumping.

He stumbled across Jionathan in the Northern District, in a inn built against the wall. Here, just like the slums, the people rarely saw daylight, and secrets could go unchecked. Rufus hadn't meant to come here, but he'd been on his way home when he'd caught Jionathan's trail, like a scent nearby. Of course, it wasn't unusual for Jionathan to be out among the people—he was their much beloved Prince, their voice in the nobility, someone who spoke out for them. Rufus knew, however, that at this hour, there was no way Jionathan's absence from the castle was sanctioned.

The Magi's suspicions were confirmed as he drew up his chair, next to the table where Jionathan was sat, hunched beneath a cloak. Rufus called for a drink, and leaned in.

"Are you planning a trip, or were you simply craving the brew of his particular haunt?"

Beneath his crude disguise, Jionathan had glowered, his grey eyes flashing. "Go away, Rufus."

Rufus exhaled, running his hand through his hair. "I don't want to make a fuss, so will you please just come back with me and we can talk about this?"

Jionathan looked away, his grip around his tankard tight. Rufus sighed again, sitting back as his drink was brought to him. He could see Jionathan eyeing him from below the rim of his hood, his mouth drawn.

"You shouldn't be here Rufus," Jionathan said.

"Neither should you."

"I can come and go as I please."

"And so can I," Rufus said flatly. Jionathan made to object before faltering. The Prince's eyes snapped to something over Rufus's shoulder, and he sat bolt upright, like he'd just seen something terrifying. Rufus twisted in his seat to look, but saw nothing. After a few moments, he turned back to find Jionathan had dropped his

gaze into his drink.

"What did you see?" Rufus asked.

"Nothing. I thought it was Zachary, but..." Jionathan gave a half shrug, pointedly avoiding Rufus's eyes. They remained like this, engaged in an awkward, taut exchange as Rufus tried to convince the Prince to return with him. Several times, Jionathan looked on the verge of saying something, but he always cut himself off.

The atmosphere in the inn was stifling, but Rufus only realised something was wrong when he tried to stand. A wave of dizziness coursed through his body, and he collapsed back into his chair, pressing a hand to his forehead. What was that? Had he stood up too quickly? No, everything was moving in and out of focus, and from beneath his hood, Jionathan was finally looking at Rufus, watching him carefully.

"I was beginning to worry it wouldn't work," Jionathan said, producing a small bottle from beneath his cloak and showing it to Rufus. Rufus swore: opiates. The Prince had drugged him. "I'm sorry, Rufus, but I refuse to go back."

He tried to stand, but Rufus lashed out his hand and grabbed him by the wrist. Jionathan stumbled, turning to object and then a pain beyond belief exploded over the top of Rufus's head. His face dropped against the table, as shards of glass clattered around his ears. Someone had bottled him.

"Go, Your Highness," a voice said, and Rufus groaned. So that's why the Prince had come here—he had allies working with him in the inn.

Through the slits of his scrunched eyes, Rufus saw Jionathan flee, the Prince stopping at the doorway to shoot him a quick, slightly apologetic look. Rufus forced himself up, stumbling to his feet after Jionathan. He could feel blood seeping down the back of his collar, but he didn't care. He had to stop Jionathan, before the idiot got himself killed. A firm hand pressed itself to his shoulder, pushing him back, and Rufus tumbled into the table, blinking blearily at the two burly men who now stood in his way.

"Get out of my way," he choked.

"You stay here," one of them replied, and then Rufus wasn't quite sure what happened. Whether it was he who threw the first punch, or whether perhaps Rufus simply fell into one of the men, and was shoved, unceremoniously, into another table, spilling someone's drink. All the Magi knew was that, very quickly, fists began to fly all around him, the inn erupting with noise as a fight broke out. Rufus felt his body being thrown this way and that, as he tried to push his way toward the door. Someone struck him hard across the back with a chair, and he collapsed onto the ground. Everything hurt, but it was getting dark outside, and Rufus had to reach Jionathan, he had to get to him before someone else did. Before Zachary did.

Forgotten in the flurry and noise, Rufus crawled across the sticky, ale-stained floor, his whole head spinning, and his mouth strangely numb as blood trickled past his ears. It took an agonisingly long time, people tripping over him, and stomping on his legs and back, but he made it to the door. Clear of the brawl, Rufus hoisted himself to his feet and staggered after Jionathan, just as the first warning bell rang. A quarter of an hour—fifteen minutes to reach the Prince and get out of the streets, before the Night Patrol arrived.

Rufus forced himself into a lolloping run, fighting back the effects of the drug. Whatever Jionathan had used, it must have come from Edwin's private store, because Rufus had never known anything commonplace that was strong enough to affect a Magi. He stumbled after Jionathan, pushing through the crowds who were now hurrying to get home. The minutes sped past, the crowds in the streets thickening, and then dissipating until at last Rufus squeezed his way into a back alley, where he found Jionathan crouching in the corner, watching the patrolling soldiers ushering the last stragglers into their homes. The Prince, stiffening at the sound of Rufus's scuffled footsteps, whirled around. His eyes bulged.

"Rufus!"

Rufus half-collapsed against the wall, his whole head

thundering—oh Healing Septus it hurt!—and swallowed thickly. "Not safe," he forced out, before crumpling into a heap.

"Rufus, can you hear me? I need you open your eyes."

Rufus shifted between the world of memory as a new, outside voice washed over him, strange and warbled as if being spoken underwater.

"Come on, wake up. Look at me."

Rufus shook his head, the drowsy, heavy feeling persisting, as if he'd been drugged. His memories clogged his brain, making it difficult to orientate himself. He remembered now, he remembered what had happened the previous night, why Jionathan had failed another escape attempt. And yet, the unsettling feeling hadn't gone away despite his newly recovered memories. There was something else he needed to do, something else that lay forgotten. Something he needed to find.

And suddenly there was a wringing clarity to the world around him, and he was conscious of a set of hands on his face. From the crack below his eyelids, he could see a pair of figures knelt beside him.

"Rufus, please, can you hear me?" Edwin asked with concern. From beside him another young Magi with long blond hair, tan skin and a pipe sticking idly out of his mouth, leant in.

"He has been struck from behind," the blond, Marcel Hathely, said with a bored tone, his voice lightly accented. East-Réneian. Edwin pressed his fingers into Rufus's temple, making it sting. A warm flood of magic spread from Edwin's hand, and Rufus knew he was being healed.

"So it would appear. Rufus, respond. Can you hear me?"

Rufus blinked his eyes open a little more firmly and gave a long groan.

"Good, you are with us still," Edwin said. "You appear to have taken a nasty wound to the head. How do you feel?"

"I…" Rufus began, and furrowed his brow as he tried to recall why he was strewn against the wall, with a head wound, in Jionathan's chambers. *In Jionathan's chambers…Jionathan…* Rufus's eyes narrowed, as Edwin drew back. "Oh that little bastard."

"This is a disaster!" Pheolus Patrude barked for the third time as he strode the expanse of the room, pacing furiously up and down. Rufus kept his eyes ahead, his face set. Edwin had attended to his wounds, but had warned Rufus that he needed time to fully heal, and shouldn't over-exert himself. Rufus's head still ached dully, and stung if he turned too quickly or blinked too hard. The pain, however, was nothing in comparison to his acute humiliation.

Jionathan had fled the castle, stolen a horse, and was now out in the wilderness. When the guards made it apparent that they'd lost the boy's trail in the mouth of the Myrithian Forest, an urgent meeting had been called.

Outside, darkness was already falling on the city, and the last rays of light were streaking through the western windows, onto the stone floor. The council room was small, but decorated grandly, with arched doorways and a thick red carpet leading to a small wooden throne. A set of lit beacons were put on each wall, and a warm, open fireplace basked the room with a deep, orange glow.

Rufus could feel a vein throbbing in his head as Pheolus kept up his furious tirade. "The Prince has escaped the city, and great Malak only knows where he intends to go! He could be anywhere in Bethean by tomorrow. We'll have to send a whole army out to find him." The short, balding man finally stopped and turned on Rufus. "How is it that one such as yourself could have fallen for such an easy trick? Such child's play? Well? Hah—is this the new generation of Magi then?" Pheolus demanded, spitting. Rufus didn't give him the satisfaction of a response, which only enraged the little man more. "I am thoroughly frightened for this city's future if *yours* are the kind to claim it!" He clutched Rufus by the front of the uniform, like he meant to shake him, but was only able to tug limply at his clothing, Rufus being significantly taller. Pheolus's moustache quivered in rage.

In the corner of the room, Zachary had settled in the shadows and watched in unsupportive silence, a faint smile on his face. Rufus caught his eye, and Zachary's smile widened as he darted his eyes down to Pheolus and then back up to Rufus again, his face alight with mirth. He waggled his eyebrows. Rufus almost laughed, but schooled himself. It wouldn't do well to laugh now.

"Pheolus, please, Rufus is not to blame," Belphegore said. "The Prince took him by surprise."

"He is the apprentice of the *leader* of the Magi, and he was taken by *surprise*?" Pheolus demanded.

From his corner, Zachary spoke, "Lord Patrude, you must appreciate that my little brother is a *scholar* specialising in magical theory and the healing arts. He's not a warrior."

Pheolus scowled at Zachary, and then returned to the other side of the room with dismissive snort. Rufus resisted the urge to brush himself down.

"Lord Merle, repeat to me again the circumstances which preceded my son attacking you," Thestian requested, his expression guarded, and Rufus straightened. He, amongst everybody else, had been surprised when the King himself accompanied his two wives to the meeting. When questioned with concerns about his health, Thestian had retorted that Jionathan was his son, and he had no intention of lying in bed knowing his only child was out alone, unprotected in the wilderness.

"When I entered the Prince's chambers," Rufus began, "he was lying in bed, Your Majesty. As I approached, I noticed there seemed to be something strange about his..." Rufus drew off, struggling to collect his thoughts. "His behaviour," he finally said. "As Lord Zachary stated, I'm learned in the basic forms of healing and medicine. Examining the Prince, I saw his behaviour to be distinctly feverish, or fit-like."

"A fine actor, your son," Reine purred at Éliane, who didn't dignify her with a response. The King paid no heed to his wives and gestured for Rufus to continue.

Rufus hesitated. "If I may be so bold, I'm certain that he wasn't acting."

There had been a terror about Jionathan when Rufus had seen him, a true pulsing fear emanating from his very skin.

"Oh my!" The Queen leant forward. "Do you mean to say that the heir of the Harmatian throne has the falling sickness?" Her eyes were predatory.

"No, I'm under no impression that Jionat—Prince Jionathan—suffers from the falling sickness. I simply described his symptoms as fit-like."

"But you claim they were symptoms," Reine pushed, and Rufus put his hands behind his back, clasping them tightly together.

"It's the best word I could find," he said. "At the time I was worried for the Prince's wellbeing, and as such I sent the guards to fetch Lord Edwin. As I turned to examine the Prince, he struck me over the head. I stumbled, and he struck me again. I don't recall any events that followed."

"I see." The King leaned back in his throne, his face thoughtful.

From his side Reine spoke again—like a viper preparing to strike. "When you told the guards to fetch Lord Edwin, you gave them no other reason to leave their post than that the Prince was taken ill. Is that correct?"

"Yes," replied Rufus warily, feeling his stomach squeeze as the Queen pressed on.

"You gave no details of the ailment?"

"No."

"Strange." She smiled at him pleasantly. "All magical ability aside, am I not understood that you are, in fact, a former physician yourself? Why, then, did you simply not examine him first, and then call for the appropriate help?"

"I was a physician's *apprentice* for a short while as a child, and I'm no great healer yet, that I could rely on my knowledge alone."

"If that is the case, Lord Merle, then why did you take it upon yourself to diagnose the Prince in the first place, if you are so much a novice?"

Rufus swallowed, his expression tightening. His fingers squeezed into fists behind his back. "I did only what I thought was best for him," he said stubbornly, keeping his temper in check. He wasn't a violent man, but his tongue was sharp, and sometimes a little too quick.

"Of course. You did only what you thought was best for the Prince, but according to whom?" Reine was enjoying her inquisition, but the King raised his hand and drew her to silence.

"Reine," he warned. Immediately the Queen settled in her seat, and Thestian turned back to Rufus. "I believe you, Rufus Merle, have no fear of that. I am not suspicious of what others might deem to be 'your part' in my son's flight from this city. I will speak plainly now with you all, as I have grown tired. I have heard the word 'escape' too many times today. My son is not a criminal, he is not a prisoner, and he was not being held here against his will. This is his home, and he may come and go as he wishes. The fact that he felt the need to *flee*, on his own, sickens me. I would like to see my son returned safely, but I would like to see him do so willingly. I will not have my own flesh and blood paraded up to this castle as a fugitive in chains. I will not send forces after him. I want to help Jionathan, not detain him." He paused. "Éliane, you have been very quiet. What say you on the matter?"

Rufus didn't dare look at the Lady as she raised her head, casting her gaze accusingly down at him.

"My son must be made to realise the error of his ways," she said, after consideration. "Whilst he possess the right to leave as he wishes, his conduct toward Lord Merle was of ill intent, and I cannot abide that."

"Your Ladyship," Rufus interrupted, his mouth dry. "If you might indulge me, I don't believe the Prince's actions were of ill intent."

"He bludgeoned you with a candelabrum," Reine laughed. "If you do not consider that ill intent, Lord Merle, then I pity your childhood."

But he saved me, Rufus wanted to say. *It can't have bee ill-intent, because yesterday, when he could've escaped, he saved me instead. He could've left me to the Night Patrol, he could've fled the city, but he stayed behind to hide me first. Never mind that it was all his fault in the first place, never mind that he drugged me and got me bottled—he sacrificed his escape to make sure I was safe.*

Everyone in the room was watching Rufus expectantly, waiting for his response. He swallowed, choosing his words carefully. "I don't consider Prince Jionathan's actions to be of ill intent, Your Grace," he said, "because as he struck me, the Prince apologised. I know his character—he's not malicious or cruel, just frightened. That he attacked me in such a way today—those were the actions of a desperate man, I warrant you." Rufus knelt before the King. "Your Majesty, I implore you, let me go after him."

"You must be jesting, man!" Pheolus intruded before the King could speak. "It was your incompetence that led us to this fine mess. Who are you to demand such favours of redemption?"

"He's an esteemed member of the Magi who stands at equal rank to you, Lord Patrude," Zachary said from his corner, where Rufus had all but forgotten him. His brothering apprentice leant out from the shadows, eerie and threatening. "And he is also a genius, and the favourite of our master, so watch what you say."

Rufus sighed. "Favourites, Zachary? Really?"

"I am *defending* you, Merle," Zachary replied, and to Pheolus he said, "I need not speak for my master when I say that he wasn't idle in his choice of apprentice. Merle may not possess skills for the blade, but if the future of Harmatia's history is to be written, it will be his hand that shapes it, *Pheolus.*"

"Arlen," Belphegore scolded as Pheolus, trouble by Zachary's natural menace, stuttered an apology. Zachary returned triumphantly to his corner. "Excuse my first-chosen and his running mouth, Your Majesty." Belphegore bowed. "But he is right. If there is a man capable of retrieving your son safely, it is Rufus."

"And what if Lord Merle should fail?" Éliane said suddenly, her eyes burning like a clear winter sky. "Then you both would be left unprotected in the Myrithian Forest, with no others capable of seeking you out. It is too dangerous—take some guards with you, at the very least."

"If I take guards, then the retrieval becomes a capture," Rufus said. "And if we capture the Prince, all he'll do is run away again. There's a reason for this behaviour, but how can we expect to discover it if the Prince can't trust us? Please, Your Ladyship, trust me—I'll find him. I always do."

"The forest is vast, it is different to the city. Can you be certain?" she pressed, and he finally caught her crystalline eyes.

"I have a sense for it," he assured. "I won't fail."

A great stillness came over the room as its occupants awaited the King's verdict. Thestian spoke. "Very well, I charge you, Rufus Merle, with the task of finding my son and, when you deem right, bringing him safely home."

Rufus pressed a hand to his chest, his head bowed. "It shall be done."

CHAPTER 5

"You're not going," Nora Merle said firmly, as Rufus folded his clothes carefully and tucked them into his bag. He'd arrived home and explained to his parents, in brief, the circumstances of his departure. Whilst his father had gone immediately to fetch one of their horses from the local stable, Rufus's mother had stayed, adamant to dissuade him. "They've mistaken you for a mercenary—and you're still injured!"

"Lord Edwin saw to my wound. I'm all but healed."

"All but!" Nora cried. "Rufus, you're not equipped for this."

"Mother," Rufus caught her fretting hands and held them still, "I've made the journey to Bethean a thousand times. I know the way."

"You know the *roads*." Nora pulled her fingers free and gripped Rufus's wrists in turn. "But you're going into the Myrithian Forest, with no clear destination, and the wyld fae *prey* on those who wander."

"All the more reason for me to reach Jionathan before something else does." He returned to his packing. "Have no fear, Mother. I can defend myself, should I need to."

"Without magic, Rufus?" Nora caught his chin, her face

steady. "Or did you think you're father and I wouldn't notice? You haven't practised your skill in almost a year."

Rufus dropped his gaze. "I…" He stopped himself. He couldn't lie to his mother—she always saw right through him. "If the need comes, I'll do what I have to, to preserve myself. I promise."

Nora didn't seem satisfied, a deep frown marring her brow. Rufus reached forward and pulled her into an embrace. She was small in his arms, small enough that he could place his chin atop her head and kiss her dark, auburn hair.

"I'll pack you some food, silly boy," she whispered into his chest, and left him to his preparations.

He continued his packing, and then stood in his room, surveying it. In the darkness, he could make out the shape of his bed, set beneath the south facing window. Cracks of moonlight seeped between gaps in the shutters and illuminated the patchwork quilt.

Adjacent to him, his desk stood busy with papers and documents of all kinds, a small stack of drawings and diagrams weighed down beneath a bronze inkwell. A bookcase, heaving with manuscripts, ledgers of sketches, and scrolls, stood to the right of that, and above—all across the room—maps of the sky and earth littered the walls. Rufus stared at them, almost longingly, and then tore himself from the comforts of his room and walked out onto the landing.

Descending the narrow wooden stairs, Rufus was met by his mother at the bottom, who handed him a hefty bundle of blankets and provisions.

"Mother, I need to travel light—"

She squeezed his face once more between thumb and forefinger. "You'll be glad of it when the cold strikes," she said.

"Thank you." He accepted the bundle gratefully, and then stooped down so that she could kiss his forehead. He embraced her tightly. "I'll return soon."

"For my health, do. Travel safely," she sighed. "Your father's outside, waiting for you. And you've got another visitor as well."

"Someone else?" Rufus frowned, but his mother simply smiled and cupped his face in her hand again.

"May Aramathea's eyes watch over you. Go," she instructed softly, and he kissed her fingers before stalking out through the shop into the open street.

As he stepped onto the cobbles, he was greeted by his father, who held the reins of a large black mare. The horse snorted fondly to him, its breath curling in the cold air, and Rufus patted the mare's nose. "Hello Moyna. Are you ready for a long journey?"

The horse rubbed its face into his shoulder. Securing the blankets to the saddle, Rufus turned to see the third, hooded figure who stood waiting in the gloom behind him. She lifted her hood as he approached, and he straightened in surprise.

"Lady Éliane?" He made to bow, but she caught his wrist and silenced him with a shake of her head, glancing warily down the streets.

"Good evening, Rufus."

"I…I didn't expect to see you," Rufus said dumbly.

"I had no intention of coming." She placed her hands lightly against her belly. "And yet, here I am."

The pair stood in stony silence. Rufus fingered his collar. "Was there something you required of me?"

Éliane sighed. "This venture is foolish and dangerous."

"I know."

"And yet you insist on going?"

"I do."

"Even though my son has not been your friend in almost two years?"

Rufus frowned. "Just because he stopped seeing me as his friend, doesn't mean I stopped being one. However difficult it's become."

Éliane stared at him, and then laughed faintly. "I see your mind is set," she huffed. "Then all I can do now is have faith that

60

you will succeed. But know this, Rufus—the Queen will send others after you, the moment the King retires to his chambers. She would have Jionathan locked in the dungeons if she could. You must take care, I beg you. If either you or Jionathan were hurt..." Éliane gripped her stomach tightly with a small gasp. "Oh, he always kicks when you're nearby," she said breathily. "Could you calm him?"

Wordlessly, Rufus pressed his palm to her womb. Beyond the veil of flesh, he felt the child stir. "Be nice to your mother," he whispered to the baby, and felt it kick his hand in response, before growing comfortably still.

"He wishes you well," Éliane whispered. "As do I."

Rufus smiled up at her, and then remembered himself, retracting his hand. "I..." He straightened his clothes. "I didn't think that you...that you ever thought very much of me."

Éliane's lips trembled, and before Rufus knew it she had leant into him and placed a gentle kiss on his cheek. She stroked her finger down his chin and cupped it.

"I am sorry, Rufus. I know it is not fair, but I cannot deny myself, not when you are *so* close." Her lips parted in sorrow, as if she longed to hold him. As if she'd deprived herself for years. Rufus could scarcely breathe.

"I hate to interrupt, but time isn't our ally." Rufus's father stepped out from behind the horse, leading it by the reins. "It's almost curfew, and the gates'll be closed soon. I'm sorry, Your Ladyship, but Rufus has to go."

"No, you are quite right." Éliane hastily removed her hands, stepping back. "Thank you, Torin. I must too return before I am missed." She gave Rufus one last lingering look. "Goodbye Rufus. May Malak guide you on your path."

"Lady Éliane," he breathed, and watched as she departed, ghost-like, down the cobbled streets, almost soundless in the moonlight. "I...I didn't expect that..."

"Nor I." Torin appeared at his side, watching. "You're not in love with her, are you Rufus?" he asked faintly.

Rufus jolted. "No."

"*Good,*" Torin stated. "Because if you were…"

"I refuse to have this conversation with you." Rufus snatched the reins from his father's hands. "I should get on."

"Aye, I'd wager that'd be wise." Torin crossed his arms, his face pensive. "You watch yourself, Rufus-lad, for our sakes, if not for your own. Your mother and I love you."

Rufus's expression softened. "I know." He embraced his father. "For all my sins, I know."

"Good. Then get gone, and if you can, come back a little less sulky and pompous in the mouth, eh?"

"I'll endeavour to change my vernacular, the day you cease your cussing and perversions, Father." Rufus climbed up onto the horse, securing his feet into the stirrups.

Torin laughed again. "You little shite. Accusing *me* of perversion? Go on then, Rufus—and by Athea, *take care.*"

Rufus bowed his head. "You're as bad as mother."

"That's because I'm your father."

"On that we can be sure," Nora agreed, from where she'd appeared in the doorway of the shop. Rufus looked longingly at her, and the home she stood before. He wanted to lie in bed. He wanted to sleep to the gentle sounds of his parent's speaking downstairs. He wanted the relief of their presence, and the assurance of a threshold. And yet he was going to forfeit such comforts now for a forest that was infested with bandits, wyld fae, and hidden marshes. Rufus sighed, and turned Moyna around to face the city gates.

It was going to be a long ride.

"Éliane?"

She froze in the doorway, her breath caged in her throat. From within the dark room, she could see Thestian sitting beside the dying fire, his chair turned toward the window. She removed her cloak carefully.

"Your Majesty." She curtsied as best she could. "I did not expect you to be waiting for me."

"I was tired, but I wanted to speak with you," the King replied, gesturing for Éliane to come and to sit beside him. The Lady did as she was bid, perching on the edge of her seat, upright and stiff. "I saw you go out earlier this evening."

"I needed to clear my head." She remained composed, her voice steady.

Thestian watched her carefully, his hands clasped in front of his mouth. "You needed to see Rufus Merle," he corrected.

Dread filled Éliane, but she swallowed it down, nodding minutely. "I did, Your Majesty."

Thestian didn't speak a while, his gaze cast out through the window, watching the rising moon. "I know, Éliane," he told her quietly. Éliane's jaw tightened, her lips pursing slightly. But the King didn't appear angry. He smiled. "You try so hard to disguise your heart, but I know. I have seen it. The way you shun him, and yet steal guilty glances when you think no one knows. The way your eyes linger on him, as if you were dreaming of a different life. The regality and coldness you hide behind when he addresses you. You birthed my son, and will soon give me another—I *know* what these looks mean, Éliane. I am not a fool."

Éliane didn't reply, but sat poised like a statue. To all others, she would appear unperturbed, but she knew Thestian saw the tightness in her shoulders and the frightened grip of her hands.

"You love him."

"Of course, I love him." Éliane couldn't contain it. "How could I supress it?"

"He's a handsome boy, I grant you." Thestian watched his wife carefully, and finally raised a hand to her face, tucking a strand of her hair behind her ear. "Do not fret, I am not angry with you," he assured. Éliane raised a hand to her mouth and inhaled shakily, closing her eyes.

"I am sorry," she whispered urgently. "I am so very, very sorry."

"I understand. Perhaps some years ago I would not have, but I am tired now, my love…so very tired…"

"I do love you, Thestian." Éliane leant forward and clasped his hands desperately. "Truly, I do. You are my husband, and I am yours, faithfully."

"I do not doubt it, my love." He smiled for her, his cheeks folding along the lines left by years of laughter. His eyes were warm. "That boy is merely one of life's many complications. But I know you will honour me, and remain faithful as you have always done. However, Éliane," he took her hand in his and kissed it, "soon I will part from this word, and your obligation to me—to the Delphi—will be no more. You will be free."

"I do not want to be free," she cried.

"On that day, sweet love, I pray you will seek happiness again."

"Thestian." Éliane rested her face on his shoulder. "I could never…I will never…" she began, but her husband merely squeezed her fingers.

"For me, you must," he insisted. "You have denied yourself for many years now. For us both, let your heart flourish."

Éliane gasped, her throat tight. Thestian kissed her forehead and placed his hand on her stomach.

"As for this child of mine, may your chosen be to him the father that I cannot."

～☙～

Jionathan woke to the merry sound of birdsong. For a moment he lay, his head resting against his satchel, and simply admired the beauty of his liberation. It was cold, barely light, and his body was stiff from sleeping on the ground, but Jionathan couldn't remember a time he'd been so happy.

Finally rising, he stood and stretched his aching back. Beside him, the bay, who stood tethered to a nearby tree, raised its head and snorted faintly in greeting.

"Good morning to you." Jionathan crossed over to it and rubbed its neck down, looking around him. Everything was as he'd left it the previous night. His saddle, sword, and provisions were untouched whilst the remnants of a fire glowed with dying embers. Jionathan was surprised—he'd expected to encounter at least a few faeries by now, but the forest had yielded nothing but trees, birds, and small foragers. For that, Jionathan considered himself extremely lucky.

He had no intention of staying another night in these woods. By his estimate, he was already halfway through the forest. All Jionathan had to do was follow the river down into the valley, and he'd be in Bethean before the day ended.

Looking back at the bay, he saw the horse had been gorging itself on the foliage at hand. "Well, you're fed." Jionathan placed the bridle back over its head. "Let's get you saddled and watered, and we can be on our way."

Leading the horse down to the river, he let it drink, while he ate a portion of his rations and filled his drinking pouch. The water was cold and sent shivers up his arm. Jionathan took the opportunity to freshen himself and, dipping both hands into the stream, cupped the water and splashed it over his face. Icy droplets trickled down his collar, and he gasped, sitting back and tilting his head to the lightening sky. It was a peaceful place, and for a moment Jionathan closed his eyes and let his mind wander, enjoying the gentle tinkle and hum of the running water. It was almost like a song—sweet and melodic.

Jionathan opened his eyes abruptly. It wasn't the river that sang—someone was singing close by. Immediately alert, Jionathan rose to his feet and looked around. At first he saw nothing but innocent trees and the bay, who huffed at him and began to graze, and then Jionathan caught sight of the culprit—a figure further downstream that he'd mistaken for a tree.

She was a young, willowy woman, with delicate arms the

colour of tanned oak, and a sweeping cascade of ebony hair that obscured most of her face. Her voice lilting with the most mournful song—so sweet, so clear, it rang like a trickle of tears, stirring Jionathan's heart.

"What's that song?" he called out to her, but his voice was either lost to the sound of the river, or she paid him no mind.

For a moment, Jionathan was almost driven to step into the moving water and cross to her, but then he noticed what she held in her hands. A chemise, stained across the chest with dark streaks of blood.

Jionathan watched, petrified, as she lowered the garment into the water and let the stream run over it, gently scrubbing at the stain, trying to wash it away. Jionathan could scarcely breathe.

It wasn't the blood on the shirt that made him falter, but the resigned way she attempted to wash it—as if she were already defeated, as if she knew the inevitability of her task—yet persisted.

Jionathan knew he ought to turn away. He was looking at something unearthly, something sinister, and yet her song was hypnotic. And she seemed so sad, so very, very sad.

She raised her head, and for a moment her dark hair glimmered with a rosewood sheen, and he saw her eyes, human and alive and full of tears—

And then, very suddenly, a hunting horn blared in the distance, and Jionathan reached for his sword, instantly alert. A battle cry followed, and the chorus of triumphant men. Jionathan looked out toward where the sounds grew distant, and then turned back to see if the commotion had disturbed the washing woman. But where she'd once been, the bank was empty, and no trace of her remained.

A dark feeling trembled through him, like the finger of a phantom caressing his spine, and Jionathan quickly retreated.

Leading the bay back up to their camp, he hurriedly saddled the horse and mounted it. In the distance he could hear the sounds of battle, and Jionathan deliberated on what to do. He could circle around the commotion, but he risked getting lost in the process. Whereas if he drew too near and chanced upon an enemy, he'd be outnumbered.

Yet curiosity spurred him on, and turning the bay's nose toward the sounds of combat, Jionathan urged the horse forward. They rode a few minutes through the dense foliage, until they approached a clearing. Jionathan dismounted carefully, and leading the horse to a clump of trees, hid there. Beyond the veil of leaves, he could hear the clash of blades, and the roar of falling water. It appeared he'd reached the Myrithian Jaws—a deep gorge that ran through the eastern part of the Myrithian forest, splitting it in half, and leading down into the valleys of Bethean. He was closer to his destination than he'd thought.

Tying his horse, Jionathan clambered quickly up into a tree to see what was happening beyond the protective wall of leaves. He was expecting to see a battle of sorts, perhaps between two faerie clans, or another mystical creature of the forest. Instead, below him, a group of thirty or so vagrants danced around a young woman, who stood caged in the centre of them. The bandits— for that's what Jionathan assumed they were—were armed with spears, and thick shimmering nets, which they whipped out threateningly at the woman. Jionathan watched, intrigued by the display.

The woman seemed calm, despite her situation, and there was something about the offensive set of her shoulders which implied she wasn't in as much danger as her captors thought.

Her head shifted quickly from side to side, almost cat-like, as the bandits leapt around her. From behind, one bold, young fool made to strike her across the back with the base of his spear, and stepped in too close. As swift as a darting fish, the woman brought her leg up behind her in a dramatic arabesque and snapped her boot hard into her attacker's face. Jionathan's stomach lurched as the bandit's head snapped back with force, and he collapsed to the ground, his face bloody and eyes vacant.

The woman retreated to her original stance, unmindful of the fresh corpse at her feet.

Jionathan slid down from the tree. "Whoever those bandits are, I can at least say *she's* not human," he whispered to the bay, who watched him dully. Jionathan pondered a moment and then, against his better judgement, slipped through trees out onto the edge of the clearing.

The bandits, who seemed oblivious even to the death of their comrade, were working themselves into a gleeful frenzy, hollering and laughing. Jionathan stood, confident that he wouldn't be noticed amongst the ruckus.

Past the merry circle of men, the Prince could see the edge of the gorge, overlooking a sea of trees far below. Beyond, the forest opened up onto a band of green fields and speckled yellow towns—the Kingdom of Bethean within reach.

Another bandit moved in closer to the woman, jabbing his spear at her side. This time, she drew a weapon—one of a set of duelling swords she wore on her back—and, catching the neck of the spear, cut it in half. Then, bringing her back leg up and around, she snapped it across the bandit's face. Jionathan winced again, as the attacker, like his comrade, crumpled to the floor. She'd crushed his eye-socket with one blow.

The woman resumed her stance, but Jionathan caught her looking out toward the forest, and then across to the perilous ledge less than a hundred strides away. She was trying to escape. What was more, Jionathan could now see that she was lagging on her right leg. Blood blossomed over her thigh. She was injured.

Quietly, Jionathan moved a little closer and watched as the bandits become more ferocious in their attacks. Strong as the woman was—whatever she was—she was lacking the proper use of one leg, and Jionathan didn't like the look of the nets her attackers wielded either.

I can't afford to intervene, he decided. *No matter what I witness here now.*

"Bring it down!" one of the bandits said, a thick burly man with red hair. The men around him did as instructed, lashing out once more. Jionathan watched, awestruck, as the woman sprung impossibly high into the air, and landed on the shoulders of one of her attackers, clamping her knees around his head. With a sharp twist of her body, she snapped his neck, and drew her blades, leaping from one victim to the shoulders of the next. Jionathan understood what she was doing. The floor was littered with nets, laid down to ensnare her. If her injured leg got caught it one, all it would take was one tug to bring her down. And so she remained in the air, light as a feather.

Bringing her fifth victim down, she stood on his buckled body, her feet planted firmly in his gut. But she was too slow in moving to her next target, as someone drove the blunt of their spear into the back of her injured knee. She collapsed forward with a cry. Immediately several men leapt on her, pinning her down.

Above her, a bandit armed with a heavy-looking mace brought it down toward her head. She veered back, pulling against the hands that held her, and the mace caught the tendrils of her hair. Several more men lurched forward and threw themselves at her. She struggled and writhed against their hold. The bandit raised his mace again, in preparation for the final blow.

Jionathan didn't stop to think. He grabbed the dirk from his belt, and charging forward, he threw it as hard as he could. The knife shot through the air, and met its mark, planting itself into the soft tissue of the bandit's gullet. The bandit choked, blood spurting from the wound, and then he collapsed with a thud, twitching. In frightening unison, the remaining bandits and the woman all turned to Jionathan. He stared back, wincing.

Overcoming her surprise at this intervention, the woman used the distraction to her advantage. Tugging her captors on the left forward, she angled toward them, using her shoulder to break through the rubble of tumbling bodies, and breaking free.

Meanwhile, a handful of the bandits abandoned their quarry in favour of the Prince. Jionathan drew his sword, cursing his decision to intervene.

The first bandit swung at him with an axe. Jionathan flinched, instinctual terror racing through him, but then years of training took control, and he let his body move without thought.

As the axe came in, Jionathan stepped into the attacker, out of his striking range. The bandit faltered, thrown off, and Jionathan used this second of confusion to launch the hilt of his sword into the base of the bandit's chin, paralysing his throat. Jionathan wasn't as strong as his attackers, but it took very little to bring even the burliest man to his knees, if you knew where to hit.

The bandit toppled forward, clutching his throat, and Jionathan dove down and out of the way, delivering the killing blow to the base of the bandit's neck.

The next bandit was easier, leaving his abdomen unguarded as he jabbed clumsily out. Jionathan deflected the blow easily, and struck back, his blade tearing through flesh. He shuddered slightly as a fresh splatter of blood struck his cheek. The bandit collapsed, intestines falling loose, and Jionathan turned away quickly.

His heart was beating fast, his tongue thick and heavy in his mouth as he swallowed. He couldn't afford to indulge his disgust or terror, so he pushed them down, tumbling into the next opponent.

Don't look, just fight. Fight for your life!

He slashed and struck, almost blindly as the battle thickened, more men lurching toward Jionathan, and surrounding him.

You've fought and defeated men with more skill than these, Jionathan told himself, as he twisted this way and that. It was little comfort. The wave of bandits seemed endless and, in his hunting armour, Jionathan wasn't equipped for the fight. If he miscalculated, if he missed a step, they would kill him in a second.

With all the confusion, the bandits' tight circle had broken and they flocked in. From the corner of his eye, Jionathan saw the young woman take her opportunity and break away from the rabble. Instead of running toward the tree line however, she veered toward the jagged edge of the Jaws.

"Wait!" Jionathan cried. Hadn't she seen how high they were? Didn't she know that, even if she survived the fall, below the rippling water of the river, a jaw of rocks was waiting to rip her apart? Around him, the bandits mimicked his distress.

"It's getting away!"

"Stop it!"

At the edge, the woman faltered, skidding to a halt. She turned back to Jionathan. Beyond her, the sunrise burst out in its full glory, and she was suddenly haloed in a blazing shower of light. Jionathan stared, and it was as if he had been transported, the rest of the world ebbing away.

It was the most peculiar feeling. As if he was stood on an entirely different plane, in a different time, as if he was looking at her through the eyes of somebody else. In that moment, she was godly, her hair a fiery gold as it caught the wind, seeming to burn. Her skin shimmered, glowing with strength and power—and her eyes! Her eyes were the most piercing, unearthly green he'd ever seen. Jionathan's breath caught, his heart in this throat, blood rushing through his ears. He *knew* her. For a split second, he knew her so well his heart was bursting with love…

And then she turned and dove from the cliff.

"No!" Jionathan cried, as she disappeared down the jagged gorge.

A gloved hand clamped across his mouth, and Jionathan was dragged back into the gaggle of bandits.

CHAPTER 6

His ears hadn't stopped ringing all day, and Rufus was in danger of dropping off his horse. Like his mother had warned, the night before had been cold, and though Rufus had benefitted from her blankets, he'd scarcely dared to sleep. The forest, for its part, had wielded very little at him, though Rufus was sure to stay on course and travel only south along the river. Several times he narrowly missed marshland only through the sensibility of his horse who would, somehow sensing the danger, refuse to move forward. Rufus chatted to the mare as they rode, gladder of her company than even the food his mother had packed. Without the mare, Rufus was sure he'd have lost courage amongst the looming trees long ago.

By the time he reached the Myrithian Jaws, Notameer was already beginning to set on the horizon, and the cold was sweeping in once more. "I have a theory, you know," Rufus muttered irritably to Moyna as they stopped on the edge of the bloodied clearing, littered with corpses. "I think he actually *enjoys* getting into trouble."

The horse stomped it's hooves in sceptical silence, and Rufus sighed, as if the mare was slighting him.

"Why else would he put so much effort into it?" he insisted. The horse gave an exasperated snort, and he dismounted, chuckling. "Very well, agree to disagree."

Tying the mare at the side of the clearing, he stalked forward amongst the corpses, trying not to look too hard at their fatal injuries as he searched for any evidence of the Prince. "And once again," Rufus crossed to the body of a bandit, and tugged a dirk out from where it was lodged deeply in the man's throat, "my senses have not failed me." In the dimming light, he examined the weapon and found the royal crest embedded on its hilt. He bent down and cleaned the blade on the deceased's shirt. "May Athea have mercy on you all."

From behind him, Moyna whinnied loudly at something through the trees. Carefully, Rufus stood and, after a moment's hesitation, approached.

Moving past a curtain of foliage, Rufus found what Moyna had seen. A large bay stallion stood, tugging at its reins, which were looped around a tree branch. As Rufus approached, the bay nickered in soft greeting.

It was a beautiful horse with a full coat and a powerful build. Had Rufus not known better, he might have mistaken it for a kelpie—a mean water spirit which disguised itself as a horse, enticed victims onto its back, and then dove into the water close by and drowned them.

Fortunately, Rufus recognised this particular beast from the royal stables. It was the horse Jionathan had stolen. "But why has he left you here?"

Rufus untied the impatient creature, which tossed its head irritably from side to side as he led it back to his own horse.

"Would it be foolishly optimistic to think he intends to return?" Rufus thought aloud, and the bay nickered again, almost laughing. Rufus snorted. "Yes, I thought so. In which case... where are you, Jionat?" he murmured darkly, sitting back on the trunk of a fallen tree. The bay nuzzled Moyna's side in greeting, and the mare whipped her tail into the stallion's face in return.

Rufus closed his eyes, concentrating. "Where are you?"

For a moment there was no response, but for the gentle brush of wind whispering unhelpfully in his ear. And then Rufus stood, almost in a trance, and walked out into the clearing. He kept his eyes closed, and began to move without thinking, his feet weaving him around in a peculiar pattern—like a strange dance. He followed the footsteps of the battle, like Jionathan was pulling him through it, turning and twisting until he lurched to a stop. Rufus's eyes flew open.

Ahead, the jagged edge of the gorge stood empty, but for the briefest moment Rufus felt like he'd just seen something incredibly important. The strange sensation was gone the next second, and Rufus shook his head. He turned back to the horses.

"We go west," he announced, and at their scepticism added, "don't ask how I know." He scanned the fallen. "He's not here, which means they've probably taken him. Seems he put up a valiant fight first though..." Rufus's eyes gliding across the disturbed earth and grass. "At least we can take heart—from the look of them, they're bandits. It's unlikely our Prince has been eaten. No, instead," Rufus grimaced, "he'll probably be tortured, disfigured, and sold as a slave into Isnydea, or onto some ship in a Betheanian port, never to see Mag Mell again." Rufus paused, his head aching under the weight of two concussions and the grim possibilities. Whatever fate awaited Jionathan, it was not a happy one if Rufus didn't reach him soon. "That stupid brat!"

The bandits clamoured around the cage, and Jionathan sat in solemn silence, awaiting his punishment. Already nursing bruised ribs, among other things, Jionathan wasn't optimistic about his situation. His current prison, a stout rectangular cage, with solid metal bars and a wooden base, had wheels and looked like it had once belonged to some exotic animal trader. Lanterns hung from each corner, illuminating Jionathan and the cage, and making him feel like an exhibition.

"You know what we're goin' to do to you, brat?" one of the bandits sneered. He was a particularly ugly specimen, with red hair and a nose that looked like it had been broken at birth, and a few times since.

"Torture me for your troubles and sell me as a slave, I suppose," Jionathan replied offhandedly. He knew it was irrational, but despite the steady ache of his bruised body, he felt too numb to be afraid.

His nonchalant response seemed to rally the men all the more, several reaching for their weapons as they glowered. It was clear they wanted to provoke a response, and Jionathan might have been more obliging, if he hadn't felt so separate from everything—as if it were all unreal. Even the pain down his body and the promise of more was not enough to bring him into sharp reality.

In some ways, this disassociation was a blessing. It allowed him to look at his situation analytically without fear or panic, neither of which would help. If he didn't escape soon, he'd likely find himself aboard a ship setting sail for the Serpent Islands or the distant lands of the Black Sun. That was, of course, providing he was spared the thousand mile trek through Kathra to Isnydea— the land of the damned—and not sold to the Shin instead. The thought was strong enough to make Jionathan shudder. He doubted he'd survive the journey, let alone being a Shinny slave. Between the pair, he'd face the uncharted ocean any day.

"Aye, we'll sell you. Bit by bit if it'll earn us our profit." The ugly bandit leered through the bars of the cage. "You should've stayed out of sight, boy. Now darkness is all you're ever goin' to know."

Jionathan heaved a sigh. "So be it," he said. "Better darkness than cowardice."

But better a coward than a dead man.

"You've a brave one." From the shadow of the trees, another bandit shifted. He was quieter than the rest, better spoken, and there was something slippery about his voice—deadly soft and serpentine. Jionathan had identified him as the leader the moment they'd entered the camp, and of the lot, the Prince was the most wary of him. Not least because, in the gloom of the forest, this one's eyes glowed bright yellow. "That, or you're just another heroic fool. Tell me, do you even know what you saved today?"

"No," Jionathan admitted. "But it wasn't your dignity."

The leader laughed. "Quick tongue—I like that in a man. Much less in noble-blooded brats who think it makes them superior."

Jionathan raised an eyebrow and gestured to the gaggle around him. "Amongst these? I would say it does."

From outside the cage, the ugly bandit reached in and seized Jionathan by his battered collar, dragging him hard against the bars. Jionathan grimaced as his chest struck the metal.

"Pretty words won't save your pretty face," the bandit hissed.

"They certainly didn't save yours," Jionathan replied, and gasped as he was thrashed up against the bars again, and dropped back to the floor of his cage. He touched his throat and coughed, rubbing his collar.

The bandit turned to his leader. "Bruatar, give me a half-hour with this son of a whore. I'll make him bleed for the brother he killed."

Bruatar considered this, his yellow eyes gleaming in the darkness. "He stays in the cage, Jak," he eventually said. "Otherwise, do as you will."

Jak grinned crookedly and reached for Jionathan again. This time, Jionathan was prepared. As he was dragged against the bars, he slipped his bound hands between them and seized the weapon on Jak's belt. It was a baton of sorts—a long rod of iron with a spiked, bulbous head.

All too late Jak realised what the Prince was doing, and as he drew away to reclaim his weapon, Jionathan brought it up and across Jak's face, clipping his cheek and nose.

Jak howled, and Jionathan pulled the baton back into his cage and retreated to the centre, brandishing his new weapon. Around him, the other bandits broke into laughter as Jak pulled his hand from his face to reveal several lines of torn flesh and a freshly broken nose.

"That's for calling my mother a whore," Jionathan said, and Jak shrieked with rage and lunged at the cage, reaching for Jionathan's leg. Jionathan brought the baton down on his outstretched hand, and Jak wrenched himself away with a scream, the crowd laughing. The offending hand turned bright purple, blood pouring between the fingers. Jionathan wouldn't be surprised if he'd broken it.

"How can it be," Bruatar smirked, as his comrades continued to cackle, "that in trying to beat him, you succeeded in *arming* him, Jak?"

"I'll kill you, brat!"

"You will not." Bruatar's smile fell. "Get this milk-faced drunkard bandaged up and out of my sight. And you," he pointed to another in the crowd, "get me those two worthless alchemists."

"But they charge their weight in gold," the chosen bandit argued, and Bruatar clucked his tongue.

"Tell them they can have Jak's weight in gold if they get here before sunrise," he replied and, at the astonishment of his men, sighed. "You don't seem to understand the value of our prisoner—or did you think I kept him for the pleasure of his *wit*? He's worth a hundred and more of those alchemists, and I'm going to rinse him for every drop."

Jionathan's stomach lurched. Bruatar knew who he was. Sensing the Prince's sudden panic, Bruatar gave him an eerie grin—his teeth sharp and white in the darkness—and then turned back to his men.

"Now get on with you. We may have made a fine catch today, but we lost another. I want it found, and I want it skinned. Clear?"

The bandits grumbled, Jak still cradling his cheek and hand.

"Good. Then go," Bruatar ordered, and his eyes flared threateningly. Quickly, the bandits scurried away, Jak following after them with one last growl at Jionathan. Jionathan waved the baton warningly and Jak's cheeks flamed red with anger.

"As for you…" Bruatar was suddenly leaning into the cage, and Jionathan gave a start—the man moved inhumanely fast. "You'd best behave yourself. You'll serve me just as well beaten as not. If you'd like to keep the privilege of both your hands, I suggest you return that to me." He gestured to the baton, but Jionathan held it fiercely. Bruatar smiled. His lips were impossibly long and thin, and he reminded Jionathan of an eel. "I'll give you some time to reconsider," he said, and then departed after his brethren. Jionathan watched him, the baton clutched so tightly, the spines dug into his skin.

He'd been discovered. So soon after escaping, he was in the hands of men who'd sell him back to his prison. Jionathan felt his chest squeeze tightly, and for the first time he truly felt afraid—afraid and bitterly alone.

After all the fortune they'd given him, the gods had revealed the affair to be nothing but a mockery—a lesson in obedience. Jionathan ground his teeth. They plagued him with visions and nightmares, made his days a ceaseless torment, and then, having goaded him with false liberty, they abandoned him when he needed them most.

Perhaps it was punishment. Jionathan thought of Rufus, collapsed against the wall, blood streaming down the side of his face. The Magi were acolytes of the ten sacred gods, chosen and schooled to wield their power. Perhaps in hurting Rufus, Jionathan had doomed himself in the gods' omnipotent eyes.

He looked up at the sky. Above him, he could see the bright star of Aramathea hanging in the north. She was the great mother of the gods, bringer of life and light. If all the other gods saw sport in his suffering, surely she—a mother and figure of warmth—would show him mercy?

"I've done little to deserve your aid, and much to procure your anger, but if you will hear me still, everything I've done, I've done out of fear. I never wanted to hurt those who love me, and I don't ask for forgiveness. All I want, all I ask, is that I might reach Bethean and find sanctuary there. That I might sleep in peace, without dreams, and come to know my own mind—that I might finally learn to face my father's kingdom with the heart to make it mine."

He closed his eyes tightly and reached down to the small pouch hidden in his armour. Inside, his fingers touched the cold band of a golden signet ring, and he drew it out and stared at it.

It was engraved with the Royal Harmatian Crest, the image of a sword thrust into a stone. The ring had been Sverrin's—a gift on his eighteenth birthday—but in his dying moments he'd passed it to Jionathan with a solemn whisper.

"*It's yours now. Harmatia is yours.*"

"Help me, Sverrin," Jionathan breathed, and some of the fear left him. "Please guide me."

"Prayin' to your gods?"

Jionathan stiffened and lurched around, hiding the ring from sight as Jak lumbered toward him from the camp. The bandit's hand and face were bandaged, and there was a murderous gleam in his eye.

"So you should," Jak said. "Because I don't care if you're worth more than the Prince of Harmatia."

"Funny you should say that."

"I'm goin' to stick you like a pig, boy."

Jionathan looked down at the baton in his hands and bit his bottom lip. "You mean with a knife?" he said. "Because with a face like that, I can see why you might resort to pigs—" He flung himself back as Jak jabbed a burning torch through the bars of the cage. Jionathan's heart seized—apparently Jak wasn't as stupid as he'd hoped.

"I'm goin' to roast you!"

"I'll scream." Jionathan forced himself as far back as he could go. "Bruatar won't like it."

"Bruatar gave me his blessin'," Jak replied keenly. "Said to keep your eyes, and face, but the rest of you's fair game. Don't worry—you'll live, though you'll wish you hadn't."

"Stop!" Jionathan ordered, his voice strained. He knew if he kicked or lashed out, he struck every possibility of making Jak drop the torch. And if the flames touched the floor of the wooden-based cage, straw-laden as it was, Jionathan would be cooked alive in minutes. "Stay back."

"Not so cocky now, are we?" Jak leered, but before he could say, or do any more, the flames on the torch disappeared, as if smothered.

Both Jak and Jionathan froze, their eyes on the scorched wood which curled with smoke.

"You do that?" Jak demanded, and Jionathan shook his head dumbly. The bandit slowly pulled the torch out of the cage and examined it. No sooner had he brought it out, did it burst into flames again, and with such ferocity Jak's eyebrows caught alight. He screamed, and Jionathan saw his opportunity. Diving forward, he slipped the baton between the bars and brought it hard against Jak's temple. Jak dropped like a stone. The burning torch rolled from his hand toward the cage and then—to Jionathan's immediate relief—extinguished once more. Jionathan hunched, barely breathing, the baton trembling in his hand as below him, Jak gave a gurgling groan and twitched.

"You're getting sickeningly good at that," Rufus said from behind him, his voice hushed.

Jionathan heard the cage door squeal open. His turned slowly, his breath caught in his throat, eyes wide in disbelief.

"Well, are you coming?" Rufus asked, and Jionathan blinked

stupidly.

"How did you…"

"I used magic." Rufus pointed to himself. "Magi, yes?"

"But the door…" Jionathan looked at the latch, which Rufus had sprung open, but saw no key.

"Jionat, I broke into the royal archives when I was *fifteen*." Rufus scowled. "I can unbolt a door."

Jionathan sat, too stunned to move, as Rufus stared at him in the dark. His blue eyes almost seemed to glow. It occurred to Jionathan that something within him had actually been *waiting* for Rufus to arrive.

"You're late," he said, and allowed Rufus to help him out of the cage.

"I'm *here*," Rufus snapped, "you ingrate." He took Jionathan by the face and examined him closely, his brow furrowed. "Your eyes are dilated," he murmured. "Did they hurt you?"

"I thought he was going to burn me," Jionathan muttered, "but I wasn't afraid. Two years of never-ending fear, and faced with fire, I wasn't afraid." He tore his face away from Rufus's hands, swatting them away. "I need my sword."

"We don't have time."

"I *need* it." Jionathan darted away. "Wait here."

The bandits' camp consisted of a small circle of mismatching tents. The commotion at the cage had gone unnoticed only because most of the bandits appeared to have gathered in a blind-spot to eat—a small blessing. Jionathan moved deftly through the shadows toward a white linen tent where he'd seen the bandits take his sword. Moving to the back, he unpegged a corner and peeked in. A horde of valuables stared back, and Jionathan wriggled through the gap and crouched amongst piles of silks—no doubt stolen from tradesmen along the roads. He found his sword a moment later, and taking it, hurried quickly back to the cage. Rufus had loaded Jak into it, in Jionathan's place.

"He's still alive," Rufus said grimly.

"Then we'd better go before he comes to." Jionathan secured his sword to his belt and started out into the safety of the trees. Rufus followed him uneasily, casting anxious looks behind him.

Beyond the foliage, Jionathan was surprised to find his bay waiting for him, beside a pretty black mare that nickered softly in greeting.

"You found my horse."

"Yes, at the Jaws when you abandoned it for those bandits."

"I was trying to help someone." Jionathan thought back to the golden-haired warrior. "You wouldn't understand."

"Jionathan," Rufus called faintly, and he swivelled back just as palm connected with his cheek. The slap wasn't hard, but Jionathan found himself sprawled on the floor regardless, his face stinging. He blinked, stunned, as everything came into focus. It was like waking from a vivid dream, the dregs of a nightmare ebbing away to the unfriendly face of reality.

"You…" he gasped. "You *pale-faced sycophant!*"

"Oh good, it is you." Rufus lowered his hand. "I had to be sure."

"How dare you!"

"You drugged me and had me bottled. Then you bludgeoned me. Unconscious. *With a candelabrum.*"

Jionathan rose unsteadily to his feet, reliving the sick memory. He hadn't enjoyed hurting Rufus, but he doubted the Magi would believe him if he said so. "Where are the rest of them?"

"Who?"

"Zachary and his band of monsters, of course." The Prince folded his arms tightly. "Or am I to believe you came alone?"

Rufus shifted, folding his own arms. "I did."

Jionathan might have laughed if a sick misery hadn't filled him. He'd escaped his cage, but never his fate. "Of course."

"I *did*. Jionat—" Rufus went to take his arm, but Jionathan pulled away.

"It's *Jionathan,*" he growled.

Rufus's lips pinched into an angry white line, his jaw clenched. In the streaking moonlight, Jionathan could see the dark bruises around Rufus's right eye.

"You arrogant brat," Rufus snarled. "Do you have any idea— *any idea*—of the pain you've caused?"

The Prince took a step back, surprised by the intensity of Rufus's voice.

"Your parents," Rufus went on, "do you know what you put them through?"

Jionathan winced. These words, more than anything, cut him. "I know well enough."

"Clearly."

"I will not be lectured by you," Jionathan hissed. "What would you know about it? What would you know about *anything?* You're just here as the Queen's little blood-hound. You have one function, man—one mindless purpose on which you excel. I should have left you to be torn apart by the Night Patrol the other night. Maybe then I would have escaped without you stalking behind me like the pestilence you are!"

No sooner had he said it, did Jionathan regret even opening his mouth. Rufus stood, speechless, his face white in disbelief.

Jionathan swallowed dryly, his heart clenching. "I...I didn't mean that."

"Yes, you did," Rufus said sharply, and Jionathan flinched. The Magi turned away. "I had to fight," he murmured. "I had to fight to convince them that, what you did, you did through desperation. I *fought* to come after you alone."

"*Why?*" The pain in Jionathan's chest doubled. "What difference does it make? Either way, I'll go back. Either way, by Zachary's jaws or your hand—and for what? To face my parents with another empty excuse? At least if it were Zachary, I might have bled to death first!"

The silence that followed resonated through the forest with an uncomfortable clarity, and Jionathan once again regretted speaking.

"*What*?" Rufus breathed, his pale eyes wide.

Jionathan turned and rested his head against the trunk of a tree, dizzy with exhaustion. "Aren't you sick of this, Rufus—the endless chase between us? Aren't you as tired as I am? Let me go. Please, let me go."

"I'm not going to leave you here."

"No." Jionathan had guessed as much. "Then do as you must. You've caught me."

There was another resounding silence, and then Rufus gave a weary sigh. "Listen, we're both tired. We'll rest a night, heal, and decide where to go in the morning. Be that Bethean or Harmatia."

Jionathan turned back in surprise, and Rufus gave him a terse, humourless smile. Producing Jionathan's dirk from his belt, he handed it over.

"I didn't come to capture you, Jionat. Only to make sure you were safe."

Jionathan took the dirk, allowing the familiar weight to fill his hands as Rufus's words sunk in. He was almost ready to believe Rufus, but before he had a chance to settle his faith, Bruatar's slithering voice broke through the quiet, startling them both.

"That is a great pity." The leader of the bandits stood amongst the trees, his yellow eyes luminous in the dark. Around him, the bandits moved through the shadows, a wall surrounding them.

Rufus cursed and dragged Jionathan behind him, as if he could protect him from all of them.

"A valiant escape, but a wasted one," Bruatar said.

Rufus glowered. "And you are?"

"Bruatar—the humble leader of this raggle-taggle band, if it pleases milord." Bruatar bowed, and Jionathan tugged Rufus's sleeve urgently.

"He knows who I am. And he's not human."

"I can see that," Rufus said, his eyes fixed on Bruatar. "My charge says you know him."

"I recognise a Delphi when I see one." Bruatar grinned. Around him, his men crept further forward, but Rufus spun, one hand outstretched.

"Back!" he ordered. "I'm a Magi. Stay back."

Several of them faltered. Whilst alchemists and those learned in magic were not entirely uncommon in Harmatia or Bethean, the Magi were an elite force with access to boundless knowledge and precise training. They were what a champion knight would be to an untrained farm-lad with a pitchfork.

What was more, with rumours of the Night Patrol spreading throughout the lands, people were more wary now of Magi than ever.

"A *Magi*." Bruatar's eyebrows rose. "Stands to reason. You've seen battle recently, milord?"

Rufus touched the healing wound on his face. Edwin had clearly seen to it, but the skin around the cut was still puckered and dark, and Jionathan could see how haggard Rufus was.

"Name your price," Rufus said. "Harmatia will reward you well for returning their Prince."

Bruatar threw his head back and laughed. "Etheus blind me— you insult me, sir! You think I kept him for a ransom?"

"You said I was worth gold, and you would rinse me for all of it," Jionathan said.

"Stupid boy." Bruatar's face was still cracked in a gleeful grin. "You're worth more gold than I could count, but it's the blood that runs through your veins that's worth diamonds. Powerful blood. The blood of the Tuatha de Danaan. The blood of Niamh."

"Blood of Niamh?" Jionathan furrowed his brow. He'd never heard the name, and yet it resonated through him as if it ought to be familiar.

"Niamh is a faerie goddess," Rufus said. "The Delphi are said to have originated from the ancient Sidhe. But that story is unprecedented, and centuries old."

Bruatar seemed surprised by Rufus's words. "Is such

knowledge so privileged in Harmatia that people have turned it to myth? Have you forgotten your ancestors?" He shook his head. "Brothers," he said mockingly to his comrades, "it's a sad day indeed when a Delphi doesn't know himself."

"Enough," Rufus said. "Whatever you hope to gain from him, you'll profit more by letting us go. I'm a man of my word, and I'll see you rich."

"Riches get spent," Bruatar said. "I want the eternal future."

An uneasy feeling settled over Jionathan. Suddenly he understood exactly what Bruatar wanted.

"Let's compromise, milord," Bruatar offered. "I'll let you keep your lives, and your gold. And in exchange, I'll take his *eyes.*" He pointed to Jionathan, who jerked back.

"Not as long as I breathe," Rufus said.

"It's a bargain!" Bruatar cried, and the bandits flocked in toward them.

Jionathan drew his sword. But before anyone could reach their enemy, the silence of the forest was broken by a horrified scream. Jionathan spun on the spot, and went cold.

Through the trees a humongous, black shape was moving toward them, eyes burning like bright green lanterns. The bandits scattered, Bruatar staring in horror.

"No…" he croaked. "No, not now. Stop it! Kill it!"

The faerie advanced on them, unfurling its black, feathered wings as it raised its head— feline in shape—and roared.

CHAPTER 7

~⟨⟩~

In the heat of the bandits' panic, Rufus and Jionathan were forgotten. They sat, sprawled like children on the ground where they'd fallen in their surprise, and watched the violent scene unfurl before them.

Jionathan shook Rufus's shoulder, silver eyes wide. "What is it?"

Rufus watched as the faerie clenched its teeth around an attacking bandit and tossed the corpse from side to side, like a playful kitten killing its first mouse.

"A Cat Sidhe," Rufus said slowly, his voice foggy to his own ears. He felt like he'd taken another heavy blow to the head.

"A cat-she?" Jionathan frowned, as a bandit was flung, screaming, over their heads and landed hard on the rocks behind them, his skull cracked open.

"No, a Cat *Sidhe!*" Rufus found his feet, hiccupping. Seizing Jionathan by the back of his collar, he hoisted him to his feet. "Now run! *Run!*"

Jionathan took no persuading. The pair threw themselves onto the backs of their respective mounts, and with hard kicks, spurred the horses into a gallop, charging into the forest like the

Wild Hunt was chasing them.

Even as they fled the chaos, Rufus was wary. Whilst he wanted nothing more than to put as much distance between himself and the feline monstrosity that had unintentionally saved them, Rufus also knew that dashing head-first into a faerie forest without a clear destination was dangerous.

No sooner had he acknowledged this, did Rufus realise that there was something strange about their surroundings. He slowed his gallop to a canter, and then down into an uneven plod, twisting around in his saddle to take in the scenery. Up ahead of him Jionathan glanced back.

"Come on!" Jionathan cried. "Why are you stopping?"

Rufus realised that Moyna had come to a standstill. "We're going in the wrong direction."

Jionathan pulled his horse back around. "Does it matter? We can turn south when we've made some distance."

Rufus shook his head, trying to clear it as a veil of fog began to fall over his usually sharp senses. "In the presence of the fae, walk steady on. For if you lose your way, they'll take your tongue."

"Now isn't the time for children's rhymes," Jionathan said, the bay tossing its head. "We need to go!"

Rufus felt as if his mind were numb. Gone was his fear, replaced now with a dreadful emptiness—that cruel feeling of realisation. "It's a cautionary tale," he said. "Never lose your way in a faerie wood."

"We *aren't* lost." Jionathan pointed to the starry sky above, where the star of Aramathea hung high in the horizon. "See, north. That's all we need."

Rufus blinked slowly. He suddenly felt very aware of his head wounds, and feared for a moment that he was going to topple off his horse. He'd ridden so hard in pursuit of Jionathan, he hadn't permitted himself the time to heal or rest. Now when his wits were needed most, he could feel them failing him. "That isn't north."

"What do you mean it *isn't north*?" Jionathan demanded, and then lurched forward in his saddle, steadying Rufus as he began to tumble to the left. "Didn't Edwin see to your wounds?"

"He did." Rufus corrected himself. He felt opiated and lethargic. "I simply…" He blinked again, trying to banish the feeling from his body. There was something strange about the foggy confusion, and he realised with a sinking heart that it wasn't caused by any concussion. "Glamour."

"What?"

"Glamour." Rufus winced again, drooping forward on his horse. "I'm such a fool."

"I don't understand."

"Faerie glamour." Rufus tried to be patient, clenching the reins tightly. "We've escaped one trap and fallen straight into another."

The world around them seemed to shimmer. It was the perfect illusion, but Rufus was trained to know the stars. Up above them, the heavens boasted the Septus constellation, a group of stars which weren't supposed to rise for another six hours, as well as the blue star Haylix, which should've disappeared shortly after the hours of sunset.

"Look around you—we've ridden through this spot three times already. We're going in circles," Rufus said unsteadily, his head spinning.

"What's wrong with you?" Jionathan leant in.

"The glamour is reflecting the stars' power erratically. It's confusing my senses." Worse than that, Rufus thought, it was beginning to affect his depth of perception. The Magi learnt to depend wholly on their sense of the stars—it was a second sight, and in this case a great weakness. "I hope this isn't that changeling's work."

"Changeling?"

"Bruatar." Rufus closed his eyes and felt himself sway dangerously again. He forced them open, trying to hold back the wave of dizziness that overcame him. As if the earth was spinning beneath his feet—perhaps it was?

"Bruatar was a changeling?" Jionathan whistled.

"I can only assume. He was a faerie, but his demeanour was human." Rufus groaned. "Jionat…I'm going to fall."

"Don't."

Rufus slid off his saddle and tumbled to the ground. Jionathan cursed and, leaping down from the bay, came to his side.

"Rufus." He rolled him onto his back, making Rufus's stomach churn ungratefully. "Get up."

Rufus groaned again. "The earth is tipping…I'm tired…and my head hurts."

"Well, my body hurts, too," Jionathan said, impatiently.

"Yes, but that's probably your own fault." Rufus slumped back, breathing slowly. "A moment, please…a moment to adjust."

Jionathan obliged him, and after a blissful minute of peace, Rufus allowed himself to be hoisted up and manoeuvred onto a tree stump, where he sat as Jionathan paced in front of him.

"So we've entered a faerie trap that guides us in circles back to this point, no matter which direction we take?"

"Yes," Rufus said. "We're going to die."

"We're *not* going to die," Jionathan barked. "If you have nothing useful to say, then don't speak."

Rufus sat in silence as Jionathan continued to pace, murmuring to himself quietly as he thought. Rufus didn't have the heart to tell Jionathan that, unless a faerie came to either guide them out of the glamour or eat them, they would starve to death long before they managed to escape.

"Something's coming," Jionathan's hand was suddenly on his sword and his eyes were closed, as if he were concentrating on a distant sound. Rufus listened closely, but heard nothing to substantiate Jionathan's claim.

"What are you—" he began, but he wasn't given the chance to complete his sentence. The canopy above them parted like set of curtains, and through it the Cat Sidhe leapt down. It landed in front of them, stretching its majestic wings before folding them against its back. The horses reared in terror, pulling at their tethers.

Rufus tumbled back from his squat, and then scrabbled to his feet. Jionathan drew his sword in defence. The Cat Sidhe looked between them and seemed to smile, fangs gleaming. Rufus might have said it laughed, if he hadn't known better.

"Young Prince," a booming female voice made the leaves shiver in the trees, "would you attack me now, when I came to your aid?"

Jionathan almost dropped his sword in surprise, and Rufus fell back, his legs weak. The Cat Sidhe rested her head in her mighty paws.

"Put away your sword. I mean you no harm."

"Y-you…" Jionathan scrabbled back, so that he was behind Rufus. "You can speak?"

Again, the Cat Sidhe seemed to laugh. Though her voice was loud, it had a pleasant tone to it.

"Yes." She elongated the vowel mockingly, and Jionathan jabbed his weapon out toward her. She focused her piercing green eyes on the blade, but made no move to defend herself. Jionathan drew back warily.

"What do you mean…come to my aid?" he finally asked. "Why would you do that?"

"I owe you a debt—you saved my life," the Cat Sidhe purred. "Or perhaps you don't recognise me?"

"I think I would remember…" Jionathan's voice quivered, and the Cat Sidhe stood again, her tail flicking the branches behind her so that they hissed. Rufus repressed a nervous, shrill laugh. Upright, on all four legs, she stood taller than him and boasted a thick coat of obsidian fur, broken only by a blood-matted white star in the centre of her chest. Her claws were as long as a human hand and her teeth were very sharp. Rufus had to agree, that if they had met, Jionathan would have surely remembered such an encounter.

"I should hope you do," she replied, and then something peculiar happened. All at once, the place she stood was enveloped in a cloud of dark mist, and her looming form began to shrink. The lightless veil of smoke curled elegantly around her as she shifted, her body morphing so that—where once stood a ferocious beast—a striking young woman took its place.

The first thing that struck Rufus about her was that she was heavily armed. Boasting a significant arsenal of twin blades, an unstrung bow with a cluster of arrows, a belt of throwing knives, and a small axe at her hip, she moved soundlessly, as if their weight and size didn't trouble her. Rufus watched, transfixed, as she stepped into the waxing moonlight. Her body was compact and powerful, skin like living marble, with all the beauty of its veins and scars. Her eyes, as in her cat form, glowed green like enchanted sea mist and Rufus couldn't help but stare into them, almost as a man stares into the depths of the bottomless ocean. On her left wrist a crescent-shaped birthmark broke the stretch of pale skin, which was otherwise littered with the white scars and blemishes of a seasoned warrior. This one, Rufus realised, had seen the multiple faces of battle, and in a human form—no taller than Jionathan, with a similar build—she was suddenly more frightening than she'd been before.

"You," Jionathan breathed, and Rufus jolted with surprise as the Prince lowered his sword, mouth agape. "From the Jaws."

"So you *do* remember," she said. "I apologise for leaving you there, but I had been fighting for the better part of the night, and stood in increasing peril of capture. I have been waiting for the opportunity to rescue you in turn." She frowned. "I hope that they didn't hurt you too badly?"

"You jumped." Jionathan didn't hear her words, his eyes glazed with astonishment. "I watched you jump down the gorge. Nothing could survive that fall. And your leg, you were injured...?"

"Wounds heal, and my wings aren't decoration. I couldn't transform and fly away before your interference because of those nets. They were especially enchanted to sap me of my strength and bind my power. I would have been dead and skinned by nightfall, had you not saved me. And for that, you have my gratitude and my favour."

She inclined her head, and Rufus had the odd sensation that he was watching a mountain bow. He sat, petrified to his post, mouth dry and fingers trembling in his lap. Never mind that his senses were still confused by the spinning sky and ground, he was now sat in the presence of a Sidhe, the most powerful of all the faerie, and it wouldn't be long before she discovered what he was.

"You called me Prince. I assume you know me, then?" Jionathan spoke carefully, and though he'd put away his sword, his hand remained on the hilt.

"Jionathan of the Delphi," the Cat Sidhe replied.

Jionathan grunted and released his blade, moving out from behind Rufus. "It seems every faerie in this wood knows me."

"Some know the scent of your blood."

"And you?"

"I recognised the crest on your sword." She smiled. "And I overheard Bruatar name you." She turned then on Rufus, who clenched his shivering hands, bowing his head with a wince, as if her stare alone had whipped him. "And this would be?"

"Nobody worth killing." Rufus shied away from her as far as he dared. Her eyes seemed to ignite with green fire, and if Rufus weren't so frightened, he might have been captivated.

"Under whose judgment?"

When he didn't respond, the Cat Sidhe turned once more to Jionathan, her expression softening slightly.

"If this one is your enemy, I will dispose of him."

For a moment, Rufus thought he might faint. He imagined his father, sitting at home, murmuring a prayer for Rufus's safe

93

return. Who would tell his parents that he'd perished? Would they be left awaiting his return for months, hoping against hope that he'd somehow lived?

"No," Jionathan said quickly. "No, he was sent after me from Harmatia. He freed me from that cage."

Rufus breathed again, closing his eyes. He could see his parents still, sat together in the darkened kitchen, the howl of the Night Patrol just beyond the shutters. He realised with a start that it had been some years since he'd been out so late under the stars.

"Then he's a mercenary?" The Cat Sidhe examined Rufus's lean form doubtfully. "A Knight perhaps?"

Jionathan snorted. Rufus tried to make himself smaller.

The Cat Sidhe leant down, her brow lowering. "You smell of fire."

"I used it to distract the bandit who guarded Jionat," Rufus said, before Jionathan could. "As for who I am—only a lowly lord."

"And tell me, what business does a 'lowly lord' have following a Prince into a faerie wood?"

"I volunteered." Rufus swallowed.

"And how is it you found the Prince, when this forest is so vast and dangerous?"

Rufus had been asked such a question many times before, though never under so much threat. He could never truthfully answer or explain the strange sense he had of Jionathan, and the way that—no matter where the Prince hid—Rufus could always find him. He shrugged, running his fingers through his fringe. "I have a knack for finding what's lost."

The Cat Sidhe wasn't impressed. "And have you found yourself then, lowly lord?"

Rufus gave a tight smile. "The glamour forbade me from doing so."

At this she laughed. "As it has forbidden many before you,

but you did well to recognise it, and you're fortunate that I am unaffected by its veil." She turned back to Jionathan. "Your bravery has earned you my favour. In return for it, I will deliver you from this forest back to Harmatia."

"No!" Jionathan spoke so ferociously, Rufus almost fell off his perch again. The Cat Sidhe drew back, her hands twitching toward her swords. Jionathan paled, a thin sheet of perspiration on his face, eyes wide with a sudden panic. "Not there," he begged. "Don't return me there."

"Jionat." Rufus stood, still a little unsteady on his feet. "It's alright."

"No," Jionathan said. "If I return to the capital, then I return to die. And for thirteen years darkness will rule Harmatia." Once more, Jionathan's pupils dilated, and in the half-light of the leaf-shrouded moon, his grey eyes seemed to glow.

"Calm down," Rufus said. "Death isn't waiting for you in Harmatia. I promise you."

"The descendants of death killed my brother, and my own will be its cure. And so it bides its time at the heart of my city." Jionathan's voice became hollow, a foreboding echo that made Rufus's body erupt with shivers.

"Jionat..." Rufus said, but beside him the Cat Sidhe shook her head solemnly.

"Heed the words of a Delphi," she said. "Prince Jionathan, if Harmatia is dangerous, then let me deliver you elsewhere. Though," she hesitated, "I will ask that you permit me a day to complete my business here first?"

Jionathan blinked, and his pupils shrank a little. Rufus ran his hand through his hair anxiously.

"Your business?" Jionathan asked.

The Cat Sidhe seemed to consider them a moment, and then spoke. "You are no doubt aware that some weeks ago, Princess Aurora, daughter of King Markus of Bethean, ran away from home into these woods."

"I heard something of that nature," Jionathan said. "My father ordered several platoons of soldiers and Magi to help carry out the search. It was fruitless."

Rufus didn't miss the slight twitch of distaste in the Cat Sidhe's cheek when the Prince said the word 'Magi', and he quietly retreated once more to his post and sat, invisible.

"Indeed." The Cat Sidhe gestured to the woods around her. "Those who become lost here are rarely seen again. However, the guarded truth is that the Princess didn't run away—she was kidnapped."

"Kidnapped?" Rufus cursed his own mouth as the Cat Sidhe looked around at him.

"Yes," she said, "by an old associate of mine. As you may know, the treaty between the Seelie Court and the Kingdom of Bethean, binds us to protect the Betheanian people from the malevolent ones of our kind. When evidence arose as to the perpetrator of the kidnap, I was commissioned to find him and return the Princess home."

"Why you?" Jionathan was blunt with his curiosity.

"My kind are a branch of the Sidhe akin to mercenaries. We are deployed when the delicate nature of a situation requires the power and skill of an army, but the subtlety of one man. As to my involvement, my personal relationship with the kidnapper makes me suited to the task."

Even before he spoke, Rufus had a dark suspicion he knew what Jionathan was about to say. But, for a blissful moment, Rufus allowed himself to conjure the fanciful idea that Jionathan wasn't so damned eager to get them both killed.

"We can help," Jionathan offered brightly, and all the darkness in his face faded into transparent glee.

"Oh, I hate you so much sometimes!" Rufus said into his hands. "Athea strike me dead."

"That can be arranged," Jionathan said jovially, suddenly so playful it was as if he'd forgotten his own dark prophecy. To the

Cat Sidhe he continued, "I know my skill is unmatched to yours, but I would like to help. Bethean is Harmatia's sistering country, and if I can assist you in saving the Princess, then let me. And forget Rufus—he has to do as I say, so he'll follow regardless. Even if he protests until his teeth fall out."

"I'll make *your* teeth fall out," Rufus growled into his hands.

The Cat Sidhe considered him. "Young Prince…"

"Please—Jionathan." Jionathan offered his hand. "I'm no more a Prince in these woods than Rufus is a god."

The Cat Sidhe took his outstretched hand, their fingers locking together. She smiled warmly, and Rufus looked between the pair as Jionathan's own expression softened.

Sweet Haylix, he thought despairingly. *Could the boy be so stupid?*

"Jionathan," the Cat Sidhe said, "you have done enough already. But if it's your wish to help me, then I would be honoured to keep your company." She dropped into a shallow curtsey, her head bowed. "My name is Fae Ó Murchadha, Cat Sidhe of the Neve, and I would be happy for your assistance."

CHAPTER
8

Fae led them, as promised, out of the faerie trap and to a small glade where she deemed it safe to rest for the night. For Jionathan's part, he was relieved at the chance to rest. After the excitement of his escape, his abused body was tired and ready for sleep.

Rufus offered both of them a portion of bread and salted pork from his saddle bag. Then, whilst Fae and Jionathan ate, he set about building a fire, struggling with a set of fire-flints as he tried to get the kindling to light.

"Will you stop and eat something? Your struggle is positively exhausting." Jionathan winced as Rufus struck the stones together again, the sparks spraying uselessly to the ground.

"I haven't the stomach."

"You should eat. You will need your strength, if you mean to escape this forest alive," Fae warned.

Rufus peered warily up at her, and dropped his head quickly, his shoulders hunched. He still seemed fearful of her, and Jionathan couldn't conceive why. What evil agenda could Fae have, when she'd fought so hard to free them both from the bandits, and led them out to safety? Jionathan wasn't gullible, he knew the forest was full of danger, but he sensed genuine kindness from Fae. Moreover, he couldn't forget the way he'd seen her at the Jaws, or the feelings that had overcome him. He might not have been able to name how, but he was certain his destiny was deeply entwined with hers, and he delighted in that.

She was certainly a refreshing change to Rufus, who'd remained in gloomy silence for the duration of the evening.

"Take this." Fae broke Jionathan from his thoughts. She drew something small and silver from her belt—a tiny whistle. "In case we're separated. Mine use it when we're hunting, to coordinate attacks."

"Thank you." Jionathan admired it, releasing the signet ring he'd been swivelling on his finger.

"You have it, don't you?" Fae peered into his face curiously.

"What?"

"The Sight." She tilted her head, her green eyes inquisitive and feline. "You seem to know things."

The Prince's throat tightened. "I couldn't say. It's not that I know. I simply…sometimes I have sense of something, a feeling. I can't explain."

"And when you intervened in my battle, did you do that on a feeling?"

"You must think me impulsive?"

"No," Fae said. "Stupid, perhaps but…"

Jionathan balked at the sincerity in her tone, and she laughed at his expression. He relaxed again. "You're mocking me," he realised, with his own smile.

"You make yourself an easy target."

Jionathan grunted. "It's true that I must have looked rather foolish."

"Perhaps, but why should that matter? You know best why you came to my aid and why you are sat here with me now, when most civilised Harmatians might have run ten miles." She offered him a draught of water, which he accepted gratefully.

"Yes, but in such a trap as we were, ten miles wouldn't have gotten either of us very far." Jionathan drank eagerly. The bandits had stripped him of his water pouch, and his throat was dry and parched. "Thank you."

"For the water?"

"For everything."

In the moonlight, he wasn't sure if she blushed. She suddenly appeared youthful, perhaps no older than he.

"You saved my life."

"I had to." He leaned in toward her so that they spoke in whispers.

"A feeling?"

"Yes," he breathed.

Across the glade the sharp clatter of fire-flints broke the peace.

"Hexias give me strength—will you *desist*?" Jionathan cried to Rufus, who struck the stones against one another again.

Rufus scowled. "Do you want to go cold?"

"You made Jak's torch extinguish and then burst into flame with a wave of your hand. So will you stop hitting those rocks together like you have a clue how to use them, and just light the damn fire?"

Rufus gave Jionathan a glum look and went back to striking the fire-flints together. From across him, Fae, who'd moved as if to relieve Rufus of the burden, grew still.

"You can use elemental magic?" she asked softly.

Rufus flinched, as if she'd drawn a weapon. "I can." His voice was impossibly small. "A little. Poorly."

"Will you relax, she won't hurt you," Jionathan said, and Rufus seemed to grow even smaller, his face pale. "They say he's a prodigy—some sort of genius—though you wouldn't know it."

Rufus gave a small whine. "Please."

"Please, what?" Fae's voice dropped dangerously, and she rose to her feet, her face dark with anger. "Remind me again, lowly lord, what position do you hold in the court?"

Jionathan rose cautiously, Rufus stumbling to his own feet as he retreated shakily back toward the horses. Fae advanced, her shoulders rippling, as if she were preparing to pounce.

"I…" Rufus raised his hands, his voice squeaking. "I…I'm…" His back hit a tree, and he stood, pinned to the trunk. He grew still and exhaled shakily, closing his eyes. "I'm a Magi."

Fae moved so swiftly, Jionathan wasn't given the chance to protest. She leapt on Rufus, her hands latching around his throat. She thrust him hard against the tree, and then up, his legs hanging above the roots.

"Stop!" Jionathan dove after them. "No, stop!"

"Magi?" Fae hissed as Rufus choked, his legs kicking uselessly as he dangled, suspended from her fierce fingers. "Treasure this sensation, it is your last."

"Let go! Let him go!" Jionathan released his sword, sensing Fae would have no fear of it, and grabbed her arm instead. "Fae, *please!*"

Fae's grip tightened, and Rufus clawed frantically at her hand, his blue eyes wide with terror. His cheeks had begun to tinge purple. Jionathan pulled at her arm urgently.

"Please," he begged. "Let him go. Please."

Fae snapped her eyes around to Jionathan, her face contorted with fury. At his expression, her own changed, the burning ferocity seeping away into something cooler. With a small snarl, she released Rufus and stepped back. Rufus dropped to his hands and knees, gasping and coughing.

"I should kill you," she hissed. "I should kill you now."

Rufus might have responded, but his words were lost in his splutters as he heaved in a painful breath, collapsing to the floor.

"You didn't say you rode with a Magi," Fae growled at Jionathan, and he shuddered at the furious betrayal in her face.

"I didn't know it was important. He's not really a—no, I mean he *is* a Magi, but," Jionathan stammered, "he's not *really*. He's just—Rufus is just…Rufus."

On the floor Rufus coughed, sitting back against the tree, his white throat angry now with bruises. With the marks around his face, he looked like he'd been left in the stocks a week. Jionathan eyed him with concern. At the side, Rufus's horse tossed its head urgently, pawing at the ground and trying to break free from its tether.

"Do you know what they have done?" Fae's voice quivered with rage, her hands gripping the hilts of her swords tightly, as if she still longed to be throttling Rufus. "His kind have skinned my kin for coats!" Her rage overcame her and, seizing Rufus by the collar of his cloak once more, she hoisted him to his feet. "If Bruatar had his way, he would have skinned me alive and one of your brothering Magi would be wearing my fur on the next moon. You *humans*."

Jionathan stood, aghast. "Is this true?"

"A century ago," Rufus wheezed, his voice crackling and frail, "Lord Graver, a General in the military was set upon in the mountains by a Cat Sidhe. He managed to defeat it, and wore its pelt as a sign of victory." He coughed, his eyes watering. "Since then, some Magi have followed his example, and wear Cat Sidhe fur as a sign of power..." Rufus looked up, eyes pleading. "But I never..."

"No." Fae dropped him, stalking to the other side of the glade. "They're expensive things, our skin." She stood, staring out into the trees, as if she might abandon them and return to her mission. A thought seemed to occur to her, and she turned accusingly back. "Or perhaps you didn't know that we're not mindless animals, that we mourn our dead?"

Rufus sat, defeated. "I didn't know," he confessed faintly. "Or that Cat Sidhe could take the likeness of a human. I didn't know."

"The *likeness*?" A fresh rage took over Fae, and for a moment Jionathan feared she would take Rufus's head. "This is not a human *likeness*." She gestured to herself. "This form is no more an illusion than my other—both are mine. My bodies. A part of my being."

"I didn't know."

"Of course not," she spat. "You're ignorant. Ignorant to the suffering you have caused my people—my family! For your Magi fashion I have lost friends, cousins, a *sister* to the blade!" Her jaw was clenched. "But you can be forgiven because you 'didn't know'? Is that the way of it?"

"I didn't ask forgiveness." Rufus voice grew stronger, and he rose to his full height, looming over Jionathan. His face was severe. "But you judge me on the culpabilities of others. I'm no villain."

"All Magi are villains," Fae said, and Jionathan watched helplessly as the pair stood off against one another. "Don't think because I am from Avalon that I don't know your practices, know about your Night Patrol, or that you worship the Red Star—the harbinger of death among your own people."

On this, Jionathan could agree. The Red Star, known to the Harmatians as Athea, was the ruler of the night and goddess of death. Whilst Jionathan knew she maintained the balance between the ruling powers, she nevertheless was only worshiped directly by the Magi. The priests chose only to call upon her during the rites of death, or to warn sinners of punishment.

"It's my duty as a Magi to pay tribute to all the gods," Rufus said, exasperated. "Death is as much part of our existence as life, and it's only our fear of it that paints Athea as anything more than what she is."

Fae laughed. "Your religion is corrupted."

"That is the definition of any religion!" Rufus's voice grew, and for a moment his eyes seemed to catch light, burning fiercely. "But would you judge me on something you know nothing about?"

For a moment, Jionathan feared this outburst would be Rufus's last, but Fae merely stood in silence, so still she could have been made of stone. Then she strode to the fire-place, and seizing the fire-flints she sat and struck them quickly together, her back to the pair. Where once her shoulders had been taut with rage, they were now relaxed, and her face was as solemn and impenetrable as a marble death-mask.

"You're wrong," she said softly. "I can't hate indiscriminately. The Magi have killed my kin this past century, but I won't judge you based on your stock. Clearly something of your character has endeared you to Jionathan, and on that merit I won't kill you. However," she struck the flints together and the kindling lit, the fire growing from its meagre sparks, "if you give me so much as *one* reason to mistrust you, then know I will rip your tongue out and then choke you with it."

Rufus bowed his head resignedly, gently rubbing at his tender throat. "I understand." He stumbled away in the dark toward the horses, where his mare whinnied loudly in distress. He touched the horse's nose and calmed it, pressing his face to its coat. Jionathan remained a moment where he was, and then joined Fae by the new fire. He sat beside her.

"Forgive me," she murmured, her hands twisted into the front of her chemise. Though her face was passive, her eyes were downcast into the flames, too concentrated to be relaxed.

"I didn't know about…what the Magi did," Jionathan said. "Were I you, I think I would have probably killed him on the spot. But I'm glad you didn't."

"You care for him?"

"No, it's not…" Jionathan pursed his lips. "I don't know," he said. "I don't know if I can trust him. But at the same time, I don't think my mother would like it if she found out I stood by and watched him die."

Fae's lips twitched. "Is that all that motivates you?"

Jionathan glanced back at Rufus, who was now engaged in a deep conversation with his horse, his back to them both. "He is what he is. I don't know where his loyalties lie, but he did follow me into these woods, so I suppose by delegation I hold some responsibility in seeing us both out."

"I respect that." Fae tugged at the bindings that held her long mane of golden hair back. "But, if you should change your mind on the matter—"

"You'll be the first to know," Jionathan said, and then yawned. Fae smiled at him.

"You should rest," she urged. "There will be plenty more adventure for you tomorrow."

"I almost dread it." Jionathan lay back on the ground, and watched as, once more, the all-knowing colours of his nightmares began to dance behind his eyelids, teasing him mischievously. He turned his back to the fire, Fae, and Rufus.

Darkness overcame him with his sleep, and before him flashed a blinding battle, banners flaring in the sky as below the heavens men died, shields splintering together as swords collided and soldiers screamed for their gods.

And in the trees, far beyond the boundaries of their conflict, as the stench of death and war rose with the heat of the day, a single dark-haired woman sat hopelessly upon the riverbank, and washed her bloodied clothes.

CHAPTER
9

Jionathan awoke to the gentle weight of a warm, thick blanket over his body. He lay, his head rested in the crook of his arm as the morning light peeped through his curls, dappling across his face. He closed his fingers around the soft, unfamiliar coverlet, and breathed in its sweet scent. It smelled faintly of lavender, and he closed his eyes a moment, dozing comfortably.

When he opened his eyes next, it was to the sight of Fae, lying asleep in her cat form across the fire from him. In the early sun, her silky black coat shimmered with each steady breath, and Jionathan realised that he had indeed seen several Magi proudly adorned in a similar fur. When he was King, he could outlaw the barbaric custom.

More alert now, Jionathan turned his attention to the blanket he'd cocooned himself in. It certainly wasn't his own, which was thinner and meaner to the skin, so it must have been one of the pair Rufus brought with him.

Rufus—Jionathan realised the Magi wasn't in the camp. To the left Moyna stood with the bay, the horse's saddle and Rufus's bags bundled along with Jionathan's own, but though all his things were there, Rufus was nowhere in sight.

With a soft grumble, Jionathan sat up and scanned the area again, this time spotting a set of light tracks leading away from their camp. He thought of returning to his slumbers, but with his rest now disturbed, curiosity got the best of him. Hugging the blankets about him like a child in a father's cloak, Jionathan set off after Rufus.

The trail led him down to the river. At its side a set of clothes were neatly folded, and Jionathan considered them, rolling his aching shoulder. The peaceful surface of the water suddenly broke, and from its midst Rufus stood, taking in a long gulp of air.

"Isn't a little cold for a bath?" Jionathan said, and Rufus started.

Blinking the water from his eyes, he glanced around, spotting Jionathan. "You're awake."

"A masterful observation." Jionathan sat on the bank as Rufus pulled himself out from the river and stood, water cascading down his white body. "Etheus blind me—would you cover up?"

"With what—my clean, dry clothes?" Rufus dropped down beside him, and sat cross-legged, his head tipped back toward the sun. In the cold morning light, Jionathan could have sworn he could see gentle curls of steam evaporating from Rufus's body.

"You have no shame," Jionathan said, and Rufus examined himself. His chest and back were littered with a cluster of faded bruises and scars, and Jionathan could see the distinct outline of Rufus's ribs. He shuddered.

"How does it look?" Rufus gestured to the injured side of his face. The once-darkened skin had turned a pale shade of maroon, whilst the wound itself had receded to a thin, white line. Across his neck, the inflamed, purple lines from Fae's fingers were also fading fast to a sickening yellow.

"You're healing quickly."

"Always do." Rufus almost seemed a little irritated by the fact. "And you, how are yours?"

Jionathan, unwilling to part from the blanket, burrowed his head beneath it and examined his own shoulder and chest. The bandits' beating had left him with several vivid blemishes, but whilst his body ached, his freedom tasted too fine to dwell on the price.

"I'll do." He remerged from the bundle.

"And your shoulder?"

"Edwin saw to it before I left. It's stiff, but manageable." Jionathan frowned. "How did you know about it?" Rufus hadn't been present during Zachary's vicious attack.

"I saw when I saved you from the Queen." Rufus sat back, drying in the sun—though for all the bright, chilly air, he seemed to have already purged himself of most of the water.

"You'll get sick," Jionathan warned. "Sat like that. And not eating."

Rufus laughed. The sound was oddly hollow. "Jionat, when was the last time you saw any Magi fall so easily ill?"

Jionathan thought on this. It was true—he'd never known a single of his father's regular Magi courtiers to display signs of even a cough or cold. "Can you not?"

"We can," Rufus said. "But it's uncommon. Any illness a Magi falls prey to is a cruel one. Though a Magi can still overexert themselves, of course." Rufus examined his hands almost curiously, turning them over. "They're only men."

Jionathan raised his eyebrow. "And you're...what exactly, then?"

"I—oh, yes. A man, as well. Of course. A Magi." Rufus's eyes became unfocused, and then he squinted down at himself again. "I'm dry." He seemed surprised and cursed faintly.

"Another masterful deduction," Jionathan said. "You're getting good at those."

Rufus dressed himself, his white chemise sticking lightly to his damp hair which, wet as it was, hung down to the back of his neck. Rufus ruffled it and tugged at his fringe, so that it stuck up

at odd angles.

"What's wrong?" Jionathan asked.

"Nothing," Rufus replied, and digging his hands into his pocket, he removed a long chain and pulled it around his neck. A pendant swung from it, but Jionathan didn't get the chance to identify what it was before Rufus tucked it under his chemise. "Let me see your shoulder."

Jionathan clung protectively to the blankets, and then conceded, letting them drop. He removed his shirt and allowed Rufus to take a look. The severed skin was mended, and all that was left was an angry red scar, dark with bruises and puckered. Rufus raised his hand slowly, looking at Jionathan for permission. Jionathan gave him a one-armed shrug, and Rufus placed his fingers gently on the wound.

"Ouch," Jionathan complained as Rufus gingerly kneaded the skin. A warm feeling swept over his shoulder, and where once the cold dregs of a steady ache had worried the muscle and skin, Jionathan felt the strain ease. He realised with a jolt that Rufus was using magic. "You can heal?"

"I've been studying a little under Lord Edwin." Rufus frowned in concentration. "I can't heal nearly as well as him, but I've learnt how to ease pain and encourage the natural healing process. There, does that help a little?"

It had helped a great deal. Only now when he was free of it did Jionathan realise how painful the ache in his shoulder had been. "Thank you."

"It was Zachary, wasn't it?" Rufus's voice sounded pained. "He did this."

Jionathan was surprised Rufus needed to ask. Zachary had taken responsibility for the majority of injuries Jionathan sustained during his many escape attempts.

"I heard you were almost out. That they pinned you at the gates."

"Yes, but I'm under no illusion that was by any stroke of

fortune," Jionathan said, bitterly. "They let me get that far. Your beast of a brother was toying with me."

"Zachary isn't my—" Rufus cut himself off and sighed. "I'm sorry for what he's done to you. You'll never forgive him, I know, and he'll be too stubborn to ask for it when he realises he's done wrong. So for him, I'll say sorry. He's not…He's not in his right mind."

Jionathan laughed in disbelief. "Not in his right mind—that's his excuse? Rufus, he leads a band of monsters through my city, killing innocents by night and feasting on their corpses. He's a wild murderer with no concept of consequence or justice. Athea herself might as well have spawned him onto the earth."

Rufus turned and began to wash his hands in the river as Jionathan dressed, pulling the blanket back around himself.

"He's not like that. Not really," Rufus said softly, almost to himself. "He's not a monster."

"He doesn't even feel *pain*, Rufus. I know—I watched him training Sverrin those years ago. No matter the strike, your half-man of a brother never even cried out—never flinched."

"There is a vast difference between not feeling and feigning."

"Have *you* ever seen him cry out?" Jionathan demanded, and Rufus deflated, his shoulders hunching.

"Not as a result of a wound," he admitted, shaking his hands dry and then tugging them through his hair. "But…"

"But?" Jionathan pressed, and again Rufus sighed, the sound bone-weary.

"The night your brother died."

A cold feeling came over Jionathan. He remembered it well—the sound of Reine wailing, Sverrin's open eyes vacant and empty, the King lain across his chest in petrified sorrow.

Rufus continued, "The four Magi guards who allowed the assassin to pass through into the chambers…they fled from Harmatia. Zachary went after them, my master and myself not far behind. He reached them first. Tore them to scraps himself—

four to one, but Zachary's strong." A strange expression came over Rufus's face, haunted and distant. "We reached him, and he was sat amidst their corpses, and…" Rufus drew off, his face grey.

Jionathan waited a moment and then kicked his knee gently. "And?"

"He was laughing."

Jionathan barely contained his disgust. "*Laughing?*"

Rufus shook his head, mouth oddly slack, like he was about to be sick. "The sound…" His voice was hoarse. "If you'd heard it, Jionat…it was like a *howl*. He was laughing, and it was like he was being flayed alive."

Jionathan locked his teeth together, his fingers curling into fists. "Perhaps he shouldn't have let Sverrin die, then."

"Jionat—"

"No," Jionathan said. "I will *not* feel pity for that man." And suddenly he was shrouded in a red mist of anger, and the words spilled from his mouth like poison. "He doesn't *deserve* pity. He's a blood-sucking monster who plagues Harmatia with his fellow band of killers!"

"Please, Jionat, don't do this," Rufus breathed, but Jionathan ignored him.

"Those same murderers who your beloved Master Odin shelters—hiding their identities 'for the safety of those who do the cruel duty of the law'. As if they don't enjoy it, as if we can't hear their shrieks of delight every night."

"Please, stop."

But Jionathan was already on his feet, the blanket slipping from his shoulders. "Do you think 'sorry' is enough to excuse him? When I've seen what they do? Hysterical women leaving their homes in the morning to find their tardy husbands strewn—*strewn*—along the streets, strides of intestines hanging loose, blood splattered across the walls of the houses—"

"Jionat—"

"And Odin *protects* them! He protects them, whilst my people stand, gagged by their terror, and that widowed woman is left to shovel the remains of her husband off her door—"

"JIONATHAN, *PLEASE!*"

Jionathan stopped abruptly. Below him, Rufus was hunched forward on his knees, arms wound about his stomach. He was deathly white, his dark hair emphasising the sickly pallor of his face. Beneath his chemise and jerkin, his shoulders shook, and with a start Jionathan realised why.

"You're scared of them, too." His eyes widened. "They're your comrades, but you're scared of them, too."

"*Scared of them*?" Rufus spat, as if he were about to retch. "I live in the Southern Quarters, you brat. Every night I hear them pass by my window, all the lights in the house put out for fear they'll be attracted to it through the cracks in the door. Sometimes, my windowpanes *rattle* they're so close. Up in your castle, you nobles could never understand—listening to the shrieks of some poor soul who got caught out, knowing you can't do anything but wait for dawn, to bury them. I live every day in fear that Zachary will finally lose control of his men and one of them will burst into my home and murder my family. And you dare ask me if I'm scared of them?" He raised his head, eyes wild. "Jionat, I'm *terrified.*"

Jionathan stood, too stunned to speak. Rufus pushed himself straight, turning his face away as he wiped his mouth like he'd been sick. His fingers quivered, and he reached down to his things and fished out a small flask, which he flicked open. A potent smell stung Jionathan's nose.

"Is that *alcohol?*" he asked incredulously, as Rufus took a swig. "You shouldn't be drinking this early in the morning."

"As the position of the stars and Earth hold very little bearing on the bodily effects of dehydrating and poisoning myself, I am confident it doesn't matter *where* or *when* I chose to drink," Rufus said, stiffly.

"Of course it matters—Etheus, what is that?" Jionathan covered his nose.

"Poitín." Rufus took another long draught, staring off into the river, blank-faced.

"Well it smells awful," Jionathan said. And then, after a beat, added, "Can I try some?"

"Only if you want to go blind." Rufus seemed to be in no mood to joke after Jionathan's outburst.

The Prince hesitated and then sat again, pulling the blanket back around him. His anger had evaporated, and he felt cold and guilty. "Look, I never said it, but thank you for following me out here, Rufus. Regardless of what I said, I would rather you than Zachary."

Rufus snorted and took another swing of the Poitín before replacing his flask. Jionathan fidgeted uncomfortably at his side.

"I saw something strange yesterday," he said, again attempting to drive the conversation away from the Night Patrol, and clear the dark mood.

Rufus grunted. "Oh?"

"Yes—a woman."

"That's spectacularly strange, yes."

Jionathan ignored Rufus's sarcastic tone. "I saw her sitting on the bank of the river. She was singing such a sad song."

Rufus stiffened, his hands caught in his fringe, which he'd been gently tugging. "Was she doing anything else?"

"That was the strange thing—she was washing clothes soiled in blood."

Before Jionathan knew what was happening, Rufus had grabbed him by the collar and was dragging him in urgently. "Did you recognise them?"

"Ow!" Jionathan slapped Rufus's hands away as they jarred his injury. "Get off me—*that hurts!*"

"The clothes, did you recognise them? Were they yours?" Rufus persisted, his fingers tight around the front of Jionathan's chemise.

"My clothes?" Jionathan spluttered a laugh. "Of course they

113

weren't mine, where on earth would she have gotten them?"

"Oh thank Aramathea." Rufus released him, sagging with relief.

Jionathan picked at his chemise, ironing out the new creases. "Mothering Prospan, Rufus—how much of that stuff have you been drinking?"

"I'm not drunk," Rufus said, turning back to the river. At Jionathan's accusatory silence, he growled. "There are stories of such women. Bean Nighe, they're called."

"Ben Neeyah?" Jionathan rolled his tongue awkwardly across the Betheanian words. He caught Rufus about to speak. "If you correct my pronunciation—Malak, so help me—I will push you into that river," he warned, and Rufus cleared his throat, hiding a smile behind his hand. "So they're faeries then, these—er—"

"Bean Nighe? Yes. It's believed they're the haunted souls of women who died in pregnancy, or childbirth, cursed by their grief to walk the Earth for the remainder of what would've been their natural lives." He gave a grim smile. "It's said a Bean Nighe is born of sorrow, either their own or by the love of one who cannot let them go in death. And so they play out their days warning the living of their oncoming deaths."

"How?"

"The bloodied clothing. Whenever a Bean Nighe washes a set of clothes, whomever those clothes belong to is doomed to die."

"You mean they kill people?"

"No. Merely foretell the inevitable. The blood they wash away is yours, and just as they can't scrub it clean, your fate is sealed."

His words echoed harrowingly through Jionathan. "You know, come to think of it, those clothes looked an awful lot like yours."

"You are immensely unfunny," Rufus said, and Jionathan cackled.

"And for a breath, I dared to hope he spoke in earnest," Fae said from behind them, and the pair leapt to their feet, Rufus almost tumbling back into the river.

"Athea, woman—you're inhuman!" Rufus gasped, clamping a hand to his chest as Jionathan drew in several long breaths.

"You noticed. I'm thrilled." Fae gave a short, dour smile, starting back toward the camp. "If the pair of you are finished, we'd best set out."

"Your wound," Rufus called after her.

Fae stopped, and turned back to him, looking like she wanted nothing more than to drag him into the river, and hold his head under the water. Rufus gulped.

"That is to say, Jionat mentioned you had a wound yesterday. Would you let me attend to it? I can heal, well…I can…well."

"It's quite healed, thank you," Fae said, and at Rufus's surprise added, "I am—as you so masterfully perceived—not human."

Jionathan saw her eyes flick quickly to the marks on Rufus's neck as he apologised sheepishly. Her cheek twitched, and Jionathan sensed that Fae didn't appreciate Rufus's equal gift for recovery.

"Gather your things," she ordered. "He's at his weakest when the sun first rises."

"Aren't we all?" Jionathan yawned, regretting his decision to forfeit the few minutes of sleep he'd sacrificed for Rufus. Wrapping himself tightly in the blanket, he followed Fae back up toward their camp, leaving Rufus by the riverside.

∼⚬∽

They took pause to break their fast as Rufus saw to the horses, loading the packed saddlebags onto their backs and watering them down at the river. Then, without further delay, under Fae's insistence, they set off.

Rufus held back as they rode, allowing Jionathan and Fae to lead, the Prince on horseback as the Cat Sidhe walked at his side. They chattered as they went, shooting stray glances and smiles at one another. Rufus knew that for the safety of his own head, his silence would be his greatest virtue.

"If I were to be dragged away now, how long do you suppose it'd be before they noticed?" he mumbled to Moyna, leaning back in the saddle as he bit into a piece of bread. "An hour?"

The mare's ears flicked, one forward the other back, and Rufus tore off another chunk of the bread and, leaning forward, fed it to her.

"You're right, of course." He patted her neck. "A day, at least."

"Rufus!" Jionathan shouted from ahead. "Would you hurry up?"

Rufus urged Moyna on, recovering the few strides he'd lost between the pair. He had no desire to be caught between them, not when Jionathan had already formed such a sickening attachment to Fae. He kept smiling at her giddily, when he thought she wasn't looking.

Haylix, this is nauseating, Rufus thought, pulling out of a trot as he approached, still maintaining a few strides distance.

"Fae was telling me a little of the foe we're about to face," Jionathan said, and Rufus took another bite from his bread, trying to quench his fear. He was wary of any enemy that a Cat Sidhe brought allies to remove.

"His name is Embarr Reagon." Fae seemed bitter to repeat the information, her tone brusque. "He's a faerie whose powers lie in the manipulation of lust. You may know him as—"

"A Gancanagh?" Rufus said.

Despite her passive revulsion, Fae raised an eyebrow, modestly impressed. "You know of them? I didn't think there were many in Harmatia."

"What's a Gancanagh?" Jionathan said. "Forgive my ignorance."

"The Gancanagh are faeries who feed on amorous feelings," Fae said. "They excrete a toxin from their flesh which, to any mortal, surfaces feeling of love and trust. Before the treaty of Bethean was signed, many Gancanagh left trails of bodies in

116

their wake, feasting on humans until they lost all strength and died in depression. Now, the Gancanagh may walk freely among the people and feed, So long as they don't feed more than twice on one human and break all magical connection thereafter."

"There was a Saphar book about such a creature, wasn't there?" Jionathan asked Rufus, who nodded.

"*The Lovers' Sin,* yes—the story of a Gancanagh who falls in-love with a human, and subsequently drains her of life. It's a cautionary tale about how even well-intentioned love can end in disaster." Rufus's voice died as an abrupt, almost tangible feeling of grief suddenly came over him. He gave a start, the very breath in his throat growing cold, like he'd dropped into a basin of icy water.

"Saphar was a Harmatian writer, yes? I have heard of his works in Bethean." Fae's voice grew distant as she and Jionathan continued to chatter idly, oblivious to Rufus, who'd erupted into a frenzy of shivers.

He released a shuddering breath, which seemed to curl before him, the world swimming. For a moment, Rufus wondered if he'd been subjected to glamour again, but he didn't feel so much dizzy as detached. His chest ached and his belly felt empty, like his organs had been carved out.

Sensing him grow still, Moyna paused in her step, looking back to her master. It had felt, for just a moment, as if something had tried to touch Rufus—a ghostly arm which, having reached for his shoulder, had passed through his human flesh and strummed his heartstrings instead, tugging at his soul.

"*Rufus.*" The name reverberated through him, like the call of a lost love, and he turned back in his saddle to the woods behind him, mouth dry in sickened anticipation. Through the shadows of the trees, nothing moved, silence pressing against his ears in a muffling embrace. The presence lingered, a handprint in wet earth as Rufus reached for it, like a man reaching for his poison.

"Rufus!" Jionathan shouted, and he jolted, the world coming

alive with colour again as he blinked, the warm, damp smell of the forest enveloping him. "What is it?"

Rufus turned back, dropping his hand and urging Moyna on. "Nothing," he said, and the trio continued on in silence.

CHAPTER
10

Jionathan was no fool. Despite Rufus's quick dismissal, there had been an almost fury in his eyes as he'd turned back to them, as if he'd been pulled away from a happy dream. And yet, the drained pallor of his face suggested otherwise—a coldness, a fresh fear.

"Did we pass through glamour?" Jionathan asked Fae, who looked back at their path and shook her head. Jionathan chewed on his bottom lip and cast the worry from his mind. If something were truly wrong, Rufus would surely say so.

"We're near," Fae suddenly warned. "Dismount. I wouldn't put it past him to spook your horses. You'll be safer on foot." She waited until both had obeyed before continuing. "Pay heed, you're safe from him only so long as he doesn't form a magical connection with you. Keep your eyes on the ground. Don't look him directly in the face for too long and try not to concentrate on how he sounds, or smells. Do not submit to feelings of desire or companionship and all will be well. If you feel in danger of losing yourself to him, leave as quickly as you can, or he will take advantage of it."

Jionathan pulled the reins over his horse's head, his mouth

a grim line. "He's a dark creature indeed, if he can induce such unnatural feelings in another man."

From behind him Rufus laughed, but when Jionathan turned back, the Magi had pressed his face into his mare's neck, sniggering quietly. Fae ignored him.

"Move cautiously now." She ushered for them to follow, her eyes glowing a vivid green. Darting out, she swept nimbly into the dense foliage, almost disappearing from sight. Jionathan and Rufus followed quickly, leading the stubborn horses, who'd suddenly grown restless, tossing their heads. Whatever creature they approached, it was upsetting them.

As they broke forward, they came upon Fae who'd stopped ahead of them, standing so still she might have been one of the trees of the forest, rooted to her spot for many hundreds of years.

"Where now?" Jionathan asked, but Rufus touched his shoulder, his grip nervous. His eyes were trained up past Jionathan, to the branches of a large tree ahead. Jionathan followed his gaze, and there, in the crook of a branch, a man lounged above them.

The first thing that struck Jionathan about the Gancanagh was that, like Fae, he seemed remarkably human. Jionathan had always imagined the faerie-folk to either tower over the heads of men, or to stoop a great deal smaller. And yet this one might have easily blended into a crowd if it weren't for the fact his eyes were blacker than coal, and beneath his high-necked, studded jerkin—Kathrak in style—his skin seemed to shimmer blue in the dappled light. Embarr smelled of sandalwood and the taste of fresh water.

"Welcome, welcome, welcome, dear friends!" he cried at the sight of them, a long, unlit pipe of red wood dangling precariously from his lips. "And may the gods bless you all this fine morning."

He had a handsome face, framed by a sharp jaw like Rufus's, and a wild tousle of dark brown hair. He was boyish in his good looks—fresh and youthful—though dark lines marked his eyes, his chin grizzly with unattended stubble. As their eyes met, Jionathan's tongue locked and a strange feeling overcame him. Heeding Fae's warning, he dropped his head, his heart palpitating in his throat. There was a warmth in the air, a softness that seemed to almost make Jionathan delirious, and yet elevated him all at once. Happy memories came, unbidden, to his mind, and were he not conscious of the Gancanagh's manipulative power, Jionathan might have started to relax, as if in the company of an old friend. But he knew these feelings were not natural. Embarr had called them up to serve his dark purpose, and so Jionathan forced them away and gritted his teeth.

"Embarr Reagon, surrender now and no more harm need be done." Fae's voice was soft, and yet it thundered like a brewing storm.

"Alas, that harm need be done to see me surrender," Embarr sang playfully. "Darling, darling Fae, my love and my light. Unbind your fists, for our friendship's sake. Let us speak."

Fae's shoulders rippled, as if she were about to transform, and then she straightened, letting her hands fall open. "Where is the Princess?"

"Why, she's stood before me now, armed with her beautiful scowl—the only Princess that matters to me."

A small tremor crept into Fae's voice, the first crackle of lightening in her tense constitution. "Are you so far fallen, Embarr—so far descended into darkness? To have *kidnapped* the Princess of Bethean—have you inherited this madness?"

Though Jionathan had trained his eyes to his feet for fear of the strange stroke of temptation that the Gancanagh induced, he sensed the playfulness drain from Embarr's composure.

"Turn back now, Fae," Embarr said. "While you can. Go home."

"You know I can't." Fae's anger was tangible, a sharp strum that filled the air and seemed to make the leaves tremble. "Tell me where she is now, or Titania be my witness, I will carve it out of you."

"Please." Embarr seemed to struggle, and Jionathan dared to glance up at him.

Without his jovial smile, Embarr seemed muted and sunken beneath his beauty. His eyes truly were colourless, and reminded Jionathan of a dream he'd once had of a man with eyes like obsidian, battling a dragon. He shook the foolish memory away, and dropped his gaze.

"Please leave, Fae," Embarr said. "I cannot stand your accusations. We were friends once. You used to say 'go siorai'—*forever*. Forever has passed by very quickly."

Fae seemed to struggle with her rage, her fingers bound into fists once more. "You dare to bring up the past? *Months*, Embarr—no sign or word, and I thought you were dead. Yet, as I might have begun to mourn you, you returned like this? No, you forfeited the right to my friendship when you candidly committed treason. So forgive me the accusations, but yours was the first spear to fly."

"Fae—"

"Don't interrupt me," Fae snapped. "If you truly have any love left for the childhood we shared, tell me where Princess Aurora is. Now."

Embarr didn't speak a while, but by the gentle croak of his breath, and the occasional crack of unfinished words, it wasn't for lack of trying. Jionathan, though desperately curious to see Embarr's expression, didn't look up. He couldn't shake the strange attraction that came over him—the infuriating need to smile and laugh. It made his skin crawl. To be forced to feel desire like this wasn't right. It was unnatural.

Craving a distraction, Jionathan peered across at Rufus, who had trained his eyes to the base of the tree. But though Rufus didn't look up at Embarr with the unaffected ease that Fae did, there was nothing in his expression to indicate he was struggling. In-fact, he seemed perfectly relaxed, almost comfortable—in contrast to Jionathan, who now took to rocking backward and forward on his heels, his hands wound into his chemise.

"Embarr, please, tell me," Fae said. "We can mend this still, I beg you."

"Forgive me." Embarr's voice was so small it might have been a trick of the mind. The air seemed to grow colder, and Jionathan found his mind clearing, the foreign endearment fading.

Fae inhaled. "No." For a moment, she seemed dampened with defeat, and then a clatter alerted Jionathan to the fact that she'd drawn her swords. "What have you done?"

"Forgive me," Embarr repeated, and then broke into a fit of coughing, wet and painful. On instinct, Jionathan looked up to see Embarr doubled over, clutching his stomach as he spluttered. Fae lowered her swords slowly, straightening from her stance. Embarr's blue pallor was broken by a feverish flare, high on each cheek, and as he brought his hand away from his mouth, it was spotted with blood.

The allurement seemed all but gone, the illusion breaking. "What...what's wrong with him?" Jionathan asked Fae cautiously. She re-sheathed her weapons.

"He's dying." Her voice was even, but the vivacity of her eyes seemed to dampen beneath her expression. Jionathan's stomach tightened.

Beside them, Rufus placed the tips of his fingers together, bowing his head. "May Notameer preserve you, and Athea guide you," he prayed, and Embarr watched him with a half-fondness on his drawn face.

"Are you giving me my final blessings, human?" It was the first time Embarr had acknowledged either of them since his greeting.

Rufus looked the faerie straight in his lightless eyes, without a flicker of trepidation. "And if I am?"

Embarr laughed and then coughed again. "I don't keep your True Gods. I am a Fomorii."

"Does it matter?" Rufus shrugged.

Again, Embarr cackled and something of his joviality returned to his face. "Magi, are you?"

"How—"

"I can sense your power." Embarr settled back against the trunk of the tree, one leg dangling from his branch.

By now, the oppressive desire that'd been so suffocating had decreased to a mere trickle, and Jionathan found himself able to look around with ease.

"Thank you for your blessings," Embarr said.

"You shouldn't have," Fae rebuked Rufus, and his face darkened.

He folded his arms tightly across his chest. "All men deserve some comfort in the hours of their death."

"He's an enemy of humans, and now all the Seelie Court," Fae snarled, and Jionathan could see sadness in her suddenly dull eyes. "He's dying only because he broke the rules of his kind."

"The rules of his kind?" Jionathan frowned. It troubled him how little he knew about the faerie-folk. He'd assumed it was a general ignorance shared amongst most Harmatians, but even Rufus seemed to know more than he.

Fae turned to him, her face seeming to soften. "He fell in love with a human."

"The ultimate sin," Rufus snarled, and Fae turned on him, her teeth bared.

"It is," she hissed. "Or have we not already established what happens to humans who suffer that kind of love?"

Rufus didn't respond. His arms clenched tighter around his chest as he trained his eyes once more to the roots of the tree. He looked very sick all of a sudden.

"Gancanagh's are forbidden from falling in-love with humans, because as rare as it is, a Gancanagh who falls in-love, can never feed on anyone else again. A faerie might survive being fed on daily, but a human?" Fae directed her anger back on Embarr.

"Did you kill her?"

"No!" Embarr wailed. "No, I swear. She was…she was so beautiful. So full of life. The little Princess of Bethean—my own sun. She made me good." He dropped his head into his hands. "She made me good when I wanted to feast," he wheezed, his voice so full of sorrow. Jionathan saw Rufus flinch.

"Clear your head," Fae commanded. "If you're in such a state, it can only mean you're not feeding. If you haven't killed her yet, then what has separated you?"

"I released her!" Embarr tore his hands from his face. "I let her go before I left Bethean. I swear it, Fae. I did betray you, I did. I crawled to the capital, wanting and hungry…but she was so kind, so very gentle. I released her and fled to these woods, and I resigned myself to death instead. But," fat tears welled in Embarr's eyes, "she *followed* me. My little love. She knew it meant her death, and yet, for love of me, she came."

The sorrow in Embarr's voice was so raw, it made Jionathan shiver. Rufus seemed to have shrunken in his looming stance, and was staring adamantly at the roots of the tree, his face solemn and set.

Fae's shoulders quivered. "What happened?" her words were gentle, her voice almost leashed. "If she followed you here, and you didn't kill her, then where is she?"

A darkness seemed to descend upon the glade, the clouds muffling the sky. Embarr closed his eyes. "I was too weak to even spirit away, too weak to walk. I was powerless when they came for her…when they took her."

"Who took her?"

"Who do you think?" Embarr gave a lightless laugh. "The Korrigans."

Fae tensed, a balanced panic seeming to come over her as she stood alert. "Korrigans?" she whispered, and then swore.

"Mothering Prospan," Rufus murmured, his eyes wide.

Jionathan cursed his ignorance again. "I presume that

Korrigans are bad?"

"Yes," all three replied simultaneously.

Fae explained, "Korrigans are priestesses of one of the Tuatha de Danaan—a Sidhe goddess I don't dare to name presently. They were excluded from the Betheanian treaty in light of their malevolent history. If they've taken the Princess, it can be for no good cause. What's more, they're beings of power, and are great in number."

"I told you to turn back." Embarr exhaled, coughing faintly. "You're no match for them, Fae, powerful as you may be."

"I can't leave her." Fae began to pace. Jionathan imagined that, were she in her cat form, her tail would've been twitching from side to side. "I was sent. I won't fail."

"You cannot fight them alone, Fae!" Panic filled Embarr's voice. "Please, don't be so rash. Send for help from your brothers? Or Reilly, surely he will—"

"There's no time!" Fae roared. "I have to face them. It's the Princess's only hope."

"They'll already know you're here. You're outnumbered and outmatched. If you fight them, you could die." Embarr drew away. "But perhaps you could lay a trap? Trick your way in and liberate the Princess before they know it."

"And how, pray, do I achieve such a feat? As you said, they won't fall for any tricks of mine. They know me—they've no doubt *seen* me."

"Use him." Embarr removed his pipe from his teeth and pointed it down at Rufus, who jumped.

"Excuse me?" he squeaked.

Embarr replaced his pipe in his mouth, chewing it. "For some weeks now, I have watched a number of Magi come and go, visiting their nest. The whisperings in the forest suggest that they've commissioned something from the Korrigans, and have been in dealings with them for some months."

"That's impossible," Rufus scoffed. "It can't be."

"I've seen them with my own two eyes," Embarr said.

"With the greatest respect, you're hardly a reliable source." Rufus appealed to Fae, "He's sick—dying, you said. He's delusional."

"I'm not so certain," Jionathan mused, and Rufus's face twisted in indignation.

"I'm Master Odin's apprentice. Do you really think if the *Magi* were in dealings with the Korrigans, I wouldn't notice? I'm loyal, you little git, not stupid."

Jionathan rolled his eyes. "Reagon didn't say he saw *all* the Magi marching into the forest, did he? Can you really account for every single one of them?"

"It's true, I've only seen a select few come by," Embarr said. "Three, perhaps. No more. Always the same ones."

Rufus seemed to calm, but a troubled look clung to him. "No," he agreed. "I can't account for all them. It could well be a conspiracy. Regardless, if any Magi are involved, I'm duty bound to discover the truth." He turned to Fae. "If I can be of assistance, then I resign myself to your hands, however tremulously."

Fae considered him coolly. "I could use you," she admitted. "If the Korrigans are indeed conspiring with Magi, their purpose must be discovered. But the Princess comes first—she's been their prisoner for too long already."

"You mentioned their nest," Jionathan said to Embarr. "Do you know where it is? How many entrances there are? The more we know, the better chance we have of getting in and out successfully."

Embarr eyed the Prince, forcing Jionathan to duck his head. "Fae," the Gancanagh almost accused, "I am either running mad in my approach to death, or the Prince of Harmatia is stood before me."

"*Everybody*," Jionathan growled to himself. "The *entire* forest."

"Prince Jionathan of the Delphi," Fae confirmed. "We met yesterday. He saved my life."

"What a strange pride you travel with," Embarr laughed. "I know your face, Prince, because I passed through your court once on my way to Kathra. My humblest apologies that I did not call you straight and show all due respect."

"I don't want your respect—I want to know how to get into the Korrigans' nest."

"The Magi and my darling Fae both have grave reason to venture into that horror, but what is your purpose?"

Jionathan dared to look up. "My purpose is my promise—I came to aid Fae in her quest, and I will see it through. Bethean is my sistering country, and King Markus a friend of my father. I will find his daughter."

Embarr hummed thoughtfully. "You have *power* in your eyes, Delphi Prince—yes, great power. How much you must see. But beware, you are almost equally matched by your foes. They have long had that gift." He broke into another bout of coughs. "You have strong allies with you Fae. It is a blessing. I couldn't, with a clean heart, let you face the Korrigans alone, but with these, I submit myself to your will." He wiped a line of blood from the corner of his lip. "Listen closely then, and I will impart everything I know."

CHAPTER 11

❧

They took leave of Embarr in order to start their planning, the three agreeing that the Gancanagh was too distracting for the delicate design of their mission. They returned to their former camp and made a war table from the stump of a fallen tree. To his companions' surprise, Rufus was quick to participate in their planning, reminding the Prince again that he *had* broken into the royal archives when he was only fifteen.

"You seem oddly proud of this felony," Jionathan muttered, and Rufus shrugged, unable to disagree.

Fae leant forward with apparent, if begrudging, interest. "You don't strike me as a man who breaks rules."

"The progression of society rather relies on someone doing it occasionally," Rufus said, and Jionathan cut between them as Fae gave a small 'hmph' of approval and even a slim smile.

"If you're done boasting, I would actually like to hear this plan of yours."

Rufus obliged, pulling out a piece of paper from his satchel. Jionathan balked.

"You brought *paper* with you?"

"I bring paper everywhere. Now be quiet a minute." Rufus

began to draw. There were six entrances into the nest. Embarr had told him their distance from one another, and which direction they faced. Rufus marked out the points of the compass on the page, and began to sketch a map with the information they'd been given. He used a scale of fifty-strides per thumb-width, and measured out the distances, plotting each of the entrances. "There," he said, when he'd finished. "It's crude, but we have a map of the entrances now, at least."

"That's good—but it isn't going to be enough to get us both in and out," Jionathan said.

"Which is why we now need a map of the inside." Rufus swallowed down his fear, knowing already what he had to do. "Fae, Embarr said that the conspirators used the entrance closest to the main road. Which is that?"

Fae skimmed over the sketchy map, tracing her finger absently across it. "The majority of this is covered by water, and marshland—and here, I know this entrance is beneath a waterfall." She pointed to the south-eastern entrance. "Which would mean...yes, this, the southern entrance. I think that's where your Magi conspirators would approach. It's the only one accessible by foot, and closest to the road."

"In which case, I'll approach from here." Rufus pushed his fringe out of his eyes, running his fingers through it. Fae and Jionathan watched him expectantly. "It's simple," he said. "I'll negotiate my way in on the pretence of being a conspirator. I'll find out what those Magi are doing, whilst memorising the layout of the nest. When I have that, and have located where they keep the Princess, I'll return to you. With the information, we'll be able to plot our route and save her, undetected."

"No," Jionathan said. "That's a ridiculous plan."

"Why?"

"Three reasons—first, you're a coward, and yet it relies entirely on you facing the Korrigans alone. Second, you have no concept of what the conspiracy is, so how do you intend to convince them to let you in, reveal everything, *and* show you where the Princess is? Finally, according to Reagon, those tunnels are a maze, yet you want to lead us in having only walked them once?"

Rufus tapped the pencil harder against the paper, the tip crumbling. He blew the shards away, the graphite leaving pale streaks of black along the white surface. "It's not ideal, but I can improvise. As for the tunnels, I have a good memory. I'm confident I'll only need to walk them once."

Fae shook her head. "Whatever confidence you have, the risk is too great. If you were to be discovered—as you will be, for they're not fools—the Princess would be lost to us."

"I won't be discovered."

"You will," Fae said. "The Korrigans are in their element, and they're *watching me.*" She paused. "Whilst your conspiracy is important, Princess Aurora takes precedence."

"Agreed," Jionathan chimed, and Rufus threw the pencil down.

"Than what would you propose? We go in, trousers down?"

"No, Magi, that's what *you* proposed."

"I may have an idea," Jionathan said, his brow pinched. "But you won't like it, Rufus."

Rufus sighed, but waved for Jionathan to continue.

"Reagon said the Korrigans haven't left their nest in over two hundred years," Jionathan said to Fae.

"That is so."

"Then perhaps we can use that to our advantage?" Jionathan caught the pencil as it rolled over the surface of the paper, disturbed by the breeze. "Do you recall another Saphar book called *The Barrel Men*?"

Fae frowned. "I can't say I know it," she admitted, but beside her Rufus cursed, as he caught Jionathan's train of thought.

"Are you *drunk*?" he demanded. "Or merely keen to die?"

"It's the best way," Jionathan replied. "It'll cut down our time by half."

"It would separate us. In a maze of tunnels we don't yet know how to navigate!"

"All the more reason to use what time we have sparingly."

"You're adamant, aren't you?" Rufus crossed his arms.

Fae turned between them, perplexed. "To what do you refer, exactly?"

"Madness," Rufus snarled. "A—a *cuckoo's nest* of a plan!"

Fae made to speak and drew off. "Is that a Harmatian saying?"

Jionathan bowed his head, tracing his fingers across the map as he chewed on the tip of his thumb, and then dropped his hand against his pocket, tapping it twice.

Fae narrowed her eyes. "I see."

"This is a stupid plan," Rufus said.

"No worse than yours," Jionathan replied. "Fae, we need to know that Reagon's information was accurate."

Fae took the map. "I will make sure all of the entrances are there." She crossed over to Rufus and, unclasping one of the swords on her back, dropped it into his lap.

He jumped, flailing, and let the sword drop the floor. Fae raised an eyebrow, and Rufus gingerly picked up the blade, wincing. "What do you want me to do with this?"

"Use it," Fae said.

Rufus turned the sheathed blade over in his hands. It was light and slightly curved, shorter than a Harmatian sword. "How?"

Fae looked at Jionathan. "And they call this one a genius?"

"I have magic." Rufus held himself straight.

"Which you won't even use to light a fire," Jionathan said.

"I can use fire-flints, so why should I?"

"Because apparently you *can't*."

"If the worst comes to it, I will." Rufus held the sword up, tilting the hilt back toward Fae. "And should that fail, my charm will have to suffice."

"And I am sure your untimely death will be all the merrier for it." Fae took the sword, and in a sudden burst of black mist, she transformed into her cat form. Drawing a few steps back, she beat her powerful wings, forcing Rufus and Jionathan to cover their eyes as a cloud of dust and dirt rose from the ground. Taking several strides forward, she galloped into the air, and took off through the canopy.

Rufus and Jionathan sprang to their feet to watch her go, mesmerised. Through the leaves, Fae disappeared into the sky, and Rufus slowly settled down again, his inside churning. It was all moving very fast, and a part of him was glad of that—it didn't give him time to dwell on the insanity of what he was about to do. Once more, Jionathan had put him in a difficult position, and Rufus had to fight his natural instinct to just flee and hide.

Pulling out his drink flask, he took a swig to steady his nerves.

Jionathan coughed in objection. "*More* alcohol? You know we're about to face the Korrigans, don't you?"

Rufus took an even longer draught. "If I'm going to die, I'd rather not be sober."

Jionathan settled beside him, wrapping his arms about his knees. "You're not going to die," he said, and Rufus laughed grimly.

"What an awful thing to say," he murmured, and rose to his feet. "I trust you still have my robes?"

"Saddlebag."

Rufus strode across and tugged the long black garment out from where it had been unceremoniously bundled at the bottom of the bag. He shook the robe out, ironing his hands over the sea of creases. When he turned back, it was to find that Jionathan had taken hold of the journal Rufus had torn his page from and was looking through it. Rufus might have been angry, if Jionathan hadn't suddenly looked so pale and grim. Like Rufus, he was trying to distract himself.

"Maps..." Jionathan said, turning the pages. "Why do you have so many drawings of maps?"

Rufus pulled on his robe. "I copied them from the library atlas.

I've always wanted to travel—to taste different air, experience a new culture, see a different sky..."

"Then why only draw them? Why not go?"

"If I did, who'd come find you when you ran away?"

Jionathan glowered. "Malak, is that your god-given duty?"

"No, only my impossible skill." Rufus chuckled.

Jionathan didn't look up from the pages, and Rufus came and sat beside him, ducking his head to look into the Prince's face.

"And so then," he continued, "perhaps it *is* my responsibility. But if it assures you, I feel that after today's misadventure, I may change my tune. At which time, you may go out and do as many stupid things as you can fathom, and I shan't follow you."

Jionathan snorted. "Yes, you will. You always do." He turned another page and added in a small voice, "These drawings are good."

"Gracious, a compliment?"

Jionathan sneered and turned another page. Rufus saw the silhouette of a body, lying broken in a pool of blood sketched angrily on the paper, and he snatched the book from Jionathan's hands before he could examine it.

"What was that?" Jionathan grabbed for the journal.

"Nothing," Rufus dismissed, his chest aching.

"No, Rufus—what *was* that?"

"*Nothing*," Rufus repeated, almost a little breathless. "Only a dream. Nothing more. A terrible, terrible dream." He fingered the binding of the journal.

Jionathan stared at him in horror. He'd seen enough of the graphic drawing—the writhing body, the blood, the fear, the tangible grief in each stroke of the pencil. "Why did you draw it?"

Rufus inhaled slowly, and then sighed. "My mother used to tell me that if we draw out our nightmares, they'll stop."

Jionathan dropped his hand. He looked even paler than before. "Did it?"

Rufus returned the book to his saddlebag. "Sometimes I'm

not sure it makes a difference," he said soberly, suddenly very tired. A dark feeling came over him, and he wondered if—all jibes aside—he'd live to see the end of the day. He wondered, suddenly, if he really cared.

The glade fell quiet, a gloomy air filling it until—clearly eager to break from his own depression—Jionathan spoke. "How did you do it, Rufus?"

"Do what?"

"When we were with Embarr Reagon." Jionathan's face pinched. "He had no effect on you."

"Of course he did." Rufus returned to his perch, taking a small handful of bread with him to eat.

"But you were so tranquil," Jionathan said. "I have never been subjected to such discomfort in my life, but you were calm. We can't have felt the same thing."

"An almost irresistible desire to submit myself to a faerie I knew might kill me—no, I'm quite certain we did."

"Yes, but a *male* faerie…" Jionathan muttered to himself.

Rufus's mouth curled into a smile. "Yes," he hummed. "Though perhaps what really troubles you is Embarr's history with Fae?"

Jionathan's face brightened like a burn. "What are you implying?"

"Jionat, you must really take me for a fool, if you think that I haven't noticed your attraction to the woman."

"I—I…how dare you!" Jionathan stuttered. "I have no—that is—she doesn't…how *dare* you!"

"With abhorrent ease." Rufus ripped a chunk of bread off and chewed it slowly like an old man with tobacco leaf. "Come, settle down. I might question your choice, but certainly not your taste. She's a beautiful woman. Any man would be a fool to say otherwise."

"You have no right to question anything!" Jionathan barked, and then lowered his voice cautiously, ducking his head in a sinister whisper. "Nor to make your own assumptions. That she happens to be beautiful doesn't mean that my behaviour is anything more than polite. After all, you're polite to her—does that mean you're making advances?"

Rufus choked, the bruises on his throat stinging. "Gracious, Jionat, she'd break my neck if I tried."

Jionathan seemed to grow more guarded. "You mean to say, you would otherwise?"

"No, Jionat. I recognise her beauty, but…" Rufus drew off, and suddenly the gloom was upon him again. "But it's different for me."

"How so?"

Rufus considered the bread in his hand, and his stomach turned. He tore it into crumbs and threw it to the birds. "Because sometimes when you experience something wonderful, everything else loses its shine."

Jionathan seemed lost. "What could be more wonderful?" he wondered aloud, and then flushed bright red, biting his lip as if to try and retract the words.

"At the least she *tolerates* you," Rufus said. "But tread carefully, Jionat, she's still a Sidhe, and you…well."

"I'm the Prince of Harmatia."

"Quite." Rufus folded his arms and squinted down at the Prince. "By the by, may I ask you what you're doing?"

Jionathan's hands paused in their task. "Unravelling this blanket," he replied innocently.

"Yes, I can see that." Rufus looked pointedly at the rough coverlet. "*Why*?"

"As a precaution."

Rufus raised an eyebrow. "I see. You mean to bribe the Korrigans with yarn?"

"Yes, Rufus. Exactly."

Snorting, Rufus crossed over into the woodland. He collected a branch and returned, removing one of the stirrups from his saddle. Carefully, he removed the leather cords and, taking

Jionathan's knife, broke the stick to the right length, carving two small knobbles either side. He lodged it into the stirrup, and flicked it, making the wood spin on its new axis. Pleased, he handed it to Jionathan, who considered it a moment, and then tied the end of the string to it, winding it in.

"When Fae returns, we ought to also take a closer look at the entrances," Rufus suggested casually as Jionathan worked. Jionathan grunted in agreement, and Rufus watched him, heavy-hearted.

CHAPTER 12

~~~

"What are you thinking about, Lord Zachary?"

Zachary glanced back to the Queen, who stood in the doorway of the circular chamber. He turned from the window and bowed deeply.

"How beautiful the light looks reflecting on the rooftops, Your Grace. There will be a glorious sunset tonight."

Reine tittered, the hem of her amber gown trailing along the yellow stone floor as she moved. She took Zachary's hand fearlessly in her own, squeezing his fingers like a shackle clamped around his wrist. "Please, Lord Zachary, you need not think me so dainty that you have to add poetry to your words. We understand each other, you and I."

"Then I was thinking about blood," Zachary replied dutifully, fighting the urge to roll his eyes. "Does that please Your Grace?"

"So long as it's the right blood." She released his hand, patting his cheek. "You're so very hollow, Zachary," she whispered, caressing his face. "As only a motherless babe could be."

"My mother might take issue with that accusation."

"From what I recall of Elizabeth DuMorne, I am not inclined to agree."

Zachary snorted, waiting for her games to end.

"Your Grace," Belphegore appeared in the doorway. He caught Zachary's gaze, and his apprentice dutifully freed himself from the Queen's grip and turned back to the window, his hands clasped behind his back. "To what do we owe this pleasure?"

Reine circled the room. It was a study of sorts—Lord Odin's private chamber and sanctuary, where he could attend to his Magi duties in peace. The walls were lined with books and a handsome desk homed mounds of documents and papers, held down with bronze paperweights and foreign artefacts. The thick red curtains were drawn back across the various windows, letting fresh air and light into the otherwise enclosed chamber.

In the corner, a fireplace glowed with the embers of a dead fire and Zachary wondered vaguely what his master had been burning.

"It's two nights now since that Delphi boy lost himself in the woods and your youngest was sent after him," Reine said. "I expect it will be longer still before we see either return."

"The woods are vast," Belphegore said. "But the King's decision to send Rufus was a wise one. I assure you, he will find Jionathan."

"Or die trying," Zachary murmured, earning a hard look from his master.

"My husband is indeed wise, but he is also sickly," the Queen said. "I want that Delphi boy back in Harmatia, where I can see him." She glanced back to Zachary. "A task I am sure the captain of the Night Patrol could perform with ease."

"I can assure you, I wouldn't find him any quicker than Merle," Zachary said.

"Perhaps not, but I would know with confidence that you would bring him home." The Queen's voice was edged with anger now. "I fear that Éliane spoke with Lord Merle. I think the pair have conspired to smuggle the Prince back to her ancestor's homeland in Avalon."

Belphegore closed the door behind him carefully. "My apprentice is not so foolish."

"Love is foolish, and I would wager your Lord Merle has feelings of that effect for the Lady. It wouldn't be hard for Éliane to use that to her advantage."

"I do not think so." Belphegore frowned deeply. "And the Lady Éliane is as anxious as you to see her son returned safely, of that I am sure."

"I do not care what you think. I want Zachary to go after them. He can take two of his men with him, if he likes." She moved toward Zachary, stepping in uncomfortably close. "Perhaps Marcel Hathely and that sweet-looking apprentice of his—Emeric Fold, is it?" she breathed into his face. "Find the boy. Bring him home."

"The King made his orders clear." Zachary wasn't frightened by the Queen's unspoken threats. So she knew the names of his men—what of it? By the same token Zachary knew things as well, had witnessed them here in this very room. Small, captured moments between Belphegore and Reine that would see them both executed if they were discovered.

"And I am making *mine* clear. Go after him. Now!" Reine was losing her temper, her voice rising.

Belphegore crossed over to her, taking her gently by the arm and drawing her away. Zachary was careful to keep his eyes on the window, but he could see their reflection. Belphegore's grip on her elbow was tender, and he spoke in soft, gentle tones.

"Not yet," Belphegore said. "Give it time. We will keep our ears open for any sign

of them, but unless we have definitive proof that Jionathan is fleeing to Avalon, trust Rufus. He will guide the Prince home soon enough. My apprentice is loyal."

Reine seemed to calm, but her shoulders remained taut. "He had better be. Or else I will have him executed."

"That is not your decision to make," Belphegore spoke too

fiercely, and the Queen laughed.

"You ought to disguise your favouritism a little better, Belphegore," she warned. "Or you will lose the loyalty of your first."

Zachary felt their eyes turn on him. "A soldier knows his place," he assured his master, and it was as the Queen had said— he was hollow.

"Yes," Reine said, "until he's abandoned on the battlefield." She turned and strode away. As the door closed after her, Belphegore released a heavy sigh and joined Zachary at the window.

"What should I do?" Zachary asked.

"For now, nothing.

"And if Merle does betray us?"

"Then you will have to save both the Prince and your brother, and stop Jionathan before he crosses the border."

Zachary watched a student run down the stairs below into the courtyard, a book held fiercely to his chest. Just like Rufus the first time Zachary had ever seen him, clean-shaven and bright-eyed.

"Merle's stubborn. I may not be able to sway him."

"Do not hurt him, Arlen," Belphegore warned, and Zachary left the window and crossed to the door.

"The Queen is right—you could at least *try* to disguise your favouritism."

"Arlen," Belphegore sighed, "Rufus is not—"

Zachary held up his hand. "I don't care anymore. I understand my role in this. Regardless, I will do what I have to," he said. "And for all my sins and failings, Master, you cannot think any less of me for that."

By the time they reached the lake, Fae had left them, not daring to go any closer. Jionathan moved ahead, his feet slipping on the wet earth as Rufus trailed behind, almost solemn. Several times, Jionathan was forced to dart back, so as not to be separated. Finally, Rufus lost his temper.

"You're like an uncut hound. Come here!" he ordered, and Jionathan returned reluctantly to his side. The ground was becoming increasingly marshy below their feet, and Rufus was taking each step like it was his last.

"Would you hurry up? Fae will think we're dead if we don't get back soon."

"Fool is the man who hurries his step on a path unknown," Rufus quoted sagely. "Give me your sword."

"What?"

"Your sword. Give it to me."

"You wouldn't have Fae's, but you'll take mine?" Jionathan said, and Rufus extended his hand.

"I changed my mind. Give it to me."

Wordlessly, Jionathan removed the sword, and then laughed as Rufus tried to put it onto his back. "It's not a broadsword, you ass—wear it on your hip. You look ridiculous."

Rufus renegotiated it to his side, securing the belt around his waist. Jionathan continued on toward the entrance, dropping his height as they got closer. Rufus stalked after him, also ducking his head, for all the good it did him.

Up ahead, jutting out from the watery marshland, was a cavernous entrance that led down into the nest. Jionathan knelt down behind the curtain of one of the many weeping willows bowing into the lake.

"There it is," he whispered, hearing Rufus approach. "We ought to go back—this area has good cover, but the last stretch is too open." He heard the clatter of a sword being drawn clumsily, and then the point of the blade was pressing gently into the small of his back. Even through his leather armour, he felt the sharp edge. Jionathan raised his hands in surrender, his breath stilled.

"Move," Rufus instructed, and Jionathan looked back at him, wide-eyed.

"What are you doing?"

"I'm sorry," Rufus's voice was remorseful, but brisk, "but I must do this. Move, now." He pressed the sword harder, and Jionathan rose to his feet, stepping out through the veil of draping leaves. "I'm going to put the sword away. Keep walking."

Jionathan nodded faintly, and Rufus replaced the weapon in its sheath. Almost immediately, Jionathan darted and ran back toward the forest. "Fae!" he shouted. "FAE!"

Rufus seized him by the waist, so the hilt of his sword bludgeoned Jionathan in the kidney. He yelped in pain, and Rufus clamped his other hand over Jionathan's mouth. The Prince struggled, kicking desperately, trying to catch Rufus's shins.

"If you struggle, I'll use magic to subdue you. For both our sakes, Jionat, don't make me resort to that."

Jionathan grew limp, his chest heaving, and Rufus let him go. "Arms," he instructed, and Jionathan dutifully held them out, allowing Rufus to bind them together with his belt-sash.

"Why are you doing this?" Jionathan demanded as Rufus worked, avoiding his gaze. "You were sent to protect me!"

"I was sent to bring you home. And I would have. But now you've gone and discovered too much."

Jionathan choked. "You're *part* of this?"

Rufus sighed wearily. "It isn't that simple."

"But when we were with Reagon—"

"I was no match for you, the Cat Sidhe, *and* the Gancanagh. You should've gone on, Jionat. If you'd only gone on, I wouldn't have had to do this."

"You *lied* to me."

"You gave me no choice," Rufus snapped. "So now I need to rectify this mess. And then we return to Harmatia."

"No, please," Jionathan begged, trembling. "Please, don't do this."

"You gave me no choice," Rufus repeated fervently. "I'm loyal to my cause first."

143

Jionathan tried to wriggle free again, but Rufus gave the bonds a sharp tug, and Jionathan settled, hissing in pain.

"You were trying to separate us," he said, between gritted teeth. "All along, you were trying to separate us and I enabled you."

"That's enough." Rufus pushed him on toward the cavern. "Be quiet now."

They walked until their feet touched stone, and they came to the rocks, the cavern entrance wide and black. Rufus drew to a halt before it, forcing Jionathan down onto his knees. "I'm here," he announced into the gloom. For a moment nothing happened, and then—

It seemed to Jionathan that the Korrigan shimmered into existence. One minute there was nothing, and then she stood in the shadow of the cavern, her robes rippling like water in the still air. The material was so frail on her delicate frame it seemed almost translucent at the ends, fraying into nothing. Indeed, it was hard to say what was fabric and what was skin, because she was the colour of moonlight, and her long hair was so pale and soft, it looked like a cascade of thin, silken threads, spilling over her white shoulders. She might have been a ghost, but there was something about her stillness that was even more frightening than that. It wasn't the stillness of a statue—it was the stillness of a pike biding its time.

In the darkness her eyes glowed crimson—the colour of Athea's star.

Jionathan's stomach grew hard as stone, and he was almost overcome by his instinct to flee. He'd been prepared for a faerie like Embarr, or Fae, but the Korrigan was something else. Something unearthly. Something dead.

"We are discovered," Rufus said, his grip tight on Jionathan's shoulder. His voice didn't tremble, but his fingers did slightly. The Korrigan considered Rufus and Jionathan, and when she spoke, her mouth didn't seem to move, her voice the echo of the drowned, whispering like the tide.

"Your name?" she asked Rufus.

"You'll have that when you give me yours." Rufus was curt, and the Korrigan again grew silent, for longer this time. Jionathan could feel his breath getting short. He didn't want to descend into the nest, he wanted to flee and never look back.

"We have no names," she said at last, almost mournfully, always softly. Her voice crept beneath Jionathan's flesh and settled there, a soft, cold dew all down his body.

"Then neither shall I."

The Korrigan was unblinking, hovering in the darkness. "There is death and fire within you," she said, and Jionathan recognised the words to be scripture, from the book of Athea.

Rufus's hand tightened on his shoulder, his fingers digging into the flesh.

"In death and fire I dwell," Rufus chanted back fluently, and this seemed to please the Korrigan, for she strayed a breath closer, though never leaving the sanctuary of the cave's shadow.

"We have been waiting, Rufus Merle."

Jionathan felt Rufus's grip grow slack, and he twisted his head back, teeth gritted. "You *are* a conspirator," he gasped, his heart stuttering in his chest. Rufus closed his eyes, mouth pinched, like he was trying to stop himself being sick.

"Be quiet," he eventually commanded, composing himself. "This one needs to be detained. I have to return him to Harmatia, where he belongs."

The Korrigan's eyes were upon Jionathan, and as she looked into his face, she smiled. It was no ordinary smile. Jionathan recoiled, crying out. Where the corner of her lips naturally ended, it was as if someone had taken a knife to each side of her face and carved into the soft tissue of the cheek. The line drew almost all the way back to her ears, the skin curling back to reveal rows of long, needle-like teeth, set in black gums. "Delphi," she said.

Jionathan lost all feeling in his legs, perspiration dripping down his back. His mind went white with terror, and then he forced himself to focus. He didn't have time to be afraid—he had faced monsters plenty of times. What was a Korrigan to the Night Patrol? What was a Korrigan to the beast in the heart of his city—to his impending doom? Jionathan squared his shoulders.

"I'm not afraid of you," he told her. She ignored him, gesturing for Rufus follow as she retreating back into the darkness. "I'm *not* afraid of you!"

"Up," Rufus snarled, heaving Jionathan to his feet. "Forward. And be quiet."

"You traitor!" Jionathan twisted. "You son-of-a-whore traitor! The gods piss on you! I'll kill you for this, I swear it! I won't forget!"

Rufus didn't meet his eye. "Come calmly, or I'll gag you, too."

Jionathan clenched his teeth and allowed himself to be pushed forward. Together they descended into the nest.

The Korrigan led the way into the depths, and though no sunlight reached this far, the tunnels seemed strangely lit. A silence clamped around them, and Jionathan could hear Rufus's breath behind him, short and soft. The walls on either side were of solid rock and sparkled with miniscule black stones. Jionathan realised what it was.

"Mica…" he breathed.

There were very few materials known to man that could effectively block or dispel elemental magic, but mica was one such stone. In Harmatia, criminals with the ability to wield elemental magic would be manacled with special mica shackles, effectively restricting any use of their power. Whilst the Magi didn't like to publicise mica's effect, there'd also been talk of weapons and tools made by third parties—things such as mica-blades, designed to shatter within the body so that it couldn't be healed, or mica-chord, a chain rope which could be used to tie, ensnare, or effectively throttle a Magi. Jionathan couldn't claim to know much on the matter, but if so little mica could paralyse a man's ability to use magic, then Rufus must have now been powerless.

They walked for what seemed to be an age, and then the tunnel opened out into a wide hallway. Jionathan couldn't identify what lit these corridors, but the light was eerie and seemed to shift like disturbed water. It might have been beautiful, if he hadn't felt like he was slowly being starved of oxygen.

Another Korrigan was suddenly with them, as if she'd stepped out of living rock itself. Like her companion, she was garbed all in white, and it seemed her feet didn't the touch the ground. Her eyes were equally crimson, but something of her face was different. If Jionathan looked close, it was almost like he could see an echo of a woman behind the sea-foam skin. And yet, if there was, she was long gone.

"Take him to your dungeon. I'll collect him when I'm done." Rufus passed Jionathan to her, and she looked silently at her companion for verification. The first Korrigan didn't speak, but something of her must have approved of the action, for the second took Jionathan by his bound hands. Her fingers were so cold, he hissed.

"He's not to be harmed," Rufus added sharply, a slight tremor in his voice. The Korrigan smiled, her face splitting, and led Jionathan away, his hands turning blue under her own.

He ripped himself free of her, tumbling back into the wall. "The gods damn you! Athea damn you!" he shouted back to Rufus. "I should have never trusted you, Rufus! I should have never trusted you!"

Rufus didn't look back, and the Korrigan calmly caught Jionathan by his bound hands and drew him away down the tunnel with an impossible strength in her lax, white arm.

"You'll suffer for this!" Jionathan swore, as he was dragged into the darkness. "Athea be my witness, you'll wish you were dead!"

CHAPTER 13

The tunnel seemed to drift on forever, Jionathan shivering under the frozen touch of the Korrigan's hand. She moved ahead of him with ease, unconcerned that he might try to free himself. No, Jionathan knew better than that—her fingers brushed his warm skin like feathers of snow. He was in no doubt that, should he make any move to escape, she'd snap his arm, regardless of Rufus's half-hearted warning.

The walls grew closer on either side of him, and Jionathan shifted further into the claustrophobic tunnels, wondering how it was that the Korrigan didn't mind the stone skimming her shoulders. It was almost as if she moved through them.

Finally, having traversed down perilous stone stairs—half-crumbled and ancient—through stout rough-cut tunnels, and then long corridors of carved stone, they came upon a chamber.

It wasn't as Jionathan imagined it, and certainly nothing like the catacombs and dungeons in Harmatia. In fact, the room looked more like a merchant's shop, or a bandit's horde. Tapestries and carpets lined the walls, some hanging loose, others rolled and leant upright. Huge collections of glorious clothes were strewn in piles of silk and fur, velvets gleaming in the torchlight. On the far side, a table was set with a wealth of golden trinkets and jewels, whilst beneath them there sat bags of rich spices, filling the room with a cacophony of aromas.

It was a warm chamber, the only one to contain firelight in the form of burning torches on each wall. It might have even been pleasant if not for the skeleton dangling from the far corner, long-forgotten in its shackles.

"Charming," Jionathan muttered as the Korrigan drew him toward one of the tapestries and, pulling it back, revealed a row of cells. She placed a hand to one of the cell doors, and it sprang open. Where her hand had been, Jionathan saw a seal burning red. No chance of stealing a key then—the doors were bound with faerie magic. The Korrigan threw Jionathan inside the cell and closed the door gently after him, locking it with another touch from her hand. Then, with an almost pleasant smile, she allowed the tapestry to fall closed, blotting out the light.

Jionathan sat in the darkness a minute, listening out for signs that she was still beyond the wall of fabric. There was no sound, but the Korrigan was so silent anyway that Jionathan dropped to his knees and, pressing his face against the floor, peered out through the crack below the carpet. The room appeared empty.

Sitting back up, he looked into the cells on either side of him. There was a set of bones in the far corner, and Jionathan's stomach twisted. Something about them—they were too clean—told him that it was unlikely the flesh had rotted. No, it looked more like it had been carved and picked delicately away.

Jionathan thought back to those devastating, black-gummed teeth in the Korrigan's mouth, and shuddered, looking over his shoulder. At first he thought the cell beside him was empty, but then he spotted a figure in the darkness, huddled in a tiny bundle. Jionathan approached, dropping down and reaching his bound hands through the cage toward her.

"Psst," he hissed. "Can you hear me?"

The bundle stirred, and then lifted her head weakly, looking around at him. The first thing that struck Jionathan about the Princess of Bethean was that she was very young. No more than thirteen summers, she had a heart-shaped face, youthfully rounded, but beginning to mature. In the grimy darkness, Jionathan imagined she must have been very pretty, were she not so drained and weak. Her delicate nose was snubbed with dirt, obscuring the faint freckles Jionathan could make out in the tiny streaks of light. From behind a curtain of wild red hair, she looked at him mournfully, almost as if he was just another skeleton amongst the collection in the room—which, perhaps, Jionathan conceded, was precisely what he was supposed to become.

"Princess Aurora," he greeted softly.

The Princess blinked her wide eyes twice and edged a little closer as he beckoned her.

"You are Princess Aurora, aren't you?"

"I…" Her voice broke. It was dry and small. She cleared her throat and nodded. Jionathan found the water pouch at his side. Removing it with difficulty, he passed it through the bars to her.

"Here, drink," he said, and she took the pouch with slow suspicion. "I came here to save you. Drink. It's not poisoned, I promise."

Aurora studied it a long moment, and in the gloom, there was something about her expression that reminded Jionathan of Rufus. He cast the thought from his mind and watched as Aurora carefully uncapped the pouch and, with shaking fingers, raised it to her mouth. She took a dainty sip, and then, as the water touched her lips, suddenly grew ravenously thirsty, tipping the pouch back.

"Slow," Jionathan eased. "Slow, you'll choke."

Aurora drew the pouch away guiltily, and then brought it to her lips again, taking smaller gulps.

Jionathan drew his hands back toward him, putting his teeth against the bonds on his wrist. "You hurt?"

"No." Aurora finished drinking, her voice stronger and thick with an eastern Betheanian accent. "Who are you?"

"My name is Jionathan," he said between clenched teeth, pulling at the fabric. "I was sent to rescue you."

"I heard mention you were coming…" Aurora slumped a little, her eyes downcast. "You should not have. Now you're trapped as well."

"My friend will come for us, have no fear."

"The Korrigans have eyes everywhere. Any plan you might have made, they will know already. They will have heard!"

Jionathan snorted faintly. "We know," he murmured, pulling at his bonds, Fae's green eyes clear in his mind.

"They're in their element, and they're watching me." Jionathan remembered her words.

He found the end of the sash and pulled it between his teeth, until his bindings fell loose. He could still feel Rufus's anxious hands tying them together, careful to pull it taut, but not too tight.

"You know?" Aurora's voice hitched.

"We know." Jionathan raised his free hands triumphantly. "And that's precisely why we never spoke it."

Fishing his dirk out from where it was hidden in his boot, Jionathan leant between the bars and slipped the dagger between the Princess's bound hands. Aurora sat perfectly still, watching intently as her binds were cut. The moment she was free, Jionathan dove his hand into his side pocket, fishing out the silver whistle Fae had given him. He brought it up to his mouth.

"What is that?" Aurora's voice was barely a whisper, and in the darkness he could see hope rising in her pale cheeks.

"A whistle." Jionathan grinned, his lips pursed around the metal. "A whistle that only my friend can hear. Don't be frightened, Aurora." He caught her hand between the bars, her fingers cold and small in his own. "I promise you, we'll get you free."

The forest was utterly still. It was almost as if all the inhabitants were holding their breath. Fae sat amongst the trees, perched on a branch overlooking the Korrigans' nest in the distance. In the quiet air, she could see the water rippling faintly from movement beneath its surface. A Kelpie, no doubt, rising up for air or perhaps something larger and fiercer, biding its time.

Embarr coughed wetly, and Fae glanced across to him on his branch. His leg dangled loose as if, at any moment, he might tumble down. He caught her gaze and gave her a slim smile, blood at the corner of his lip. Fae turned away, leaning against the trunk of her own tree, her arms folded.

"Are we simply going to remain in silence?" Embarr asked softly. "We cannot be seen or heard here, not by Korrigan, or Sidhe or…or worse. I've seen to that. Please, Fae, in my final moments, do not deny me the comfort of your voice."

"And what would you have me say?" Fae spoke easily, her voice fluid. "That I forgive you? That I *understand* why you've done this thing?"

Embarr didn't respond, and again silence fell. "Can you trust them?" he eventually asked. "The Magi and the Prince?"

"Jionathan, perhaps." Fae let her arms drop to her sides, gazing out from her vantage point to the lake far beyond. "The Magi, however…"

"He has power, that one," Embarr conceded. "You'd do well to be cautious of him. You might also do well to recognise your own prejudice. Not all Harmatians have dark hearts."

Fae didn't acknowledge the remark, and Embarr chuckled, as if pleased by her wilfulness.

"I notice you're not wearing your ring."

"Be quiet. I must listen." Fae folded her arms tightly over her chest.

"I'm sorry for you, sweet love."

"Others will have cause to be sorry for *you* in a minute, if you're not careful," Fae said, allowing her voice to swell. Embarr grew still, and she returned her attention to the lake. Some time ago, she thought she'd heard a disturbance, but now there was silence again. She sat patiently, waiting. Embarr invaded her peace once again.

"Are you sure of his plan?"

Fae scowled. "Is there no threat I could muster to silence you?"

"You'd silence a dying man?"

"I would."

"Then by all means." He threw his arms out in invitation, almost causing himself to topple out of his branch like a sick baby bird. Fae took in his withered body, from the unsteady, wet sound of his heart, to his ruddy cheeks—unhealthy against his usual, bluish pallor. She turned back to the lake.

"I am not sure of it," she said. "And yet, Jionathan believed it was our greatest chance of success, and I trust his foresight. He and the Magi enter first, and whilst the 'conspirator' discovers the true nature of the plot, Jionathan infiltrates under the guise of a prisoner and finds the Princess. From there, he will signal me, and I will be able to locate them both."

"And that contraption on your hip?"

Fae glanced down to the roll of thread attached to her belt. Jionathan had pressed it into her hands with a passing comment about catching salmon. The thread rolled easily free from its axis, and smelt so strongly of the Prince, Fae could follow it even in the dark. "I will fish it behind me, so we can follow the trail out."

Embarr whistled. "And all this you managed to plan without speaking a word?"

Fae closed her eyes. She remembered the way Jionathan's fingers had traced the map, two entering through the main entrance and then dividing. It might have meant nothing, if it were not for the third finger that trailed in after them as Jionathan gently tapped the whistle at his side, as if only to check it were still there.

"*It's a cuckoo's nest of a plan!*" Rufus had exclaimed, and Fae understood.

"Do you know what a Harmatian means when he says something is a cuckoo's nest?" she asked, and Embarr frowned in puzzlement.

"It means something is fraudulent, does it not? Or fictional? Though I never understood why."

Fae smiled. "Because cuckoos don't *have* nests."

Embarr considered this information a moment and then roared with laughter, the sound dying into a harsh, bloodied cough. "This Prince of yours is really rather clever."

"It's only clever if we survive—" Fae froze, a clear sound piercing through the forest. She leapt down from her vantage point. "That's my signal."

"I didn't hear it."

"Good," Fae transformed in a swirl of black mist. "Then neither did the Korrigans."

"Good luck," Embarr offered, and Fae leapt into the air, flying up toward the sun so that she could circle the lake. She glided in the air, waiting. Another whistle blast came, strongest from the eastern entrance. Fae dove down toward it and, dropping to the ground, transformed again—the tunnel was too narrow to accommodate her full size.

Looking around, she secured the end of her thread to one of the many stark trees that grew, gnarled and bare, at the water's edge. Then she crouched at the opening, glancing warily in. Darkness greeted her, and through the hum of the stone and air, she could hear it was empty. Deciding it was safe to enter, she moved cautiously in, her hands on her swords. In her current state, she might be able to face one Korrigan, or even two at a time if she kept her wits about her. But any confrontation would alert her enemies to her presence. The Korrigans knew when one of their own was slain—they were of one flesh and one bone, cursed to live by their bond and in their darkness for eternity.

Fae kept her back to the wall as she descended, her eyes adjusting quickly to the thin veil of ethereal light, which seemed to throb far below her. A whistle came again, and she quickened her pace, listening to the sound as it bounced along the tunnel walls.

She met nothing on her descent, though she didn't lax her guard. Reaching the mouth of the tunnel, she peered out into a grand corridor. It was tall and thin, a part of the original structure, once a place of great comfort and sanctuary.

The whistle blasted one more, and she followed it, listening carefully. Her step grew faster, but she checked herself—it wouldn't do to fall into the haze of overconfidence now. The Korrigans weren't bandits to simply be tricked—they were more ancient than she was, wiser and crueller. Fae had a rich ancestry and powerful blood, but she was many centuries too young to think herself an equal match.

Turning into another tunnel—more rugged this time—she descended a broken staircase and caught her first scent of Jionathan. She followed it, moving cautiously just as a Korrigan appeared down the far corridor, a white figure in the darkness. Fae stepped back into the shadow, holding her breath, and waited for the creature to pass. It did so, gliding up the stairs as easily as if it were flying. Fae thought her heartbeat might betray her, but the Korrigan didn't look back, her expression serene.

Checking that the coast was clear, Fae continued, cautiously following Jionathan's scent. Another whistle blast echoed across the stone-walls, and she darted toward the chamber from which it originated.

Letting herself in, she observed the room guardedly before a hushed voice ushered her over to the wall of tapestries. Drawing it back, Jionathan grinned at her from the other side of his prison. Princess Aurora sat adjacent to him, their hands clasped. For the first time, Fae allowed a rush of warm hope to seep through her body, the tight knot in her chest releasing a little.

"Your gods must love you, Jionathan." She crossed to the doors and stared intently at the lock. It was magically bound, but the enchantment—strong enough to contain a human—was nothing to her. Fae rubbed a thumb across the seal, willing some of her magic to pass into the metal. Then, with a hard tug, she pulled the door free, allowing it to swing open. Jionathan didn't step out, but kept his fingers tightly around Aurora's in gentle comfort. Fae crossed to her door and did the same, wincing as the metal clattered in her hands. Allowing the door to fall open, she leant into the prison and offered her own hand to the Princess.

"Princess, my name is Fae Ó Murchadha," she said. "I was sent by your father."

Jionathan released Aurora's hand, allowing her to reach for Fae's. Fae scooped her out of the cell, and Aurora wrapped her arms around Fae's neck, trembling in relief.

Fae smiled to Jionathan as he stepped out. "I thought for a time the Magi may have truly betrayed you. Your act was rather exaggerated. Where is he now?"

"With the Korrigans, and you're not the only one. They knew him, Fae. They knew his name." Jionathan's mouth pinched. "He may be in danger."

"As will we, if we don't leave now. Are you sure he can be trusted?"

"Yes. And if he betrays us and we die, then Athea willing, I will haunt him for the rest of his long and miserable life."

Fae snorted. "Come, Princess." She settled Aurora onto her feet. "Can you walk?"

Aurora wiped the corner of her eyes daintily and nodded, her fiery curls bouncing. "I can."

"Then we should hurr—FAE!" Jionathan cried, and Fae's hands flew to her swords.

In the doorway, a Korrigan stopped in her path and observed

the three, her eyes unblinking.

Fae attacked, spinning in toward the Korrigan, who let her hideous jaw fall open, and emitted a long screech—so inhuman that Jionathan lunged toward Aurora and pulled her back. Fae didn't let herself flinch at the sound, but lurched forward, decapitating the Korrigan in one, swift blow. The Korrigan's head rolled from her shoulders, and blackened blood oozed from the stump of her neck, the corpse tumbling to the ground.

Fae flicked her blade clean, her mouth drawn tightly. "They know now," she said, and Jionathan sighed.

"Never trust good fortune." He clutched Aurora's fingers in his own and followed Fae out into the tunnel. "Its only purpose is to turn."

CHAPTER
14

~⚬~

It was a good plan, Rufus had conceded. It relied too heavily on Fae remaining undetected, and Rufus's ability to lie, but it was a good plan nonetheless. And then the Korrigan had said his name, and Rufus had regretted ever agreeing to anything.

Now, too late to retreat, Rufus knew better than to break character or show fear, though it drummed through him like nausea. A terrible suspicion began to rise in his stomach, his palms clammy with sweat as his hands shook—their deception was going far too smoothly, and he didn't trust a moment of it.

Down in the nest, the darkness was suffocating, and Rufus had never felt so lonely as when—slipping further into the tunnels—his sense of the stars had slowly ebbed away. Here, without elemental magic, he was truly at the mercy of his hosts—these cursed priestesses that could wield their own faerie magic as he stood, defenceless in his humanity.

He thought of how frightened Princess Aurora must've been, trapped in this solitude. Her fear gave him the strength to keep his voice even, even as Jionathan was dragged away, shouting curses at him as he went.

It's hard to know if he's a convincing actor, or if he truly believes

I've betrayed him, Rufus thought grimly, Jionathan's voice echoing behind him. Rufus turned to the Korrigan.

"I would like to see your progression," he said, in what he hoped was an authoritative tone. The Korrigan inclined her head, and turning, she led him further into the nest, through their sunken temple. "You know me," he said, as his guide directed him toward a grand staircase, half in ruin, the victim of time and corrosion. "How is that?"

She didn't respond and Rufus resisted the urge to fidget and run his hands through his hair, aware that they weren't alone. Though he couldn't see anyone else, he was conscious of others, watching from the corners, beneath the flickering light. The Korrigan leading him stopped at the top of the stairs and looked patiently back. Rufus followed her and faltered as he reached the end.

Where he'd expected another hallway there was a ledge overhanging into an enormous hall below. He stood and marvelled, struck by its architectural beauty, ancient and crumbling as it was. The space was hundreds of strides wide and tall, layers of balconies and doorways spiralling up to the dome ceiling and overlooking the wide floor from varying levels. And yet, it was the ceiling that was most impressive, and proved to be the source of the mysterious blue light. It appeared to be entirely made of glass, almost like the domed roof of the Great Library. Rufus thought at first that the shifting blue was from the lake above, but then he realised that rather than glass, the ceiling was formed of layers of bright blue and green crystals, merged and melted together, burning brightly. They pulsed, shimmering and twinkling like stars from the ocean floor. It was the most beautiful thing Rufus had ever seen.

"A light for the dead." His guide brushed his arm. "To keep them on their path."

Rufus glanced down below and almost cried out. At the floor, gathered like a swarm, a hundred Korrigans stared back up, their faces lit, mouths hanging open, silent in their deathly pallor.

"What're they looking at?"

His guide only smiled and ushered him after her, leading him along the narrow ledge to another, smaller chamber.

This one was circular, and lit by torchlight. He recognised it as a sacrificial chamber, and it appeared to be the best preserved space within the sunken temple. The room was beautifully decorated, the pale, yellow stone carved with intricate shapes and knots, spirals etched onto the ceiling. Rufus swallowed thickly, the sweat trickling down his back. Was she going to kill him? Eat him, perhaps?

In the centre, an altar carved of the same stone was set with an impressive polished top of labradorite, rainbows swirling in the dark mass. A dish of glowing embers had been placed before it, heating incense so that it wafted gently into the room, filling it with a smoky, blue haze.

I've been here before, Rufus thought, turning slowly to examine each wall. *I know this place.*

He looked back at the altar, and his legs locked beneath him, his heart stopping. A wash of terror consumed him, paralyzing him to the spot.

Hanging above the beautiful stone was a complex magical diagram, etched into what Rufus could only identify as human skin. It was like nothing he'd ever seen before, yet he recognised its elements—the symbols for Athea and Notameer, the constellations drawn as they would be at the hour of sunset. But the image was a bastardisation of olden texts, and it was combined with something more—symbols he didn't know, writing in tongues so archaic they might have been lost to all memory.

The little Rufus had read into faerie magic had been sparse, half-fabled and speculative, but he'd come to recognise its distinctive shape. Faerie magic had a natural curvature to it, a subtlety that inspired him in his own craft—the power of the

True Gods bending under his will. He'd always thought both arts to be beautiful in their individuality, and yet this—this profane merge, this mutation of the True Gods and the ancient magics—slipped between his teeth and settled tightly in his gullet.

"What is this unholy thing?" he said before he could check himself, unable to tear his eyes from the sinister display. It spelled death in its spirals, death and something worse—something unspeakable he couldn't name. A kind of darkness, that only grew and didn't end.

"It is what was asked of us, by unholy men." The Korrigan seemed to find a bitter pleasure in her patron's hubris, her mouth curling cruelly.

"This...it's unnatural." Rufus lost control of his voice. Gone was his false authority and pomposity. He submitted to his fright, his knees close to buckling. "It's an abomination."

"As were we in our creation." His guide brushed the top of the altar with her frozen hand. The stone grew black under her touch, the colours fading away. "We are at the whims of our masters. As are you." She leant across and touched his chin. Her fingers were freezing, and a heavy wave of fatigue drifted over Rufus.

"What do you mean?"

"I know what you are." The Korrigan drew close to him, so that he twisted, his back against the altar behind. Her lips were tinged with pink beneath her white skin, and she was so beautiful in her hollowness, with her blood-red eyes and flowing hair. "Abnormal child. Feared child. Others do not understand your gift."

Rufus shuddered. "How do you know me?"

She tipped his head down, her mouth close to his own. "You ask with a heart that says you do not wish to know."

Rufus closed his eyes. "Am I so easily read?" When she didn't reply, he continued, "I don't care by which dark art you came by my name, but you know *me*. You know what I am. How? I've never spoken it, not to a soul."

"It runs through your blood. You may try to stifle it, but you cannot smother it. I see it as if you wore it on your skin. The fire is within you, child. Hide it if you will, but it will always burn bright. And if you do not feed and tend to the fire, it will consume you one day."

"You speak wisely, for a villain." Rufus was lulled by her voice. Her touch seemed less cold now, her skin less white, and there was a familiar hue to her face—someone he knew, someone he loved.

"Am I a villain?" Her voice was gentle, and the room grew warm around him, the burning incense becoming the sweet smell of an orchid. In the forepart of his mind Rufus saw wheat fields, apples ripe and heavy in their trees, the skirt of a dress disappearing ahead as a figure ran, laughing.

"You're a Korrigan." His eyes slid shut, content in their dream as the rich sensation of home took him. "You eat men alive… kidnap…" He tried to focus, but felt himself slipping further into his reverie. It wouldn't hurt to dream a moment, would it? What harm could it do?

A blood-chilling screech broke the serenity, echoing from deep down within the nest. The Korrigan drew away, her expression coy, and Rufus jolted from his dream.

"It seems your Prince has escaped."

The room grew icy again in an instant. The cheek her fingers had pressed against was glacial, and Rufus couldn't think for how cold he felt, his breath coming out in misty bursts. He composed himself, his teeth chattering slightly. "Allow me to fetch him."

"The Cat Sidhe has seen to that," the Korrigan said, and Rufus grew still. So they knew Fae was here. The Korrigan turned back to him, her jaw splitting in its petrifying grin. "Or did you think we did not know you were coming for the Princess?"

Rufus faced her crimson eyes, his back pressed hard against the altar. "If you knew, why did you let us in?"

"She is of no consequence, nor the Prince, nor even the Cat Sidhe. You, however…" Her smile widened. "How else were we to

162

lure you in, Rufus Merle?"

Rufus thrust his hand into the bowl of burning embers and, taking a fistful, flung them into the Korrigan's eyes. She screamed, stumbling back, her burnt face in her hands, and Rufus bolted from the chamber.

Reaching the narrow ledge, he almost slipped over into the pit of Korrigans below. They stood, still staring up to him, like a pool of ravenous fish. He had a dark suspicion that if he fell amongst them now, they'd strip him down to the bone in seconds. Scrabbling across the ledge, he fled down the stairs and cast out his senses, searching for Jionathan. At first, he felt nothing, and then the familiar sensation of Jionathan's presence filled him, and it was as if Rufus was stepping into Jionathan's shadow and being pulled after him.

Taking a sharp left, he slipped down the tunnel he'd come through and sprinted, terror his fuel. Though he dared not look back, he could feel the Korrigans moving after him. Shadows and flashes of white flittered in his peripheral, and though his enemy was silent, he could hear the occasional tinkling, echoing sound of water, like bells, close by. His skin prickled with a cold sweat.

Rufus reached another broken staircase, and slowed, almost tripping. The lights had faded behind him, and it was so dark he had to strain his eyes to see very much at all. He looked behind him, the dark tunnel looming. Everything was silent and very still, the tunnel staring at him, like a giant black pupil, watching him ominously.

And then a figure came clawing out of the darkness, the shadows clinging to her white garb as the Korrigan ripped herself free from the blackness and snatched out toward him. Rufus screamed, stumbled back, and missed his step. His insides swooped, his arms flailing as his balance shifted, and before he could right himself he was crashing down the stairs. His arms flew around his head as tumbled over the broken stones, and landed in a heap at the bottom, sprawled in the dirt.

He gasped, curling around himself, his brain trying to catch up with him. He thought he heard someone call his name, but his mind was blank, still caught in the dreadful moment of pre-tumble. He looked up to see the Korrigan descending on him, her long fingers reaching out as she flew down the stairs. Rufus yelped, throwing his hands up in defence just as something leapt over Rufus from the other side. He saw a stream of golden hair, and the flash of a blade, as Fae brought her sword around and, with a roar, cut the Korrigan in half.

Someone grabbed him by the shoulder, and began to drag him back. Rufus gave a violent jerk, trying to tear himself free, only to find Jionathan leaming over him, his face twisted in a scowl.

"It's me, you idiot!" Jionathan said, and it took all of Rufus's strength not to fling his arms around the Prince in relief. "Are you hurt?"

"No, I think—ow!—I'm alright," Rufus said breathily, still winded as Jionathan helped heave him to his feet. His body was bruised, but everything felt unbroken. His bad habit of trying to run down stairs in long robes, and with stacks of books, had actually given him a great deal of practise on tripping safely. "The Princess?"

"Right here." Jionathan moved aside to show a young red-head kneeling on the floor behind him. "She's safe, but she needs healing—she's very weak."

"I'm sorry—I can't use elemental magic down here," Rufus said.

"I-I am al-alright, thank you…" Aurora stuttered, her voice a little slurred. She was clearly dehydrated, and malnourished, her heart-shaped face a little sunken. After a few minutes in the nest, Rufus felt on the verge of losing his mind. He couldn't imagine what it had been like for a child to be trapped down in these dank tunnels for days on end.

"They're coming this way—you have led them right to us,"

Fae snarled, tearing the coil of string away from where it was attached to her belt, the line leading back up the stairs. She went to Aurora's side and helped her stand, the Princess leaning heavily against her, breath ragged. "We need to find another way out."

"But—" Jionathan began, but was cut off as Aurora screamed, pointing up to the stairway. At the top, a group of Korrigans had melded out of the darkness, their mouths all hanging open, like hungry pike.

"Run," Rufus said, grabbing Jionathan's sleeve. "Run!"

They tore back into the tunnel, the Korrigans descended after them in waves. Rufus heard Aurora gasp, tripping.

"I...I cannot—" she wheezed, but Fae knelt in-front of her.

"On my back!" She commanded, and Aurora sank gracefully against her, Fae lifting her up.

"Forgive me..." Aurora moaned, her voice croaked and eyes unfocused. "Forgive me..."

They ran on, the Korrigans drifting down the tunnels behind them. They didn't run, or move quickly, gliding instead, and yet no matter how fast Rufus and the others pushed themselves, the Korrigans never seemed very far behind, catching up to them slowly like a creeping mist. The tunnels continued on ahead, growing longer and more winding, and leading them deeper and deeper down.

For the second time, a rushing feeling of familiarity filled Rufus. He'd been chased many times before, and perhaps this nightmare was echoing a similar one, from previous nights, when Jionathan and Rufus had fled through the maze of the Harmatian streets from the Night Patrol. Even so, Rufus felt like he was repeating himself—like he'd navigated these tunnels before. It was almost a similar feeling to the one he got when he was trying to find Jionathan—a sort of tug, deep in his soul.

We *need to go left,* Rufus thought with a sudden certainty. *There's a door around here, we need to go—*

"Left!" Jionathan shouted, making Rufus jump. "Go left! That door there! Through there! Hurry!"

Fae did as instructed, tearing into the chamber as Jionathan skidded past it himself, his feet slipping. Rufus caught his collar and forced Jionathan hard into the room, falling in after him. Fae threw herself against the heavy door, shouldering it closed and latching it with a thick, wooden beam. Even as she stood back from the sturdy entrance, her face was white. "It won't hold them for long."

"We're trapped," Aurora squeaked looking around her. It was an empty chamber, the walls alive with etchings and drawings, as if a madman had been unleashed upon them.

Rufus looked at the carvings, and an overwhelming feeling of exhaustion and terror rushed through him. Pain shot down his hand, as if it had been he who had carved these symbols into the wall, nails bleeding as he hit stone with stone, his body shaking from the effort. Rufus flexed his fingers and the feeling receding, his mind clearing.

"We're not trapped," Jionathan said, and walked to the far wall, his hand brushing over the walls desperately. He was trembling too, and looked as sick as Rufus felt. Had the Prince experienced the strange phenomena as well? Had he too caught the tail end of whatever had happened in this chamber? Perhaps they had been guided here? Perhaps it was haunted?

"Jionathan," Rufus said, but his charge didn't listen, his fingers painting the expanse of the wall. "Jionat."

"It's here somewhere—we're not trapped!" Jionathan's index finger came to rest upon a knoll carved in the stone. He pressed it, and it was as if the wall divided, rippling like a curtain of water and revealing an ancient stone doorway into an adjacent room. Jionathan's spectators stood in awe.

"Glamour," Rufus said, and Fae dared to swipe her hand into the doorway. It passed easily through the open air.

"Even I couldn't see it," she breathed, turning to Jionathan. "How did you—"

166

"We don't have time. Go. Quick," Jionathan urged, and Fae nodded, carrying the Princess through. Rufus went after, ducking his head under the frame, and Jionathan followed, the doorway disappearing after him as he removed his hand from the wall and stepped through.

"Where are we?" Fae looked around her.

The new chamber was pitch-black, no light permeating its walls. Rufus felt something murmur through him, and he raised his hand, his heart thundering. Concentrating hard, he drew in the whispers of energy he could feel passing through the room, like a breeze. A sparse flame flickered in his palm, flooding the chamber with light. Fae leapt back in alarm, drawing Aurora away. Rufus stared at the fire and laughed.

"Magic?" Jionathan drew near, the flame reflected in his wide eyes. Fae snuck forward, like a suspicious wildcat, Aurora's head propped on her shoulder.

"Does it not burn you?" The Princess asked, gazing at the flames which smouldered, weak and vulnerable, in the bowl of his palm.

"I don't—"

"If you're using magic, that must mean there's an exit close by." Jionathan asked loudly over them, and Rufus nodded. "Where?"

Rufus drew off, and then pushed past them, following the weak source of the magic. He raised the flame and observed wooden boarding, blocking a circular tunnel. "There. Through there," he said. "We're close to the surface. It must be another tunnel. Fae?"

She drew her axe and hacked into the wooden boards. As she did, sunlight broke through into the room. Aurora laughed, and from the chamber beyond there came the first crack of wood— the Korrigans were breaking through the door.

Rufus peered up the tunnel, and his heart sank. Up above he could see the light of day, but the tunnel was still too long.

"Go," he said. "Hurry. If you start up now, you may make it

beyond the lake before they catch you."

"Rufus?" Jionathan frowned, just as another crack of shattering wood echoed behind them. Rufus stood, trembling.

"I'll hold them off. Go," Rufus said.

Jionathan snatched him by the front, drawing him up. "We go together."

"You'll never make it out in time. I can give you a few minutes, so go!"

"I'm not leaving you—"

"It's *me* they want, Jionat!" he blurted, and Jionathan stood, stunned by the rage and terror in Rufus's face.

"What?" His voice was husky.

"This whole charade." Rufus tugged at his fringe with his free hand, running his fingers through his hair. "They knew. They've known from the start. All of this, it was to lure me in."

"*Why*?"

The fire petered out in his hand, and Rufus clutched Jionathan's sleeve, his fingers bunched in the fabric. "It doesn't matter." His voice dropped. "Listen to me. That night, Jionat, that night when the Patrol almost had us—you never left me. I was a deadweight to you, I cost you what time you had, but you didn't leave me. You didn't leave me to die. But Jionat," he smiled, his vision swimming, "this time, you must."

Jionathan stood, frozen in disbelief. Beneath his grip he could feel Rufus quivering, the Magi's pale blue eyes wide and watery.

He's not thinking clearly, Jionathan thought. "No," he said. "I refuse to leave you."

"You don't have a choice. Fae, remove him forcefully if you have to. I know I can trust you to see him safely into Bethean." Rufus pried Jionathan's hands from his front.

Fae inclined her head solemnly as Rufus stepped back, his long form caged in shadow.

"Rufus," Jionathan said, feeling sick. "Don't do this."

"It's done. They're almost here. Go. If I'm right, as long as I remain, they won't pursue you."

"Rufus—"

"I *have* to protect you. Please don't make it any harder. Go, Athea damn you!" Rufus was visibly shaking now.

Jionathan lurched. "Damn my title, and damn yours—you have no obligation to me!"

No sooner were the words out of his mouth did Jionathan feel a sharp pain across his face. He staggered back, starring at Rufus's raised hand. The Magi had struck him.

"You think I'm doing this because you're a *Prince* and I'm a *Magi*?" Rufus thundered. "It's nothing to do with obligation, I'm doing this for *you!*" He broke off, and then spoke again, his voice soft, and urgent. "Listen to me, Jionat, and if you ever trust anything I say, then trust this. Your people love you for a reason, and one day you will be a great King. I know and believe that. You're courageous, and fair, and good, just as your father is, and you will rule better than him for the loyalty you've earned in your people. No matter what others say, I know who you are, who you were *born* to be. And I trust in that future, so don't abandon it. Please."

Jionathan was struck dumb. He stood, feeling almost boneless, his mouth slack.

Rufus sucked in a deep breath, screwing his eyes closed.

"Fae," he said.

Wordlessly, Fae took Jionathan's arm, hitching Aurora higher onto her back. She led the Prince toward the tunnel, her grip tight.

"I'm sorry," she whispered, and Jionathan tried to pull half-heartedly back toward Rufus, who had turned his back on them.

"My parents," Rufus said, his voice thick. "Jionat, my parents…" He drew of, the words lost in the darkness.

"Yes?" Jionathan breathed.

"Will you tell them—" Rufus looked over his shoulder, his blue eyes catching a beam of light. They were wet. "Tell them I didn't suffer."

Jionathan barely held back his sob. Rufus was so young in that moment—a frightened boy facing his death with a straight back. He barely looked older than Jionathan, certainly not old enough to die.

Beyond their hidden chamber, they heard the door give way, and Fae drew Jionathan hard up the tunnel. "Run," she said, pushing him ahead of her. They sprinted, Rufus's voice echoing up behind them, steady but somewhat shrill.

"Ladies, I submit myself to your mercy."

There was no sound after that, and as they scrabbled toward the sunlight, Jionathan dared to glance back. A single Korrigan stood at the base on the tunnel, peering up at them. She gave Jionathan a skeletal grin, and then disappeared back into her nest.

They broke the surface of the tunnel, reaching freedom and ran until they met the treeline, stumbling toward the safety of cover.

Only then, when the lake was far behind, did Jionathan allow himself to topple to his knees. Bowing his head to the earth, he buried his face into his hands.

CHAPTER
15

Rufus's shoulders shuddered so forcefully the muscles in his arms ached. He clenched his jaw to stop his teeth chattering, and whined between them, his hands balled into fists.

They'd brought him back to their assembly hall, dragging him by the arms, and deposited him in the centre. The fantastical light above had dimmed, almost in condolence, and in the fresh, cold-blue darkness the Korrigans gathered silently around him. There they remained in their hundreds, still and soundless, jaws hanging open, eyes glowing, and their long, sharp teeth glinting.

Rufus felt their breath on the back of his neck, on his face and shoulders, and the cold was so heavy it sunk into him like he would never know warmth again. His breath came in frightened pants, breaking their hush as the sound echoed through the stone room.

His earlier guide, the Korrigan he'd burnt, took hold of his face. The skin around her eyes, which should've been swollen and red, was its natural sickly pallor, as if the embers had never kissed her.

Perhaps, Rufus thought amidst his fear, *it's a different one?*

In the darkness, glowing like spirits, the Korrigans all looked the same—a single, many-headed entity, waiting for the feast to begin.

"Calm now." Her voice was hushed like the sound of a retracting wave, and Rufus flinched involuntarily. "Be still, Magi." She brushed his face with the back of her fingers, leaving an icy trail. She traced her hand down to his chin, and then up to his cheekbone, and Rufus felt his pulse begin to slow. His mind grew pleasantly sluggish, and the Korrigan gave him a human smile.

Rufus knew he was supposed to be afraid, but all at once he couldn't quite remember why. She was so beautiful in the dark. Rufus moved into her touch, exposing the left side of his neck, and she leant in toward it and opened her mouth wider, brushing her teeth against his sensitive skin. The touch of her teeth wrenched him from his pleasant, cloudy thoughts and he shuddered and jerked away from her again.

They're trying to enchant me, he thought, fighting through the sedative feeling of her magic. If he submitted to her, it would all be over.

The guide's fingers twined into his dark hair and she held him in place as she explored, touching her nose to his skin, shifting so that she was beneath his chin, then beside his collar bone, up to his shoulder, behind his ear and finally back to the stretched muscle of his throat. Every kiss was a battle to keep his conscious mind sharp, and not submit to the poison of her allure. She skimmed her teeth once more across the flesh, seeming to enjoy what little heat radiated from him. Rufus let out a frightened whimper and it curled in front of him as mist. His throat was too cold to sob.

Something sharp touched his inner arm, and he yelped hoarsely, twitching back. Another Korrigan had appeared whilst Rufus was distracted, and drawn a knife across his skin. Blood welled from the wound, bubbling to the cold surface as several Korrigans lunged up to draw Rufus's arm taut. The blood dribbled into the groove of his elbow joint, and then down, where it was caught in a bronze bowl by the Korrigan who'd cut him. Rufus struggled weakly, hands from all around holding him in place. He opened and closed his mouth in a desperate chant—"No, no, no."

"To complete our spell," his guide whispered into his ear. The bleeding in his arm crawled to a stop, and they cut deeper into the flesh to provoke the well.

"Please," Rufus choked. "Don't do this."

"Be still." The Korrigan took his face between her fingers. "Do not fret, we will not bleed you dry. Our master has another purpose for you."

Rufus moaned as the knife cut deeper, his stubborn blood refusing to flow. The blade flashed as the Korrigan twisted her hand, and his legs grew limp with faint. The Korrigans refused to let him drop, hands supporting his whole body, like living shackles.

Finally the bronze bowl was full, and it seemed to hum, the blood turbulent and thick. It looked close to black, and rippled with agitation in its confinement.

"Don't do this," Rufus repeated, watching as the bowl was carried away. "Please. Please." His voice cracked and failed, and he was once more left amidst the mute sea of white. He closed his eyes and choked out a prayer.

"Your gods cannot reach you here," his guide said.

Slowly Rufus lost all feeling in his skin. Even the wound, still trickling with droplets of blood, didn't hurt. The numbness clung to him like the comfort of death, and again those dark thoughts reached for him—his sadness, his hunger, his emptiness.

"Submit to me now," his guide whispered, her mouth close to his own. Her breath was as cold as the winter wind. Rufus pursed his lips, and she laughed faintly at his unspoken defiance. "You will," she promised, and kissed him.

And suddenly the cold was gone. The hands that clung to him become the warm, soft body of a familiar figure, and Rufus opened his eyes.

He was laid on her lap, his head cushioned in her brown skirts, basking in the sun as cicadas sang lazily nearby. A book lay forgotten on his chest, and the figure above him leant forward, her hair tickling his nose.

"Did you fall asleep?" she teased, her accent soft, and he smiled sleepily as she cupped his face in her hands.

"Mielane," he murmured, and he reached up and caught the tip of her hair, rubbing the strands between his fingers. Something troubled him, but he couldn't think what.

"Rufus," she called him from his thoughts, her voice lilting. "What's wrong?"

"I was cold," Rufus said. "So cold. It was a dream, I think."

"Have you caught sick?" She covered his forehead. "It's hard to know when you're feverish. Your skin is always so warm."

"I'm fine." He frowned, still fiddling with her hair. He brought it to his lips and kissed it, distracted.

"You've been kept in Harmatia too long," Mielane chided. "Your mind is all addled."

"Perhaps." He glanced down at the book on his chest and picked it up, turning the pages. Mielane peered over his head to the words. "What was I reading?"

"*The Lover's Sin*. Our favourite tragedy." Mielane took the book from him, holding it open so he could scan over the familiar lines. He knew it by heart, but the writing was unintelligible and he couldn't concentrate on any one word. "What's wrong?" Mielane repeated, putting the book down, her fingers mopping his brow. She always knew when something was lingering on Rufus's mind—she always knew which balm he needed for his hurt.

"I was so cold."

She rested her forehead against his. "Perhaps you *are* falling sick. They work you too hard—even your mind needs rest occasionally. I'll have Luca prepare some soup—"

"No!" he cut over her, something urgent clawing up his throat. "No—I *am* cold."

Mielane's forehead wrinkled slightly in concern. "It's the height of the day, how can you be cold?"

"Mielane," he caught her hair again, holding it again to his lips pensively. "Why can't I smell you?"

Her crimson eyes grew wide in surprise—*they're not supposed to be so red*—and Rufus broke from the mist of the dream and inhaled sharply, gasping. His breath came out as a pool of steam in the icy air, and the Korrigans came into focus around him. The glamour faded from his mind, shattered, and he was crippled by an overwhelming exhaustion.

Rufus's guide stared into his eyes with a cold fury. She dropped her jaw and screeched, the sound ricocheting through his body. He lurched back against the wall of hands and was allowed to tumble to his knees, wheezing.

"You will submit," his guide hissed, seizing a fistful of Rufus's hair and drawing him up. "And if not to pleasure, than to pain."

The crystalline blade flashed in her hand, and Rufus screamed.

～☙～

It was Aurora who finally managed to rouse Jionathan from his misery, touching his mop of curls as he bowed. She didn't say anything, merely sat with him in his grief until he finally raised his face.

The sun was still shining. In the nest, it had seemed like hours had passed, but the woods were oddly jovial in the daylight, and it sickened Jionathan. It should have been dark, the sky turbulent and stormy. There ought to have been rain. There ought to have been something amiss in the world.

They'd lost Rufus, and to Jionathan that was the single most baffling thing. Rufus was always there to follow him—always one step behind Jionathan, chasing him, playing their endless game. Jionathan had thought he *hated* that about the Magi, but in the absence of that assurance he felt more lost than ever. Deep down, despite all his complaining, despite calling Rufus a coward, despite accusing him of being in league with the Queen, the truth was Jionathan had always relied on the fact that Rufus would find him.

"He was a good man." Fae knelt beside the Princess, taking Jionathan's hand. "He sacrificed himself nobly for us all…I can see now that he was nothing but a friend to you."

Jionathan gave a miserable laugh. "A friend?" His shoulders slumped, the laughter dying in his throat. His lips parted noiselessly. "He was my friend?" He smiled, despite himself. Hadn't the Magi come all the way into these woods for him? Hadn't he put himself in danger over and over for Jionathan's sake? Jionathan had spent so long being suspicious of Rufus, he hadn't ever stopped to consider Rufus was being sincere. It hadn't even occurred to Jionathan that Rufus's only motivation in following him, had all been for Jionathan's sake. It hadn't occurred to Jionathan that Rufus actually cared.

"Yes, I suppose you're right," Jionathan said. "I never realised." He gritted his teeth together. *What good is understanding all of this now,* he thought desperately, *when it's too late to say I'm sorry?*

"I think he knew," Aurora said, and Jionathan laughed wetly again, gazing up at her. In the open, he could see her freckles and the light tone of her face. Her red hair seemed to burn, despite the dirt which matted it, and her eyes looked almost turquoise. She had a benevolent face, compassionate and loving. She gave him the best smile she could, her fingers entwined with his, and he wondered if she could somehow feel his pain through the skin. "He knew you were friends."

"He deserves to hear me say it," Jionathan said, an urgent feeling rising in his chest. "I can't leave him. Not to die. Not like this." He found himself on his feet, the two women rising with him, Aurora's hand still in his. "I have to go back for him!" he exclaimed. "I have to—"

"Jionat!" Fae barked, and for a moment he forgot to breathe. No one else had ever called him by that name. "You can't go back."

"I have to," he insisted in a soft whisper. "We need Rufus. More than you know, more than *I* know."

"He's already dead," Fae said.

"No!" Jionathan's voice swelled, and both women drew back, startled by the ferocity of the exclamation. He released Aurora's hand and held his fist to his chest. "I refuse to believe that. Rufus isn't dead. He can't be. I would know. I would have felt it. I would have *seen* it!"

"All the same, I can't let you go. I promised to deliver you to Bethean safely. I promised Rufus."

It was the first time Fae had used Rufus's name, and it was as if—in his absence—Rufus had finally become valued.

"He followed me all the way here—I have responsibility to see him safely out of this forest," Jionathan said, and Fae gave him an exasperated smile.

"For your mother?"

"Yes," he said. "And for his parents. His family. His friends. *For him.* I can't leave him, Fae. Not if I'm in any way the man he described. He wouldn't have left me."

The woods grew quiet around them, and in their silence Jionathan truly found his resolve.

"Take the Princess," he said. "Take Aurora back to Bethean. Consider your favour paid. I can't ask anything else of you—but...but, if you would come back for us, I would be forever in your debt."

Fae sighed, shaking her head. "You ask me to come back for two corpses?"

"If that's all that's left..."

Fae pursed her lips, and then let her arms drop from where they were folded across her chest. "He was right, you know. You'll make a good King." She smiled. "Though I fear for the length of your reign."

He chuckled, an honest sound, and approached Aurora, kneeling before her. "I have no doubt you know who I am."

"Prince Jionathan of the Delphi," she recited. "Heir to Harmatia."

"Now everybody in the forest does know," he said wryly. "We're kin, you and I. Our fathers have been the strongest of allies, and in future days I should like us to be. But with the world as it is now, you must keep my part in your rescue a secret—no one can know you saw me. No one can know I was here."

"I will guard the truth," Aurora vowed. "But I will also remember this service…that you saved my life, I will not so easily forget that."

Jionathan kissed her hand tenderly. "And I will not easily forget you." He mounted to his feet and glanced to Fae who rolled her eyes.

"Go and save your lowly lord. I will return for you as soon as I can, I promise," she said, and Jionathan grinned. He knew by the time Fae returned it would be too late, but he kept his farewell light. He squeezed her fingers in unspoken appreciation, and she covered his hand with her other.

"Go." Releasing her, Jionathan turned to the Korrigans' nest and ran back across toward the lake.

CHAPTER
16

The Korrigans were not waiting for him at the end of the passage, to Jionathan's immediate relief. He paused at the bottom, the last lingering rays of sunshine peeking down into the dark room. A damp silence pressed around him, and Jionathan was all the more aware of it in his solitude. If he turned back now, he might still catch Fae before she departed.

If he turned back now, Rufus was a dead man, and Jionathan would have to live with that decision for the rest of his life.

He found the glamour wall and touched it. He wasn't sure how to pass back through it, and for a moment feared he'd stranded himself in a dead end. Touching the shadowed wall, he felt for the same engraving which decorated the inner chamber, and followed the sweeping lines, which curled into a swirl. Finding the centre he located a notch in the stone and pressed it.

The wall disappeared, allowing him to pass through into the chamber. Jionathan stood in its centre and looked over the desperately engraved walls. He wasn't sure what had driven him toward this particular room, or why he'd somehow known about the trick door, but he had the oddest sensation of familiarity. Like someone had told him about the room, long ago. Like he'd

179

watched, a passenger, as the carver had imprisoned herself in this cell, cutting into the soft rock, not in order to get out, but in order to stop something getting in. Jionathan cast the thought away, leaving the ghostly presence behind him and pacing out into the corridor alone.

With the distance they'd run to get out, Jionathan could scarcely get his bearings of the nest. The tunnels all looked eerily similar to one another, and he was given no choice but to follow his instincts.

He walked for what seemed an age and finally caught sight of a faint line of blood leading down the corridor. He stooped toward it, daring to press a finger to the liquid. It was warm and wet. Jionathan cursed.

Fingers clenched in a tight ball, he followed the trail of blood swiftly, careful at every corner to ensure no Korrigans loomed in the shadows beyond. Several times he almost lost the trail and had to go back on himself to find it again. The silence continued around him, and if it were not for the sound of his own feet, Jionathan would have thought he'd gone deaf.

Finally the blood trail ended, and Jionathan found himself in another storeroom, blander than the last, with none of the colourful tapestries or silks and jewels. Instead, the room seemed to contain a small arsenal. Blades, maces and other weapons lined the walls, and lay in disarray across the floor. None of them were clean, each spattered with old, coagulated blood, as if they'd been freshly picked from a battlefield and then left to decay. There was blood on the floor too, rotting and dark.

Is *this a torture chamber?* Jionathan picked his way across the room, stepping over a pikestaff which still had tufts of hair caught on the end, stuck in the blood. His stomach rolled in disgust.

Turning from the gruesome display, he spotted a curtained-off section of the wall. The veil was the same colour as the stonework, and blended in, but like the tapestries in the other room, it appeared to disguise a cell beyond it. Grinning triumphantly,

Jionathan leapt toward it and drew back the heavy curtain.

The smell struck him first, thick and overwhelming. He threw himself back on instinct, his hand clamping across his nose and mouth as he gagged. The smell was so powerful it made his eyes water, as he shuffled closer, the bottom of his face buried into his arm. The space beyond was no cell, but a store-room.

Huge iron hooks dangled from the ceiling, suspending the limp bodies of meat from the floor, some dripping with fresh blood still, others long dry and rotting from the inside.

Jionathan swallowed back a cry, biting into his own skin. The harvested meat was not venison, poultry, or pork. No, he was staring at the suspended carcasses of ten humans, naked and carved-out, their ribs protruding through the stretched skin. They hung like a batch of drying grapes, bodies lacerated and bunched together, still in death.

Jionathan sobbed into his hand as he looked desperately over the bodies, searching for a familiar face. He saw none, but a child's arm hung limply out from amongst the batch. With a stifled gasp, Jionathan threw the curtain closed again and fell back to the floor, shaking with terror.

He sat then for some time, unable to repress the dry sobs that raked through him, overcome with horror. Finally he licked his thumb shakily and drew it across his forehead, marking himself for protection. "Notameer preserve me, Aramathea protect—" his voice hitched, dying in his throat. Something moved behind him.

The quiet of the room was permeated by the slow sound of metal dragging against stone. Jionathan sat, petrified to his position on the floor. The sound stopped and was followed by another long silence. Slowly, hands shaking, Jionathan turned. The room was as it had been, but the pikestaff was gone from the floor.

Pushing himself to his feet, Jionathan looked hesitantly around, his pulse beating against his neck and wrists. The stillness was now suffocating, and Jionathan wished he had his sword. Instead, he drew one of the battered, rusting blades from the table beside him.

Behind his eyes the colours were back, flashing and dancing in red, threatening to take him over. He fought them back—he couldn't afford to lose consciousness now.

And that was when he saw it, tucked at the very edge of his peripheral vision. Jionathan turned his head stiffly and faced his foe, eyes wide and unblinking.

It wasn't a Korrigan. Indeed, at little over two feet tall, with gnarled skin and talons on each hand, the creature was like nothing Jionathan had ever seen before. Its eyes were large, impossibly so, and completely red, with only a tiny slit of a pupil in each. Its teeth were also long, protruding from its mouth in layers, almost forming a beak below a single nostril, which was the only indication of a nose. And it was entirely naked, but for a pair of iron-shod boots and a cap—red with fresh blood, which stained the visible outer rim of its leathery scalp. It held the pikestaff in its hands.

"I know what you are," Jionathan whispered faintly, a terrible realization dawning on him. "You're a Red Cap."

Éliane had told Jionathan stories of Red Caps when he was a young boy. She'd entertained him with many tales of hauntings, mostly to discourage him from going down into the castle dungeons or the catacombs. Even as a child, fascinated as he'd been by the macabre apparitions his mother conjured, Jionathan had never really believed in them. In the safety of Harmatia, dark faeries scarcely seemed real.

Here in the Myrithian woods, however, in the heart of the Korrigans' nest, Jionathan knew better than to dismiss the stories from his childhood.

"A Red Cap," he babbled, edging around the room, the sword still in his hands. The faerie didn't blink. "What did Mother say about Red Caps? That they haunt ruins and kill any trespassers

182

horribly." He glanced up to the creature's gruesome cap. "And that in order to survive, they wet their namesake in their victim's blood…" He paused in his movement, the colours dancing wildly across his field of vision, almost blinding him. And then, as if he'd been thrown into the midst of a vivid dream, images suddenly came to him.

The Red Cap moved without warning, throwing itself up against the wall and scurrying toward him, arms and legs scuttling sickeningly. A stride away, it leapt, weapon raised toward Jionathan.

Jionathan brought his sword up in a wild arc, but it was too late—the Red Cap latched its feet into his shoulder, and Jionathan screamed as the iron shod-boot dug into his flesh like meat-hooks. The Red Cap plunged the pikestaff into Jionathan's throat, silencing his screams as it tore through the flesh of his neck, drowning him in a thick fountain of blood.

Jionathan's sight cleared and he choked, reeling from the vision. The Red Cap threw itself up against the wall and crawled across it like a spider, scurrying toward him. A stride away, it leapt, weapon raised. Jionathan immediately dropped, diving to the side and the Red Cap tumbled onto the floor. Jionathan rolled to his feet, readying his sword.

The faerie picked itself up and let out a feral shriek, swinging its pikestaff toward Jionathan's belly. Jionathan dropped his sword, catching the creature's blade against his own. But the Red Cap was ready for this, and twisting its pikestaff, locked Jionathan's sword in place. Jionathan cried out, and then howled as, with the talons of its free hand, the Red Cap stabbed him through the abdomen. It dug its hand in deeply, grabbing his intestines, and ripped them out onto the floor in an unholy mess of blood and organ, Jionathan screaming like a man on the pyre.

Jionathan gasped, his stomach lurching as the faerie before him shrieked in outrage and attacked, swinging its pikestaff toward his unguarded stomach. Jionathan immediately dropped his sword, parrying the blow. The Red Cap twisted the pikestaff, locking Jionathan's blade, and jabbed out with its free hand. Jionathan drew his dirk from where he'd secured it to his belt and caught it between two of the creature's talons, forcing the hand back before it could rip into the soft tissue of his stomach. They struggled against each other, but the Red Cap was monstrously strong, pushing him back.

I'm going to die, Jionathan thought, with horror. *I'm going to die down here. I'm going to die down here in the darkness, and no one will ever know what happened—*

"No!" he said aloud, and with a hard twist and flick of his sword, he managed to rip the pikestaff out of the Red Cap's hands, and throw it across the room. The Red Cap lunged at him in fury, and Jionathan raised his foot, and kicked it back with a bellow, sending it sprawling to the floor.

He lost his own footing in the process, and stumbled into the wall behind him, each breath ragged with fear. His vision tipped, like he was in a ship on the turbulent sea. It was a struggle not to be sick. Everywhere he looked the colours swirled in red, and it was getting dark in the corners of his eyes.

He could still feel the phantom pain of the Red Cap digging into his intestines, and his legs went watery. Sweat dripped from his face, and he clung to the wall to stay upright.

I have to end this now. Now, before I lose all my strength. I can't die down here. I can't.

He looked down at the sword which rattled in his hand. It was too blunted and ruined to cut, more like a club than a blade. And the Red Cap was strong, and fast—stronger and faster than Jionathan, who was weakening rapidly.

Why can't these stupid eyes of mine show me how to save myself, instead of just showing me how I die? He pushed himself back against the wall, as the Red Cap slowly raised itself up, its teeth gnashing.

From behind it, something sparked, drawing Jionathan's attention. He blinked, unsure if his mind was playing tricks on him, or whether—

No. A small fire-place was carved out of the wall, filled with debris and lumps of cloth—clothing, perhaps, from the Red Cap's victims. And it was *burning*.

That wasn't lit when I came in, Jionathan thought, watching as a small flame rose up from the centre, and began to grow, eating away at the fabric. Jionathan had no idea what had caused the ignition, whether there had been embers already smouldering beneath, or whether some invisible hand had seen fit to help him, but it didn't matter. Because suddenly, he knew exactly what he had to do.

If it survives by soaking its cap in blood, what happens when the blood dries off?

Jionathan's distraction cost him. The Red Cap moved before he had a chance to think. This time no vision came to warn him.

It crashed into him with enough force to smack him back against the wall, and make his legs give way. Jionathan shouted, throwing his sword out like a bar across the Red Cap's chest. It struggled, snapping its beak-like mouth at him, gangly fingers scratching at the air barely a thumb from his face. They pushed against each other, Jionathan's arms screaming under the strain of holding the Red Cap back. If he slacked his grip, even for a moment, the Red Cap would rip him to pieces.

He darted his eyes to the fire. He only had one chance. If he missed—if he was wrong—both he and Rufus would die down here.

Hoping against hope he was right, Jionathan drew his sword in a little toward him, letting the Red Cap get in closer, so that its talons were a breath away from his nose and eyes. Jionathan grimaced as it leaned in toward him, its foul breath—rotting blood and flesh—hitting him hard in the cheek. He could see the triumph spreading across its ugly face, his mouth opening wide—and then, with a snap of his hand, Jionathan reached across and snatched the bloody cap right of the creature's head.

The Red Cap's tiny pupils shrunk to nothing and it squealed, twisting and clawing for the cap which Jionathan held out of reach. The Red Cap tried to clamber up over the sword toward it, and its iron boot crunched down on Jionathan's knee.

Jionathan yelled, but the pain fuelled him, and pushing his weight forward, he slammed the Red Cap onto the ground, pinning in by the chest with his sword. With only a second before the creature recovered itself and retaliated, Jionathan drew back the sodden cap and threw it with all his might toward the fire.

He watched it fly gracefully through the air, his heart in his mouth.

Don't miss. Don't miss. Don't miss!

It landed straight in the flames, and burst alight.

The change in the Red Cap was almost instant. From where it had pushed itself up, it stilled, and then convulsed with an agonising scream. Jionathan threw himself clear as it writhed, arms and talons flailing. In the fireplace, the cap curled in the flames, the blood on it steaming and drying up. The Red Cap gave a long squeal, clawing at the air weakly and Jionathan took his dirk and staggered back toward it.

He dropped to his knees and, with a ferocious roar, stabbed the Red Cap over and over until it ceased to squirm. Blood, rich and dark, coated his hands and Jionathan collapsed back with a moan, dropping the dirk. His chest heaved.

Done. It was done. He had won.

He tried to rise to his feet, but his leg—the one the Red Cap had stamped on—gave way, and he fell against the wall, haggard and exhausted. He rolled, so that he was facing into the room, legs splayed out in-front of him. His knee was swollen—not broken, thankfully, but badly enough hurt that he felt sick.

He had died twice in this room. Died, and then snapped back to the present only to have to fight for the very life he'd watched himself lose. Everything felt very distant then, and Jionathan found that he was numb and cold and very tired. He tipped his head back, consciousness slipping from him, and then—

He was in the training grounds. Strewn out on his side, he lay panting, his sword only a few strides from him, abandoned in the grass. A foot nudged him in the back, and he rolled slowly, staring up at the bleached sky, the sun blinding him. A figure loomed above, and Jionathan squinted, his face hot.

"You lost again." The figure's voice was familiar, and tinted with amusement.

"Yes, thank you, I was oblivious to the fact," Jionathan mumbled, and then sighed, too exhausted to be angry. "Hexias give me strength—I might as well be fighting a monster. There's no way I can win."

"Is the training that hard?"

"Yes. Now leave me alone, I've had enough."

"I quite agree. The lesson is suspended for the day." The voice once more sounded amused, and Jionathan couldn't help smile.

"I can't see your face," he said. "Move a little over, could you, Sverrin?"

"Septus, you must be concussed. And no—you just want me to blot out the sun, and act as a parasol for you."

"But it's so hot," Jionathan whined. "My skin's burning, and my armour's heavy."

"You've absolutely no right to complain—you chose to put the ridiculous thing on, so you must suffer the consequence."

Jionathan frowned. "You're not Sverrin," he said. "Sverrin doesn't speak like that."

The figure shifted, his looming silhouette dark against the bright sky. "You're quite right, I'm not. Prince Sverrin has already returned inside to change. He thought the most fitting punishment for your losing was to leave you here in the heat, unattended."

"If that's the case, why have you come to attend to me?"

"You look very uncomfortable," was the light-hearted response, and Jionathan's lips broke into a smile as he threw an arm over his eyes.

"I see," he laughed faintly. "In which case..."

"Yes?" The figure leant toward him, and Jionathan extended his arm, reaching out.

"Help me up, Rufus?" he said, and Rufus clasped the Prince's fingers and pulled him sharply up.

"Rufus!" Jionathan's head jerked up, his whole body still feeling like it was rising. He pushed himself forcibly upward away from the wall, completely forgetting about his injured leg. It collapsed beneath him the moment he applied pressure, and he toppled once more to the floor. He lay, face down, and gave a long moan before slowly pushing himself up again. This time he rose more cautiously, careful to favour his good leg.

Beside him, the fireplace seemed to have burnt itself out, and he stared at it. Ever since entering the Korrigans' nest, despite the overwhelming odds, it had been as if someone had been helping him through. First he'd had the strange sensation which had guided to him to the exit, and now something had lit the fire which had saved him.

Is the nest haunted? Jionathan wondered. *Haunted by something good?*

It didn't matter. He didn't have time to dwell. The corpse of the Red Cap lay cool and still, its blood no longer flowing. Jionathan nudged it with his foot to make sure it wouldn't spring back to life, and then he turned for the door.

As he limped out into the tunnels the air seemed to grow even colder. He had no idea which direction he'd come from, or which way he was supposed to go, but he knew he couldn't stop. If he stopped, it would be even harder to get started again. Jionathan shivered, his side pressed to the wall for support as he moved.

The cold air grew repressive around him, hopelessness descending slowly like a mist, as he pushed on further through the tunnels, alone, hurt and terribly lost.

And then, from deep within the heart of the nest, he heard Rufus scream.

CHAPTER 17

Almost as soon as the blade was withdrawn, the pain subsided, and Rufus gasped in relief over the unbroken skin. It was glamour—an illusion and nothing more—and yet the sharp bite of the crystal blade felt as real as any when it plunged into him. His guide seemed to be growing impatient beneath her serene expression, and had taken to carving the knife through him with a slow and steady precision before removing it. Rufus might almost have been glad had it been real—he would've surely bled out by now.

The Korrigan gave him a moment of repose, before asking—as she had repeatedly—whether Rufus was ready to submit. Rufus shook his head, though he wasn't so sure what it would mean to submit now. Perhaps it would peaceful?

"Will you have us play this game all night?" his guide asked, and Rufus's throat was so raw and cold he could scarce draw in breath, let alone reply. "You think this blade does you no harm, but you are wrong, for with it I cut into your very soul. Submit to me." She traced her hand down his cheek. "Submit to me, and all your pain will vanish. Submit, and you will never know emptiness again, nor hunger, nor strife."

Rufus mouthed his words almost soundlessly, and yet in the silence of the room his voice was heard. "Death plays similar cards."

The Korrigan tore into his chest with her knife, digging it into his heart. Darkness enveloped him briefly, and then a pain like no other flared through him, so grave and deep Rufus couldn't scream for his anguish. The Korrigan left the blade stuck in him and watched him as he gasped, tears streaming from his eyes. "Death will not have you," she said, and Rufus grew numb in terror, his heart pounding. The Korrigan removed the blade. "Are you not tired, Rufus Merle?"

I am, Rufus thought as his guide traced her fingers through his hair. He allowed her gentle touch to lull him for a moment, a relief after the pain. A moment was all she needed, and through his watery vision the Korrigan was replaced.

"I don't want to hurt you, Rufus. Please, let go." Mielane pressed her hands to either side of his face, stroking a gentle thumb along his cheekbones. Rufus closed his eyes, unable to move his head. It was *not* Mielane, it was a Korrigan. A Korrigan with a cruel mask. "Look at me," she begged, and it was as if the knife was stabbing into his chest again. "I'm sorry. I'm sorry I left you."

"Don't…" Rufus's voice broke.

"Forgive me. I love you. Forgive me, Rufus. I didn't mean what I said."

He dared to open his eyes. Her own were full of tears, and though he couldn't smell her sweet scent, she was warm against his frozen skin, and her face was kind, and loving again. Not twisted in pain and anguish as it had been the last time he saw her—a pain he might have prevented, an anguish he'd caused. "Mielane…" he called, and she pressed herself against him. He couldn't raise his arms to hold her, so he allowed his head to drop against her shoulder. "Mielane…*is not here,*" he hissed, and bit the Korrigan's neck with what little strength he had left.

The Korrigan threw him back against the wall of hands, which dangled him upright as Rufus spat out the bitter, salty taste of her black blood. The Korrigan pressed her hand to the wound and let her lips curl back to reveal her teeth.

Rufus knew, in that instant, that he would inevitably betray himself. The Korrigans were tireless, and he was losing strength. He was going to submit—as the cold grew, he would lose sight of his surroundings and he would fall into the fantasy the Korrigans weaved around him. And yet, were it any other, were it the contented image of his family at home, or his friends—Jionathan full of life and energy, Zachary his old self—Rufus might have given in already. But not to Mielane.

"Fool is the man who denies happiness in favour of the past, for he will surely die wretched," the Korrigan said, and Rufus laughed. It was a gut-wrenching sound, and he was glad no one he loved was there to hear it.

"Then let me die wretched."

"That is not your purpose."

"What do you want from me?" he choked, and the Korrigan pressed herself against him, like a lover and whispered into his ear.

"The world changes. Everything changes, and you cannot stop it. All you can do is change it back."

The words were familiar, but Rufus couldn't recall where he'd heard them before, as the Korrigan once more pressed her lips to his. Without her mask, she was as cold as he, and softer than water. Rufus had no more strength to fight her, no more will, or energy to push her away and endure even more pain. He let his mouth melt against hers and released the desperate stubborn stranglehold he had held over himself, preparing to submit.

"Sweet Haylix, if I'd known these were your intentions, I might have spared myself the journey back." Jionathan's voice echoed from the mouth of one of the tunnels.

The Korrigan drew back from Rufus and turned to Jionathan,

who leaned heavily against the wall. Rufus's heart stopped.

No, he thought. *No, that's not possible. He got away. No, it has to be another illusion.*

"You returned." The Korrigans seemed unsurprised.

Jionathan bowed his head. "I have. And if you can hold your desire, perhaps we can negotiate a deal?"

The Korrigan approached Jionathan with careful intrigue. Rufus wished he had the strength between his broken breaths to shout out to Jionathan, and tell him to run. Illusion or not, he couldn't bear to see Jionathan subjected to the same torture.

"You wish to negotiate, Delphi? On what grounds do you presume to have such an advantage? We can devour you whole."

"If that were your intention, I wouldn't be standing here now."

"You mean to fight through all of us?"

"I did, originally. Now I have a proposition instead. This," he drew a ring from his finger, "is the royal seal of Harmatia, worn by the heir. It was my brother's, but on his death he bestowed it to me. I offer it in exchange for Rufus."

The Korrigans didn't speak, their red eyes gleaming as they watched Jionathan with a strange satisfaction. Several of the hands holding Rufus steady grew lax, and he felt himself slump a little.

"What use is a ring to us? It bears no meaning but to a Prince."

"And you claim to be creatures of foresight?" Jionathan spat. "This ring is my promise to you—with it, I form my allegiance. Those Magi whom you serve will have no use for you soon, and you will return to the eternal darkness where you're cursed to stay. But if you return Rufus to me, Harmatia will ever be your friend."

The guide drew still. "You think we desire friendship?"

"I think you desire freedom—who would want to stay in this darkness forever?" Jionathan's voice rose until it filled their hall. "Release Rufus, and I'll free you from whatever tyrant holds you here."

192

Rufus didn't know what game Jionathan was playing, but the Korrigans hadn't yet attacked. In fact their silence was contemplative, almost respectful. They waited upon the guide, who inclined her head.

"As you wish." She reached for the ring and, after a moment's hesitation, Jionathan gave it to her. She examined it, and him. "You are wounded. Did you meet another of our guests in your venture?"

"I defeated your pet," Jionathan growled venomously.

"Not without aid—it seems the heir of Nicnivin cannot help himself but meddle," the guide said softly, her words meaning very little to Rufus, who was struggling to understand the exchange. Everything was fading in and out of focus. He didn't know what was real anymore. Jionathan couldn't be here. He couldn't be.

"Did you enjoy the taste of death?" the guide's voice purred distantly. "You will feast upon it soon."

"If you kill me, that ring is meaningless," Jionathan said.

"Yet your promise will live on." The Korrigan gestured toward her sisters, who flung Rufus forward. He collided with the floor, Jionathan darting across to cushion his head before it struck the stone. Rufus didn't fight it, exhausted and defeated. Jionathan was breathless as he heaved Rufus up and held him in place, searching his face.

"Jionat," Rufus murmured weakly. "You escaped..."

"And then I came back. It was too honourable a death for you." Jionathan's lips quivered in an uneasy smile. "You ought to die falling off a chair, or trapped under a bookcase. Sacrifice doesn't suit you at all."

"You would say that." Rufus lay back. It couldn't be real—there was no way Jionathan would have been foolish enough to return for him. And yet there was a comfort to Jionathan's presence, false or not. If this was the trick by which he submitted, Rufus decided to welcome it.

"Notameer, you're freezing." Jionathan's panicked voice broke through his serenity. "What have you done to him?"

"He resisted," the guide replied calmly.

"Rufus, open your eyes," Jionathan said. "Open them—Athea damn you!"

Rufus complied, though with difficulty, for he felt so very heavy now, and so tired. It was strange that an illusion sent to calm him was in such distress.

"Delphi," the guide said, the ring in her hand. "We have returned your friend to you, and fulfilled our promise. How now will you escape, when you have bargained away all you are worth?"

"If you kill me," Jionathan growled, his voice strange, "you will never escape this darkness."

"How can you know?"

"I know, because my eyes are stronger than yours!" Jionathan cried, and the roof above, which had been dulled to almost black, suddenly burst with light. The shimmering colours darted like startled birds across the ceiling—stars shooting through the sky.

It was like a jolt of pure energy. Rufus awoke from his stupor, and he knew then the terrible reality of what had happened. Jionathan *had* returned to save him, and in doing so, he had forfeited himself. The Korrigans grinned as one.

"Then perhaps we should take them."

Jionathan seized his sword from Rufus's hip and drew it out. And then a rumble came from above them, and the ceiling, already splayed with colour, grew into a frenzy of light as cracks began to form along the bedrock. The whole dome shook, and then shattered, rock tumbling down over their heads.

Rufus rolled to his feet and dragged Jionathan down, covering the boy's head and shoulders with his body. The roof came in, water cascading down from the lake as sunlight poured into the nest, a white blaze descending amongst them. A moment later, that blinding light was gone, and Fae stood in its place. Her skin, which had burned like molten starlight, slowly settled into its usual marble pallor. The Korrigans, those not trapped beneath the tumbling stone, stood behind the curtain of falling water. Fae transformed, her wet fur clinging slickly to her body as she drew her wings out.

"Get on!" she commanded, and Jionathan burrowed out from beneath Rufus, the water rising up to their waists and dragged him across to the Cat Sidhe. The Korrigans merely watched from the shadows, red eyes intent. "Hurry! The water is coming too fast." Fae arched her wings up to keep them dry, and Rufus heaved himself onto her back, quietly apologising as he grabbed a fistful of her fur to hoist himself up. Jionathan leapt on after him as Rufus collapsed against Fae's warm neck, his face buried in her soft fur.

"Go! Go!" Jionathan held Rufus by the waist with one arm, his sword in his other hand. Fae, unable to bound forward through the tumbling water, beat her wings hard through the air, and they lifted slowly. Rufus could feel the strain of their weight below him, but Fae didn't falter, and they rose up toward the fading sunlight.

In their flooding nest, the Korrigans stood, the water now up to their necks, and gazed up in eerie synchronicity. The guide held up the ring so that her hand was caught in the sunlight, revealing scaled and slippery skin.

"By this ring, you are bound to your promise," she cried, her voice rising like the call of a gull. "On the day the royals strike down the crow, we will return. Seek us then, in the name of Jionathan of the Delphi."

Fae snarled. The sound vibrated up through her powerful back so Rufus could feel it against his face, and then she beat her wings once more, leaving the water below them and soaring up into the sky. As the air rushed around their ears, Rufus gripped Fae and breathed in the warm, comforting smell of her fur, Jionathan whooping with joy.

CHAPTER
18

They flew out over the forest until they arrived at their camp, the horses tossing their heads in greeting as they swooped down toward them.

"Where's the Princess?" Jionathan asked as Fae landed evenly on all fours, her fur now long dry from the wind. Jionathan and Rufus clambered down, and she transformed in a cloud of black mist.

"I came upon a search party as I flew into Bethean. The Crown Prince was amongst them, so I left her in their care and hastened back to you."

"Then she's safe?" Jionathan breathed, Rufus stumbling a little behind him, uneasy on his feet.

"She'll be in the capital by nightfall," Fae assured. "You're lucky, Jionat. If I'd had to fly to the city, I would have never made it in time to save you." She glanced down to his leg, his limp obvious. His knee was visibly swollen through the materiel of his trousers. Behind them, Rufus gave a very faint whine, and Jionathan rolled his eyes.

"Rufus, we're *safe*—" he began, but Rufus fell into him, fingers curling roughly around the collar of his shirt.

"We're *alive!*" Rufus exclaimed, almost in horror.

Jionathan stumbled, blinking rapidly. There was a madness in the Magi's eyes—anger and fear too. "Yes."

"You *saved* me?"

Jionathan prickled, affronted by the accusatory tone. "I couldn't just leave you."

"You might've died!"

"You would have!"

Rufus threw his head back and laughed, and Jionathan struggled to hold his weight as Rufus fell further into him.

"Hexias give me strength—Rufus!"

Fae swooped in behind, and together they lowered Rufus to the floor as his laughter erupted into a forceful cough. Knelt on the ground, he trembled like the cold still had hold of him. Jionathan dipped down worriedly, touching Rufus's cheek. It was icy beneath his fingers.

"He's been poisoned," Fae said, taking a blanket from Rufus's saddlebag and throwing it over his shoulders.

"Poisoned?" Jionathan said, and Fae bowed her head, her mouth grim. "By what?"

"Korrigan magic is strong and toxic. Too much exposure can often lead to death. If I am frank, I honestly didn't expect him to still be alive." She knelt down beside Rufus and pulled the blanket tighter around his shoulders. "I have questions for you," she said, "but they can wait until after you have rested."

"Cold." Rufus's teeth chattered, his eyes glazed. "I'm s-so cold."

"I will build a fire." Fae got up, casting her eyes to Jionathan who stood, helplessly, between then. "You, too, have been exposed—you're two shades too pale, my friend. Wrap up warm, and both of you drink this." She drew a bottle from a pouch at her side. The liquid inside was pearly white and shimmered.

Jionathan did as instructed, taking a sip—the liquid was sweet and soothing, like milky honey—before giving the rest to Rufus, who'd toppled onto his side and was curled into a ball.

"Jionat," he croaked between his clenched teeth, when he finished drinking.

"Yes?"

"Thank you." His eyes were squeezed closed. "Thank you," he repeated fervently, voice breaking.

"Idiot," Jionathan replied, and Rufus wheezed, breaking into an uneasy smile before growing lax, his body still trembling.

Fae returned with kindling and wood, and assembled them carefully. She took up the fire-flints, but before she could strike them, Rufus had extended his hand into the pile. Fire rose from his fingers, hot and hungry, and took the branches with a great thirst. Rufus didn't remove his hand, but let it rest there, exhaling loudly.

Jionathan watched, fascinated. "Your skin really never burns, does it? Even among the Magi, you're an odd one."

"I ate a burning coal once," Rufus confessed. "As a baby—or I tried to. I cried so hard, my parents thought I'd burnt my tongue clean away...apparently it was the taste I'd found fault with."

Jionathan snorted, and Fae sat down beside them.

"Remarkable," she said, "that you didn't grow out of your idiocy."

Rufus didn't reply, and when Jionathan looked over, he was slipping off to sleep. Jionathan kicked him in the leg. "Drink and eat something first," he commanded. Rufus grunted and removed his hand from the fire, hugging it to his chest. He was asleep again in seconds, and with the colour finally returning to his slack face, Jionathan didn't have the heart to wake him.

The Prince sat, massaging his aching knee. Fae came and sat beside him.

"What happened?"

"Red Cap."

"A *Red Cap*?"

"It's fine."

Fae pinched her mouth, and edged closer. "Let me see."

Jionathan rolled up his trouser-leg, wincing as it pulled over the swollen joint. It was dark with bruising, but otherwise fine. "I don't think it's fractured. Just a sprain."

"You'll need a cold press. And to keep it elevated—here," Fae said, and reaching into a small pouch at her side, she drew out some gauze and bandage. Jionathan raised his eyebrows.

"You have medical supplies?"

"My physician in the Neve is rather fussy. He always insists I take supplies with me wherever I go, despite my natural healing ability. It seems to be serving me well currently, however." She bandaged Jionathan's knee, compressing it gently, and then dampened the gauze with some water, ringing it out, and laying it over the wound. "Here, put this under." She dragged the saddle bag over, and Jionathan lifted his leg over it, wincing.

"Ow," he hissed. "I don't suppose you have anything for the pain, in that pouch of yours?" He smiled at her.

"I have this." Fae held up a small bottle of clear liquid. "But it'll put you to sleep for an entire day."

"Maybe not then," Jionathan said. Fae chuckled, and then sighed, shaking her head.

"I truly thought I would never see you again," she said softly.

"Nor I you." Jionathan settled back on his hands. The light above them was fading rapidly, and the night air was cool and pleasant. "Fae...the Korrigans' last words to us, do you think they're true? Will they return?"

"Korrigans speak in riddles, it's their nature," Fae said briskly. "Anything that can peer into the future is cursed to never tell it clearly—the more you see, the less you can say."

"What do you mean?"

"You shouldn't be alarmed. Yes, I fear the Korrigans know of what they spoke, but the words they gave you were merely scraps. Imagine picking up a book and reading only a few sentences sporadically. Could you then summarise the whole novel with that alone? Predictions are misleading, and all the more if you fret over them."

Jionathan was comforted by this, and it wasn't only because of the Korrigans. The images and flashes that had driven him from Harmatia, hounding him for months, suddenly seemed to hold less power over him.

"What are they, Fae?" he asked. "The Korrigans? There was so much darkness in their nest, and sadness, too. You said they were cursed. What was their crime?"

Fae gazed out into the woods. "It's not a happy story."

"The true ones rarely are." Jionathan hugged the blanket around him and shifted closer to the fire, rubbing the muscle around his bound knee. Rufus moved in his sleep, but didn't wake.

"Once, the Korrigans were human," Fae said, and she dropped her eyes to the forest floor. "Betheanians to be exact, though at that time Betheanian merely meant you allied yourself with the Sidhe rather than the Fomorii—"

"What are Fomorii? Reagon called himself one," Jionathan interrupted and Fae gave him a patient smile.

"They don't teach you very much about faeries in Harmatia, do they?"

"I'm sorry."

"No, it's not your fault. There are two clans of faerie gods whom you need to be aware of. The Tuatha de Danaan—the children of Danu, of whom the Sidhe are descendants, and the Fomorii—the children of Domnu. Embarr is one of the few Fomorii who aligned himself with the Sidhe, and made peace with the humans. Most Fomorii aren't as benevolent." Fae smiled, raising her hands. "Now, a long time ago, the Korrigans were the priestesses for one of the Tuatha de Danaan named—" Fae looked quickly over her shoulders, before leaning in, her body tense like an agitated cat, "Morrigan," she said.

"Morrigan?" Jionathan repeated, a little too loudly, and Fae shushed him. Rufus stirred, and gave a faint moan in his sleep,

200

before settling down again. "Sorry," Jionathan whispered.

"Names are powerful things in this forest, Jionat. Say them with caution, or you may summon something you'll regret."

"Sorry," he repeated. "Please, go on."

Fae nodded and continued. "The nature of the Korrigans order was that of female power. Many of the women who joined or came to them for sanctuary were fleeing abusive husbands and fathers. The Korrigans focused on the arts of healing and benevolent magics. They opened their doors to any people in need—whether to shelter, heal, birth, or give them advice. They were good women. But they were also powerful, and therefor deeply feared." Fae grew silent, her brow drawn in contemplation. She seemed to be gazing deeply into the past.

Jionathan fidgeted, waiting for her to go on. Just as he was about to prompt her, she spoke again.

"The men of the village nearby began to clamour for their wives and daughters to be returned. The Korrigans wouldn't obey, and so, in a violent frenzy, some of the men stormed the Korrigans' abbey and burnt it to the ground. Those Korrigans who escaped were chased to the lake, where they were forced back into the water.

"As they were drowned, the Korrigans called upon their powers, pleading with the gods to give them retribution. And so it was given, and each one was born again from the water." Fae exhaled, and leaning forward, fed some more wood into the fire. "The Korrigans, full of anger, overpowered the men and killed them all. But their bloodlust was not sated, and so they found their way to the village and killed every man who was left, and then every boy down to the last child. The gods were so appalled by this act that they cursed the Korrigans to live underground eternally, in their sunken abbey, until their sins were redeemed.

"Now the light of day reveals their true faces, and only the love or forgiveness of a wronged man will set them free. Until then, they are doomed to live eternally in darkness."

The fire crackled, and Jionathan stared into it pensively. "Is that what I promised them?" He bit the inside of his lip.

"Promised who?" Fae asked.

"The Korrigans—in exchange for Rufus. I swore to free them from their curse. It seemed like the only thing they'd agree to. I...I sensed that's what they wanted—even before I knew anything about them. Maybe it's because we're quite similar."

Fae laughed, and then seeing Jionathan was being entirely serious, gaped at him. "Similar? Jionathan, in what way?"

Jionathan shrugged. "We see things. And we're cursed by violence in our pasts. And people hate us because...because we're both monsters of a kind."

"You? A monster?" Fae raised herself up. "Never, Jionat."

Jionathan only smiled, his stomach aching. He realised he hadn't eaten anything since breakfast that morning, but he couldn't stomach the idea of food now. "It's true we're faeries though, isn't it? The Delphi. That's what Bruatar said. And my power...It's not normal, is it?"

"The Delphi *are* descendant of the Tuatha de Danaan, yes," Fae said, and she appeared to be picking her words carefully. "But you have bred with humans so long, it's hard to believe you could call yourselves anything but." She frowned. "Why do you think you're a monster, Jionat? Why do you think you're cursed?"

"I don't know." Jionathan picked at the bandages on his knee, not looking at Fae. "Ours is a history soaked in bloodshed. The Delphi are all but gone now—tragedy after tragedy, the gods picked us off. I think that when my father married my mother, it wasn't only for love, but also for our preservation." He stopped, and swallowed. "Do you know about the Knights of the Delphi, Fae?"

"I do," Fae said. "When the Delphi first arrived in Harmatia, they brought with them a flock of loyal Knights, who served them."

"Loyal—yes," Jionathan said, bitterly. "The Delphi and the

Harmatian family built Harmatia together, you know? They combined magic and human ingenuity to create a rich and prosperous kingdom, which they agreed to rule in tandem. But when the time came for the Delphi to take their turn on the throne, the Harmatian Kings rebelled.

"They said the Delphi were too powerful, too faerie to rule mortal men. And so it was agreed, so long as the Delphi couldn't rule for their magic, any King of Harmatia was equally forbidden to practise the art. If they disobeyed, they would forfeit their right to rule under threat of death. And so it was that no King of Harmatia ever learnt magic, until one Prince—my great-uncle—broke the vow. His father refused to remove his title, and so the Delphi Knights crept past his guards one night and they murdered the Prince in his sleep, as they promised they would.

"Of course, when the news got out, there was outrage in the city. The Royal Guard stormed the Delphi household and took all of the Knights' children to put to death in retaliation.

My great-grandmother was the head of the Delphi family at the time, and she couldn't bear to see the children murdered. So she offered her own life instead, in recompense for the assassination. She was put on the wheel and beaten to death. Her parents both died of grief, and her son, my grandfather Vincent, was raised outside of the capital in solitude."

"It is a sorry tale," Fae murmured. "But what bearing do their sins have on you?"

Jionathan chewed his lip a little harder, unsure of whether to go on. "After that day," he said slowly, "the Knights of the Delphi disappeared. They retreated into the shadows, in order to make sure they were never used against the Delphi again. Many believed they disbanded, but my mother once told me they lived on in Bethean and Harmatia. Still loyal. Still serving. I didn't really believe her until…"

"Until?"

"My brother. Sverrin." Jionathan went to twist the signet

ring on his finger, but it was gone. He'd left it in the hands of the Korrigan. His hand felt naked without it, so he clutched his armour instead. "He learnt magic—or started to. I warned him against it, but he told me there were no Knights left, no Delphi family but for me and my mother. He told me that nothing would befall him..." Jionathan huffed softly. "The first warning came soon after, telling my father to renounce Sverrin's title and bestow it to me, or Sverrin would die. My father wanted to agree—I think secretly he's always thought the Delphi *should* rule, but Queen Reine forbade it. Her son was the heir and the Delphi were nothing, she said. She wasn't afraid of the Knights, and she wouldn't fall prey to their threats. She put guards on Sverrin. The *finest*..." Jionathan drew off and spat. "Arlen Zachary—one of the strongest warriors in Harmatia—remained with him at all times. And yet, the one night Zachary allowed himself to be drawn away, the assassin came. My brother fought, called for help, but the guards set to protect him were bribed and stood idly by. By the time Zachary returned and chased the assassin away, it was too late. Sverrin's injuries were..." Jionathan shuddered, seeing it all over again—his brother, huddled in a pool of his own blood, gasping desperately for air as he clutched at the gaping wounds in his stomach and chest. "Nothing could be done. He died in agony."

"Oh Jionat." Fae caught Jionathan's fretting hand and squeezed it. "I am so sorry."

He gazed at her, his mouth drawn. "I don't know them, I didn't command them, but my people killed Sverrin. They killed him for me, so that I could be King—and not even because I was better suited, but because of an antiquated law." He forced a bitter laugh. "It was beyond my control, but I am to blame, aren't I?" Jionathan dropped his head into his hands. "After Sverrin died, I started to see things—these terrible visions. I knew it was the gods punishing me. My brother died because of me! How dare I accept the crown after that? How can I ever be the King

Harmatia deserves?"

"Rufus seems to think you can," Fae said, and a small blossom of warmth grew from Jionathan's chest.

He looked around at the sleeping Magi, and laughed faintly. "Yes, though the gods only know why." He settled back onto his hands, the tight feeling in his stomach alleviating. The sky above was peppered with stars now, and it was incredibly beautiful. "When he said those words to me," Jionathan said, "it felt as if I had been forgiven, even if only a little. After all, if someone like Rufus can have faith in me, then perhaps I can make this right?" He shot Fae an apologetic look. "I'm sorry—I'm being incredibly rude, unburdening myself like this onto you. You're very easy to talk to."

"Strangers often are," Fae said simply.

"No, it's not that." Jionathan shifted a little closer to her, at the same time that she moved in toward him. "You'll think me mad, but I actually feel as if I've known you for years." He chuckled. "Perhaps the feeling is a projection of times to come?"

"That's a bold statement."

"Is a bad one?"

"No," Fae said, without hesitation. "I wouldn't mind at all."

Zachary could feel Marcel's eyes boring into the back of his skull. The blond had been stood in the chapel doorway for a minute now, but hadn't bothered to announce himself, choosing, instead, to stare at Zachary until he was acknowledged.

The back of Zachary's neck prickled under the intense gaze and, unable to withstand it any longer, he rose from his perch and turned to greet his friend.

"Hathely," he said, his voice too loud in the quiet room. "Have you come to say your prayers?"

Marcel drew his pipe from his lips, blowing out a line of smoke. His mouth was twisted indignantly on what was otherwise a blank face. "You did not attend council."

Zachary shrugged and turned back to the statue that loomed above him. "Oh Mother Aramathea," he said dramatically, "save me from my second-in-command, who has come to rebuke me." He shot Marcel a sly look. "Even if I had attended such a droll meet, pray tell me, Hathely, what could I have possibly contributed or said?"

"Too much, probably." Marcel came and sat on one of the warm wooden benches. Zachary joined him, the pair facing into the room. The chamber around them was circular and dotted with ten small alcoves, which housed an altar for each of the True Gods. On the far wall, the largest statue stood above them all, the Mother Aramathea weeping tears of pearl from behind a stone blindfold. In her outstretched arms she held a blade in one hand and a baby in the other.

"Why are you here?" Marcel asked.

"I was reminding myself of our gods," Zachary lied jovially. Standing, he crossed to the front, touching the carved walls, which were decorated with stories and tales. He knew Marcel could see through him—the blond was the most perceptive man in Harmatia, and knew every secret in the court, though he rarely repeated them. "Do you recall the story, Hathely? The origin of our gods?"

"Yes," Marcel muttered dully.

"I shall tell it all the same, if only to rehearse."

"Do not."

Zachary ignored him and, putting on all the airs of pomposity he could muster, he spoke grandly, prancing across the room. "Before the world knew life, there were four elements in existence—Fire, Water, Earth and Air." He gestured to the elaborate carvings on the ceiling as he spoke. "Together they made everything, from the trees to the oceans to the mountains and rivers. But whilst it was a beautiful land, there were no creatures to inhabit it."

"Stop," Marcel instructed.

Zachary danced around him and continued. "And so the elements sought out the goddess of all life, Aramathea, daughter of Danu, who lived upon the planes of paradise. When they showed her what they had created, Aramathea was so pleased she filled it with life and prophesised that she would have nine children by the elements, who would rule the land together, the youngest ruling over them all."

"You are insufferable."

"I thank you," Zachary bowed. "And so it was that Aramathea gave birth to her first child, a daughter born of Air, whom she named Malak and made goddess of travel and wisdom."

"I know."

"Of course you do—you were born under Malak's star." Zachary wouldn't be deterred. Marcel settled back and allowed him to go on, Zachary dancing from one statue to the other. "Then came Etheus, also of Air and the god of swiftness, subtlety, and cunning. It's no surprise he's worshiped by assassins and thieves, though I too am somewhat partial to him. He has a look of great wit." Zachary ran his hand across the statue's face and moved on. "Aha, then came Prospan, born of Earth, goddess of nurture and parenthood, deity to mothers, farmers, and sailors alike. She looks nothing like my mother, thankfully." He moved to the next. "And now comes *my* goddess—Haylix, born of Water, the face of elegance, youth, and the arts. Doesn't she suit me well, this deity for love-struck girls and children?"

"She suits your mind."

"Is that a comment on my femininity, Marcel?"

"Femininity?" Marcel rumbled, shaking his head. "Your immaturity."

Zachary cackled, and moved one. "Then there was Penthar, born of Earth. Sturdy, loyal, he became the god of pride, battle and courage—a man after my own heart. Though why one person would need to carry so many swords is beyond me."

Zachary inspected the statue. Penthar's armour was laden with six blades—two at each side and two on his back. "Sverrin was born under Penthar."

"He was." Marcel's voice seemed to soften, but the sympathy was lost in another cloud of smoke as he exhaled.

"The Queen wants me to go to the Myrithian Forest and search for that Delphi brat," Zachary said, as if it were a passing thought.

"And Lord Odin?"

"Has forbade it, for now. He has faith in Merle."

"*I* have faith in Merle," Marcel said. "What will you do?"

"Wait." Zachary paused. "If I go, will you come?"

Marcel didn't need to respond. His silence was a steady assurance, and Zachary stepped across to the next statue, his face brightening. "Next came Hexias, born of Fire. Strong and forward-minded, he became the god of will, strength, and forging, deity of the blacksmith and stonemason.

"Then there was Septus, born of Earth. He was weak of body, but strong of mind, and became the god of healing and medicine, deity to physicians and the like. It appears Lord Edwin has been to pay respects to Septus this day. Look, a candle is lit." Zachary paused again. "I would like to bring Fold with me as well. That is, if you don't object. I know he's your—" Zachary's mouth curled suggestively, "*apprentice*, after all, and it may be dangerous."

Marcel took a long drag of his pipe and released the smoke between his teeth. "Ask him. He will do as he wishes."

Zachary nodded and returned to the gods. "Finally came Octania, born of Fire. Strategic, clever, and creative, she was made the goddess of knowledge and intelligence, deity to all scholars. Merle was born under Octania, was he not?"

Marcel inclined his head, and Zachary came and stood below Aramathea, gazing up at her.

"And so eight gods were born, and they were cast into the sky to reside amongst the stars." He lowered his voice. "And then the ninth was due, the ruler of them all. And yet at that time, two of the elements, Fire and Water—who had both been courting Aramathea—grew in competition. Both had it in their mind that the ninth child ought to be theirs and threatened that, were it not, they would destroy the world. For without water or sunlight, we would all die." Zachary reached up and touched Aramathea's face, trying to brush away the pearl tears. "Poor Aramathea, pregnant with a child of whom she did not know the father... It was only natural that she sought out the help of her mother Danu, goddess of all time, truth and knowledge. Danu informed her that when the child was born, Aramathea was not to look upon it, for to look upon it would be to give it life. Instead, she had to take a sword and cut the baby in half. Only then could she gaze upon her child." Zachary allowed his voice to fall short and he turned back to Marcel who was sat, watching him silently. "Can you think of anything worse than asking a mother to cut her own baby in half?"

"When was the last time you slept?"

"This morning. Same as you, unless, perhaps, Fold was keeping you company?" Zachary said teasingly, and Marcel gave him a hard look. Zachary turned back to Aramathea and caressed her face. "Aramathea loved her children, but she also knew her duty. And so when the child came, ridden with guilt and sadness, she did as she was told and cut the baby in half." He released the statue's face. "Oh woeful woman, grieving mother, she must have wept such tears. And then there was a miracle, for when at last she turned to her child—thinking it was only to mourn it in death—she came upon two beautiful living babes instead of one! A girl, Athea, born of Fire, and a boy, Notameer, born of Water. With great joy she took the babes and introduced them to the world. But amidst the celebration, squabbles grew out—which was older? For the youngest was destined to rule all. Aramathea explained the circumstance of their birth and divided the rule between her son and daughter to quell the trouble. Notameer, god of justice, sensibility, and life would rule in the day and be the rising sun that gives light to the world. And Athea, passionate and imaginative, goddess of emotion, battle, and death would rule come night, and be the guide to the lost. And these two children, who were once one, would be joined together only twice—on the opening and close of the day and night." Zachary traced his hand over the engravings of the stars. "Just as one sets and the other rises." He finished grandly and turned to Marcel for his verdict.

His friend studied him with the exhausted look of a parent dealing with a difficult child. "What have you discerned from this, Arlen?"

Zachary came and settled himself on the seat again. "Only that I am glad my own parents didn't try to make a twin of me when I was born."

That would have been two children to hate, he thought, conscious that Marcel was studying him critically.

"It's a beautiful story," Zachary eventually concluded. "One that speaks of hope—hope that even in the darkest times a solution will present itself. And yet with so many gods, Hathely," he gestured to them all, his face sober, "you would have thought they wouldn't be so fucking useless."

"Arlen," Marcel warned sharply, and Zachary drew back, like a sulky child. "They will hear you."

"Ach, with the volume of my voice, I should hope so. Otherwise they really aren't listening." He stood again, a sudden agitation in his legs as he paced to the weeping statue of Aramathea. "If we're going to suffer, at the very least they ought to hear it."

"You are being childish."

"I am," Zachary admitted, and stalked back to Marcel again, sitting beside him. "Forgive me, my friend. The evening is slow, and I long to sink my teeth into something."

"Curfew will begin soon enough."

"Good." Zachary felt something stir within him, a curling desire and hunger. It was straining and dark, and his lips parted into a smile. "Then let us go hunting, and pray some conspirator braves the street this night. I do so hunger for their blood."

CHAPTER 19

~~~

Rufus woke to the reassuring crackle of a campfire and the hushed voices of Jionathan and Fae talking beneath their breaths. He lay a moment, content under his blanket, head resting in his arms. The cold was finally gone, and above him he felt the tug of the star, Athea, risen now to her fullest. It was a gentle comfort and, for the first time since entering the damned wood, Rufus felt truly safe. He dozed for a while until his thirst got the better of him and he opened his eyes. Fae was watching him intently as he did, as if the moment he'd stirred, she expected him to leap to his feet and attack. Jionathan followed her gaze and smiled broadly.

"You're awake," he almost congratulated, and Rufus sat up, accepting the water pouch Fae wordlessly passed him.

"So it would seem." He drank voraciously, and then passed it back, clearing his throat. "How long have I slept?"

"Some hours now—you look a little better," Jionathan said, and leaning across he touched Rufus's forehead and gave a satisfied hum. "And you seem to have returned to your usual high temperature. How do you feel?"

"More myself." Rufus pressed his hands to his cheeks, tracing the ghost of stubble on his chin and upper lip. "I never thought

I'd see the sky again." He turned to Fae. "You broke your promise to me."

She blinked languidly. "Jionat was insistent."

"And for that, I'm thankful." He moved his hand down his neck. The swelling was all but gone from Fae's attack, and he imagined that the bruising on his face and throat were clear too. He felt parched though, like he'd traversed a desert. "Is there any more water?"

"Hold on." Jionathan took the pouch and bounded off toward the stream, leaving Fae and Rufus in silence.

"He's limping," Rufus noted.

"He was injured. A muscle wound is all—it will heal. For now you might concentrate on your own recovery, Rufus." Fae's voice was almost kind, and Rufus looked at her in surprise.

"That's the first time you've ever called me by my name." He smiled. "Are we friends then?"

"I will grant you a name," Fae said stiffly, "for the service you did us all, and the friend you have been to Jionat. But if it's friendship you seek from me, you will have to try a little harder."

"But it's a start, yes?"

She rolled her eyes, and Jionathan returned, giving Rufus the pouch to drink. Rufus took it and settled back amongst his blankets, tipping his head to enjoy the breeze.

"I didn't think I'd ever feel the night air again," he admitted, and Jionathan rumbled in agreement.

"You nearly lost your life in that nest."

Rufus frowned, casting away the ghostly images of the Korrigans in his mind's eye. He could feel them on his skin, Mielane's face inches from his own. He twitched as if struck. "I don't think that was their intention."

"Which begs the question," Fae said. "What did the Korrigans want with you?"

"My blood," Rufus shivered, touching the healing wound on his arm. "More than that, I don't know."

"Why would they want *your* blood?" Jionathan flicked Rufus's ear, and Rufus slapped his hand away irritably.

"They said it was for their spell."

"The Korrigans could have taken blood from any of the Magi conspirators or victims alike," Fae said. "But it was you in particular they wanted. Indeed, you implied that this entire affair seems to have been a design only to seize you. I would like to know why."

"I can't explain it," Rufus said. "I don't know what their purpose for me was, only that it was dark."

"Are you especially powerful amongst the Magi? Your ability with fire certainly seems unique," Fae pressed, and Rufus laughed, looking back at the fireplace.

He remembered lighting it now, and the flames that he had conjured in the Korrigans' nest and in the bandit's camp too. It was the first magic he'd done in so long, and yet it came seamlessly to him, like drawing breath.

"It may be unique, but it's of no consequence," he said. "As to my power, as I am now, I can hardly be described as special. I'm only a level four."

"A level four?" Fae and Jionathan spoke in unison, and Rufus winced.

"It's a measuring system the Magi use to understand our magical capacity."

"Oh yes!" Jionathan said. "Sverrin told me about that. Belphegore Odin is a level six, isn't he?"

"Yes, which is exceptionally rare. He's a powerful and prestigious man, and a Child of Aramathea, no less. If anyone was to be marked as special, it would be he."

"What does each level mean?" Fae asked, and Rufus was delighted to hear a genuine curiosity in her question. Something about it softened her face.

"Each person has within them a capacity to do elemental magic. Levels one to three describe the most basic kind—the ability to manipulate the elements. That is the average capacity."

"Wait, you mean we can *all* do elemental magic?"

"In theory, yes."

Jionathan pondered this. "Then how does it work?"

Rufus struggled a moment, choosing his words. "The True Gods rule from the stars, and each of them has a specific time in which they reign. Each god was born of a different element, and so during their reigning time and for three hours either side of their peak, they emit a power which can be manipulated. Do you see? Any human can learn to manipulate elemental magic—it's like mathematics or music. If you understand the theory, you can put it to practise."

"So what about the other levels?"

"Well," Rufus said, "there are some who are born with a higher capacity, and can manipulate elemental magic in a different way. That's what the Magi can do—you have to be a level four, or above to join."

"And what does a level four permit you to do?" Fae asked.

"Those who are level four are capable of creating a mental barrier, which shields you from other elemental magic."

"And you can do that?"

"I can," Rufus said, feeling a little prideful. "In fact, I'm rather good at it. Holding up a strong shield can be like holding one's breath, but I'm renowned for keeping mine evenly sustained for a long period."

"What can level five do?" Fae pressed on, before he could continue to boast.

"Level five is the decomposition of objects in space."

"Excuse me?" Jionathan coughed.

"It means you can break things apart with your mind," Rufus translated. "You expand it from the inside—break apart the bonds which hold a thing together. Depending on your capacity, you can break larger things into smaller pieces at a higher rate. It can be quite explosive."

"And level six is *moving* things with your mind, isn't it?" Jionathan said, and at Rufus's surprise, added, "I've seen Odin do it."

"Yes. Level six is the ability to move objects through space. Master Odin is the only recorded man to have such a capacity in Harmatia."

"But Zachary can do it, too," Jionathan interjected.

"That's…" Rufus hesitated. "That's different."

"Is it because of the Night Patrol form?"

"Yes." Rufus fidgeted, avoiding Jionathan's gaze. "It's a strange phenomenon."

"So there are six levels," Fae said, but Rufus corrected her.

"Seven, in theory. The last is the ability to reconstruct items which have been destroyed—restore buildings, turn sand back to rock, heal a wound like it was never inflicted…"

Fae and Jionathan went slack-jawed. "I didn't know that power existed," the Prince gasped.

"It doesn't anymore. There's been no one with a capacity that high since before Horatio of the Delphi. It's no doubt an ability lost from the world. But," Rufus shrugged, "with so many people unaware of their capacities, perhaps there are yet people capable and merely uneducated."

"I am surprised," Fae said. "I didn't know that *all* humans had the potential to do elemental magic."

"With the proper instruction and understanding, humans have the ability to do anything. Magical theory—especially with a heightened capacity—grows more complex, certainly, but it's not unreasonably hard."

"Of course you would say that, you *specialise* in magical theory." Jionathan rolled his eyes. "That's why Mother calls you a genius."

"Your mother thinks me a genius?" Rufus felt his heart skip.

Something in his expression must have disturbed Jionathan, for he drew his mouth into a long line.

216

Fae spoke before any more could be said. "And you claim to be a level four?"

"I am. Currently."

"Does that mean your natural capacity can be changed?"

"No. Yes, it…no…it's complicated." Rufus turned back to the fire. "The point is, there's nothing to mark me out any more than my brethren. I have no idea why the Korrigans wanted me. In the magical spectrum, I'm of no real significance."

"Then could it be that you are one of the Night Patrol?" Fae suggested, and Jionathan laughed so loudly it carried out into the night.

Rufus winced and dropped his head. "No," he said, after a moment. "No. No I'm not."

"Why did you hesitate in that denial?" Fae scrutinised him and Jionathan ceased his laughter in surprise.

Rufus couldn't meet their eyes. "Because in truth, I intended to be."

"You, *what*?" Jionathan leapt to his feet. "You were going to be a Night Patrol?"

"It's not like that," Rufus said.

Jionathan growled, his once jovial face twisting in a sudden fierce anger. "Not *like* that? I thought you were afraid of them! You told me—you said…How *could* you?"

"You are not endearing yourself to me, Magi," Fae agreed in a softer voice, and Rufus threw his hands into the air.

"You misunderstand me."

"What is there to be misunderstood?" Jionathan cried. "They have terrorised my people—murdered and slaughtered them without mercy or restraint, and you want to be one of them! I can't believe it! I should have left you to the Korrigans!"

"Then why *didn't* you?" Rufus demanded.

Jionathan faltered, his cheeks flaring scarlet in anger. He took in several steadying breaths. "Because you're my friend," he said between clenched teeth.

"Then let me explain myself."

Jionathan clenched his fists, chewing the inside of his mouth and then sat, his shoulders taut.

Rufus leant toward him, lowering his voice. "No matter what they've done, you have to understand that before they were the Night Patrol—terror of Harmatia—their design was something more inspiring."

"You're going to have to explain yourself better than that, *Rufus*," Jionathan spat.

Rufus tugged at his fringe in agitation, wishing he'd kept the truth to himself. "What the Night Patrol were supposed to be—what Zachary intended for them to be—was an elite force. Knights, if you will—they were the *Knight* Patrol." He dared to look up at them. Fae's face was passive and unreadable, but Jionathan's still glowed with rage. Rufus rose to his feet and paced desperately, gesturing wildly in his justification. "The magic of the True Gods works by redirection. We draw in their power, and it runs through our blood. Our bodies are a mediator with which we adapt the power from its rawest form and concentrate it to our purpose. Transforming means drawing more elemental magic into you than your body can contain. That's what causes the metamorphosis. That's what causes Zachary to transcend his natural capacity, for a limited time.

"When you transform, you become a higher being. Your body grows stronger, adapts, you become more powerful. Few can do it, it's no easy process, but it creates an almost perfect form— you heal from wounds, your senses heighten, your skin is like armour. The Patrol were supposed to be the force which protected Harmatia, the line of defence that no nation could cross. Our greatest and finest. I'm no warrior, but learning to transform would mean learning the secrets beyond our natural capacity. To witness something beyond what can be imagined, to feel true freedom, to be a part of that power rather than a shepherd for it. It's conceited, I know. But I was young and ambitious, and my head was full of wonder, and I was so…so *hungry* to know." He drew off, angry with the vain boy of his youth. "I regret it. I regret how much I misunderstood of that form, how much control it takes not to lose yourself to your instinct…and the kind of beast you can be when you do. I didn't know. I was vain, and I didn't know."

For a long time all that could be heard was the crackling of the fire. Rufus stood with his back to the pair, his fingers bunched up into his hair.

Finally, Jionathan spoke, and his voice was calmer. "But you didn't join them. Why?"

"As I said," Rufus murmured, "it's not an easy thing to do, and circumstances fell which prevented me from pursuing it. The truth is, it was my choice primarily, but I resented not having that ability when there were others who wasted it, *wasted* it on unimaginative displays of brutality and destruction. They could never appreciate what they had. They never took the opportunity to further what we all might be, to re-examine the fundamental structure of magic itself. And then the curfew was set." He turned back to the pair, the firelight flickering across their face. "And you had your first escape attempt." Rufus swallowed. His outburst had strained his voice, and he felt cold again and lost. "Zachary found you in the street. Do you remember?"

Jionathan could only nod, his own face pale now in recollection. Rufus folded his arms tightly across his chest, keeping his voice steady.

"He carried you back to the castle. You were covered in blood, barely conscious and badly wounded. As Zachary brought you in, I went to attend to you, and you looked at me with such *hatred* in your eyes. I had become your enemy—by mere association. The Night Patrol almost *killed* you." Rufus clenched his teeth. "And suddenly that power, that knowledge and ability…I never wanted it again. Never, Jionat."

Jionathan stared guiltily to the ground, his mouth soft in

shame. "I'm sorry I lost my temper," he eventually said. "I got ahead of myself."

"No, *I'm* sorry." Rufus came forward and reclaimed his seat by the fire. "I'm sorry for the pain they caused you and the way I tried to justify it. There is no justification."

Jionathan gave him a weary smile, which Rufus mirrored.

Fae clasped her hands and put on a cooing voice. "It would seem the pair of you may have misjudged one another, but clarity has finally won through. Well done. Now, that being said," she dropped her babying voice, "it's late. So if there is nothing more to be learnt, might I implore you both—in the name of whichever god you choose—to be silent and to go to sleep?" She paused. "Before you wake the entire forest, that is."

The two exchanged an embarrassed look, and mumbling their apologies, they lay themselves out dutifully for sleep.

"That is well," Fae said to them both. "Goodnight, Jionathan, Rufus. Please, do not rise again until dawn."

CHAPTER 20

Even as Torin entered the shop front, he knew their home had been invaded. Standing behind the counter, he peered into the darkness, the windows still shuttered and vast folds of fabric curled and folded in bunches against the walls. He spotted the culprit and grunted irritably.

"What d'you want?" he demanded.

From where he sat almost invisible, a man unfolded himself from the shadows, stepping out into a slim strip of sunlight. He was large, and bearded, his teeth bright against his dark complexion.

"I'll have a four-stride of silk twine, if this bender'll serve," he said, his voice thick with a southern accent—Lemra'n to be precise, the vermin-infested port town in Bethean where thieves and assassins seemed to cultivate.

"I'm not selling you anything." Torin leant against the counter. "What're you doing here?"

"There's a 'cull fish' playin' rat in the slums, that my patron would have me slit before he sings us under. Thought I, cut him and leave a noticeable mark, or dangle the little bender 'til he forgets to dance, and leave him with a pretty note instead? Hence the twine, which I'll have."

Torin sighed. Lemra'n slang was in itself its own language, and Torin had long ago lost his fluent tongue.

"Couldn't he have sent your brother?"

The intruder snorted. "That boy's too hungry and fresh for this job. It's a blue-blood after all, hidin' with the fleas. No, this one's mine to corpse." He paused and sniffed the air. "Where's the fire-child? I slipped through his window, and his bed was cold."

"You stay away from my son." Torin stood straight, his shoulders tense. The assassin gave him a languid grin, his eyes colourless in the dark. "He's gone to the Myrithian Forest. The Prince—"

"I know about the Prince," the intruder grunted. "The dead chatter more than the livin' will commit. By the by, send my love to the boy—*this* slit-throat will be back for Lemra by tomorrow."

Torin glanced over his shoulder. Upstairs he could hear Nora dressing, and he chewed his lip nervously. She wouldn't abide the assassin being in the house, and Torin wasn't so loyal to their friendship to antagonise his wife.

"You shouldn't have come." He stepped out from the counter toward the intruder, who chuckled darkly, his large hands brushing over the available silks. "Harmatia has no place for you."

"And it's got one for you?" The intruder's fingers snatched Torin's wrist, forcing his hand up. "Or are these hands clean now?"

Torin wasn't intimidated. "Remove yourself."

"Why should I?"

Torin snapped his free hand up to the assassin's throat and pressed him against the wall, his fingers digging into the flesh.

The Lemra'n smiled. "Ah, there he is," he rasped. "My 'ti little blackbird. I head-scratched that havin' a son might've neutered you. There were whispers you'd changed—put your sword down for a needle. But I see it now, my old friend."

"I am what I've always been." Torin's voice grew dangerously low, and his own accent dipped to match the other's. "But what's required of me now *is* a needle. Now get out of my shop, before I gut you." He released the man and stepped back. The intruder rubbed his throat.

"Aw, you butter me up, all right," he said. "I'm gone, Torin. For now at least, but don't be so sure your sword's laid to rust. There's blood in these streets, and more'll flow soon. Can you hear it? The song of restless bones, the murdered risin' from their untimely graves."

"Get out," Torin repeated.

The intruder raised his hands in surrender, and stepped back into the shadows. He found the door and with a deft flick of his hand, unbolted it.

"Here, take it." Torin leant across, and taking a ball of twine, threw it to the intruder, who caught it eagerly. "Stay away."

"A very good day to you, sir," he mocked, and slipped out of the door just as Nora came down the stairs.

"Torin? I thought I heard a voice." She peered into the room. "Who was it?"

"An early customer," Torin lied easily, crossing over to give her a quick kiss. "He needed some twine to fix a belt."

Nora eyed him sceptically and touched a hand to his lips. "Why do you lie to me?" she sighed.

He smiled, kissing her fingers tenderly. "For the same reason I lie to Rufus," he replied. "Because you wouldn't like the truth."

～⋆～

Jionathan woke to the crisp aroma of toasting bread and sat up sleepily, following his nose.

From where he squatted by their fire, Rufus grinned in greeting. "Good morning," he saluted, and there was an uncharacteristic cheer about him.

Jionathan yawned, rubbed his eyes, and then looked at the two slices of bread, which Rufus was holding against the flames with his bare hands. For a moment Jionathan forgot that Rufus couldn't burn, and his stomach somersaulted

Rufus removed the bread and held one out for him. "Breakfast," he offered.

Jionathan eyed the thick slice, which was golden brown and burning hot, and blinked the sleep from his eyes. "I think I will wait a moment."

"As you wish." Rufus took a bite out of his own, untroubled by the scorching heat.

Jionathan lay back and tried to recall what he'd been dreaming about. It had been pleasant—which was a nice change—but he couldn't grasp the details.

"How do you feel?" he asked as Rufus swallowed his mouthful.

"Much recovered," Rufus replied. "And yourself? You were wounded yesterday."

"Fae attended to me. I'm sore and will limp a while, but other than that…" Jionathan shrugged. His injured leg was stiff, but didn't ache so much now. "Where's Fae?"

"Gone to the stream," Rufus remarked, taking another bite from his bread.

"And returned." Fae appeared behind Rufus and clapped him on the back. Rufus yelped in surprise, inhaled his food, and choked.

Fae smiled at Jionathan. "Good morning, Jionat. Did you sleep well?"

"Soundly." Jionathan stood, the world spinning a little. He rubbed his eyes. "What time is it?"

"I would—ach!—tell you, but I can't breathe," Rufus coughed, trying to dislodge the crust from his throat.

Jionathan sighed. "And yet you can speak. The small miracles of Rufus Merle." He yawned loudly and rolled his shoulder, grumbling under his breath. He picked up his own bread and took a hesitant bite. It was hot, but not burning, and seasoned with seeds and herbs. He ate it greedily, and then licked his fingers clean. "Are we to Bethean then?"

"I promised I would deliver you." Fae gave a half curtsy from where she was assembling her meagre things together. "But before we go, I must see Embarr."

"Will he still be there?" Jionathan asked.

"I think so," Fae muttered, and her voice shifted. She sounded suspicious. "Something of this affair doesn't sit right with me, and I would like to go and ask him why." She paused and then smiled. "You need not come with me—I can see to him myself."

"Nonsense!" Rufus, who at last had ceased his coughing, rose to his full height. "We've come this far together. We might as well see it through."

Fae regarded him frankly. "You think I plan to abandon you here, don't you?"

"There is that possibility," Rufus said. "But I'd actually also like to ask him if he knows anything about this." Rufus drew a folded piece of paper from his pocket and held it out. Jionathan leant across curiously as Fae took it and peeled it open.

"What is that?" Jionathan resisted the urge to recoil instinctively away from the intricate array that Rufus had drawn.

"It was in the Korrigans' nest—it's what the Magi commissioned." Rufus folded his arms. "I'm afraid it's the only thing I found."

"This is dark magic," Fae said. "Reagon may indeed be able to help you translate it. Though this—these lines here are beyond me." Fae traced her fingers over the work, and Jionathan examined the picture.

"Those are the marks of Athea," he realised. "They're etched on the ceiling in the castle crypt."

"They are," Rufus said, taking the paper back. "But they're reversed, do you see? This spell seems to be a way of cheating death."

"Magi looking for immortality?" Jionathan snorted. "Don't you live long enough as it is?"

"Two to three hundred years, yes. I can't think what calibre of man could stand to live longer."

"And what calibre of man would refuse?" a slick voice interrupted them, and the party leapt back in surprise to see Embarr Reagon peering over the page alongside them.

"Embarr!" Fae cried, as both Harmatians dropped their eyes immediately, scrabbling back.

"Dear friends, will you not lift your heads? There is no need for such alarm. So long as my intentions are true, I am quite harmless." Embarr's voice was strong and beautiful, not the broken speech of a dying man.

"Where did you come from?" Jionathan demanded. He hadn't heard the Gancanagh approach at all, and couldn't conceive how he'd slipped into their glade unnoticed.

"I spirited, dear boy," Embarr said. At Jionathan's silence he added, "My kind can appear and disappear at will. We are creatures of the air—free to roam as we please. We call it 'spiriting.'"

"Only a well-fed Gancanagh can spirit." Overcoming her initial shock, Fae didn't look nearly as surprised to see Embarr as the others. "That magic is taxing."

"Well, I have rather been gorging myself in Kathra these last months. It is a surprisingly beautiful country. I made a few friends there, too—a black-eyed Isny, who I think you might like, and a Magi. Perhaps you know him—"

"You were dying yesterday!" Fae's voice rose. "Starved of affection!"

"A falsity, I confess," Embarr sounded regretful.

Jionathan felt sick. Rufus took his arm and drew him back protectively. As before, Rufus himself seemed almost as unaffected by Embarr's power as Fae.

"Then it's as I thought." Fae clenched her fists, and Jionathan wondered if she was going to hit him.

"You always were sharp." Embarr waggled his finger.

"What's going on?" Rufus demanded, his hand still on Jionathan's shoulder, fingers tight.

Fae circled around toward them, putting herself between the Harmatians and the Gancanagh. "He manipulated us. You were never in-love with the Princess, were you? You never even made a bond with her."

"How can you know?" Embarr put his long red pipe in his mouth. "Is she not fair, after all? And so very sweet? Even as I brought her to these woods, even facing such dangers, she was a gentle soul."

"You might have been hungry enough to feed on a woman, if there were no men to steal your fancy," Fae growled. "But she was yet a child. You are strict about your preference."

"I am," Embarr agreed, and his voice dipped with sincerity, "and I am truly, in my heart of hearts, sorry to have had to lie to you. Believe me—my fright that you were to face the Korrigans was real."

"You kidnapped her," Fae said. "You kidnapped the Princess and gave her to them. You were a part of their plan."

"That, I was not." His voice grew firmer. "I assure you."

"How am I to believe anything you say?"

"You have no reason to." Embarr sat by the fire, his blueish hands extended toward the flames, which died out beneath his fingertips. "But why should I wish you harm? You know who I work for, and you know my purpose. I am a spy, and I do the bidding of my master. That the Korrigans expected me was not my business to question…but I did fear for you. I feared for you all. Especially you, Delphi Prince, when you faced that Red Cap."

"When he faced *what*?" Rufus balked, and Jionathan froze.

"You were there?" He dared to raise his eyes to Embarr's throat.

"I lit the fire," Embarr said. "Though my orders were strictly not to interfere."

"That fire saved me," Jionathan breathed. "Then was it you,

who guided us out through the tunnels as well?"

"No?" Embarr's voice lilted, almost in question. "I did no such thing. How curious."

Fae spoke over him. "But why? Why, then, if not to help the Korrigans, would you cause so much trouble? Was it your mother? Have you submitted to her?"

"Fae, darling, please, if I had submitted to her, I would be feasting on these mouth-watering humans already. The Prince, I admit, is still a few years too fresh for my taste, but the Magi... well, you would be a scrumptious treat, my dear." Embarr moved toward Rufus, taking him by the chin. "What say you, Lord Merle? Would you care to be more intimate?"

Rufus inhaled deeply. "I'm hardly in a position to refuse, am I?" he said breathily, and Fae pushed her way between them, separating Embarr from Rufus, who dropped back, his hand clutched to his chest.

Embarr returned to the conversation easily. "I am and have always been loyal to you and your family," he told Fae. "I am bound to them."

Fae wasn't impressed by his words. "You mean to say that it was Niamh who gave you this task?"

"She told me that what came to pass in these woods would change the fate of this land forever. The Korrigans, no doubt, with their own foresight, thought to take advantage of whatever plans had been made. Or perhaps it is the reverse?"

"But why? Why did she send you?" Fae demanded.

"To guarantee that it would be you, my darling Fae, who came after me. Niamh used our friendship against you...another thing I regret."

Fae seemed to struggle a moment, her arms folded. "But we achieved nothing," she finally said. "We solved only a problem that you created."

"Yes, you did, and yet something of greater value has been made. A Magi, a faerie, and a Delphi Prince working together toward a common goal—what a union!" Embarr chuckled, and Fae looked at them, her lips parted. She strayed her eyes over Rufus—still suspicious, still uncertain—and then to Jionathan. Her expression warmed at the sight of him, and then she corrected herself and turned back to Embarr.

"But how did you forge your sickness? You were truly dying yesterday. I felt it."

Embarr lounged back, resting his head on one of the saddlebags where Rufus had been sleeping. He spread himself seductively, the top of his chemise hanging low, so that it exposed his bare chest. Embarr stroked his fingers lightly up and down the muscle, as if unaware of what he was doing. Jionathan turned his back, staring out into the woods, his face burning. Beside him, Rufus didn't move, but made a small, appreciative noise in the back of his throat. The Gancanagh chuckled.

"I knew no glamour or spell that could fool your senses," Embarr admitted to Fae. "So I used a poison to bring myself to the brink of death. It was carefully constructed to mimic all the symptoms of starvation. My suffering was quite genuine. I resolved not to take the antidote until I knew you were safe. I could not have lived with myself if I'd had any part in your death."

"Of *course* not."

Embarr laughed again. "I sense you may be angry with me."

"No, no." Fae's voice was acidic. "After the anguish you put me through for the folly of my grandmother—the months of worry, the betrayal, the torn despair that you were dying… no, Embarr, why should I be angry?"

"Excellent." Embarr clapped his hands. "You are a better woman than e'er I did know!"

Fae made a small noise in the back of her throat, like an agitated cat.

Jionathan dared to look back. "Would you like me to break his legs?"

"I'll hold him," Rufus offered in turn, still sounding a little breathy. "Very, very gladly hold him."

Jionathan could have sworn he saw a flicker of smile dance on Fae's lips, and Embarr laughed again, the sound like running water.

"Will you let me see what it is you have discovered?" he asked. "Perhaps I can redeem myself in that?" He gestured to Rufus who, turning to Fae for her blessing, handed Embarr the drawing. Embarr studied it awhile, and something of his aura changed—the joviality slipping away to a more serious tone.

"This is indeed grave," he agreed. "It is as you say, a spell which meddles with the nature of death…but it is uniquely constructed, far beyond me." Embarr trained his eyes on Rufus's face, and Rufus dropped his gaze, somehow looking more coy than cautious. "They took your blood, I heard. What an interesting brew they must have concocted." He returned to the drawing. "This is centuries of work—old, *old* magic combined with new. I am afraid even with my lineage I could not help you. My mother might, but for your preservation, I do not think it wise to introduce you."

"Who's your mother?" Jionathan frowned.

"Speak her name in these woods?" Embarr said. "I might as well fetch her. She is a true Fomorii and no friend to the Delphi. No, take what you have and be content with your findings for now."

"And what will you do?" Fae asked, her voice still bitter.

"It seems my work has been accomplished, so I will be on my way." Embarr rose to his feet. "But before I go, allow me to make you a solemn vow. Never again will I knowingly trick you in such a way. Take this as token of my affection and my word." He drew his pipe from his lips and threw it. Rufus caught it awkwardly as it dropped through the air. "May your gods be with you on your journey. Now, darling Fae, if I might?"

Fae's brow furrowed. "If you might—" she began, and in the next second, Embarr had somehow crossed the distance between them and pressed his lips against Fae's own. She stood, eyes wide in shock as Embarr cupped her chin, and then she drove him away with a powerful shove. Embarr fell back a few steps, massaging his chest with a giddy little laugh.

"A quick meal to get me by. I thank you, my love, for the kind donation."

"You mongrel-pig of a man!" Fae swore. "How dare you feed on me!" she advanced toward him. "I will remove your jaw!"

"And on that threat—Prince Jionathan," he winked at Rufus, "Lord Merle," he retreated several steps, his hands raised, "darling, darling Fae, I bid you all a loving farewell, and may we meet again!" And, like that, he was nothing but the air, disappearing in a flurry of wind, his laughter lingering after him.

"Return and face me this instant! Embarr!" Fae shouted, grabbing at the space he'd been, her eyes darting across the glade. "You pervert!"

But he was gone, and with an angry growl Fae kicked the dirt and turned back to Rufus and Jionathan. Behind her burning eyes and skin-deep fury, Jionathan could see laughter, and he knew that whatever may be, Fae was glad Embarr Reagon would live. Though he suspected Fae would still gladly dislocate both his shoulders if Embarr presumed to return too soon.

"Are you well?" Rufus asked.

"Fine," Fae huffed. "It appears our work in the forest is truly at an end. You can give me that." She gestured to the long red pipe Rufus still held in his hands. Jionathan peered at it, but didn't dare touch, in case something of Embarr's toxicity lingered. Rufus held it tighter to his chest.

"If it's all the same to you, I should like to keep it—a memento for this bizarre and dangerous adventure."

"As you wish, it holds no other value." Fae stomped out the fire, and Rufus beamed and tucked the pipe away safely, like it was a treasure.

CHAPTER
21

He was running down the dungeon stairs, his heart fluttering in his little body. Small hands pressed against the wet stone as he slipped, almost tumbling down the ragged stairway. Far below he heard the sharp crack of the whip again and a scream of pain. He kept running. "Katrina!" He turned a corner, but the stairs seemed to wind endlessly on, shifting under his feet. He could hear her sobbing, the stairs elongating and growing until his seven-year-old legs could no longer reach down them and he had to jump from stone to stone. The whip kept cracking, and he felt it on his own shoulders, an icy burn. She was begging now, pleading, and Arlen stopped, looking desperately down. He could see the end, the bottom of the stairs, but even as he ran toward it, it didn't get any closer. "Katrina!" he shouted. "Katrina!"

Suddenly something cold and hard struck against his back, and he found himself pressed into the stone. He struggled to sit up, but the great weight grew over him as the tumbling rocks slowly covered his back, and then his head. Earth shifted through the cracks, binding him down in his grave. Panic settled in. They were burying him alive! He kicked out, trying to twist desperately around, but it was too heavy. He couldn't move. He couldn't breathe! He opened *his mouth to scream and—*

A sharp rap on the door woke him, and Zachary lay, tangled in the bedclothes, his face pressed into the pillow. He lifted his head and looked around, his mind still muted by sleep.

"Arlen," a strict voice called from beyond the door. "I'm coming in."

Zachary grunted, and let his head drop back against the pillow, dragging the covers up over his bare shoulders, though he had nothing to hide from Heather Benson. As his childhood nurse and current housekeeper, she'd seen all of him.

She bustled in, her usual black frock pristine and tight about her little body. Closing the door behind her, she moved to the bed and folded the covers away from where Zachary had dramatically thrown them over his head. "It's almost noon," she told him.

"And I came to bed at dawn, woman." Zachary wrestled with her over the covers, until she won over and stripped him of them completely. He rolled, naked, from the bed, and hid behind the bedpost, scowling.

"Where are your robes?" she asked, her grey eyes dark in the lightless room. Zachary pointed to a bundle on the floor, tossed in an unceremonious heap. Heather bent to pick them up, and Zachary covered himself with his sheet—conscious even in her presence of his bare skin. She paused and, running her hands along the dark fabric of his robe, glanced worriedly up at him.

"There's blood on this," she said, and Zachary shrugged.

"Someone broke curfew," he muttered, reaching into the wardrobe for a clean chemise.

Heather silently filled his washing bowl, her thin mouth pinched in disapproval.

"Oh don't look at me like that." Zachary heated the water with a touch of his hand and cleaned his face.

"Would you prefer I return later, Lord Zachary?" She bowed her head, and Zachary winced, water dribbling down his nose.

"*Lord* Zachary, am I, all of a sudden?" he chided. "Woken like a child, and then judged as a man. Decide, woman, which am I?"

"The way you behave, both." Heather seemed to relax at his playful tone. When Zachary glanced back to her, though, something of her narrow face was sad. He could see his sister Katrina in that expression.

"Well, I had to fit a childhood in somewhere," he laughed, and tried not to make it bitter. His back hurt, and again he was conscious of his nakedness and pulled the fresh chemise over his body.

"Why did you wake me?" he asked as he dressed. Heather turned her back to give him his privacy, though it was more of a gesture than to save his dignity. He'd lost that to her nineteen years ago, the night he'd urinated in his sleep and she'd caught him in the desperate, comical act of trying to change his own sheets. He'd been an impossibly small child at the time, his bed so vast that he'd struggled to even climb into it at night. Now he slept comfortably, his head against the rest board and feet brushing the end. Who knew such a meagre scrap of a child could grow so tall?

"Her Grace, Queen Reine, had this delivered by courier." Heather produced a note from her apron and held it over her shoulder for him. Zachary took it, sliding his thumb under the wax seal. He squinted at the writing, Heather opening the shutters on the far windows. Sunlight poured into the room, and Zachary—dismayed by the sight of the outside world—continued dressing hurriedly before returning to the letter.

It was a simple enough order. Information had been gathered that there was a man hiding in the slums who was believed to be associated with the Knights of the Delphi. Zachary read the description two times through, before giving his eyes a cursory rub and throwing the note into his fireplace. He set it alight with a flick of his fingers and watched it curl into ash. Moving to his desk, he fetched a piece of paper, found his quill and began to write a note. Heather watched him.

"Left hand," she warned, and Zachary cussed and swapped the quill to his right hand, taking longer over each word.

"Ach, it's not like he'd be any the wiser," he said between his teeth, allowing the ink to dry before folding the note and passing it to Heather. "Have this sent on to my master," he instructed.

"Will you go out?" Heather asked.

"Yes. Duty calls. Have a drink prepared for me when I return." Zachary straitened his uniform, and then threw his robe over the top, smoothing his hair back. "I shan't be gone long."

Exiting his chambers, he strode across the extensive landing and down the grandiose staircase that led to the hallway. His horse was already waiting for him outside—Heather must've had it prepared, she knew the way of things.

He made his way down through the city until he was in the Southern Quarter, where—the streets narrow and bustling as they were—he dismounted and led the horse on foot. Around him, the shops were sprung open, vendors calling out of their doors and windows, children dashing out between the streets, unattended and joyful. Zachary watched out for them, keeping his nickering stallion on a tight lead as the smallest ones dove out in front and behind him. A young girl stopped to admire the horse, with its gleaming dapple-grey coat, but ran away and hid shyly behind her mother's skirts when Zachary spotted her. He gestured mother and child toward him, the woman stepping across fretfully, her gloves twisted in her hands.

"Where are you going?" Zachary asked, and the woman pointed to the end of the street. Zachary lifted the young girl up and put her on the back of the horse. She squealed with delight, gripping the saddle tightly between her fingers. Her mother gave a wan smile, and Zachary walked with them to their destination before helping the child dismount, and wishing her a happy morning. The girl waved as he passed by, and Zachary hummed to himself. On the street corner opposite, an offensive blood splatter was smeared across the ground and adjacent houses.

Zachary glanced at it. So this was where he'd been last night? The streets looked different in the daylight.

Walking on, he caught a boy trying to pickpocket him and sent him on his merry way with a cuff over the head and a coin to keep him out of trouble. The sun was beating down on the stone city, baking the paving stones below him. A child playing in the doorstop, banged a spoon against a pot, and the sudden noise almost sent his horse into a frenzy. Zachary struggled with it a moment, dragging it down and calming it.

"And you're supposed to be battle-worthy," he scolded, holding its nose. It tried to nibble his fingers, and he turned back to continue on with his way. Stepping out, he almost collided with a tall, dark-haired man. Zachary drew away, surprised.

"Merle?" he said, the other man also pulling away with an apology. Zachary's eyes adjusted and he realised his mistake. "I apologise, I thought you were someone else."

"Rufus Merle?" the stranger chuckled. His eyes were pale green, and his features were so similar to Rufus's that Zachary had to consider him again. He realised a moment later who the stranger was.

"You must be Torin—Torin Merle."

"And you are Lord Arlen Zachary, if I'm not mistaken." Torin beamed. "My son speaks very highly of you."

"Well either he's lying, or you are," Zachary said. "It's good to meet you at last."

They shook hands, and Zachary noted the strength of Torin's grip. *He's held a sword before,* he thought, *and more than once.*

"It's been a few days since Rufus left Harmatia now," Torin said. "I don't suppose anyone in the castle has heard after him?"

"I was about to ask you the same question."

Torin's face grew more sombre. "Nothing, as of yet," he admitted, and Zachary was amused to see how similar Rufus was to his father in his manner. Indeed, Zachary might have passed the pair off as brothers if he hadn't known better.

236

"I am sure he is with the Prince," Zachary said, and there was no doubt of that. He had faith that Rufus would find Jionathan—it was merely whether he'd wade out of the Myrithian Forest alive to tell of it.

"Aye, I'm sure they'll be home soon." Torin smiled, but his brow seemed heavy regardless. "Well then, Lord Zachary, if you'll excuse me..."

"Of course. Good day to you," Zachary bowed his head on instinct, and Torin did the same.

"And to you." He started back up the street, and Zachary watched him go, lost in thought, before returning to his task.

Quickening his pace now, he found his way out of the Southern Quarter at last and into the slums. Here the air was thick with dust and sand, and the people were scarce and shadowy. Zachary was not perturbed by the eyes that watched him in the gloom, and moved on with confidence.

Coming to the southernmost sentry, he found an old, abandoned whorehouse and stood outside, conscious that if he left his horse unattended, it would undoubtedly be stolen. Deciding that it didn't matter, he led the creature into the building instead, passing the occupants until he came to an old man. He drew out a coin.

"I am looking for a man—blond hair, brown eyes. He doesn't belong." He waved the coin temptingly, and the old man took it, pointing with his thumb to a room in the far back. He grinned to Zachary. Only two of his teeth remained. Zachary went on his way, guiding the horse through the narrow corridor, so that it stomped and huffed angrily.

Coming to the door, Zachary pushed the slim wood open and stepped into the square room. A corpse waited for him, swinging from the crooked rafters on silk twine. Zachary gazed up to the purple-faced dead man, and then down to the toppled stool beneath him. A letter was placed atop a pile of well-embroidered clothes, and Zachary opened it curiously, picking up the stool and taking a seat beside the hanging man's legs.

"*Forgive me*," Zachary read the letter aloud and grunted. "Not a man of many words." He turned back to the hanging man and touched his ankle. The skin was cold—he'd been dead some hours. Zachary stood and cut down the corpse, letting it drop unceremoniously to the floor. Then, leaving the body to the rats, he led his horse back out again, passing the curious beggars as he did. "Free clothes," he dutifully told them, thumbing back toward the room. He heard them scrabble to reach the dead man first and left them at that.

Getting back out into the street, Zachary looked back at the note in his hand and threw it away—there was no truth to it, either way. The whole affair was a cunningly designed murder, not suicide. After all, the note might have been in a fair hand, and the stool and noose all rightly set, but the victim had been much too small to reach and tie the twine to the rafters himself. Besides which, the indents on his fingers had shown he once wore rings, forcefully removed no doubt, and not by any of the slum rats, either—they wouldn't have left him his clothes. An assassin then, looking to fill his pockets, but not burden his arms. Zachary scowled and, mounting his horse, he left the city, deciding to forfeit the street and take the longer route out and around the capital itself, across the moor. It had been a wasted journey, so he might as well make something of it.

Out in the clear air he pressed his horse on, his mind set on the murdered man. Could he have been a Delphi Knight? If so, he'd been a sword-less one—his hands were smooth and delicate. But then the Delphi Knights hadn't seen battle in near a century. Zachary thought what the Queen would say about his findings, and mused that he might have at least taken the man's head. But then, Zachary thought, it was too warm a day to be carrying a decapitated skull through Harmatia. No, the victim, whether affiliated with the Knights or not, was dead, and his secrets had gone with him. Zachary's duty was to torture and coax information, not investigate whatever ill had befallen the man first. He would leave that to the Royal Guard.

He caught sight of a pyre as he rode by, a flock of mourners gathered around the burning body, some wailing and others stoic in their grief. The wind caught the smoke and brought it over toward the city. Zachary breathed in the putrid scent of burning flesh and recalled that he hadn't eaten yet today. The corpse smelt tender, and Zachary lingered, staring out to the fire, the air rich with blood. He realised what he was doing a moment later, and pressed himself onward. He wondered whether perhaps he should forgo doing the Patrol for a night and leave the men to Marcel Hathely instead. He banished the notion instantly—he was their captain, and the thought of missing the hunt made his skin crawl. Perhaps tonight the rats would crawl out of their conspiring nests, and they would be his to devour.

His pulse quickened with excitement, and he checked himself, spotting a group of children ahead. They were picking flowers together in groups. Lily-of-the-valley, to be precise, and Zachary realised with a jolt that it must already be the month of Haylix. He paused to watch them in their work, the late spring heat making their laughter and chatter rise and banish the earlier smell of charred flesh. The ritual of gathering Lily-of-the-Valley was an ancient one that children did every year. They picked the white flowers and presented them to their mothers as thanks for their love and kindness.

Zachary couldn't help but find it amusing that such an innocent flower, gathered for such a sweet purpose, could be quite as poisonous as it was.

As he approached, the children ran away, wary of his tall, grim figure. Zachary dismounted and, looking over the clumps of white flowers, gathered a handful and sat cross-legged in the grass, binding them together. Lily-of-the-Valley was one of the few flowers he could tolerate being close to, without breaking into sneezes. Its arrival on the moors, however, signalled the start of a season where Zachary would have to stick close to the city, or else be perpetually red-eyed and irritable.

The children watched Zachary curiously as he worked, edging ever closer until they were peering over his shoulders and knees. He plaited the flowers together into a crown and, pleased with his work, placed the finished garland onto his head, securing it in place. The children all giggled at him as he mounted his war-horse, and winking at them, set off back toward the capital.

He entered through the eastern gate, his face sombre again as he passed through the vigorous line of guards. They saw the crown of flowers resting on his head and wisely kept their words to themselves, even though Zachary would have invited their ridicule—he cherished any chance he could to scare men witless.

Once in the city, the private road back to the castle was a short one. He made his way home, letting a stable hand take his horse from him at the door as he climbed the stairs.

Heather was waiting for him inside—a tray in her hands with a cup of wine prepared. "Did you find what you were looking for?" she asked, and he grunted.

"A dead man swinging," he replied, and gently removing it, he placed the crown of flowers onto her head in turn. He kissed her cheek tenderly and took the wine, draining it. "I am returning to bed," he informed. "Don't wake me until it's time for me to kill someone again."

It was nearing the heavier part of the afternoon, and Rufus could see Jionathan was struggling. His cheeks were visibly pink, even in the shade of the overgrowth, and perspiration dewed on his forehead as he furiously kneading his knee and thigh.

"Do you need to stop awhile?" Rufus inquired, and Jionathan shook his head sluggishly, taking a draught of water. Rufus had conceded to performing magic, only to ensure they all remained hydrated on their travels. Both his companions had been surprised by his ability to draw water from seemingly nowhere, but as Rufus had reminded them, there was water in the air. It was no great task, under Notameer, to condense it to something tangible. Though, admittedly, it did not produce great quantities, and Rufus struggled with water above all the elements.

"It's too hot," Jionathan huffed, and Rufus grunted in agreement. Jionathan rolled his eyes sceptically. "How would you know? You don't even burn."

"I may not burn, but I'm perfectly capable of feeling temperature. The heat might not hurt me, but prolonged, it can be just as uncomfortable as the cold. Here, you need to rest. You're in pain." Rufus fretted, looking out for Fae. She'd scouted on ahead to ensure there were no unpleasant surprises on the path, and she was nowhere in sight.

"I'm fine. The sooner we reach Bethean, the better."

"A moment's pause won't delay us anymore than you collapsing from your horse," Rufus insisted, drawing Moyna up in front of the bay, so that he cut Jionathan off.

Jionathan growled. "Rufus, if I get off this horse, I won't be able to mount it again."

"Of course, you will. I'll throw you over like a saddlebag if I have to. Come, rest." Rufus dismounted and coaxed Jionathan down. "Fae!" he called into the forest. "Fae! We're stopping a moment! Fae!"

"I heard you," Fae's voice said, close to his ear, and Rufus jumped as she stepped out from behind him, appearing from nowhere. She took Jionathan's other arm and eased him down.

"I'm fine," Jionathan insisted, but his limp had grown heavier, clearly aggravated by the ride.

"We could all do with a rest," Fae said. "It isn't far now. An hour at most and we'll be clear of this forest."

Jionathan exhaled with relief. "Thank the gods, I thought we'd be travelling until nightfall."

"Well that rather depends on where you plan to go." Fae sat

beside him as Rufus tied off their horses, and then attended to Jionathan's leg. The knee was swollen and tender. "If it's the capital you want, I would suggest taking shelter somewhere tonight, and going on tomorrow."

"The capital's too dangerous, and any other large cities likewise." Jionathan shook his head. "They'll have Magi Ambassadors there, and who knows who they answer to."

Fae frowned. "Magi Ambassadors?"

Jionathan rolled his shoulder. The injury Zachary had inflicted was probably also still sore. "From what I gather, due to the Magi being so advanced and secretive with their magic, they...loan out Magi to other countries sometimes."

"It's a little more complicated than that," Rufus said. "But certainly, simplistically, that is the way. Magi Ambassadors provide services for other Kings and Queens and in return are given land, titles, and wealth."

"Some of which," Jionathan added, "obviously goes back to the Magi Institute in Harmatia."

"Yes, we make a tidy profit of them. Though there are more in Kathra than in Bethean." Rufus drew on the stars' power, and let it flow in gentle waves through Jionathan's skin, easing the pain and swelling in the knee. Jionathan smiled at him gratefully.

"Where do you wish to go?" Fae asked.

"What's the closest town?"

"That would be Sarrin, wouldn't it?" Rufus said and Fae, looking up to calculate their position, nodded.

"What's Sarrin?"

"Sarrin town is a small farming community who profit on the trade of wheat, mead, and apples."

"So that's why *you* know about it," Jionathan said to Rufus. He shot a look up to Fae. "He's obsessed with them, you know. Apples. Come Autumn, it's all I ever see him eating."

"There's nothing wrong with liking apples. They are an exceptional fruit," Rufus said, without shame. "And Sarrin apples, in particular, are famous, because they grow almost all year around. In-fact, the apples you find in the castle in Harmatia often come from Sarrin."

"Fascinating," Jionathan drawled. "What's this Sarrin town like then, other than full of apples?"

"The patron of most of the land is a man named Michael Rossignol," said Fae. "He is a cloth merchant I believe, and an exceptionally friendly gentleman."

Rufus was surprised. "You know Michael Rossignol?"

"I have met him in passing, yes," Fae said. "He offered me a bed in his home once, but I was forced to decline. Still, I spent a happy hour resting in the town."

"How extraordinary," Rufus murmured, and Jionathan scratched his chin thoughtfully.

"Is it a good place to rest for the night?"

"Certainly, I'd highly recommend it," said Rufus. It had been a long time since he'd passed through Sarrin town, and the thought of its golden fields and rolling orchards made him happy.

Fae too seemed of a similar mind. "I concur. It's a friendly but discreet town, off the main road. It's ideal for your circumstances."

"Sarrin town it is then." Jionathan pushed himself up to his feet with a small groan. "I'm anxious to return to civilisation."

"They're Betheanians," Rufus warned. "It won't be the 'civilisation' you're accustomed to." He caught Fae's glower and added, "They are of a much warmer sort."

Jionathan hummed longingly. "All I want is a bed. If they can give me that and a warm meal, then you can consider me content." He reached up for his saddle and looked guiltily back to Rufus. "Can you…?"

Rufus made a step with his hands and hoisted Jionathan back up onto the bay.

"Follow me," Fae instructed, leading them back toward the path. Rufus leapt onto Moyna's back, his spirits lifted as they pressed on toward their new destination.

CHAPTER 22

As they entered Sarrin town, Jionathan's first thought was to how welcoming it looked. In the orange light of the late afternoon sun, the earth appeared to glow, making the town look comfortably homely.

As they passed through the gates, which were nothing but a gap in a waist-high stone wall, Jionathan marvelled at the simple, natural beauty of the place. Where in Harmatia houses were bundled close, pale stone baking, there was a spaciousness about Sarrin. Flowers grew on the side of the road, trees and long grass reaching up to houses. The buildings were roofed with straw thatch and brightly coloured tiles. The town was alive with colour and noise, stalls and shops packing away their wares as the evening drew in, a lone blacksmith hammering away in his forge, his doors thrown open. Children played gaily, clambering the trees and walking along the town wall in turns. All their faces were either sun-kissed or naturally dark, their eyes bright as the wild birdsong. And there was a lot of birdsong—it struck Jionathan how little he heard it in Harmatia.

There were no soldiers in Sarrin town, only a set of town guards, who were engaging in a board game. Father and son by the look of it. *No*—Jionathan corrected himself, stunned— *mother and son*. The woman's hair was tucked into the back of her armour.

Rufus caught him staring. "Bethean's the only human country in Mag Mell that lets women into its armed forces," he said. "It's not an unusual sight here."

The idea was perplexing, but Jionathan found himself smiling at the thought. Something about Sarrin cheered his weary heart, like the sound of music. For the first time in a very long time, Jionathan felt inspired.

"It's beautiful, isn't it?" Rufus grinned.

"I should be very happy to stay here," Jionathan said, his mood light.

"We must find an inn first." Fae peered up the street, which turned to cobbles ahead of them.

"Do you know where it is?" Jionathan asked Rufus, but the Magi's attention had been drawn away. He was staring over his shoulder, ignoring Jionathan completely.

"Rufus?"

"Hm…sorry, what?" Rufus turned back, distracted. In the distance, a young woman was attending a stall of rather juicy-looking apples. Rufus had clearly been eying the fruit, his lip caught mischievously in his teeth.

"Oh Hexias give me strength," Jionathan muttered. "Rufus, we need to find the inn. Do you know where it is?"

"No, I've never stayed at the inn here." Rufus glanced back. "Let's go and ask." Leaping off his horse, he tied the reins to a wooden fence and strode toward the apple stall. Jionathan sighed and followed his example, limping impatiently after him, Fae close behind.

They approached the apple stall together. The young woman who watched it had her back to them and was gathering the empty baskets in preparation to pack up. She was of a slight build, with dark, tawny skin and rich brown hair, which she worn in a long plait down to her waist. Rufus cleared his throat.

"Excuse me, young lady?" He put on an air of pomposity, his tone authoritative and words over-pronounced. "My friends and I have been travelling all day, and are looking for the town inn. Might you direct us to it?"

"Of course, one moment," the woman replied in a sweet, lulling voice, her accent full and melodic. She straightened and, dusting her petite hands on her apron, turned back to them. "Now, if you follow the road back up and take the first turning on your right…" Her voice died in her throat as she took in the three, her apron—which had been twisted in her fingers—falling slack over her maroon skirt.

"Perhaps we could buy some apples then?" Rufus grinned and threw his arms open as, with a delighted cry, the woman dashed out from behind the stall and leapt into an embrace.

"Rufus!" She wound her arms around his neck, her legs bent at the knees as he lifted her clean off her feet, rocking her from side to side before, with a firm kiss to her cheek, allowing her back down again.

"Luca." He placed her gently on the ground, his eyes gleaming. "How d'you do?"

"All the better for seeing you, you daft loon! Haylix, man, look at you—you've changed."

"Not so much."

"And what's all this then?" She pinched his chin, running her thumb over the stubble on his cheeks and upper lip.

"I've not had any chance to shave these past few days. Does it suit me ill?"

"To the contrary, you look just like your father."

"I'd be pleased to do so. You're certainly looking more beautiful than ever."

Luca hugged him fiercely again, her head against his chest. "Oh, it's been so long. What are you doing here?"

Rufus feigned offence. "Can't a man visit his family if the

feeling takes him?"

"A regular man might, but you…" She reached up and flicked his nose.

"Ow!"

"It's been close two years," she said, and he rubbed his face sheepishly.

"Gracious, two years."

"You might've at least been more diligent with your letters." Luca turned to Jionathan and Fae, who'd remained silent spectators.

Rufus stepped in. "How rude of me. Please, Jionat, Fae, allow me to introduce you to my cousin, Luca."

"Cousin, he says." Luca shook her head. "But it's our parents who are so. Luca Rossignol, welcome to Sarrin." She bobbed into a curtsey.

"Miss Rossignol, it is an honour. I am Fae of the Neve." Fae bowed in return. "I know your father, Michael, though I had no idea Rufus was a relation." She snapped her eyes accusingly to Rufus, whose mischievous grin widened.

"Oh, he probably withheld it for some wicked purpose—it's in the Merle nature to always be up to no good," Luca said, and Rufus raised his arms in silent surrender. "I've heard your name, Lady Fae, and am honoured to meet you. Any Sidhe of your good standing is a welcome guest in our town."

"You're very kind, and please—Fae will suffice."

"Then call me Luca." Luca turned to Jionathan. Her eyes were heavily lashed, and the colour of mahogany, burning a cherry red in the sunlight.

"Good day," she greeted him, smiling. Her face was amiable, and somehow familiar.

"And to you. It's a pleasure to make your acquaintance. I'm a friend of Rufus's."

"The pleasure's all mine. Jionat, was it?" She extended out a petite hand, which he shook. Her fingers were surprisingly strong for their size. "I must confess, Rufus hadn't mentioned you before, though he's so irregular with his letters it's hard to get anything from him these days." Luca laughed. "Though, come to think of it, he does mention *a* Jionat, but that can't be in reference to you, because that's what he calls...it's what he calls the..." She drew off, a growing panic in her eyes as her words caught up with her. "Oh Etheus blind me—you're Jionathan of the Delphi, aren't you?"

"Yes." Jionathan smiled self-consciously, and Rufus roared with laughter, throwing his head back.

Luca whirled around and struck him across the chest. "You little bastard!" she shouted, and then lowered her voice. "You might've warned me! Here I am rambling like some fool, and he's Crown Prince of Harmatia!"

"Please!" Jionathan lurched forward, conscious of the people around them. "Please, don't call me that. I'm not supposed to be here. If the Queen finds out where I am, I'll be dragged back to Harmatia without say or word. I implore you, just call me...call me Jionat."

Luca seemed lost a moment, looking between the Prince and Rufus. She nodded slowly. "I understand...Jionat," she said with difficulty. "Though I can't say the same of this union. Rufus, why are you travelling with a Neve courier and the..." She gestured to Jionathan.

Rufus, who had since helped himself to an apple from the stall, smiled through his mouthful. "I kidnapped him," he said. "Fae helped."

"You *what*?" Luca squeaked, and Jionathan flicked his fist out and punched Rufus in the stomach. Rufus doubled over, and Jionathan reassured Luca, who was working herself into a dizzy frenzy.

"Ignore the fool, he's teasing you. I would be more than happy to tell you the truth of it, but first, we're all tired and in need of a good meal and a rest. If you'll tell us where the inn is—"

"The *inn*." Luca snorted, a surprising sound coming from such a delicate woman. "You'd have me send you to an inn?" She laughed, like it was ludicrous. "Highness, if my father discovered I'd given you directions to that spider-infested dust-heap, he'd disown me. No, you're both—well, all three of you," she eyed Rufus angrily, "honoured guests, and you'll dine and rest in our home and nothing less."

"That's very kind of you, but—"

"Nothing less," Luca insisted. Turning back, she gathered the last basket of apples and, thrusting it into Rufus's arms, marched up the path with a sweeping gesture that they should follow. Jionathan ran back to fetch the horses, and Fae gave a little smile.

"Your cousin," she told Rufus as she passed him, struggling with the apples. "I *like* her."

In the end, composed as she was trying to be, Luca couldn't help but run up to the house as they approached, and call out to her family within. Rufus watched her fondly, following her up the path as she threw open the heavy door of the yellow-stoned house and shouted in. Rufus was given only a breath to relieve himself of the heavy apple basket before two young children came charging out, roused from their evening meal.

"Uncle Rufus!" The taller of his two youngest cousins, a girl of eight years, reached him first, her six-year-old brother struggling after her. Rufus dropped to his knees and caught the pair in his arms as they dove into him, their faces bright with delight.

"Annabelle, Rowan!" He held them fiercely, his heart soaring at the sound of their laughter. "Gods, but you've grown!" He released them, ruffling their dark hair in turn and kissing them. "I thought I told you to stop that. Next time I come, you'll be bigger than me!"

Both giggled gleefully at his exclamation as, from the doorway, their mother, Lily-Anne appeared. She, like Luca, wore an apron over her teal skirt, though while Luca's chemise spilled over her shoulders, showing as much of her collar and cleavage as was conceivable without being indecent, Lily-Anne's was more modest in its cut and shape. She moved gracefully down the path and took his hands as he stood. Her face was weathered by the sun, skin and hair fairer than that of her children, and eyes a similar colour to her skirt. She smiled warmly, clearly pleased by the sight of him. But then, the last she'd seen Rufus, he'd been grey-faced, sunken and dark-eyed with grief and heartache. He'd gained weight since then and his complexion and air was certainly healthier now.

"Rufus, my dear," she said as he stooped to let her kiss both his cheeks. "You look well."

"As do you. It's good to see you, Aunt." He glanced back to see Fae and Jionathan approach, the Prince leading the horses up the path.

"What's all the noise about?" Back at the house a tall, broad-shouldered figure stepped out, and Rufus excused himself to run up and greet his uncle.

"Rufus-lad!" Michael's voice boomed, and he engulfed Rufus in a back-numbing embrace. "My boy! Welcome home!"

"It's good to be here, Uncle."

Michael released Rufus and, stepping back, they inspected each other. Clad in fine clothes, Michael Rossignol stood a little taller than Rufus himself, but was built like a bear, with thick arms and a wide back and torso. Square faced, with a strong jaw half invaded by a thick, dark beard, his skin was dark, and wrinkled by years of sun and laughter. That, and the softness around his belly, gave him a constant air of cheerfulness and joy.

Michael, in turn, studied Rufus and—clearly pleased—clapped him across the shoulder, almost sending him into the nearby rosebush. At the bottom of the garden, Lily-Anne introduced herself to Fae and Jionathan, the latter of whom seemed slightly dazed by all the warm hospitality. Rowan had taken shelter behind his mother's skirts, but peered out in wonder at Fae. She stuck her tongue out quickly, and Rowan giggled. Rufus turned back to his uncle.

"Oh, Rufus-lad," Michael's voice boomed like thunder, "it's really been far too long! Where've you been? No, never mind that, you're here now! Let me fetch you a cup of fresh brewed mead, the finest taste in all o' Bethean!"

"Uncle," Rufus laughed, "I see you haven't changed. I thought the physician told you to stop drinking." He smiled at Michael's reproachful expression. "Yes, Luca told me all about it. Said the physician was quite insistent."

"Hah! That physician doesn't know his own head from his arse," Michael roared cheerily. "He's a nosey, superior-minded cock of a man, with enough conceit in him to damn a town! I'll tell you what, I'd rather be diagnosed by my own good judgement, and my judgement comes from what my body demands—good food, intelligent conversation, and long beautiful working hours."

"And alcohol?"

"I said intelligent conversation, didn't I?"

Rufus snorted, and Michael grinned, his teeth bright white against his dark face. Looking over Rufus's shoulder he grew still with surprise.

"You've brought friends with you. Ah, I know the woman. That's the most esteemed Fae of the Neve. And the other..." He squinted, as the group moved up the path toward them. "Etheus blind me," he gasped. "That's the son of the Lady Éliane of the Delphi, I'd wager my life on it. The Prince of Harmatia is coming up to my door."

"You recognised him quickly." Rufus was surprised.

Michael gave a dazed nod. "Aye, I know him. I see his mother in his every step...though the turn of his head and eyes, they're his father's. A natural commander," Michael huffed proudly. "This is a wondrous day indeed! My long-wayward nephew returned to me, a fine Sidhe approaching my door, and the Prince of

Harmatia come to dine in my home. I cannot begin to guess how you three came to be here together."

"That's a story for later," Rufus promised, and Michael descended the stairs to greet his guests, taking Annabelle lovingly in his arms as he did.

"Good husband," Lily-Anne said plainly, "I have taken it upon myself to invite these people to dine with us, and remain in our home as long as they please. I trust this does not oppose any plans you've concocted in the darkness of your study, away from prying ears."

"Good wife!" Michael chortled. "You accuse me of conspiracy! I am a simple man of simple needs and simple pleasures. So do not talk of dark studies and quiet murmurings. The night is young and the mood growing bright! Honoured guests—*honoured guests!*—you need not introduce yourselves, for I know you well already. I am Michael Rossignol, today the happiest man in all of Sarrin town!" He took Fae's and Jionathan's hand in turn, shaking them vigorously. "Today is truly a fortuitous one—to be graced in such excellent company! Come, please, make yourselves at home! I am delighted to invite you in." He ushered them to door, Lily-Anne relieving Jionathan of the horses as Michael called in.

"Luca! Luca-girl! Prepare some drinks—there is a toast to be had! A welcome to a brave Sidhe warrior, our long-lost cousin, and the Prince of Harmatia, who will dine and rest with us this night! Luca-girl, get to it!"

"The physician said no alcohol!" Luca shouted down the stairs, and Michael stormed into the house, Annabelle clinging to his back like he was a moving mountain.

"Aye, and the abstinent bugger can live a long life of misery. I will die a happy man!"

Rufus laughed and caught eyes with Jionathan, who seemed stunned by the display.

"He's been at his pipe, hasn't he?" Rufus asked, and Lily-Anne gave him a secretive smile, throwing her hair over her shoulder as she led the horses away.

"It was a warm, lovely day," was all she said, and Rufus stooped down and picked up Rowan.

"Are we celebrating?" Rowan asked, his lips clumsy over the words.

"We're celebrating," Rufus replied, and putting his arm lightly over Jionathan's shoulder, he guided the Prince in. "I told you Sarrin was an excellent place to rest a while."

"You did this on purpose," Jionathan accused.

Within the house, Michael was shouting for Luca to find bigger glasses and to fetch some fresh bread and butter.

"Yes," Rufus admitted shamelessly. "Yes, I did."

CHAPTER 23

~~~~~

"I hope you'll be comfortable."

Fae looked back at Luca, who stood in the doorway, an extra coverlet folded in her arms. She brought it over, laying it on the edge of the bed.

"It may be hot in the day, but the house gets rather cool at night," she said and Fae thanked her, touching the soft fabric. It was warm under her fingers, no doubt recently ironed. "Also, I hope you don't mind sharing the room. We have a guest chamber downstairs, but..." Luca drew off, and Fae rose, moving to the window. The garden outside was spilt with pale moonlight, making the orchards look silver.

"I am very comfortable, thank you. This evening has been a pleasure," she said earnestly, aware that her demeanour might appear cold. She forced herself to relax her guard a little, turning back to Luca, who had dropped onto her own bed. She sat, a pillow clutched in her arms. "The meal was truly delicious."

"Oh, that was nothing. Tomorrow we'll have time to prepare something much more spectacular. Do you like venison?" Luca's smile was contagious, and yet Fae couldn't allow herself to share its warmth.

"I do, but I fear tomorrow I may have to move on," she admitted. "My duty in the Myrithian Forest is complete, and I ought to return home."

Luca appeared crestfallen. "I'm sorry to hear that," she said. "Is there no way I can convince you to delay your return awhile? It's been so long since we've had company in the house, and I've never had the chance to talk with a Sidhe before. That is to say, you're welcome to rest here longer. It'd be our pleasure, truly."

Fae considered the invitation. She'd thought to leave for the Betheanian capital in the morning, to see that Princess Aurora was safely delivered. And yet somehow, after the glorious meal they'd just shared, made colourful with laughter and stories, Fae felt reluctant to leave so quickly. Her place was not amongst humans, but the entire affair in the forest had been so surreal in nature that it hardly seemed right to abandon Rufus and Jionathan so suddenly afterwards. Perhaps it would do no harm to rest a while longer, to heal and recuperate. For a few days at least. She'd earned that much.

"How long have you lived in Sarrin town?" Fae returned to her own bed and sat on it, facing Luca, who was brushing through her long, dark hair. It was truly a beautiful mane, shimmering and vibrant, like strands of dyed silk. Fae knew several Sidhe who would be jealous of such hair.

"Oh, I was born in Sarrin." Luca's brush caught in a knot, and she tore it forcefully through. "Lived here all my life. I thought I might like to go to Harmatia some time, but the older I get the more it loses its appeal. You know," she leant in conspiratorially, "they marry as young as fifteen there sometimes? Imagine that, and with no proper engagement either? And no sex before the marital bed." Luca shook her head. "It's ludicrous. How can anyone vow themselves to another, if they're not given the chance to fully know each other until the deed is done?"

Fae laughed. "How, indeed," she agreed, and she clutched her left hand in her right tightly. She kept her voice light. "Harmatia is a strange place…bordering civil and yet somehow still on the edge of savage."

"Well, until they are decided which to be, I shall remain a happy resident in Sarrin," Luca concluded. "It's small, but it has everything I might need…" She trailed off wistfully, and Fae suspected that despite her words, Luca had ambitions beyond the walls of her home. Fae admired that.

A knock on the door interrupted them, and Lily-Anne let herself into the room. Luca threw her pillow at her mother. "The purpose of a knock is to ask invitation," she scolded, "not declare invasion."

"So dramatic, girl." Lily-Anne threw the pillow back. "Lady Fae, I trust you'll be comfortable here. If my daughter grows wearisome, do feel free to banish her elsewhere."

Luca grumbled, and Fae couldn't help but smile. "To the contrary, I find her to be excellent company."

"Well, may she remain so. I have some clothes here that might suit you, should you wish to remain with us a few days. I've no doubt Luca's already extended our invitation?"

"She has." Fae accepted the bundle of skirts and dresses, surprised by the easy manner in which the Rossignol family conducted themselves. She'd heard of the hospitality of the Betheanian folk, but had rarely had the opportunity to enjoy it. She sensed for Jionathan, it had been a similar shock.

"This is very kind of you." She looked over the clothes again, pondering the last time she'd had occasion to wear a dress. The skirts were not as vibrant in colour as Luca's own selection, but had a more subtle, mature tone to them. Luca came and relieved her of them, and stored them in a chest at the end of Fae's bed. "I don't know how to repay you."

"You freed our Princess from the clutches of a great evil," Lily-Anne said. "It is we who repay you, and with all our hearts."

"I was only doing my duty."

"Perhaps in saving the Princess, but when you returned for

my nephew and Prince Jionathan, that was of your own choice. For that, we are in your debt."

Fae cheeks flushed at the candour in her host's voice. Lily-Anne smiled, and addressed Luca, returning to her purpose.

"Have you seen our copy of *The Lover's Sin*?" she asked, crossing to a bookshelf on the far wall. It was laden with a heavy selection of beautifully bound novels. Already, Fae could see much of Luca's character through her taste in books, though— she reasoned—the bed she now occupied must have belonged to another at some time. A sister perhaps, older no doubt, gone on and married. Fae had caught a name a few times during the course of the evening—Mielane. Though by Luca's subtle tone and conduct it was easy to see something ill had passed between them.

"It's with the other Saphar works." Luca lounged dramatically across her bed, staring up to the ceiling as her mother rummaged through the bookshelf. Fae had a sudden thought.

"*The Barrel Men*," she said. "That's a work by Saphar, is it not? Do you perhaps have a copy?"

"Certainly." Lily-Anne drew a volume from the shelf.

"Thank you." Fae accepted it gratefully. Jionathan and Rufus had made reference to it in the forest, and she was curious to understand how their own scheme had been born of it. At the shelf, Lily-Anne finally located *The Lover's Sin*, buried at the bottom of a dusty pile. She departed, wishing both women a good night.

Glancing back at the shelf, Fae noticed a fiddle sat beneath it, nestled comfortably in its case. Luca followed her curious gaze.

"Do you play?" Fae asked.

Luca picked up the instrument to examine it, like she'd not held it in an age. "I do," she said, and there was a deftness about her hands as she raised the instrument to her chin, letting her fingers drum along the board so the strings hummed. It was clear Luca did more than play. "And you?"

"No," Fae said regretfully. There were few musicians in her family. Hers was a clan now of all brothers, and few were interested in laying down their weapons to pluck the strings of a harp. "I like to dance though," Fae admitted. "Very much."

"Then we have that in common," Luca said brightly, and replaced her instrument. Fae was almost disappointed—the thought of music gladdened her. But it was late, and if she were to stay a day or more, perhaps she could convince Luca to perform for her. It was certainly incentive to delay her return.

In her distraction, she didn't notice Luca cross over to the chair where she'd laid her weapons. Luca examined her swords, and with an easy boldness, drew one from its sheath. Fae felt her gut tighten protectively, but for all her intrusion in the Rossignol home and Luca's bedroom, she didn't say anything. Luca handled the sword with care, holding it up to candlelight. She caught sight of Fae over the blade and dipped her head apologetically.

"I'm sorry." She replaced the sword quickly and carefully. "I'm a curious creature. They're very fine blades."

"Yes," Fae agreed. "I have a set of twin brothers close to my age—Eadoin and Arton. When I was young, we were very close, and for my birthday they both set it in their minds to buy me a sword, without consulting each other." Fae smiled at the memory. Her brothers had since grown distant, but perhaps that fault lay with her rather than them. "And so they gave me one each, and being of similar tastes, the blades were almost identical. I was so frightened of offending my brothers I learnt to use both." She looked fondly back at the weapons. It was rare for her to speak of her family to others. Her loved ones were a weakness that could be extorted, so Fae usually kept silent. But drunk on the meal and the kindness of the Rossignols, Fae couldn't see any harm in imparting some detail. It was refreshing to speak without fear of judgement or danger.

"What about the bow? It's an odd shape." Luca peered at the offending item, small and compact, and much too strong for a human to easily draw.

"Specially made for my skill and build. My older brother Korrick had it commissioned when I finished training with him. He was a mentor of sorts." Fae thought back to the stern, somewhat overbearing man. "He taught me everything I know."

"You must be a fearsome warrior."

"I am certainly a warrior," Fae said. "And you? You know how to fight."

Luca raised her eyebrow. "What gives you that impression?"

"The way you held the sword." Fae glanced at the blade, safely tucked away again. "It wasn't your first time."

Luca gave her a mischievous smile. "It wasn't," she admitted. "In truth, my father has this old broadsword in his study that I used to take into the barn to play with. It was almost as tall as I was, and my mother caught me trying to swing it one day. She wasn't best pleased. But," Luca checked the door, her eyes glimmering, "my father told me that if I was going to insist on trying to use it, best I learn to do it right. He gave me a few instructions—with a smaller sword of course—and every now and again when the feeling takes him, he'll take me for another lesson. My mother doesn't know...or if she does, she disapproves in silence." Luca clenched her fingers into fists. "My hands are yet too small and soft, but one day I'd like to see that right."

"You might lose a finger," Fae warned. "Then how would you play the fiddle again?"

Luca glanced guiltily back at the instrument. "I suppose I'll just have to be careful that I lose a finger on my right hand, then."

Fae couldn't help but smile at Luca's conviction, and decided that, should time permit, she would give Luca some instruction of her own.

～～～

Rufus settled back in the chair with a huff, letting the ink dry as he read over his words again. After their gargantuan supper,

Michael had lent Rufus his study, so he could write a letter to his parents and assure them all was well. Jionathan, exhausted after the day's events, had already retired to bed. Rufus planned to do the same soon.

Scanning the words, Rufus wished he could have said more. Unwilling to reveal too much, in-case the letter was intercepted, he'd been sparse with the details of their adventure. He didn't speak much of the Korrigans, or what they'd done to him— the memory of it still made his skin turn cold—but meagrely recounted his rescue and recovery, hailing Jionathan and Fae as heroes. He couldn't imagine his attempted sacrifice would be well received by his mother, though his father would certainly be proud. Rufus would have the letter delivered in the morning.

Leaving the study, he snuffed out the candles and wandered down through the hall. Michael was still in their parlour, dozing in his favourite chair, head tipped back and mouth agape. Rufus might have roused him, but he suspected Lily-Anne would do so when she came down to bed. The smell of fresh bread, roasted vegetables and marinated poultry lingered in the air, and Rufus thought back to the delicious meal. His aunt had always had a talent for making feasts out of nothing, and there'd been so much food the table had been overrun with dishes. He thought of Jionathan's laughter, and the easy way in which he ate. Such a change from the suspicious, surly Prince he'd been in Harmatia, wary that each meal might be poisoned. It had warmed Rufus to the bone. He himself had also eaten well, Lily-Anne's subtle attempts to refill his emptying plate not going unnoticed. She hadn't said it, but she still thought him too thin.

Rufus snorted to himself, patting his hands across his waist. He *was* too thin, though not by design—food simply didn't hold its usual fervour for him these days. Tonight had been a pleasant exception.

Climbing the stairway, he paused in the doorway of Annabelle and Rowan's room. Inside, Lily-Anne was perched on a chair between their beds, reading to them. Rufus leant against the frame and listened to her hushed voice. It was a chapter from *The Lover's Sin*, the story of a human woman, Sophia, and a Gancanagh named Ciarán, whose love for one another ultimately led to their deaths. A censored version of the cautionary tale had also been read to Rufus as a child too, but the full text was graphic with its sex and violence. Lily-Anne was careful to only follow the poetry.

"Oh, Time, thou art a plague," Lily-Anne's voice rose. "For as soon as sweet dawn touches the brow o' the earth I might be free of confinement, my soul trapped in bitter waiting! Oh, all you unfortunate souls who do not know love, never seek confinement. Thou art a villain if thou doest. My love—you whom I adore before recompense, I lie and wait, spurned by my affection and ensnared by my longing, unable to sleep. Oh, sweet Love, thou bitter potion, so good art thou that I should call thy name a thousand times and not be satisfied. But enough, the lark has bedded and the owl cries low—'tis time that I lay my head to slumber, if slumber will have me so."

Rufus recognised the verse. It was Sophia's words to Ciarán the night before their wedding day. Rufus found his mouth curling over the letters.

"But say my name again, the sound upon your lips is foreign to any ear—the sweet music from your royal tongue yet alien to mortal sense. No other man may know my heart, nor might he ever again hereafter. Good man, kiss me and hold me 'til the 'morrow. Hold me, Love, 'til our wedding bells chime and at last to our vows we commit. For if my bed be cold at sunrise, than e'er to my sweet tomb will I in sorrow submit."

Rufus opened his eyes reluctantly, his breath caught painfully in his throat. He was suddenly aware of a tearing pain in his abdomen, and looking down he thought he might see a dagger jutting out of the flesh. His stomach was smooth and unblemished, and yet he fought hard not to cry out as Lily-Anne continued to read, the pain intensifying.

"You think this blade does you no harm, but you are wrong, for with it I cut into your very soul." The Korrigan's words reverberated through him, and Rufus drew in a sharp breath, his hand clutched to his heart. Down the hallway, a door opened, and a familiar figure stepped out.

Oh Mielane, he thought. *Thank the gods you're here.*

"Rufus?" Luca called with concern. "Are you alright?"

Rufus felt himself jolt, and he straightened immediately, his voice caught. Luca watched him, worried, and he smiled despite his pain. "Fine," he said, "I'm fine. I must've eaten too much."

The lie was feeble, and his hands were shaking again. He felt as fragile as the skin of a dried leaf, and slowly he opened his arms.

"Come here."

Luca was only too happy to oblige. She buried herself against his chest, and he clung to her with a sudden desperation, dropping his head down into the nape of her neck. He breathed in her scent, like Mielane's—warm, sweet and full of life. And with the scent, the haunting remnants of the Korrigans were gone, and he was holding his beautiful cousin again—just the wrong one.

The stabbing pain subsided, but the dull ache of guilt didn't leave, and Rufus released her, trying to maintain his smile. "More than eat, I think the mead went to my head…sweet Luca." He touched her face. "I'm so glad to be home."

"Welcome back," Luca whispered, her lips moist. She slipped a finger down the collar of his shirt and it caught against something. Luca blinked, and then pulled up the chain there. A ring slid across and down. "You kept the engagement ring?" Luca sighed. "Why do you punish yourself like this? You have to stop. It's been three years Rufus. Mielane—"

He covered her mouth with his fingers, cutting off her words. Her eyes softened with pity and Rufus closed his own, tipping his forehead against hers.

"Does it still hurt?" Luca pressed a hand to his chest, her fingers hovering over his beating heart. He gripped her wrist tightly.

"Yes," he choked, and kissed her forehead, his lips lingering on her skin. A hunger flared up within him, but it was not for food. How long had it been since he had tasted the flesh of a lover? How long since he'd taken, or been taken, since he'd run his tongue along a willing throat and kissed until his mouth was bruised and swollen with want? The Merle men found comfort in touch when they were hurt—that's what his mother always told him. It was how they healed.

Heal, something purred within Rufus, and he brushed his lips against Luca's hair, aware of a ravenous power coming over him. He opened his eyes and caught sight of her face, so sweet, golden in the dark light, her hair hallowed in a red hue. She watched him curiously, trustingly, and he felt his stomach turn. He released her, stepping back, conscious of how close they'd been. Guilt festered in him again, and Rufus cleared his throat, trying for a weak smile. "Goodnight, Luca." He bowed his head. "Sleep well."

She frowned, confused, her lips still wet and parted. Rufus couldn't think about taking those lips now, couldn't bear to look at her with another name playing on his tongue. He slipped past her and hurried toward his own room, her eyes hot on his back. Rufus might have apologised, but somehow in that moment, explaining himself seemed so much worse.

CHAPTER 24

The silence pressed down hard as if to smother him, and Jionathan crept forward, feeling that he too must keep quiet, or else be noticed.

There was a river close by, he could feel it, and he placed each foot cautiously, careful not to fall. He didn't want to be seen. It wouldn't do to be seen.

Finally he found the bank and stopped, staring into the water. White, soul-like shapes stared back, floating past him, some passive, others clawing at the surface of their glassy prison, as if trying to break out. Jionathan watched them wordlessly, the thin layer separating the two worlds within arm's reach. Jionathan knew that he could easily bend forward and dip his hand into this pit of wandering spirits, but he also knew he shouldn't. If he did, a balance would be disturbed—these souls needed to remain beneath, otherwise they might escape through him. He couldn't control them, nor should he touch them, though the power was within his grasp.

He ignored the angry and pleading faces, and gazed into his own reflection instead, studying his face—he really did look like his father.

Suddenly the reflection shimmered, and he watched, spellbound, as another face took his place. He stared in horror, before dropping to his knees, his eyes bound by the reflection—his other half, his other soul.

"Sverrin…" he choked, and his brother looked back.

Jionathan began to shake, face draining of colour. Sverrin was soundless, his expression cold, as if he couldn't see Jionathan, or as if he and Jionathan had reversed places. Jionathan felt crushed, the suffocating grasp around him growing like he was being pulled forcibly through a crowd. He couldn't breathe. It was freezing—the feelings overwhelmed him.

"Jionat?"

He lurched back, breathing hard as the air stirred, the trance broken, his reflection disappearing. Jionathan put his head in his hands and gasped, shivering violently.

A muffled hum filled the air, creeping out from the mist. Jionathan searched for the source and saw a woman on the other side of the bank. She knelt, washing bloodied clothing in the river, scrubbing the life of the wearer into the realm of the dead. An ever-constant omen. Jionathan stood, his stomach tight.

"Jionathan," a voice called again, louder this time, but Jionathan couldn't be torn away. He knew those clothes—he recognised them.

"Jionat, wake up—you're having a dream," Rufus told him firmly from beyond, and Jionathan sank to his knees as the Bean Nighe dipped Rufus's robes into the river again, streaks of blood seeping out.

Jionathan woke twice in the night, his dreams overpowered by monstrous waves of colour that left him breathless, choking and shaking in his bed. Twice he'd tried to grip onto the harrowing nightmare, but the evasive images had slipped away before he could make sense of them. At that time, clammy-skinned and shivering, he'd looked over at Rufus whose eyes were always open, the Magi quietly roused by Jionathan's violent dreams.

"Are you all right?" Rufus asked each time.

Jionathan had forced himself back beneath the covers with a curt, but grateful, "Yes."

Rufus would nod and close his eyes again, though Jionathan doubted he slept.

The third time he woke from his violent dreams, daylight was creeping through tiny cracks in the shutters, and Rufus's bed was empty.

Jionathan lay still, the echoes of his visions still straining through him. His eyes rolled back and he moaned faintly. In a sudden wave of heat, he kicked away the suffocating covers and tossed his head from side to side, pressing his palms into his eye sockets. All at once his body erupted into shivers, and his injured leg throbbed, but he was too preoccupied by the dull ache in his head to care. The colours mocked him behind his lids, and he snarled, curling onto one side tightly, wishing them away. They were not perturbed by this feeble attempt.

The room seemed to tilt sickeningly from side to side, and in his mind's eye Jionathan saw hordes of dark shadows dancing madly in some terrifying ritual. A black presence loomed over him, reaching for his shoulder as he curled in tighter, clutching his chest.

A short, sharp rap at the door broke him from the glassy surface of his torment and he froze, breath caught. The knock came again, and Fae spoke.

"Jionat, are you awake?"

Her voice was so sweet that Jionathan sagged, releasing a long breath. "I...I am," he eventually said, and he heard her pause.

"Are you well?" She sounded strange through the wood, distant and distorted.

Jionathan clambered from the bed and dropped onto the floor, sitting helplessly. His legs were weak. The door opened and Fae peered in. She had a basin of water in her hands, and when she saw him on the floor, she hurried across.

"Jionat?"

"Its fine," he said, as she knelt beside him, placing the basin down. Jionathan noticed that, rather than her armour, she was wearing a sleek beige skirt and a fresh white chemise that smelt of spring water and wildflower. Her hair was pulled into a thick plait, which hung over her shoulder, and Jionathan guessed— by the daisies and poppies plaited into it—that Annabelle was responsible.

"You look flushed," Fae said.

"It was just a bad dream." He wiped his brow. "Really, I'm fine. Thank you."

Fae covered his hand, her thumb stroking across his knuckles before she released him and stepped back.

"I brought you some water to wash. It's almost noon."

Jionathan rose and limped across to the windows, throwing open the shutters. Sunlight poured into the room, and the world outside was glorious. He breathed in the fresh air, and it seemed to chase away the lingering shadows. Leaning out of the window he peered into the garden. Below he could see Annabelle and Rowan playing court tennis, or some variant of it, with a cork ball. They spotted him, and Annabelle waved enthusiastically, whilst Rowan hid shyly behind his racket.

"*Joshua*," Jionathan suddenly said, puzzled.

"Who?" Fae came and stood beside him, smiling down at the children.

"I don't know. I had a dream." He let the statement hang as Fae studied him. "I'm sorry." He shook the thought away. "Let me dress, I'll be down shortly."

"Lily-Anne has prepared an early luncheon. Luca tells me there's a market in town today, with some merchants come from Avalon and East Réne. She thought we might like to see it."

Jionathan would. He'd seen markets in Harmatia—large, colourful ones in the great forum, but he could never wander through them as 'Prince Jionathan'. Perhaps now as simply 'Jionat' he might. Fae seemed to sense his excitement, because she left him to wash and dress with a smile and a light step. She paused in the doorway. "Sarrin town," she mused, "is a good place."

Jionathan found a clean shirt amongst his belongings, and taking careful time to wash, he readied himself excitedly.

Downstairs, he found the children had come in from their games and were dining messily already. Fae had taken the duty of seeing Rowan fed, whilst Lily-Anne bustled about the room, chiding Annabelle, who had crumbs in her hair.

"Good morning," Jionathan said, a little nervously, unsure of how to fit himself into this domestic scene.

"Jionat! Did you sleep well?" Luca greeted. She was dressed in a bright crimson bodice, with a cream-dress, that hung off her shoulders. Jionathan couldn't help but stare. Women in Harmatia didn't dress like that at all, and the bareness of her drew his eye. Luca noticed the attention, and seemed pleased.

"Frivolous girl," Lily-Anne murmured as she passed, and Luca threw her loose hair over her shoulder and stuck her nose in the air.

"I can wear whatever I wish." She patted the seat beside her, and Jionathan slipped into it, helping himself to the fresh bread and butter. The smell was rich, and Jionathan was greedy with his portions.

"Where's Rufus?" he asked as he ate.

"Oh, he went to have a letter delivered."

"He's been gone for a long time." Fae frowned, and Luca and Lily-Anne exchanged a devious look.

"I imagine he might have...gone seeking some company in the town," Luca said carefully, looking pointedly to Rowan and Annabelle, who ignored their chatter.

"An old friend?" Jionathan asked.

"Rather..." Luca giggled." Company of a more intimate and fleeting nature."

Jionathan spluttered. "You mean he's gone to a—" he broke off and mouthed, "a *whore house*?"

Lily-Anne and Luca simultaneously threw their heads back with laughter just as Michael came into the room, his broad form filling the doorway.

"Prince Jionathan, you cannot know my nephew well if you think he needs to *pay* for such services." Michael grinned, and picking up Annabelle he placed her on his knee and sat at the table.

Luca leant in toward Jionathan. "I think half the town are in love with him," she said. "They say all it takes is one kiss. He's like a Gancanagh himself."

Jionathan was shocked. He could hardly imagine such a side to Rufus—the Magi was too bookish, too composed for such activity. Yet, when Jionathan considered Rufus's demeanour with Embarr Reagon, it stood to reason that, relaxed, Rufus *did* have all the potential to be a deviant. Jionathan shuddered at the thought. "I never thought him the type."

"His father was same." Michael began helping himself to the food. "Torin is, and has always been, the finest friend I've ever had, but he didn't half drive me to distraction as a youth."

"Uncle Torin certainly started early," Luca agreed, helping herself to another serving before her father could take the rest.

"How would you know, girl?" Lily-Anne began to clean Rowan's face, which was sticky with food.

"Well, he had Rufus at seventeen, and by all accounts he was no stranger to women by then, either."

"He was not," Michael chortled. "But until then he'd been void of responsibility. The night he found out Rufus's mother was pregnant...Lords, I've never seen a man more in need of a drink."

"Seventeen." Fae shook her head with dismay. "So young."

"He was. We were quite worried, weren't we my dear?" Michael caught Lily-Anne as she sauntered past and drew her in for a kiss. "I trusted Torin Merle with my life, but I didn't trust him as a father. We even offered to take the baby—Lily-Anne was already a few months along with our first, Mielane. Another babe would've been no great task."

"To you perhaps," Lily-Anne chided, and tore herself away from Michael's embrace with a secretive smile.

"What about his mother? Surely she wasn't so willing to give away her child?" Fae's brow lowered disapprovingly.

"Her? She wanted him even less than Torin did. A Betheanian lass, merchant's daughter named Ella, supposed for greater things. The whole pregnancy was great a scandal. My cousin—Torin's wife now, Nora—was her midwife, and the first to hold Rufus when he was born. His mother wouldn't even look at him, refused. Probably for the best. Torin might've done the same, but Nora was so angry she threatened to beat him into the next day unless he held his son." Michael chuckled. "Aye the Rossignol women aren't so easily tamed when enraged, eh, my girl?" He flicked Luca's cheek, and she gave him a smug smile. "I think, too, that was the moment Torin realised his feelings for her. For all their flippancy, the Merle men like their partners to tell them what to do. So Torin held Rufus…and you know I never saw a man change so quickly. He was a reckless, stubborn arse of a boy was Torin. My greatest friend but also my personal bane—always ready to launch himself into a next adventure, get involved in things that were better left alone. He gave me a scare or two in his youth, I tell you. But he took one look at Rufus, with those bonny blue eyes, and he fell in love. Overnight he was changed—became a man. He took responsibilities, good work, married Nora. Having children will change you—bring out the best in you." Michael bounced his knee up and down so that Annabelle, who was perched there, giggled with delight. "Or the very worst!" He engulfed the girl in his arms, like a bear, and she squealed, batting him playfully away.

"Stop it, you'll make her sick." Luca wrestled her sister free and held her protectively away, Annabelle laughing almost drunkenly. Jionathan thought of his mother and father in Harmatia, and wished they were with him. Surely the fresh Sarrin air would revive his father's health, and his mother would no doubt delight in the Rossignol's company. A hand found his beneath the table, and Jionathan realised he must have appeared forlorn. He brightened his expression and squeezed Fae's fingers gratefully.

"Should we go to market?" Fae suggested, and Michael clapped his hands with enthusiasm.

"Ah yes! Our famous Sarrin market—you must go indeed! There'll be many a pretty thing abound. Luca-girl, keep an eye out for that silk vendor. Hah! If you could call it silk! I'd have words with him."

"Yes, father." Luca rolled her eyes, and Jionathan felt his spirits brighten as he quickly finished off the last on his plate, the sunlight sparkling through the open windows.

~~~

Rufus hummed, enjoying the warm beat of the sun as he descended into the market place. He'd had a fruitful morning— delivered his letter, made a few purchases, and then met a friend, with whom he'd spent several happy hours in a naked sweat, tangled in bed sheets. Feeling refreshed, and fuller than he had in many weeks, Rufus took pause at the fountain in the square to drink. Splashing his face, he heard the sound of laughter, and spotted Luca, Fae, and Jionathan resting in the shadow of a building.

"You paid *how* much?" Luca was saying to Jionathan, who held a new dirk in his hands.

Jionathan looked between her and Fae, baffled. "Eighteen silver. Is that not right?"

"Not right? It's positively criminal!" Luca snorted, and then caught sight of Rufus and halloed him enthusiastically. "Rufus— good morning, cousin. Come and join us out of the sun before you burn."

"Hilarious." Rufus moved over to them, leaning down to kiss Luca on the brow.

She pinched his cheek playfully. "Which poor soul did my Gancanagh of a cousin feed on today, hm? Man or woman?" she whispered up to him.

"Hush you," he scolded. "You lecherous soul."

"Quite right. What woman would have you with my scent on your shirt?" Luca mused, ignoring him.

Rufus changed the subject. "So have you been robbed, Jionat?"

"Apparently." Jionathan looked glumly down at the dirk in his hands.

"You've not experienced a true market until you have," Rufus said, and that seemed to bring something of Jionathan's spirit back. "I heard news on the main road—there are celebrations throughout the land. Princess Aurora is safely home, 'recovered and rescued' by her brother."

"Malak be praised," Jionathan huffed with relief as Fae gave a discreet, but pleased, sigh.

"How sad that I know the truth of the affair, but can never tell a living soul," Luca lamented. "That it was you three who rescued her...and from Korrigans no less!"

"One day the world may know." Jionathan gestured for her to lower her voice. "But for now, I'm happy just to know she's home at last."

"On that we can agree," Rufus said. "Fae, Luca, if you might permit me, I would like to borrow Jionat a moment."

"And what if I don't want to be borrowed?" Jionathan said.

"Don't be contrary," Rufus snipped. "I have something for you."

"A secretive bunch, aren't they, these Harmatians? Come along then, Fae, let's go find a more interesting distraction away from these droll men," Luca suggested, and Fae took her arm, the pair moving off together. Rufus marvelled at their friendship,

Jionathan watching after them.

"They've barely known each other a day."

"Luca will break any formality that impedes comfort. Why waste time on social convention if you both laugh at the same jokes?" Rufus said, almost proudly, and Jionathan chuckled.

"That takes a certain courage, I think." He turned back to Rufus. "What is it then? This thing that you've used to rob me of good company?"

Rufus drew it from his satchel, and Jionathan huffed.

"A book. What a surprise."

"Just take it, you ingrate." Rufus knocked it into Jionathan's chest

Jionathan looked over the leather-bound journal. His hands flittered across the careful craftsmanship, admiring it before he flicked the book open. "It's empty," he said, incredulously.

"For now." Rufus produced a pencil from his bag and handed it to him. "But when you're through with it, it should be a book of dreams."

Jionathan took the pencil suspiciously. "A book of dreams?"

"You've not been sleeping very well, have you? And my mother used to say—"

"That if you draw out the bad dreams, they'll stop," Jionathan recalled. "Yes, but you said it didn't work."

"I said that I wasn't sure it made a difference, but the dream did stop. Hopefully yours will too."

"Thank you." Jionathan's voice was deep with gratitude.

Rufus's eyebrows rose. "Heavens—that actually sounded sincere. Are you feverish?" he goaded, but Jionathan didn't rise to the bait. Rufus frowned. "It really wasn't any trouble."

"Maybe, but you didn't have to do it. You didn't have to do any of this. Rescuing me in the forest, sacrificing yourself, and then bringing me here…" Jionathan drew off. Rufus's frown deepened.

"What's changed?" he asked. Jionathan had clearly learnt something that morning, something pitiful. Rufus prayed it wasn't what he feared. "The Rossignols have told you something about me, haven't they?"

"Your mother," Jionathan confessed, and Rufus's chest lightened.

"*Oh*. Her."

"I'm sorry about what happened."

"You needn't be," Rufus dismissed. "The best thing she ever did was forfeit me to parents who love me. I had a good childhood. I don't miss her."

Jionathan looked up, disbelieving. "But you must wonder."

"I did, when I was your age. Now, not really. My father told me she married a Réneian tradesman, and has brats of her own."

"You mean you have brothers and sisters?"

"I suppose. I don't really think about it much." He shrugged. "It's no great loss to me."

The sound of music suddenly filled the square, and a merry party passed them by, children throwing blossoms as bells chimed in the distance. "A wedding!" Jionathan cried, looking at the two beautifully-clad women who were being happily paraded under an arch of flowers. "A double wedding? But where are the grooms?"

"I rather think the brides are marrying each other."

"They...excuse me?" Jionathan demanded, spinning on his heel.

"Marriage laws are different in Bethean," Rufus laughed. "The introduction of the True Gods into the country is still relatively new, and so there remain many old traditions. For instance, Betheanians still bury their dead in accordance with the old custom, rather than burning the body. Equally, marriage is not a union for the purpose of children, but rather a vow of eternal love, not to be made lightly. Many wait until long after they've had children before making such a vow—my uncle and aunt included."

"You mean to say that the Rossignol children are bastards?"

"There's no such word in Betheanian," Rufus said sternly. "But by Harmatian translation, yes, Luca and…and Mielane were. Annabelle and Rowan were born in wedlock."

"It's a strange practice," Jionathan said. "Though I suppose it makes sense. But women *marrying* each other?"

"Certainly. And men, too. It's a pact of love."

"But then anybody could marry anybody!" Jionathan protested. "A man might marry his dog."

"Jionat, I hardly think that a dog is capable of making a vow of eternal love."

Jionathan stood in contemplative silence. "They look so happy."

"Wouldn't you be, on your wedding day?"

Jionathan seemed to struggle a moment. "I suppose so," he agreed, his face brightening. "This is a strange place, Rufus. And yet, I can't find any fault with it. It's just so different. I *like* it."

"Good." Rufus grinned, and the pair watched the procession go by, hearts light.

"What happened to Mielane?" Jionathan asked, absentmindedly.

It was like the Korrigan had plunged the dagger back into Rufus's chest. He went cold, his body petrified.

"You must be close to her. She's the same age as you, isn't she? But she doesn't live with the Rossignols anymore."

"She…" Rufus's mind was blank, nulled of inspiration. He found the ring on the chain around his neck and tugged it, running a hand up through his hair. "She left," he eventually said.

"Left?" Jionathan frowned, scanning Rufus's face. "Rufus, what's wrong?"

"She married," Rufus said quickly, a claustrophobic panic coming over him as the words tumbled out, confused and thick. "She married. Young. Very young. Too young. A man from a village nearby. She left." He drew off. "She left us." He gritted his teeth, anxious. "It's best not to talk about it. Don't mention her.

When she left, it wasn't under good circumstances. Not good at all. The whole thing was…" Rufus swallowed. "Don't talk about her. Please. Not to the Rossignols. Not to me."

"I won't, I'm sorry. Septus, man, you're white." Jionathan peered anxiously up to his face.

"I must've been out too long. I'm going back to the house," Rufus said, moving off away from the jovial crowd.

"Rufus," Jionathan objected, but Rufus gave him a final, terse smile.

"I'm fine," he lied. "I just need to eat something, maybe rest a while. Don't worry—enjoy the market." He squeezed Jionathan's shoulder, and then fled back to the house, the cold following him all the way.

CHAPTER
25

The Queen wasn't content with Zachary's discovery when he gave her the details of the hanging man. Nor was she happy that Zachary had neglected to investigate the death any further.

"I want whatever is left of those Delphi Knights run from this city. Run, or put on the wheel for my pleasure. Do you understand me?"

And thus, Zachary found himself once more walking through the slums in search of a cold trail. This time, Marcel Hathely joined him.

"What does she expect us to find?" Zachary grunted as they looked over the empty room. The corpse had since been burned, and any remaining artefacts masterfully cleared. Even if the room had been left as it was, Zachary doubted any more could have been discerned from the assassination. The key to the investigation lay now in the chatter and whispers of the under city, and the Queen's ears through the capital were better suited to that task.

"It is punishment," Marcel grunted, and Zachary snorted. The Queen also hadn't been pleased when he'd failed to bring the perpetrator's head, but Zachary had expected that.

"He was assassinated." He stood beneath the spot where the body once hung.

"Are you certain?"

"Positive," Zachary said. "This investigation would be swifter, therefore, if we knew who the victim was..." He broke off and coughed into his elbow. "Ach, the air is putrid in here." He slapped his chest twice to clear it and continued. "If we knew who he was, we could find out why he was killed, and who did it."

"That is ambitious," Marcel grumbled, and Zachary knew he was tired. Despite being born under Malak, who reigned from sunrise through most of the morning, Marcel didn't tend to greet the day with great enthusiasm. He was a sour man come daybreak, and would usually remain so until he took luncheon. Zachary, too, would have rather stayed in bed. His chest had felt heavy all morning, and he'd woken—for the fourth time in so many weeks—to a heavy nosebleed and bloodshot eyes. A day's rest would have been welcome.

Struggling to keep his eyes open, Marcel stifled a sudden yawn, and Zachary shot him a look.

"You know, you didn't have to come with me," he said. "The Queen would have been none the wiser."

"*You* asked me. I came." Marcel came and stood beside him, peering up into the rafters. "What was he hanging from?"

"I don't recall. Twine, I think. Must have been silk. It was very thin. Lucky the man had a thick neck." Zachary tried to call back on the image, and something moved in his peripheral vision. Zachary turned his head sharply, looking up to the rafters behind. The corners were dark with shadows, but there seemed to be nothing else there. Marcel raised his eyebrow, and Zachary shrugged. "Rats," he said.

"What do you remember of him?"

Zachary cleared his throat, massaging his chest. "The victim? Well-fed, simply dressed, but I should say wealthy. He had several rings, removed, and he wore a signet, I think—there was a large indent on one finger—so old family. Clean-shaven, too, so Harmatian by my guess—they're all sporting beards in the Betheanian court now."

"He may have shaved."

"No, his face was too smooth. He kept it like that. Besides, he was too pale for a Betheanian." The beams creaked above them, and Zachary grew stiff, sure that something was moving in the corner of his eye. Before he knew it, he was summoning magic into his body, preparing to transform. As the power built up inside, the first thing he noticed was a heightening in his senses. His sight grew sharper, his hearing clearer, and the smell—he could appreciate the putrid air of unwashed bodies all the more.

And he could also smell the inconspicuous, but ever-present scent of another human being in the room. Zachary turned on his heel just as a figure dropped from the rafters and planted a hard kick into Marcel's back, throwing him to the side, before darting out of the door.

Marcel rolled quickly to his feet, Zachary already in pursuit as the hooded figure tore out of the building and onto the slum streets.

Zachary sprinted after them, his blood racing as the figure moved nimbly forward. Zachary had no idea who he was after, but this was no ordinary slum rat—they were trained, and clothed all in black for the purpose of going unseen, face masked. Whatever this spy's reasons for listening in, Zachary wanted to know.

The spy turned a sharp corner, and Zachary followed, watching amazed as—with great dexterity—they lunged up the side of a building and onto the rooftop. Whoever they were, they moved like a professional assassin.

Zachary scaled up the building as effortlessly as his foe, following the path. He too had learnt how to navigate the terrain of a city at speed, and was unhindered by obstacles that would stop another dead.

Reaching the top of the building, he sprinted after the spy, who leapt onto the next roof, and then jumped back down into an alley between two of the houses. Far behind, Zachary could hear Marcel calling his name, but he pressed on.

Jumping down after the spy into the alley, Zachary landed effortlessly, magic racing through his blood. Dismissing his initial instinct to summon a wall of flames—fire in the proximity of so many houses could be catastrophic—he concentrated on water instead, and drawing on the moisture in the air. Two, long thin whips of water began to form, and he grasped one in each hand and lashed out. They snapped and hissed, marking the walls either side as they sliced forward. The spy looked back just in time to see them, and dove out of the way. One of the water whips caught their arm, and the rich scent of blood filled the air. The spy didn't betray their voice, but stumbled back, clamping a hand to the wound. Zachary drew more magic into himself, a hunger flaring up just as a scream caught him off guard.

A young girl had come out into the street to see the commotion and caught sight of Zachary's face. The girl, no more than seven years old, stood, mouth agape, frozen to the spot in absolute terror, staring into Zachary's eyes. Zachary realised they had turned black. He was beginning to transform into his Night Patrol form.

No! he thought sharply. It was one thing to transform during curfew, but here in the day with the scent of blood driving him half-wild? He released the magic building up inside of him, and as he did the thick, coagulated feeling in his chest intensified. With a retch he dropped to his knees, coughing desperately. The spy took their chance and fled, and Zachary choked, trying to clear his airway. A moment later, the feeling subsided, and he sat up straight, footsteps hurrying up behind him. The little girl had bolted back into her house, and the spy was gone.

"Arlen!" Marcel shouted roughly, as he ran up to him.

Zachary waved his hand in assurance. "I'm fine…but they got

away."

Marcel dropped to his side and seizing Zachary's hand raised it into the air. Zachary was surprised to find it covered with blood.

"What…" Zachary frowned, and then touched his free hand to his face. It was slick. He wiped blood from his chin and lips. His blood. His own. "Oh." He stared up at Marcel in shock. "Oh."

Marcel huffed in agreement and dragged him to his feet. "We return to the castle, now," he said, and Zachary—glancing down to the patches of red along the path beneath him—knew better than to argue.

⁓

He'd barely made it through the window before Nora stormed into the room, her face pinched with fury. "Torin Merle!" she shouted as he shrank back, dropping onto Rufus's bed guiltily. "Where, in Athea's name, have you been?"

Torin drew the mask down from his face and smiled ruefully. "In the slums…" he admitted, and Nora cuffed him around the head. He rolled away defensively, backing toward the bookcase. "I'm sorry, Nora."

"Sorry? *Sorry?* Mothering Prospan, Torin, what were you *doing* there? You're covered in dust."

"Mostly being chased by Magi…"

Nora's eyes bulged. "Chased by—" She cut herself off. "Why?"

"It was a misunderstanding, that's all."

"Not 'why were you chased'—*why* were you *there?*"

Torin gritted his teeth, looking around the room for inspiration. Nora pinched his chin between her fingers and forced his gaze back to her.

"*Why?*" she demanded again.

He exhaled. "There was an assassination. A man was in hiding there—some noble. He was killed."

"And what's that got to do with you precisely?"

"I may…have supplied the murder weapon," Torin confessed.

"The twine?" Nora moaned.

"The twine."

"It was that Lemra'n, wasn't it?"

"…Yes."

"You—" Nora swallowed the curse. "Why did you have to get involved?"

"Look, I gave him the twine and told him to leave. I didn't *intend* to get involved but…" he looked over at Rufus's empty bed. Somehow, with Rufus gone from the house, Torin had found himself getting restless for old habits. "I was curious. What was special about this one that they sent an assassin like that?"

Nora paced. Torin knew she was torn between scolding him and asking questions. She chose the latter. "Who was he then? Another assassin? A traitor?" She paused. "A Knight?"

"An informant, I think."

"Of what?"

"I don't know. But neither do the Magi. I wasn't expecting them to be there today. Arh!" He raised his left arm and felt pain streak through it. Blood was already seeping out through the make-shift bandage he'd bound around his arm. "Oh, I'm getting old." He removed the bandage, and his shirt to observe the cut better. It was long, and deep.

Nora pinched her mouth, and leaving the room, she returned with a bowl of hot water, fresh bandages, a needle and thread.

"You don't have to," Torin said, but Nora made him sit. Kneeling beside him she began to work, binding the skin together again.

"You forget, Torin, that I didn't first learn to stitch on fabric."

"I don't forget, Nora." Torin rested his head back against the wall, looking at the diagrams and maps that Rufus had pinned up. He felt a flare of pride for his son, and was ashamed to be in his room as he was. "I think Rufus's brothering apprentice, Arlen Zachary, is a Night Patrol."

"Why?"

"When he attacked me...something happened. There was an air about him, Nora, I can't explain. His eyes turned black, his face was fierce—the air seemed to thicken."

"You're lucky to have escaped with your life."

"It *was* luck—I didn't fell him, he collapsed. He's well trained that one, and not just by any master of sword in Harmatia. If he'd caught me, I'd have been dead in seconds," Torin said. "Something doesn't sit right about all this, Nora."

"I nearly lost a husband and Rufus a father for your foolishness. It doesn't sit right with me either." Nora tightened the thread, drawing it taut.

"That's not it," Torin said. "Something's happening. I can feel it. Everything's shifting again. I can't sit idle any more. I need to get back onto the streets. I need to resume my work."

"And what do I tell your son when you get caught up and killed?" Nora demanded, and Torin dropped his head back against the wall.

"The truth," he muttered. "The gods know I owe it to him. Nora, between the Knights, the Magi, the Queen, and the Kathraks, I swear King Thestian's the only thing standing between us and all-out war. When he dies, if Prince Jionathan isn't here to take the throne, the capital will suffer. It won't be safe here. You and Rufus should take cover elsewhere."

"Torin." Nora pressed her forehead into his shoulder. "This is *our* post. I won't abandon it." She pressed a kiss to his arm. "We will do what we have to, what we've *always* done, to survive."

Torin rested the side of his head on hers, and found her hand, squeezing it. "And Rufus?"

"When he's home, we'll tell him. Tell him everything."

"Yes," Torin said. "It's long overdue."

As the evening drew in on Sarrin town, Rufus found himself walking through the orchards at the back of the Rossignol house. The amber sky made for a fine horizon over the knolls, setting them ablaze with a dark, golden light.

He found Fae, sat reading beneath his favourite tree, unmindful of the growing dark, her features pinched in concentration.

"*The Barrel Men*?" he asked, and she was so engrossed she jumped slightly at the disturbance.

"Yes." She held the book against her chest protectively. "Luca lent it to me."

"And what do you think?"

She glanced down to the book. "I have reached the part where Dellatania sneaks into the dungeon to find his brother, by having Ardios and Vespus pretend to arrest him. I presume that was the inspiration for our own little plan."

Rufus came and stood beside her. "May I sit with you?"

She eyed him up and down. "You may," she granted at last and he settled amongst the roots, Fae returning to her book.

Rufus studied her. "You look confused."

"Dellatania's brother is something called a *Child of Aramathea*. I have not heard such a term before. Well, no." Fae closed the book. "Today in the market I heard it. The priestesses of the next village were selling wreaths to raise money for the restoration of a statue."

"The statue of Alywn the Gentle, yes. She was a famous child of Aramathea in these parts a few hundred years ago."

"What is a Child of Aramathea?"

"Simply put? A prophet." Rufus shifted and lay back, gazing at the foliage above, the leaves opaque and glowing, so he could see their veins. "Every person is born under an elemental star, and it not only affects who we are and how we behave, but our natural affiliation. There are two gods, however—Athea and Notameer—who were supposed to be one, but were divided. One rules during the day, the other at night. However, twice a day they meet, at the

284

dawning of the night, and at the end of it."

"Sunset and sunrise."

Rufus nodded. "For a brief moment, they are conjoined, and babies born at that time are known as Children of Aramathea. Those born at sunrise are of Notameer, and those born at sunset belong to Athea. It's unclear what Children of Aramathea are, exactly. Some say they're the vessels of the gods themselves— their speakers and bodies on our plane. Others say that they *are* the gods, but in human form—a small drop of divinity. Regardless, Children of Aramathea tend to mark the world, for better or worse."

Fae listened to him intently. "You mentioned having such person in Harmatia?"

"Yes," Rufus said. "My master, Belphegore Odin. He was born of Notameer, and is a very powerful man. He leads the Magi, and since doing so has brought prosperity to the whole city. By his invention, every sector in the capital now has easy access to clean water and a working sewage system—people both rich and poor."

"If the technology is available, then that just seems like common decency," Fae snubbed, and Rufus chuckled.

"Yes, I suppose," he agreed. "But you'd be surprised how few people are capable of that."

"If Children of Aramathea are so heralded, then why in the book is Dellatania's brother imprisoned and to be put to death?" Fae returned to the book, finding her page once more. "He's committed no named crime."

"They're afraid of him." Rufus's voice lowered.

"Because of his power? Is he not a prophet of your True Gods?"

"He was born at sunset, under Athea—the Red Star."

"Your god of death?" Fae recalled, frowning at the pages of the book. "He seems so innocent."

"Athea is about more than death. She's raw emotion—love,

285

fear, anger. Above all, she's the guide to the lost. Everything ends, Fae, but that doesn't mean it's bad." Rufus took the book from her, brushing his hand over the illustration of Dellatania and his brother, embracing in the cell. "But it's true that those born under Notameer tend toward a more peaceful existence, content to help and serve justice, whilst those under Athea are…of a more vibrant stock. There are rare incidents documented of Children of Aramathea displaying incredible feats of power, channelling the gods. It's a phenomenon that can only occur twice during the cycle, as the god rises and at the moment they stand highest in the sky. Those born under Notameer are said to have performed miracles—produced rivers of water in barren lands, or stopped a raging flood. Whilst those under Athea have been documented to burn entire cities to the ground and cause mountains to erupt. The incidents are scarce, but of course they're remembered."

"So…they fear him for the potential power he might possess?"

Rufus shrugged. "In history, it wasn't uncommon for babies born under Athea to be killed at birth. They become harder to kill as they grow older, so to prevent a potential evil, many villages nullified the problem instead. The practice is all but gone now though, and there have been several named prophets born under Athea who are revered. Still," Rufus smiled ruefully, "fool is the man who openly admits to being born under such a dark star, for his every action will be judged by it. Better to live a lie, if it means living a normal life."

Fae's expression was pinched again, her thumb stroking over the cover of the book as she reclaimed it from Rufus. "How old are you, Rufus?" she eventually asked.

"I was twenty-three this year. Why?" Rufus peered into her face, which had darkened, brow furrowing. "You're surprised," he said. "Surprised that I'm older than you."

Fae's eyebrows rose sharply, her lips curling back so that he saw a flash of her dangerous teeth. "You assume that very quickly." Her voice was dark with offense. "What would a Magi like you know of my true age?"

Rufus sat up, raising his hands. "Peace," he said quickly. "Peace, please! I know that the Sidhe age differently to humans. Your mental development is twice as fast in youth, and physically three times as slow at prime age. It was merely an insight. You are timeless in most senses, but…you've only lived a few years. I would say twenty? Nineteen, perhaps. Like Luca."

Fae was silent, and then gave a soft grumble, placing her chin in her hands. "This year will be my twentieth summer."

"Well, you won't have to wait long then. The days are getting warmer." He reached his hand up to the sky, as if to touch it and then let his arm drop. "I haven't said it yet, but you really do look lovely in that dress."

"That side of the conversation ends now." Although soft, there was something heavy and firm in her voice.

"Naturally." He looked away. "I'm a Magi, after all."

"Yes. You're a Magi," she said tonelessly, and Rufus sighed and lay back down against the roots, cushioning his head in his hands. "You think me overly suspicious."

"Not overly."

"You're right to." Fae opened the book once more and continued to read. "I have barely known you a few days and have been betrayed by those I played with as a child."

"I'm sorry."

"Don't misunderstand—it's not something which burdens me. Either way, you have no right to judge me. You are incapable of being candid even with those closest to you."

Rufus sat up again, this time in surprise. "How so?"

Fae made a guttural noise somewhere between amusement and frustration. "Don't think that, because you're expressive with your feelings, I haven't seen the shroud of secrets and half-lies you wrap yourself in. You may think it protects you, but it will only hurt you in the end."

Rufus felt his mouth go dry, and he realised it was hanging

open. "I…" He blinked, and then forced himself to smile, tugging his fringe. "Being secretive is just my nature I suppose. Runs in the family. But then," he eyed her, "aren't you the same?"

"*I* am protecting myself." Fae turned another page. "You are simply pushing people away. It wouldn't matter, if you could at least be honest with yourself."

Rufus laughed to cover the hurtful pang of truth. "You read me as easily as that book."

"No. But you have been slack these past days. Something of this town softens you. It doesn't concern me, but you have no reason to be secretive with Jionat." Fae spoke distantly, like she was not fully invested in the conversation, her eyes still darting across the page.

"It's not a matter of trusting in him." Rufus lay back down and closed his eyes. "It's just that I'm a coward. And, as you say, there are some truths I'm not yet prepared to face."

"That is no life."

"I have a few centuries to organise myself." Rufus gave an exaggerated yawn, and Fae turned another page.

"Jionat doesn't have that time to wait for you," she said, and Rufus turned on his side, studying her. In the fading half-light he could see a line of white, star-like marks framing her eyes, a quiet proof of her Cat Sidhe heritage, though Rufus didn't know what they meant.

"Fae, what will you do now?"

"Finish this book, if you'll let me," Fae muttered.

"Will you stay in Sarrin a while longer?"

"I have no reason to." She spoke a little too readily, but Rufus caught the brief, longing look she took over the orchards. How long, he wondered, since this warrior had had a chance to rest? To dress comfortably, stroll through the markets, laugh, and chatter with new friends? Rufus wasn't foolish enough to imagine that Fae's ambition lay in a quiet town like this, and yet he couldn't shake the impression that Fae was, somehow, tired.

Like a howling sea storm that wanted to curl open to blue sky, if only for a day.

"Stay with us," Rufus said quietly. "You did your duty, now stay with us a while. Stay with Jionat."

"As a guest?" she asked. "A friend?"

Rufus gave her a crooked smile, shrugging awkwardly from where he lay. "I know Jionat would like it if you did."

"Do not lightly make claims on another's behalf."

"I do it with all sincerity. He wants you to stay. I know it," Rufus insisted, and Fae seemed to consider the proposition.

"And you?" she eventually asked. "Would you like it?"

"Yes," he confessed. "Very much."

"I see." Fae gave a curt nod. "You mean to wait until I transform, unaware, and then kill and skin me when my back is turned."

Rufus's face contorted with horror. "No!" he cried. "Never! I would never—" he cut himself off as Fae tilted her head back with a hearty laugh. It sounded like a bell, melodic and warming. "You're wicked." Rufus cussed, and she rose to her feet, slapping the book closed.

"I think I will stay a while longer," she decided, straightening her skirts. "Sarrin agrees with me." She dared to give Rufus a little smile. He returned it, beaming at her. She shook her head slightly, still tittering and walked off into the orchard to read in peace. Rufus followed her graceful figure departing through the trees, and dropped back with a grunt.

"Mother would like her," he said to himself.

CHAPTER
26

"Oh sons of the gods, is this necessary?" Zachary griped as Edwin forced his jaw open and peered into his mouth.

"How much blood was it?" the physician asked. Zachary tried to talk around the intrusive fingers, but his response came out a garbled mess.

Marcel replied in his stead. "A few mouthfuls. Enough to cause concern."

Zachary grunted a retort about causing real concern, but it was lost again to Edwin's fingers. Finally the physician relented, pulling away, and Zachary rubbed his jaw irritably. He had waited the better part of the day to be seen by Edwin, despite other healers in the sect being available. Edwin had been his physician from childhood and was one of the few men Zachary truly trusted. He wouldn't be seen by anyone else.

"There seems to be no tearing in the throat," Edwin murmured. "Was it all blood, or was there mucus, bile?"

"Just blood." Zachary kicked his legs with boredom. He already had some idea of what was wrong, but Edwin had his routine, and Marcel wouldn't be happy until the examination was complete.

"Any discomfort in the stomach? Bowel?" Edwin took Zachary's wrist, pressing fingers to the pulse line as he placed his other hand across Zachary's forehead.

"I am the picture of immaculate health."

"Hm, no fever." Edwin removed his hand.

"Obviously."

"Any pain in the chest?"

Zachary hesitated. "My lungs felt a little heavy."

Edwin paused, still counting Zachary's pulse. "For how long?"

Zachary exhaled through his nose. "Since this morning."

Edwin released his wrist, and sighed heavily. "And yet you went out on this ridiculous escapade instead of coming to me?"

"This isn't East Réne," Zachary said. "We don't live in a democracy. I was given my orders, I did them. Besides, I thought it was caused by the flowers and dust."

"Men do not cough blood for flowers and dust."

"Hence why I came to you."

The door behind them opened, and Belphegore stepped into the room. Zachary shrank back at the sight of him, his master's gait long.

"I came as soon as I heard. Is he alright?" Belphegore demanded, and Zachary glanced accusingly at Marcel, who stood by the window. The blond blew out a line of smoke, his pipe sticking out of the corner of his mouth, and shrugged.

"Hathely," Zachary said. "It will be nightfall soon. Go and prepare for the Patrol. I will be with you shortly."

Marcel bowed his head and left the room soundlessly, billows of smoke following in his wake. The moment the door closed, Zachary turned to Edwin.

"May I get off this table?" He asked, in a voice that said it wasn't really a question. Edwin conceded with a shallow nod, and Zachary stood, fetching his jerkin and putting it back over his chemise.

"Will somebody please explain what happened?" Belphegore

demanded. "Arlen, don't be petulant," he added as Zachary grumbled, rolling his eyes. "I was told my apprentice was ill."

"He collapsed this morning."

"I did not collapse."

"And was coughing blood," Edwin continued, unperturbed. "Fortunately, I do not think it is anything serious. Not yet, anyway," he warned Zachary, who threw his hands in the air, halfway through buttoning his jerkin up.

"What caused it?" Belphegore asked, as Zachary pulled his robe on over his uniform, patting it down. Tiny fumes of dust rose from the black fabric.

"I believe it was an after effect of repetitive transformation. The excess magic has caused the body to create a surplus of blood. There was literally too much in his body," Edwin said, and Zachary nodded. He'd suspected as much. "That doesn't surprise you?" Edwin noted.

"It explains the nosebleeds."

"*Nosebleeds*, Arlen?" Edwin fumed. "For how long?"

"Oh Healing Septus, am I to come to you every time I scrape my knee?"

"*Yes,* you incompetent child, because apparently you can't tell the difference!" Edwin shouted, and Zachary twitched. "Forgive me," Edwin apologised immediately. "It has been a very long day. But Arlen, if there had been too much blood, you might have drowned. It was in your *lungs*."

"What do you recommend?" Belphegore came between them, touching Zachary's shoulder, almost as if to assure himself his apprentice was standing straight and strong. Zachary found the strangest comfort in it.

"He's been transforming every night for months. Two years almost. Seeing as none of the other men who patrol on routine have displayed any similar symptoms, the transforming is clearly not the problem. It is the proximity and frequency. I would recommend you take a few days rest from the patrol."

Zachary ignored the momentary panic that came over him, and remained calm. "Then who would lead them?"

"Lord Hathely is capable."

"No," Zachary answered shortly. "I won't abandon my men."

"Arlen, you're playing a dangerous game."

"And it is my pleasure."

"Enough!" Belphegore's patience ran thin. "This need," he warned Zachary, "it is an addiction. You will control it."

"What are you going to do? Cap me?" Zachary asked coolly. "Like you capped Merle?"

Zachary couldn't name the emotion that flared in Belphegore's eyes, but it wasn't pleasant. "Don't you dare twist my actions," Belphegore growled, his jaw clenched. "What I did to Rufus, I did because he begged me to."

Zachary snorted. "What Magi *begs* to have their capacity capped?" To be capped should have been any Magi's living nightmare, and it seemed to Zachary that Belphegore had conceded all too easily to the desperate request of a head-sick man. "He's starving himself, and you let him."

"And you are gorging." Belphegore refused to be shaken. "Recognise that there are many forms of grief, Arlen."

"Grief?" Zachary laughed. "You think I am *grieving*?" He leant in toward his master, finally letting his voice rise. "I don't have a doubt in my heart, Master. Not one. I began this, and I will damned well end it."

"You dig your own grave and ask me to idly stand back and watch?"

"So close your eyes," Zachary hissed.

Belphegore exhaled angrily, turning away.

"If there's too much blood, bleed me," Zachary instructed Edwin, rolling up the sleeve of his chemise and holding his arm out. "Master," he hesitated. "I am not your responsibility anymore. Everything I do, from here onward, is with my hands alone."

There was a moment of silence. Both Magi watched Belphegore quietly for his verdict. Belphegore gave a long breath and threw his hands in the air. "Do as he asks," he ordered Edwin. "I won't argue with him. Arlen…" He reached forward and squeezed Zachary's shoulder. "You will always be my apprentice, and my responsibility. I chose you, and as much as you like to make us think otherwise, I was *not* wrong." He left the room before any more could be said, and Edwin fetched a small knife.

"He's right, you know. It's an addiction. All magic is by nature, but—"

"It's not the magic I am addicted to," Zachary said firmly, holding out his arm. Edwin sighed. He couldn't see past the stubborn, frightened eight-year-old boy Zachary had been.

"You're better than this." The physician cut into his skin, and Zachary watched as blood pooled out greedily, gushing like a fresh spring. Zachary's mouth watered, and he suppressed the mixed shudder of disgust, and hunger that sprang through him.

"Am I?"

"Joshua."

Jionathan leapt in surprise and turned back to find Fae peering over his shoulder. He hadn't heard her approach. "Excuse me?"

"You said it this morning—Joshua." Fae held up the copy of *The Barrel Men* triumphantly. "I finished it."

"You read quickly." Jionathan closed the book of dreams, which had been balanced on his lap.

"When I have the chance." Fae hopped up and joined him on the wall, overlooking the market that was being packed away. "Joshua's the name of the forgotten Prince at the end of the book, who overthrows the tyranny and becomes King."

"Yes, that's right." Jionathan took the book and flicked to the end. "It's been so long since I read it, and he appears so fleetingly." He exhaled, relieved. "That must be why I thought of the name.

Did you enjoy it?"

"It was educational." Fae reclaimed the book and looked down at Jionathan's own. "What were you doing?"

"Drawing," he confessed. "Well, ruining perfectly good paper. I was never taught to draw. Only to kill." He couldn't keep the reproachfulness from his voice.

"You're not a man who rejoices in battle?"

"The best place for a sword is in its sheath. I won't decorate its purpose—its design is to kill. I am happy to use it, but it shouldn't be drawn idly."

"You drew your sword for me," Fae said.

"You were a good cause." Jionathan turned the book over in his hands. "I'm not foolish. I know the way of the world, and I know that some men will never be happy with words. There will always be a time when a sword must be used to protect or defeat. But you can't build a kingdom on death and bones alone. The man who wins a battle without drawing a sword is a man more worthy of respect than he who must flaunt his to be heard."

"You're very wise," Fae said. "Harmatia will benefit from that."

"Just as long as I keep my temper," Jionathan huffed, twirling the pencil in his hand. "Would you walk with me?" He leapt down from the wall. His leg twinged in complaint, but he ignored the dull pain. "The sun is setting, but there's still enough light." He held up his hand and Fae took it, jumping down after him. They set off, arm in arm, up toward the wheat fields, their fingers knotted together. "It's strange," Jionathan said as they walked. "For the first time in so long I feel like I can breathe. I didn't realise how suffocating Harmatia had become."

"You seem in finer spirits," Fae said. "This is a good place. I am glad we chose to rest here."

"The Rossignols surprise me. They're so kind, such good people." Jionathan stopped at the top of the hill, looking down. Below they could see the Rossignol house—the children playing out in the front, Lily-Anne and Michael sat on the bench outside, watching them together. In the orchards, Luca and Rufus were walking, arms around each other, lost in earnest conversation. There was a warmth and love in the air so sweet it was almost tangible.

"This," Jionathan breathed. "This is what I want to create in Harmatia. Not fear. Not silence. This peace. If I could make my kingdom even a shadow of what Sarrin town is, I would be happy."

"You can. You will. I believe that." Several strands of Fae's golden curls had fallen loose from her plait, and blew around her shoulders. Jionathan watched, captivated. Reaching forward, he caught a strand between his fingers.

"I worry the world may be too complicated for such simple ideals," he murmured, tucking the hair behind her ear. "Princess Aurora is safely home. Will you be leaving now?"

"No." She caught his hand and held it against her cheek. It was soft, and cool to the touch. "No," she repeated, and reaching forward she brushed his face with her own fingers, tracing them down. "What reason do I have to leave?"

His relief was overwhelming, and before he knew it, he had taken her by the back of the head and drawn her in. She wrapped her arms wordlessly around his back, and he buried his face into the nape of her neck. She smelt of a long, long-forgotten home. "Fae..."

"I have you," she promised, and Jionathan didn't know if it was he who was crying, or her tears on his face as their lips met for the first time, two entwined figures silhouetted by the sun.

CHAPTER
27

"Where has the sunshine gone? Where has the beauty of spring hidden? Behind the deceiving clouds perhaps? They who have stolen all joy from me and left only a plague in this land..." Mielane put the book down with a scowl as Rufus chuckled. "Stop laughing, you've ruined it," she complained, though her voice was light and her eyes sparkled merrily.

Rufus shrugged, his head resting on her lap and then laughed again as she raised the book to recommence.

"That's it, I'm not reading."

"No, please don't stop! You've nearly finished. I'm sorry, I'll be quiet," he promised.

"No, no, you've killed the entire thing," Mielane said. "Saphar is disgraced."

"Oh, don't say it like that. You know how much I adore the works of Saphar—well, as much as an honest man should." Rufus rolled onto his front and leant up on his elbows.

Mielane shifted, elegantly holding the book in place. "You are hardly an honest man, Rufus Merle," she said. "And I don't see what's so humorous about my reading."

"There is nothing humorous about your reading, I wasn't laughing at you. You're wonderful," Rufus said with as much sincerity as he could muster, and *then laughed again despite himself.*

Mielane gave him a look of mock horror and clutched at her chest like she'd been gravely injured.

"I'm sorry, truly you read wonderfully," Rufus said. "I just marvel at how much passion you put into it, I can't help myself. It's so beautiful that I laugh."

"Well, of course I put passion into it!" Mielane pouted. "I need to. Ciarán's begging for death in this passage, not asking for his laundry to be done."

Rufus pretended to frown. "You're very quick to assume a man cannot be passionate about his laundry."

"Honest men don't fret about their laundry."

"Then I suppose I'm not an honest man, and neither is Ciarán for that matter."

"Ciarán is begging to be joined with his dead lover," Mielane snapped. "And he's my favourite character, so think carefully before you criticise him."

"Naturally your favourite is the dashing Gancanagh."

"Oh, stop it, Rufus. It's just a story, and it's romantic," Mielane cooed.

Rufus rolled his eyes, waving his hand dismissively. "Romantic you say. Pah! That's what Sophia thought! As for Ciarán, he's only mourning her because she failed to do his washing up before inconveniently dropping dead."

"Rufus!" Mielane slapped him with the book, and he cackled.

"Your misconception lies in the fact you believe he's passionate at all. No, men can only be passionate about food, lust, or war—or knowledge in my case. If a woman believes that a man is capable of a passion, such as a romantic like Saphar would write, then she's sorely mistaken. Or indeed, if not, then the passion is akin to that a man gets when his laundry isn't done properly."

Mielane struck him across the shoulder again. "Rufus Merle, you're a terrible person!"

"I'm sorry, my dear. It's a sad truth, but your girlish ideals of romance are quite misguided. Men don't have passion from the heart, only the groin."

"You read it then, as clearly I know nothing of males and their capacity for passion." Mielane thrust the book toward Rufus who sat up and took it, still chuckling. Mielane's face flushed with a mixture of amusement and anger. Rufus looked down the page and, finding the beginning of the passage, cleared his throat.

"Where has the sunshine gone? Where has the beauty of spring hidden? Behind the deceiving clouds perhaps? They who have stolen all joy from me and left only a plague in this land...Ah, cruel fates, did you feel it? A droplet of rain—yes, it is not a tear on my cheeks. I have wept no such thing for a human. It is the heavens who howl, it was the rain. I do not cry.

"Sophia, sweet Sophia my love. The sun may lull over our heads, spilling its warmth, but within me it is dead. My soul has been carved—my existence superseded. Let me die, too. Let me die, for this world is empty without your hand in mine. I cannot breathe, I cannot see—my words are broken at the lips you last kissed. Oh gods, let me die, too. I would rather face death than a life so hollow. I cannot fathom it. Day and night are meaningless. I am lost without you. Sweet Sophia, do not leave me here in emptiness—Oh gods, let me die with you. Good gods of the heavenly world, let me die with you. I cannot be alone now." Rufus finished, his voice stilled as his eyes fell on the final passage where, broken and sobbing, Ciarán cradles Sophia in his arms and is granted his wish. Rufus fingered the page for a moment, almost hoping that on the next there might be a reprise, but he knew it was blank. Finally he looked up.

Mielane watched him, her cheeks wet and red eyes brimming with tears. She gave him a watery smile.

"There. And you said that men couldn't be passionate." Her hands interlocked with his.

~⚬~

"A letter arrived for you this morning," Michael said between mouthfuls.

Rufus lowered his cutlery with interest, and Luca scowled, slapping her father's arm.

"I told you not to tell him until after he'd finished his meal," she said. "Now he's going to—"

Rufus rose from the table eagerly. "That was awfully fast. I'd better go and see."

"I told you!" Luca hissed, as Rufus excused himself.

"It's in the study," Michael called after him, and Rufus let himself into the room at the back of the house. Sure enough, a letter sat waiting for him in the perfect centre of the desk—almost as if Michael had made a great ceremony of placing it there. Rufus reached for it with excitement and fingered the familiar wax seal. It was the depiction of a blackbird in flight, a sprig of leaves in its beak.

He slipped his fingers under the paper and opened the sealed envelope. He tried, as he always did, to do it without breaking the wax seal. Somehow, breaking it always seemed like a terrible omen.

Unfolding the page, Rufus gave a wry smile at his father's careful script. It was almost identical to his own, Torin taking great pains not to be outmatched by his son. In several places however, Rufus could see that his father had rushed, the words slanted and smudged. He read with pleasure.

Rufus-lad,

I cannot begin to tell you how relieved we were to receive your letter. Your mother has been fretting and, needless to say, I have fared no better since you departed. It was of great comfort to know that you and the Prince are safe in Sarrin.

It sounds to me like you've been playing some mighty heroics, my lad. I expect the fine detail when you return, as you have been unreasonably sparse. Regardless, it seems you have made an interesting friend in Fae, and I am glad your relationship with the Prince is improved. Please, take care—something is brewing, and I fear you may be caught up in it. Sarrin may be the eye of the storm, but it is beginning to thunder around you. I fear for all your safety.

Harmatia is ill at ease. The King has not been seen for some days, and the curfew is now an hour earlier than before. It is harder than ever to leave the city. This letter will be arriving with some deliveries, and I suggest you reply in the same way. I have burnt the one you sent.

Stay prudent, but take advantage of your time in Sarrin to rest. I am sure the Rossignols are very glad to have you.

I do not have much time, so I must finish here. Our love to you all, and please Rufus, take your chance now, and go and see Mielane. It is long, long overdue.

Signed your loving and proud parents,
Torin & Nora

Rufus placed the letter down and scanning over the words again, ran his fingers up through his hair.

Go and see Mielane.

He touched the dry ink and then folded the letter quickly, closing his eyes. The nervous, tight knot in his chest bobbed as he swallowed, and he covered his face, resting his chin in his elbow and leaning heavily on the desk. He regretted, in that moment, not sharing the detail of his encounter with the Korrigans more clearly. Had his father known about the freshly opened wound, he might not have made his suggestion. The mere thought of seeing Mielane now made Rufus's stomach turn. He felt vulnerable—weak even, weaker to the temptation of a quick release. Drink, insomnia, emptiness—he'd seen better men fall to that fate, and he wondered, as his hands began to shake, whether he was already slipping.

"Sweet Haylix, when did I become so helpless?" He laughed at himself, at the vanity of his youth. He hadn't thought he could become so hopelessly fixated on a single person, but then he hadn't thought Mielane would leave him. They'd both gone their separate ways in the past, both experimented, both known the touch of another lover—Mielane had been Rufus's greatest councillor in love. And yet, every time she spoke, every time he felt her skin on his own, her smell, her touch, the taste of her when they were together, Rufus couldn't think of anyone else. As sweethearts or simply friends, she was his soul, and the rest of the world paled in comparison.

Perhaps, he reasoned, that was what frightened him—because if he went to see her now, he would still feel the same way. That he belonged with her.

She wouldn't share that sentiment, and Rufus couldn't stand the thought of it. He'd rather have his memories than risk them to say goodbye.

"Rufus?"

Rufus jerked to his feet and looked at Luca, who stood in the doorway, watching him shrewdly, frowning. His heart almost stopped for how much she looked like Mielane in that instant.

"Is everything alright?" Luca asked, her eyes dropping to the letter. "Has something happened to your parents?"

"No. No, no," Rufus said, checking his expression. "They're well. I was simply lost in thought…" He trailed off, the tight feeling in his chest not leaving. It seemed to grow more each day he stayed in Sarrin, and suddenly he wished he could bury himself in the archives in Harmatia again. A thought occurred to him—he'd done no serious research into the dark spell from the Korrigans' nest. Perhaps he could go to the next village and see if there were any books that could aid him. The concept of a project was a relief. "I need to go out."

"You haven't finished your meal," Luca berated, but it was half-hearted. She could already see he'd settled on leaving.

"I'll be back soon, I promise." Rufus made to move past her, but she caught his arm. Her fingers seemed cold against his skin. He wondered how long she'd stood outside the study with her hand on the door handle.

"Drink plenty of water." She didn't meet his eye. "Today will be a hot one."

"Thank you," he kissed her on the side of the head, closing his eyes so he didn't have to see her dark hair. It was soft under his lips, and she leaned in to him. "Luca," he forced himself to say. Then, tearing away from her, he strode down the hallway to the front door.

Luca isn't Mielane, Rufus told himself, *Luca isn't Mielane. But, Athea, she's so much like her.*

CHAPTER 28

Jionathan squinted at the drawing on his knees, twirling his pencil thoughtfully. He was sat on his usual perch on the town wall, where he retreated most afternoons to draw. Fae was always training at this time, and Luca took to her room for an hour or two to 'practise', though Jionathan didn't know what. Rufus usually disappeared into the orchards to steal apples and read, while the children were occupied with their studies. It was a peaceful time of the day and, though alone, Jionathan cherished the brief solitude.

The last week in Sarrin had been a joyful one, and Jionathan had found himself becoming firm friends with his hosts. A few days ago they'd gone on a fishing expedition to the river. Jionathan thought they were looking for dinner, but in fact the young ones brought little glass jars to catch tadpoles, and had spent the afternoon frisking the water with homemade nets. Then they'd gone swimming, though Jionathan himself had abstained from that.

"Is the water too cold for you?" Luca had asked, and Rufus had laughed at Jionathan and explained.

"He doesn't know how to swim."

"I do know how to swim," Jionathan muttered to himself, though in truth he had very little experience. Harmatia was not known for its rivers or lakes, and Jionathan hadn't sought any opportunity to practise his skill. Luca had promised to teach him next time they went to the river and, unable to refuse her, Jionathan had conceded to try. He'd spent the rest of the afternoon watching Rufus and the Rossignols splash about, whilst he and Fae waited like patient adults on the bank. Then, whilst they dried off, the children snoozing in the sun, Luca and Fae took branches from a nearby tree and practised duelling. The exercise, which Jionathan had suspected was supposed to be serious, had turned into a farce when Annabelle awoke and insisted on joining in and making a game of it. Jionathan had found himself playing the role of hero as Rufus pretended to be a great villain, kidnapping the still-slumbering Rowan, Luca his evil lieutenant. Needless to say, the forces of good won over when Rowan, woken by the commotion, started crying, and Fae had pushed Rufus back into the river to make the boy laugh.

"*I am vanquished!*" Rufus had cried dramatically, water dripping down his face.

Jionathan grunted a laugh at the memory.

Hunching over the page, he returned to his drawing, trying to shade it from the glare of the sun. His picture of the dark-haired Bean Nighe stared back at him, her hands submerged in the flowing water that darkened around her. She was a sad figure to be drawing on a sunny day, her face still blank—Jionathan couldn't seem to get her features right.

Giving her hair a few extra strokes, Jionathan suddenly shut the book of dreams with a jolt and sat very straight. He turned and glared over his shoulder to Rufus, who drew back, raising his hands guiltily.

"Sorry." He didn't sound in the least bit apologetic. "You draw remarkably well."

"How long have you been there?" Jionathan demanded.

"Not long," Rufus said. "Your powers of foresight prevented me from having any more than a quick peak. But really, it's nothing to be ashamed of. You have a remarkable talent."

Jionathan narrowed his eyes with suspicion, but Rufus seemed sincere. Pivoting, so that his legs dangled on Rufus's side of the wall, Jionathan faced him.

"Where have you been all morning? You disappeared so suddenly."

"The next village." Rufus gave a dismissive shrug and folded his arms. "I went to see if I could find any books that might help me understand the Korrigans' spell better."

"Any success?"

"No." Rufus hoisted himself up onto the wall beside Jionathan and heaved a sigh. "I think it may well have to wait until I return to Harmatia."

Jionathan hunched his shoulders, and Rufus glanced over to him.

"You've gone grey," he noted, and knocked Jionathan's arm. "Look, don't worry yourself with it. It's not important—no doubt merely the vanity of an over ambitious Magi. There's no great urgency for us to return."

Jionathan hugged the book of dreams tightly to his chest. "Harmatia isn't safe," he muttered into the leather, and Rufus didn't reply. Jionathan sighed. "I'm sorry. You must think me totally mad."

"No."

"Fae thinks I can see it." Jionathan slowly eased his grip around the book. "The future."

"Can you?"

"...I hope not."

Rufus made a small, sympathetic noise in the back of his throat. "I think it's rather beyond hope now, don't you?"

Jionathan groaned. He'd accepted the Sight the moment he'd used it to fight the Red Cap, and yet to speak so openly about it

305

seemed strange. A part of him still wanted to pretend it wasn't real, to pretend that his drawings were conjured from nothing more than the dark corners of his mind. He didn't want admit that there may be truth in the stroke of his pencil, or in the penetrating horror of his dreams. "It began after Sverrin died," he said, in a small voice. "It shouldn't surprise me that this power was triggered by death…It's all I ever see."

Rufus didn't speak, and Jionathan was glad of that as he gathered his thoughts together.

"Colours, to begin with," he said. "I see colours. At first they made no sense, and they were so infrequent that I thought nothing of them. Then…then they started to take hold. The first time, I thought I was poisoned. My whole body…I…" He struggled with his words. "You know. You saw."

"The day you escaped?"

"Yes. When it takes hold, it takes hold of all of me. But I think perhaps that's because I was fighting it." He sighed again. "I always thought of it as something external happening to me—a punishment. Now I think, by ignoring it, I was making everything worse. If I draw it out—the dreams, the things I see…" Jionathan drew off. "I dream terrible things."

"What kind of things?"

He shook his head, and then gave a sharp cry as Rufus snatched his sketch book from his lap. He grabbed for it angrily, but Rufus had the advantage of height. "Give that back!"

"I've watched you scribble secretively in this for several days now," Rufus said. "It's good you are drawing it out. Now share it. I have wide shoulders—I can bear a little weight. Let me look."

"Fine." Jionathan slumped back. It was too hot to argue, and Rufus could always just steal the book in the night.

"Your book of dreams," Rufus said triumphantly, running his hands over the leather cover. "It's really quite heavy."

"My dreams are heavy," Jionathan griped as Rufus began to flick through the pages. He gave a low whistle.

"And dark. I dread to interpret the meaning of some of these." Rufus stopped at the picture of large dragon, which had enveloped itself around an entire city, spitting fire as blood ran from the city walls. He traced the detail of the dragon's breath. "Does drawing them help?"

"Yes." Jionathan watched a group of children chase butterflies in the square below. "One day I'll bind all of my nightmares within this book, and sleep easy."

"I pray that day comes swiftly." Rufus turned to the next page, studying each drawing carefully.

"What do you think?" Jionathan enquired, looking between the pictures and his friend.

"I think that all the misery aside, it's a pity," Rufus murmured. "The creative world lost a true artist to you, Jionat. I had no idea you had such a steady hand."

Jionathan was taken aback. "I can't draw as well as you."

"Gracious, are we complimenting each other now? How the winds have changed." Rufus turned to the next page and grew still. It was Jionathan's latest picture, the sad Bean Nighe washing her bloodied clothing.

The colour drained from Rufus's face. "Is this the one you saw?"

"I can't get her face."

Rufus shut the book. "Probably for the best." He returned it to Jionathan just as a voice called out to the pair of them from the path below.

Luca waved and hurried up to them, her skirts hitched up to her knees. She wasn't wearing any stockings, and Jionathan flushed at the sight of her bare skin. Though he ought not to have been—she'd swum in the nude.

"Boys!" She ran the last few strides and stopped before them, beaming. "Here you both are! What are you doing?"

"Nothing," they replied simultaneously, and Luca looked between them, suspicious of their almost rehearsed synchronicity.

"Are either of you hungry yet? Mother and Father have taken Annabelle and Rowan to the next village to find some new shoes—they grow so fast!—so they won't be back until later. The kitchen is at my mercy."

"I'm well enough for the moment," Rufus said.

Jionathan noticed that once again the Magi seemed uncomfortable, his eyes downcast. He'd caught Rufus with such an expression several times over the week, normally when Rufus thought no one was looking.

"If either of you are hungry, please don't wait on me. Eat. I must write a letter." Rufus jumped down from the wall and, with a brisk farewell, strode purposefully toward the house. Jionathan watched him go. When he turned back to Luca, her face was contorted as if in pain.

"Excuse me, Jionat," she said, before marching after Rufus down the hill.

"What in the name of…?" Jionathan, unable to contain his curiosity, leapt down and followed. A few hundred strides away, Luca disappeared into the bustle of the busy street, and it was only when Jionathan reached the house that he heard her again.

Her voice came fast and low from the study at the end of the entrance hall. Rufus replied, his own voice equally hushed. Moving deftly across the hall, Jionathan drew closer to the doorway. He knew it wasn't right to spy, but his curiosity won over his sense of propriety, and he peeked in through a crack.

"Don't take me for a fool, Rufus—you've been avoiding me all day. You can't even look me in the eye. What have I done to offend you so greatly?"

"Nothing, you've done nothing," Rufus insisted, but his back was to her, and he was running his hands through his hair.

There was an excruciating silence, and Jionathan considered leaving the pair be, but Luca spoke again, her voice broken with a sudden upset.

"It's Mielane, isn't it?"

The name seemed to physically cripple Rufus, and he hunched forward, his fingers squeezed into fists around his hair.

"You still love her," Luca said.

Jionathan could see Rufus's shoulders shaking. He'd figured that something of Mielane's marriage had upset Rufus personally, but he hadn't suspected it might be an issue of jealousy. There was suddenly a great grief about Rufus, cold and hopeless.

"You do," Luca said. "Your silence says it better than words." Her voice broke. "After all this time…it's been three years, Rufus! Why are you still punishing yourself? Why are you still holding onto these feelings, when I'm here now? I love you just as much— love you *more!*"

"Luca, don't."

Jionathan knew he ought to leave them to their conversation, but he couldn't tear himself away from the door. He was frozen to the spot, his surprise shackling him. A great energy had built up in the room, crackling like lightening.

Luca stood tall, her eyes burning with angry determination. "It's true," she insisted. "It's true, and you know it! You can't have her, Rufus—she's gone! She left us and she's not coming back! And it breaks my heart, as much as it does yours, but you have to let her go, for Athea's sake—let her go and be happy."

"How?" Rufus cried. "Every morning—*every morning*, I…I…" He pounded a hand against his chest, choking on his words. "I'm *trying*, Luca."

"Starving yourself? Not sleeping? Quitting magic? Oh—you think that your parents haven't told mine? That we don't know about your self-imposed famine."

"*I know!*" Rufus roared, pacing desperately. "You think that if I could, I wouldn't have ripped it out of my skin—this *feeling*? *I don't want it!*" He covered his eyes, his fingers splayed through his fringe. "I don't want to feel it anymore. I don't want to feel."

Luca caught his arm and drew him sharply in toward her. She clasped his face. "Let me help. Mothering Prospan, Rufus, I'm *here*. I love you. I've *always* loved you, and I can be everything that Mielane was—"

He tore himself away, shaking his head feverishly. "No. No, no, no, no, no. Please, Luca, don't say that."

"It's the truth."

"No. I won't. I won't do it," he whispered fervently, tugging his fringe hard.

"Rufus!"

"I can't, Luca! I *can't*."

Luca pulled him roughly back across, holding him steady. "Say it!" she demanded. "Say it, for the love of Athea."

"I can't love you!"

"*Why?*"

"Please, Luca…" Rufus groaned.

Luca stared at him, her whole body trembling. She hunched forward, and then with an almighty howl, turned and swept her arm across the desk. Papers flew up into the air in a flurry, the ink bottle smashing on the ground, as Michael's quills and pens rolled away across the floor. Slowly the paper settled, and Luca leant heavily against the desk, panting. "Maybe if I was dead… Maybe you'd love me then," she spat.

Rufus straightened. "You're probably right."

"You bastard!" Luca flew up in a rage and struck him around the face. "You bastard!" She hit him again across the chest, driving him back against the wall. "You—"

Rufus caught her wrists, and they struggled against one another until Luca relented, dropping her forehead against his chest, their breathing raw.

"Please," Rufus begged. "Please…" It turned into a whimper, and releasing her arms he slid his hands up over her shoulders and cupped her chin, tilting her head back. He stared into her face, the pair of them now shaking like they'd suffered grave wounds. Something of Rufus's resolve seemed to break, and with a sudden speed he dropped his head and pressed his lips to

Luca's, holding her tightly, his fingers tangled in her hair.

Jionathan knew he had to leave now, leave as quickly as possible—he shouldn't watch this, he had no right to see it. And yet his shoes were like lead, and he could no more leave than he could announce himself. It was as if a great hand was pinning him down, forcing him to watch. As if the truth was so desperate to be known, it had chosen him to be its witness.

Rufus broke the kiss abruptly, eyes wide in horror.

"Rufus." Luca put a hand to his face, but he pulled further away, like he had been scolded. Again, tearfully, Luca said, "Rufus, *please.*"

Rufus shook his head, and Luca allowed her hands to drop. She wrenched herself out of his arms, falling heavily against the desk. Rufus went to aid her, but she fled before he could.

Jionathan stepped back as she flung the door open and ran past him. Her sobs broke the peace of the house as she sprinted up the stairs. Jionathan turned back to the study and almost collided with Rufus.

Rufus stepped back, startled, and they stared at one another in silence, almost as if the other was about to draw a weapon.

Finally, Jionathan spoke, his voice muffled with shock. "What have you done?"

Rufus's eyes widened at the accusation, and then his face hardened with a sudden purpose. He brushed past Jionathan, striding toward the front door.

"Where are you going?" Jionathan called.

"To resolve something," Rufus replied curtly. "I've waited long enough."

CHAPTER 29

By the time Jionathan dared to breach the sanctity of Luca's room, Fae was already comforting her. Luca's head was rested on the Cat Sidhe's lap, and she was sobbing hopelessly. Jionathan wagered that Fae had probably heard the entire confrontation, and from her expression when he entered the room, she was deeply angry.

"Where is he?" she hissed.

"I don't know," Jionathan said, edging into the room. "He left the house. I'm not sure where he's gone."

"Well he had best stay *gone* until I am calmed." Fae bared her teeth. "Heartless Magi!"

"*No.*" Luca cried harder, her shoulders hitching. "No, he's not heartless—he's *never* been heartless. Rufus is *kind*, and loving, and good." She pulled herself upright, and Jionathan fetched a handkerchief from the vanity table, offering it to her. Her eyes were red and swollen from tears. "Please," Luca begged, "don't think wrongly of him. It's my fault. It's all my fault." Her lips parted, and fresh tears streamed from her eyes. "I thought I could help, I thought I could make it better. Distract him…but I'm no match. I'm not clever enough, or beautiful enough. I'm not good enough to be loved by him."

"Enough," Fae said firmly. "You are better than he is, in both soul and mind—purer *and* kinder."

"No, you don't understand." Luca shook her head insistently. "You never saw him in love." She hiccupped. "He's kind, too kind—it's abstract at times, but beneath it all, he's…" She sobbed again. "He's Rufus. *My* Rufus, Mielane's Rufus. Oh, if only you knew my sister, you'd understand. I can never be to Rufus what she was—it's not him I'm unequal to, it's *her*. I'm the person who's not naïve, but never clever. The child who knows more than her enemies, but less than her friends. The daughter who's pretty, but can never be beautiful. The girl who thinks of the witty retorts, but a few seconds too late…Everything I am is an overflow of my sister's greater talents. Of course Rufus could never love me, the plainer of us two."

"You're talking nonsense." Fae's voice rose with agitation. Something of this affair seemed to have struck a very personal chord within her. "If the Magi is so materialistic to compare your worth by your beauty, then I have lost all respect for him."

"It's not that," Luca cried. "That's not why he loves Mielane so fiercely. Oh, if only you could you see her, you would know. You'd understand. When they were together, it was as if all the powers in the world had designed them for each other…"

"The way you're talking…" Jionathan began. He knew the ills that a memory could create, the way time repainted people. "Were they really so close?"

"Close? Jionat, they were *engaged*. They were engaged when she—" Luca cut herself off, and buried her face in the handkerchief with a fresh sob. "Oh Mielane, why…why did you leave us?"

Jionathan and Fae exchanged a look of surprise, but Fae recovered quickly.

"None of that matters. Regardless of what happened, he had no right to treat you that way." Fae grasped Luca's shoulder tightly and shook her. "Despite knowing your feelings, to say he would love you only in death...!"

Luca laughed miserably. "I think he was mocking himself more than me." She rose from the bed, and going to the vanity table, drew out a small portrait from one of the drawers. She passed it silently to Fae, Jionathan peering over to the picture.

"Who is that?" Jionathan frowned. "A portrait of you?"

"No." Luca held her arms tightly over her chest, the handkerchief clutched in her fingers. "That's my sister. That's Mielane."

"But," Fae looked up, "you look so alike."

"The same hair and eyes," Luca agreed. "Even a similar voice to a faded memory. I can't be loved in my own right, so I thought, given time, I could become like her instead. But Rufus doesn't forget. He won't let me take her place, even if it's what I'm willing to do. That's a strange kindness in itself, don't you think?"

Jionathan took the portrait and studied it carefully. Dark brown hair pulled into an elegant knot, eyes piercing and intelligent, the colour of mahogany against a slightly paler face than Luca's. Yes, it was true, the sisters did look alike, but Mielane seemed to take after Lily-Anne in her posture—a more serene figure. Whereas Luca had all of the warm, welcoming qualities of her father—darker-skinned and open-hearted. Something of Mielane's more reserved expression stirred a familiarity in Jionathan. At first, he thought it was because she resembled his mother in some way, and yet the feeling ran deeper than that.

"I've seen her before," he realised.

"Pardon?"

"This woman, Mielane, I've seen her somewhere before." He paused. "Recently, I'm sure of it."

Luca gave a dry, half sob. "That's impossible."

"No, I'm certain." Jionathan began to pace. "It was from a distance, but I have seen her. In the town, perhaps? No, somewhere else...Harmatia?"

Luca's eyes started to water again. "You can't have," she murmured. "You've never visited Sarrin before, and whilst Mielane went to Harmatia several times, she would've surely told us of such an encounter."

Jionathan cursed, rubbing his eyes as he tried to concentrate.

It came to him in a triumphant flash, and his entire stomach constricted. "Oh Athea, no, that can't be right." He groaned. "Luca!" He raced to her side and clasped her hands. "You need to tell me now, where's Mielane? Please, for Rufus's sake, tell me I'm mistaken." His voice trembled. "I've seen something terrible."

~~~

Rufus approached the gates cautiously, his steps short and slow. He could feel his stomach twisting in anguish at the mere sight of them. They were painted a mournful black, vines of roses crawling their way to the top spikes. All along, a low wall was covered in similar ivy and wild flowers. Poppies nodded their heads at him as he passed, a light breeze carrying the scent of lavender from a clump nearby.

Rufus stopped outside, hands shaking. He knew what he'd set out to do, but yet a dark foreboding had come over him, and his stomach and lungs felt so tight now it was difficult to breathe. And so he stood and let his imagination run wild, looking across the wall. In the foliage he saw mocking faces watching him, shapes and memories etched deep into the stonework.

"Are you going to stay out there all day?"

Her voice was faint, but firm, and he looked up. Through the bars of the gate, Mielane stood watching him patiently, her arms folded, as if mimicking his own stubbornness. His mouth went dry, and then he shook his head.

"No," he said. "I am coming in today."

"It's been three years."

"I'm sorry."

She stood back as he reached for the gate. "Are you still angry?" she asked, and he smiled weakly.

"No. No, I was never angry. Not about this." He went to open the gate, but a sudden terror come over him. "What did I do wrong?" he blurted, before he could stop himself. "What did I do to deserve this?"

Mielane withdrew, dropped her eyes to the ground. Rufus stared at her, willing her to reply—to give him an answer, but she didn't say anything. His hand slipped from the gate, his courage waning. He shouldn't have come—he wasn't *ready* for this. He turned to flee, but then Fae's words floated into his mind.

"*That is no life.*"

She was right. This half-existence, this *abstinence* he'd lapsed into, wasn't a life. He'd slowly tried to remove himself from the world, to disappear piece by piece, but he couldn't do that anymore. He couldn't keep treating his misery like it was a punishment he deserved, or else how could he ever expect it to end?

Go and see Mielane, his father had written, and Rufus threw the gates open with such force they shrieked. He stepped into the threshold and stood within the walls. "I'm here now," he announced, and Mielane turned with a pleased smile, and silently led the way up the path, her footfall so light that her feet made no din. She stretched her hand out behind her, almost as if to take Rufus's own and guide him on. He reached forward, but didn't touch her.

"Here we are," She said at last, her white gown catching an invisible breeze and blowing like great lily petals. She sat on an upright stone and faced him. "My darling Rufus," she welcomed, tears in her eyes.

Rufus blinked, and like that, she was gone—nothing but a sweet conjuring of his own imagination.

"My sweet Mielane." He reached forward, kneeling down on the grass and touching the carved headstone, his hollow voice echoing through the empty graveyard. "It's been a long time."

At first, it was only a pain in the stomach, as women sometimes have. It might not have been anything to fret about, if Mielane hadn't been pregnant with their first. To begin with, she'd concealed the discomfort, perhaps more in self-denial than anything else, but by the time Rufus came to bed with her, she could no longer hide it.

"It's like my blood is coming," she whispered, clutching her belly. The bump was only small, but it showed on her petite frame.

Rufus held her tenderly, trying to soothe her taut shoulders. He used his magic to ease the discomfort, and Mielane cried.

"Mother lost her first, and a few between. Our hips are too narrow."

"If the baby comes too soon, then it wasn't right for this world," Rufus said. His mother was a midwife. He knew the number of women who'd lost their babes to the blood within their first months. Mielane didn't take comfort in this and didn't speak to him the rest of the night.

The pain persisted into the next day, and seemed to worsen. Rufus—his worry growing—advised her to see the physician, but Mielane refused. She avoided him all day until he found her hunched over the laundry, her face hidden miserably in the crook of her arm. She apologised for being angry, and he held her tightly, her body trembling against his own.

"Nothing bad will happen to you. I promise." Rufus stroked her hair, sure of that at least.

By that evening, the pain was gone, and Mielane seemed to brighten.

"See, babies do all sorts of horrible things to their mothers. You're lucky you haven't been losing your breakfast every morning," Rufus joked with her, the pair curled in bed together.

"Oh, and are you some expert on the pains of babies now?"

"I've been present at two births," Rufus said. It was a traumatic

317

truth from his childhood, when he'd been forced to stay with his mother as she delivered the babies. "Which is two more than you."

"Does it truly hurt so much?"

Rufus thought back to the two women he'd seen. One had writhed and screamed, and had had to be held down and supplied with copious amounts of whiskey to see her through. The other had been serene and had only grown vocal as the head had pushed through.

"Everything worth doing hurts a little," Rufus said, and Mielane sighed.

"It'll be three births then."

"Pardon?"

"When this one is born. You'll have been to three births."

They slept comfortably that night, her head resting on his shoulder, long eyelashes brushing the tops of her cheeks as she slumbered. Rufus loved her more than anything.

It was Luca's terrified screams on the third day that broke the happy reverie. Rufus and Michael, who were busying themselves in the study, heard the terrible shrieks and bolted to find the source.

They found Mielane at the bottom of the orchard, her pale skirt stained dark with blood. Luca sat beside her, holding her upright, Mielane's face was pressed into her sister's shoulder. Her whole body shuddered with the force of her sobs, the pair crying hysterically.

Michael carried Mielane back up to the house, and Rufus ran for the physician. By the time they returned, Mielane had banished both her father and sister from the room. Never before had Rufus seen her like this, so overcome by grief.

She screamed and shouted at them, told the physician to be on his way and that there was no need for him anymore.

"My baby's dead! My baby's dead!"

When Rufus tried to calm her, she turned her fury on him.

"Don't come near me—this is your fault!" she shrieked into his face, as he recoiled. "You promised me it would be fine! You used magic on me—you, an unqualified healer! You're probably the *reason this child is dead!"*

Rufus stuttered, unable to find his words as Mielane continued to throw her accusations at him. He'd never known her capable of cruelty, but loss and pain sharpened her tongue like nothing else.

"Get out!" She slapped him on the chest, driving him back. "You, with your empty promises—GET OUT! I don't want to see you! I don't ever want to see you!"

Rufus fled the room, and sat outside, listening helplessly as she cried behind the locked door. Her words swam in his mind, repeating themselves over and over in an endless mantra. By the time she stopped sobbing, Rufus's own heart was so full of sadness and anger that, when she called his name, he didn't reply.

"Rufus?" she breathed through the door, her voice frail and broken. "Rufus—I'm sorry. I didn't mean any of it...Rufus?"

His heart ached, the wounds she'd inflicted still too sharp and real for him to ignore. He punished her for her cruelty. He pretended not to hear her.

"Rufus, please...I love you."

He said nothing.

Lily-Anne returned home later that evening to the bad news and was the only one permitted into the room. She remained with Mielane some hours before emerging, pale-faced and stricken. The physician was summoned again, and this time Mielane wasn't able to stifle her moans, clutching her stomach, her breath ragged and quick.

Rufus remained with Luca at that time, his cousin curled in her bed, still shaking from the shock of the afternoon. Annabelle joined them, frightened by the commotion, and Rufus brought Rowan in when the boy woke, and began to cry.

Early the next morning, Michael burst into the room, eyes wide from sleeplessness, and told Rufus to come to Mielane's bedside now.

"Is she asking for me?" Rufus felt sick, his legs weak beneath him, barely able to hold his weight. He didn't think he had the strength to

endure another torrent of curses from Mielane, or worse, another apology. Because even if her words, spat with so much venom, had been nothing but a product of her anguish, Rufus knew there was truth to them. A terrible truth he didn't want to face.

Michael didn't answer him, but took Rufus by the arm and pulled him out of the room, down the stairs.

The Mielane Rufus found was unknown to him. She lay in a tangle of sheets, her breath uneven, eyes unfocused with growing fever and sickness.

The physician looked at him grimly. "This baby has been dead several days already."

The rest, Rufus understood. The dead body inside of Mielane had become a poison, a poison that had long since taken its hold over her blood. She stuttered and groaned incoherent nothings, tossing her head from side to side. Occasionally she would emit a strange wail—hollow and oddly songlike.

As evening drew in, her body convulsed and shook, and no amount of medicines, magic or otherwise, would reduce her fever. Rufus sat by her, watching the nightmare unfold. He spoke to her, but it was too late. If she heard him, she couldn't possibly understand through the haze of her delirium.

He might have cried then. Cried and begged, but he was too tired to be sure. He was aware of others in the room—the physician had abandoned his vigil when the reality became apparent, and the Rossignols took turns in keeping their watch. The house was full of tears and shouting that night, Michael's voice raised so that the very foundations seemed to shake.

By the next morning, Rufus had clambered into the bed beside Mielane, and held her as she trembled, unresponsive and burning hot. She'd wet the bed sometime in the night, and he'd taken great pains to clean her, her legs freshly bloodied.

Rufus must have slept at that time, his head light from dehydration, sleeplessness, and hunger. He couldn't name the exact moment he woke, nor when Mielane finally ceased to move, his hand *still stroking her hair gently. Around him, he heard the Rossignols begin their mourning. Lily-Anne gathered her remaining children to her and cried desperately, whilst Michael begged Rufus to let Mielane go now, tears rolling down his cheeks. Rufus remained with his love.*

"Shh, shh, sweet one. I have you now. All will be well. Look, your fever is finally going down."

Rufus wasn't sure how much time passed, before Torin arrived, appearing in the doorway, dirty and haggard. He'd ridden all night from Harmatia. The sight of his father filled Rufus with a great calm. With Torin there, everything could be resolved. There was no ill that a parent couldn't fix.

"Rufus…" Torin laid his hand gently on Rufus's shoulder.

"It's alright now," Rufus croaked. "I'm just going to lie with her, until she wakes up."

Torin closed his eyes, a flash of pain searing across his face, like he'd been struck. His grip on Rufus's shoulders tightened, and then he began to pull. Rufus's relief turned to panic, and he clung to Mielane as his father fought to pry him away.

"Let her go, Rufus."

"No!"

"Rufus, let her go!"

"NO!" Rufus begged as Torin peeled his hands open and pulled him off the bed. Rufus kicked and screamed, as he was dragged away, Torin's arms tight around Rufus's chest.

"She's gone. She's gone, lad. She's gone," Torin repeated until the words took hold. Rufus's screams died in his throat, and a wave of terrible exhaustion overcame him. His knees buckled, and he sagged, Torin falling back to the floor as Rufus went limp in his arms.

"But I didn't say it back," Rufus breathed, feeling like the slightest pressure would crumble him away into dust. "The last thing she said to me…I love you. She said I love you, and I didn't say it back. I was angry, and I didn't say it back."

CHAPTER 30

～～

Jionathan paced the room, almost chewing through his own lip. Luca watched him, her tears now dry, but her face drawn. The Prince turned on her, perhaps a little viciously.

"Why?" he demanded. "Why did you never speak of her? Why did you never say she was dead?"

"Jionat," Fae said in a warning tone, and he growled and turned furiously to the wall, trying to calm himself.

His anger, he knew, was at his own lack of perception. He should have very well seen the truth—the sadness at the mere mention of Mielane, the quiet absence in the house that was almost forcefully covered up by the Rossignol's cheer. Michael's drinking…Rufus's drinking.

"After Mielane died, my mother became very sick," Luca said. "Rowan was only young and needed her, so we all agreed it was best not to talk about Mielane's passing, only her life. It made everything more bearable."

Jionathan closed his eyes and rested his head against the wall, clenching his fists. "She was with child," he moaned. "Rufus's child…"

"I thought you knew," Luca said. "The careful way you avoided speaking about her, I thought Rufus had told you."

"No, he lied," Jionathan snarled. "He lied, and I believed him."

"Jionat, you can't be angry with yourself—"

"I *am* angry!" Jionathan whirled around. "Three years he suffered this! Three years he spent almost every day at my side! I should have *known*...I should've known." He pinched the bridge of his nose, holding his breath and releasing it slowly.

"But I don't understand." Luca rose to her feet, the handkerchief twisted in her hands. "If you didn't know she was dead, than how did you realise? And what do you mean when you say you saw her? How could you have seen her?"

Jionathan winced. "Sit down, please."

"I will not," Luca snapped. "Tell me. Tell me what you meant."

Fae rose and reached for Luca's arm, but Luca shook her grip away, her eyes ablaze.

Jionathan sighed heavily and surrendered. "A few days ago, I saw something in the forest. I've been dreaming about it since." He drew the book of dreams out and, finding the appropriate page, showed it to them. "A woman on the bank of the river, washing bloodied clothes. She's been haunting me ever since, and now I know why."

"A Bean Nighe?" Fae said.

Luca clasped her hand to her mouth with a gasp and sank back onto the bed. "Oh no, oh no, Mielane, not Mielane..."

"I'm so sorry." Jionathan came and knelt before her. "I'm so, so sorry." The gods knew the last thing he wanted was to bring more sorrow upon this beautiful house.

"We can't tell my parents," Luca said, her eyes watering again. "My mother...oh, my poor mother. It would break her."

"We will keep it between us," Fae agreed, drawing Luca into a comforting embrace.

"Fae..." Luca gripped her tightly. "But how am I to bear this on my own?"

"You're not alone," Fae said.

Luca made a noise that might have been somewhere between a sob and a laugh. She sat up straight again, wiping her eyes. "What about Rufus? How do we tell him? *Should* we tell him?"

"He saw the picture." Jionathan gritted his teeth. "I fear he already knows, or suspects it at least."

"He'll blame himself," Luca said. "He hasn't let go of her yet. He's still haunted by that day—he can't forgive himself."

"Where is he now?" Jionathan rose from his crouch. "I'll go and find him."

Luca still seemed too stunned, her eyes glassy and unfocused. Jionathan found her hand and forced her to look up at him. "Listen to me. I'm truly sorry for your loss," he told her. "I know the singular pain of watching your sibling die, and this news…I can't imagine the burden you're bearing. But you need to concentrate. Rufus can't be allowed to suffer this alone either. He's borne that too long already."

Something in Jionathan's voice seemed to stir Luca, and her eyes sharpened again. She looked at him closely and nodded. "Mielane's grave," she said. "I think he must have gone there. He'll feel guilty for kissing me." Luca reached forward and rested her hand on Jionathan's arm. "It's strange," she said. "They say the King of Harmatia has the voice of authority. I see now it is a trait he passed to his son. It's easy to forget you're a Prince, until you take command."

Jionathan straightened, an odd flush of pride passing through him. He'd never been compared to his father in that way before. "Her grave? Where can I find it?"

"The cemetery. It's down the main road leading south."

"I'll go there now."

"The gods be with you Jionat. When you find him, tell him I'm sorry."

"I'll bring him back." Jionathan turned to gather his things, and then paused. "When he told you he would love you in death, you said he was mocking himself. What did you mean?"

324

"For three years he's loved a dead woman, and it's only caused pain," Luca said. "That's all he thinks he's capable of now. Causing pain."

The words hung in the air, crisp and cold like a terrible promise.

Fae came to Jionathan's side. "Hurry," she said.

The journey, though long enough by foot, was short work for Jionathan on his horse. The bay seemed to sense Jionathan's urgency, for it responded to each kick anxiously, tossing its head. They galloped up the main road, and then drew into a steady canter as the path forked off, heading south. The road seemed to stretch on endlessly, until at last Jionathan spotted an enclosure ahead. He hadn't been sure what the cemetery would look like—his only experience with burial was the tombs in Harmatia where the ashes were placed—but he spotted Rufus's mare tethered outside and slowed to a trot.

The cemetery was an attractive place, by its own right, the walls decorated naturally, with ivy and flowers, and roses framing the wiry black gate. Yet Jionathan found himself oddly frightened by it. He couldn't imagine being buried. What if the soul got trapped inside, and you spent all eternity beneath the earth, rotting away? Better to be burned and let the ashes rest in the cool, open darkness of an airy tomb.

Jumping down from the bay, he tethered his horse beside Moyna, whom he petted as he passed. She, too, seemed nervous, and pulled at her reins. Jionathan left the pair and moved quickly toward the gate.

Slipping in, he followed a faint set of footprints, and found Rufus kneeling beside a grave. There was a great stillness about him that frightened Jionathan. Slowly, he lowered himself to the floor beside the Magi.

"Rufus," he said softly. "Rufus, you've not done anything

foolish, have you?"

For the longest time Rufus didn't respond, and then when he did, his voice was so impossibly small it hardly seemed real. "Luca?"

"She's fine. Fae's with her."

"She told you?"

"Yes." Jionathan sighed. "Why didn't you?"

Rufus's shoulders seemed to dip. "When I told my father I was going to marry Mielane, he asked me why. I said it was because I loved her with all my heart. He told me that couldn't be so—if you love someone to their full capacity already, then you never truly loved them. The Betheanian marriage vow is to love more each day. 'Your heart can't be full, Rufus,' my father said, 'because you will never love her again like you did on your wedding day. By your first anniversary, you will love her twice as much. That's why we celebrate them at all.'" Rufus paused. "I think it's the same even in death. Is that wrong of me to say? She's frozen in time now—but me?" He hesitated. "It's sick really, but I love her more in death than I did in life."

"Is that why you lied?" Jionathan asked, looking up at the gravestone. It was simple, but elegant, Mielane's name carved in its polished, almost glassy surface.

"I'm not sure," Rufus admitted. "I said it before I realised what I was doing."

"You could have trusted me."

"I didn't want your pity."

"To spare your pride?" Jionathan said. "Or because you want to be punished?"

Rufus didn't reply, his expression unusually blank, and slack-jawed. He looked oddly vacant. Despite this, there was a noticeable tension in his arm, and Jionathan saw that Rufus had taken hold of a rock from the ground and was holding it tightly, as if he meant to crush it.

Jionathan took the offending hand and, gripping the wrist

firmly, placed his palm beneath Rufus's curled fingers.

"Let go of it," he ordered. "You are going to hurt yourself. Let go."

Rufus hesitated, and then dropped the stone into Jionathan's hand. It was burning hot, and Jionathan threw it away, examining Rufus's palm. The skin was grazed, and marked, but not cut.

"I thought you might do something stupid," he admitted, and Rufus gave a sudden laugh, shaking his head. Jionathan shuddered at the sound—it didn't feel natural, or happy.

"No, I have a responsibility. What would you do if I were dead?" Rufus gave him a half-smile.

"Rejoice, probably. Free at last to do all the silly things I wish," Jionathan replied lightly, and this time Rufus laughed properly.

"Oh, what a pair we make." He settled back on his hands. "I fleeing the past, and you running from the future. We're thoughtless fools, aren't we?"

"Speak for yourself."

They sat side by side, shoulders lightly touching.

"Three years." Jionathan exhaled. "I remember now, you used to disappear every few months. You would come here, to be with Mielane?"

"Even a Magi is allowed leave."

"And then…I think I remember one day, you didn't return for a long while. I asked why, but they simply told me you had affairs elsewhere."

"I was in no mood to share," Rufus said.

"Does anyone in Harmatia know?"

"My master suspected something. As did Zachary—he's more observant than people like to think. But they knew enough not to question me." Rufus drew his hands up to his neck and pulled out a ring from around a chain. "This was the only evidence."

Jionathan took the ring. It was a delicate piece—gold, with a small pearl in the centre. He realised how small Mielane's hands must have been. "You recognised her in my picture, didn't you?"

"Of the Bean Nighe?"

"Yes."

Rufus reclaimed the ring and replaced it around his neck. He looked back at the grave solemnly. "I knew." He massaged a hand across his chest, as if trying to reach into his heart. "I've felt her presence several times. I…I knew, Jionat. I couldn't let her go. I couldn't lay her memory to rest, so I knew. I knew I'd damned her. The love of my life, and I damned her." He bowed his head, shaking it slightly from side to side. Jionathan could see Rufus's hands quivering. "I knew all along."

"And yet all this time, you bore it alone? Your grief?"

"Oh, sometimes I let it out," Rufus said. "Sometimes I can't help myself. Once, soon after her death, there was a lady—a wife of some Magi or other—who was pregnant with her first. They were gathered in the corridor, and my master was congratulating her. I took one look and began to shake. Arlen dragged me from the room under the guise of some menial task. He saw I was about to make an embarrassment of myself. He brought me to his home and hid with me in one of his rooms until I recovered. I almost told him…" Rufus drew off. "But there were no words. My grief began to manifest itself in my magic—my methods are precise and delicate, but suddenly there was too much emotion. I couldn't control it." Rufus ran his hands up through his hair, pulling his fringe. "It's the extensive use of magic which elongates a Magi's life, so every time I performed it I thought of living two hundred years more without her." His voice rose. "Two hundred years? I could barely sleep, food was like ash in my mouth, each day a task that grew heavier. I was so *furious* with myself. I began to quit magic. I had myself capped and—"

"Capped?" Jionathan interrupted. He'd heard the term before—it was a technique that disabled a person's magic. Usually such a device was reserved for criminals with magical ability, or rogue Magi who'd committed treason. Never before had Jionathan heard of a man asking for such a shackle. "But you can still use magic."

"Caps work by erecting a barrier of sorts within our capacity. My master put mine in deeper, leaving me at a basic level four— the lowest capacity that allows me to be a Magi."

"Is it permanent?"

"Master Odin can remove it at any time, if I ask. Or I could try to remove it myself—though I'd almost certainly die in the process."

Jionathan made a small sound of discomfort. Rufus raised his eyebrows.

"What?"

"I can't speak for you on the matter," Jionathan said, after a moment's consideration. "But repressing your power? From my experience, it only ever made things worse."

"It's a little different to your visions, Jionat."

"How?"

Rufus took Jionathan's hand and turned it over. A red mark had appeared where Jionathan had caught the boiling stone Rufus had held. "It's dangerous," Rufus said.

Silence fell again, and Jionathan curled his fingers into the cool grass, tugging it slightly. "I wish I'd known," he said eventually. "I wish I'd known about all of this in Harmatia."

"Why? Would you have been more sympathetic to me if you had?"

"I might've trusted you sooner." Jionathan spoke into his knees, which he drew up. "Not that loss is the best way to measure a man's integrity. But perhaps I would've been more patient. All I knew is that before Sverrin's death, you became distant with me, and then when he died…"

"I thought you needed a friend."

"It was too late, Rufus. You were gone for a year, and then you re-emerged as if nothing had changed—abbreviating my name, showing no respect, treating me like you always did, even though I was the Crown Prince. I thought you were a *spy*." Jionathan ripped several clumps of grass away, and then let them fall, flexing his fingers. "I thought it was all a desperate farce. How could a Magi be my friend now? Now, when the Delphi Knights had killed my own brother?" A sudden anger burned through Jionathan—fierce and hot. "If I'd known—if I'd *known!*—I might've trusted you sooner! Two years of darkness and loneliness, and I *hated* you because I needed a friend. I needed a friend, and I didn't know that that's what you were…" He exhaled heavily, and shifting forward, spoke to the gravestone. "Forgive me, Mielane. Your fiancé is a hopeless fool, and I even more so."

Rufus chuckled and the pair sat, listening to the crisp birdsong. Something of the dark mood that had blossomed over the cemetery dissipated, like a great sigh of relief.

"She would've liked you," Rufus said. "Mielane. She would've liked Fae, too."

"Luca showed us a portrait. What was she like?"

"Shy sometimes. More reserved, but very intelligent and beautiful. She used to say Luca was like a burning fire, so hot and bright people couldn't help but be drawn in. Mielane was like a river in contrast—peaceful, serene, but powerful beneath the surface. And turbulent sometimes." Rufus brushed his hand over her name on the headstone. "She had two faces, my Mielane— the outward appearance of an innocent, and a wicked humour hidden beneath. She never let me get away with anything. She wasn't afraid to scold me."

"Good, you need someone to put you in your place." Jionathan clapped his shoulder. "Luca thinks she's the plainer of the two."

"Not so." A gloom fell across Rufus again. "And yet I took advantage of their similarities, and her feelings for me. I know she loves me in a way I've never been able to reciprocate, and yet I've raised her hopes like this. I was weak. My behaviour was dishonourable to Mielane, and more so to Luca. I have hurt them beyond forgiveness."

"Oh Notameer, your guilt complex is unfathomable."

Jionathan rolled his eyes. "It wasn't your fault Mielane died."

"Perhaps not, but my actions with Luca?"

"People make mistakes, Rufus. All it would take was an apology, and your guilt would be your retribution. Luca doesn't blame you, so why must you complicate the matter?"

"Because it's my fault."

"This self-flagellation won't change what happened," Jionathan said. "I understand your struggle, I do. Every night for a year I thought of what I could've done to save Sverrin. If only I'd tried harder to discourage him from learning magic, if only I'd been stronger. But I was a child, and he my older brother, and I could no more deny him his wish than Reine could. And thus I came to a conclusion. I can't change the past, but I can shape the future. That's my gift, isn't it?" He rose to his feet and offered Rufus his hand. "As I see it, the world owes us something for this loss, and if we wait, we'll see that debt repaid. You asked me what I would do without you. Well, I would suffer your loss as hard as Sverrin's. So I'll be damned, Rufus Merle, if you dare abandon me for the easy road of death now. You found me in that forest, and in Sarrin town I have found you. Now take my hand, you coward." He seized Rufus's fingers. "Fae and Luca are waiting for us."

⁓⁕⁓

"Is it complete?" Morrigan sat back in her dark throne, and observed her priestesses as they gathered around her like seafoam. The High Priestess, a nameless white figure, came forward and laid the scroll at her feet. The Priestess stepped away, and the goddess took the scroll and looked over the spell.

"Why did you let him go?" she asked, as she examined the work.

"He was not ready for your purpose," the High Priestess replied, and Morrigan knew that beneath that truth was a cleverly concealed plot. It didn't matter. For all their eternity, the Korrigans had learnt the same patience as she, and if they deemed her Magi not to be ready, she could wait a little longer to see the future unfurl.

"Send word to Harmatia," Morrigan ordered. "Tell them their spell is ready. But be sure to keep it from the ears of the dead." She curled the spell up and passed it back. "Even voiceless, they spread word quicker than breath."

Standing, she descended amongst her own as they crowded adoringly around her. She glanced up to the shattered ceiling, moonlight pouring through. "Give him light," she said, finding pity. "May they never say I damned a Delphi to the absence of that."

CHAPTER
31

～～

"Bandits?" Zachary flopped back against his seat with a grunt. "Well this has to be the high point of my day."

Belphegore looked up from his desk, where he was filing through his paperwork. "They were spotted around Corhlam, moving back into the Myrithian forest. My informants tell me there were Alchemists among them."

"Corhlam? Then Anaes's Fortress can deal with it—it's their territory."

The borders of Harmatia had long been guarded by a string of fortresses, which framed the kingdom. In the days of war, the fortresses were connected by walls, or encampments, but now most of them had become the glorified watchtowers and castles of the wealthy. Their meagre responsibilities meant that they still protected the border from potential threat, but with treaties between Kathra and Bethean, most of the lords and ladies had become lax in their guard.

"And that is precisely why I am sending you." Belphegore eyed Zachary, who grunted and let his head drop back against the chair, jogging his leg up and down petulantly. "I admit, it does not usually fall under our jurisdiction, but the force was a large one, and the presence of Alchemists requires certain safety measures."

"If they were going into the forest, then they were moving toward Bethean."

"Which is where the Prince is," Belphegore said. "My informant says that the bandits captured him in the forest."

"Your informant says a great deal."

Belphegore ignored him. "I need to know if there is any truth to the matter."

"So you want me to dredge the forest for bandits in case they have the Delphi brat?"

"If they had him, I do not think they do so anymore." Belphegore shook his head. "In fact, I am almost certain he escaped. The miraculous return of Princess Aurora, at the same time as our Prince's disappearance? I am not so foolish to think these coincidences. Jionathan had a hand in that."

Zachary watched his master carefully, and the truth dawned on him. "You're not worried about the Delphi—you want me to look for Merle," he realised. "You think something may have happened to him, with those bandits."

"It worries me," Belphegore admitted, and Zachary laughed.

"Merle will be fine."

"There was a time, Arlen, when you would have never left any of your men's fate to such chance."

"Merle's not one of my men," Zachary said, curtly.

"No, but he is your brother."

"And your apprentice. And yet you have no faith in him." Zachary stood. "I'll go and see what I can find, if that's what you want. There are other matters I must attend to in the forest either way. May I take Hathely and Fold with me?"

"They are your men to command."

"Then, if you'll excuse us all our daily duties…" Zachary bowed with a discourteous swagger, and went for the door. He stopped as he reached it, glancing out of the nearby window.

"And what should I do if I come upon them? The Delphi and Merle, that is?"

"Leave them, for now," Belphegore said. "Unless—"

"Unless they're crossing into Avalon. Yes, yes, I recall." Zachary stared out into the courtyard below. It was rapidly darkening outside, and he could see the windows of the prayer room opposite were bright all with candle-light. Many people had been leaving offerings to the gods as the King grew weaker. Zachary had seen him only once since Rufus had left, and the man had been grey and unable to stand. "It won't be long now." He breathed on the window pane so that it obscured the sad image. "We will need the Delphi close."

This time, when the colours came, Jionathan didn't fight them. He dropped to the ground behind the town wall, trying to submit to his power's will, even as a terrible fear washed over him and he struggled to breathe.

He tried to remind himself that it was nothing but a vision, even as the cold began to creep along his body, explosions of colour and light stunning his aching eyes. He felt his body convulsing, the dirt clinging to the fine gleam of sweat that covered him. At first Jionathan tried to grip his sense of consciousness, but the feeling only grew, a heavy weight on his chest that made him heave and gasp. He threw his head from side to side, whimpering. It was coming now, he knew—the worst was about to strike. He bucked as a shock of energy passed through him like lightning, and suddenly he was no longer on the hillside in Sarrin town.

The figure loomed over him, expression torn with a mixture of fear and determination, eyes alight with a strange power. Jionathan saw the dagger as the boy above him held it over his heart. He was going to stab Jionathan, and yet when Jionathan tried to move, he found his body locked in place. His muscles wouldn't obey him. Not even his fingers twitched. And so Jionathan was forced to watch, his gaze frozen up at his assassin. His heart thumped, hard and heavy inside his chest.

"Do it," a familiar voice said.

Jionathan's very soul erupted into shivers. He felt like his body were a casket, and he was trapped inside.

"Go on, Joshua. Don't be frightened. Isn't this what you were born for—what you trained for?"

The boy didn't move, uncertainty in his blue eyes. The voice grew, stronger, more determined as Jionathan tried to beg with his eyes, unable to even blink or look away.

"Go on, do it Joshua. Your men are fighting—your brother is fighting! Isn't this the only way to end it—by killing him? Kill the King, and the fighting ends. Kill Jionathan, and the throne is yours."

The boy shifted, and his blue eyes hardened, tearing themselves away from Jionathan's face—like he couldn't bear to look at him. He drew the dagger higher.

"So tragic," the voice crooned. "To be so young, and already a cold-blooded murderer."

"This isn't murder," the boy said. "This is mercy."

And then he stabbed down.

Jionathan screamed, his spine arching up as pain bolted through him. Almost as soon as it came, it was gone, and he crumpled, lying panting on the grass. He trembled, still blinded by the whirling colours, and waited for the vision to dissipate.

When at last it did, Jionathan lay in silence, watching the clouds pass lazily above him. Slowly he moved a hand up and wiped his face. His cheeks were wet with tears and sweat.

"So if I return to Harmatia, I will become King," he told the sky, his voice hoarse. "And die, paralysed by some curse or poison."

A cold fear settled over him. He couldn't see how to avoid his fate. The vision had only shown him his death, not the circumstances around it. He knew only one thing, one fine detail—the name of his assassin.

He was going to be killed by a blue-eyed boy named Joshua.

~~~

It is time to come home.

The message had come a few days ago, slipped into her hand whilst she walked in the town. Fae had done her best to ignore it, tucking it away in the belief that she had a little more time before they would know she'd received it. And even then, the note was in no way a command. If Reilly wished her back, he would have sent her orders, and her father's signature would decorate the bottom of the page.

As it was, those were the only words written: *It is time to come home.* Fae thought it was a little late for such an invitation. In the Rossignol house she was happy, despite its hidden turmoil. She liked being a friend to Luca, and she liked being close to Jionathan. Perish the thought, but she'd even enjoyed Rufus's company, when the four of them descended into the orchards and talked as the stars appeared. It seemed so long since she'd known such peace, such a spontaneous sense of joy when Luca woke her in the mornings, or Jionathan caught her hand as they walked. She missed her brothers, but Rowan and Annabelle were such a delight that the ache was tolerable. And yet the message lay heavily on her, like a form of guilt. *It is time to come home.*

Fae stood outside the door uncertainly, her hand raised, poised to knock. Inside she could hear Jionathan's gentle breath, long and deep in slumber. His heart beat steadily, and if Fae concentrated, she could make out the sound of his hair brushing against the pillow as he shifted in sleep.

Fae pulled away and dropped her hand. She didn't want to disturb him, even though she was worried. He'd disappeared the night before, whilst Rufus had been out enjoying the company of some young man, and Luca had been helping her mother bathe Annabelle and Rowan. When the Prince had returned, he'd been pale and clammy, and had retired to bed before supper. Though he hadn't said anything, Fae suspected Jionathan had had a vision.

Turning from the door, Fae made her way quietly down the stairs. Most of the house was still abed, but in the washroom she could hear splashing water, and knew that Rufus was also awake.

She turned left at the bottom of the stairs, into the right side of the house. Passing the master bedroom, she went to the furthest door on the left and knocked. There was no response, and so she knocked again, more insistently. She heard Rufus pause.

"Yes?" He sounded tired.

"It's Fae. May I come in?"

"Yes."

Fae slipped into the washroom. Shutting the door behind her, she turned and froze in horror.

Rufus shrugged. "I never said you'd approve of what you found." He raised his arms, only emphasising his nakedness. He had stepped out of the bath, water gleaming on his body, his towel still neatly folded on the chair nearby.

Fae flushed with rage. "Most people give permission with that in mind!"

Rufus winced. "The door is behind you, if it offends you *that* much."

Fae turned her back on him, folding her arms tightly. Rufus sighed.

"There's no need to turn away—it's not as if I am doing anything indecent. And you've already seen me naked."

It was true. A fishing trip to the river had ended with Rufus and the Rossignols all stripping off their clothes to swim. Fae had greater restraint.

"It is a matter of common decency."

"I'm in a washroom, what did you expect? There," he added. "I'm back in now. Does that help?"

She looked back to find that Rufus had climbed down into the bath. It was a small but deep tiled alcove, in the base of the floor. Fae imagined that to fill the whole thing with warm water was quite a task, but Luca had demonstrated that with a base use of elemental magic it was no chore. Fae hadn't even realised Luca could also use elemental magic until that moment, and had been rather surprised.

"*Hard not to learn, when you've got that one prancing around,*" Luca had laughed, nodding toward Rufus. "*Though I'm rather bad at it, truth be told. Can't do anything complex—I mostly use it for house-hold chores!*"

In the bath, the water steamed heavily, and Fae felt the temperature of the room rise. Rufus didn't seem to notice the water boiling around him.

"Would you care to join me? There's room for another," he asked, as the silence went on.

Fae drew herself up to her full height, her fingers tightening around the skirt of her dress.

Rufus sank down into the water sheepishly. "I jest."

"Something of drink seems to make you lose control of your tongue." Fae looked up at the slanted ceiling above her, spotting a shuttered window above.

"Who said I've been drinking?"

"You haven't?" Fae followed the rope, which ran down from the window to the far wall. "Well then." She took a hold of it and gave it a sharp tug.

The shutters flew open with a clatter, sunlight pouring into the dark room. Rufus cried out and fell back into the bath, cowering into the corner with his hands over his face.

"Please," he whimpered, "for the love of Athea, close that thing."

"I have no love for Athea," Fae said. "So no."

"Yes, I drank. I had a drink. I had a drink last night. Or two. Maybe three. A few dozen. I lost count—please! Please, my head is reeling. *Please,*" Rufus begged, and Fae released the rope, the shutters closing with another clatter. Rufus sagged down into the water, the surface of the bath rippling around his body as he shook.

"I have no sympathy for you. You brought it upon yourself." Fae folded her arms again. "If you ate a quarter of what you drank, and only drank double of what you currently eat, you could be healthy person."

Rufus scowled. "What, did my father send you? My health is none of your concern."

"True," Fae agreed, and she found the rope again in the dark and tugged the shutters open. Rufus tumbled back, slipping and dropping under the water. He came up, spluttering and coughing, and retreated to the furthest corner again.

"Oh gods, mercy woman, mercy," he heaved, and Fae considered him before releasing the rope again.

"I am not here to berate how you choose to live," she told him firmly. "I know what you have suffered, and if this is how your grief is expressed, then what right do I have to comment on it? Even so, my words are not without merit."

Rufus peered out from where he'd buried himself beneath his arms, and crept forward, his eyes narrowed, as if waiting for her to open the shutters again. "It's gotten better," he said. "It has. I'm trying every day, but it isn't like climbing a staircase. It's a mountain. Sometimes the path goes down, before it rises again."

Fae's mouth twitched, but she held back her smile. "Very lyrical," she said. "I will leave the subject there then, but perhaps you should try to rely on your family and friends a little more, Rufus. It will make the climb easier."

He nodded his head, but said nothing. Fae didn't know if he would ever take her advice, but she had given it anyway, and that's all she could be expected to do. Besides, this wasn't why she'd come down to speak to him.

"Last night," she said, "Jionat disappeared quite suddenly from the house."

"Disappeared?"

340

"For an hour, or so, while you away."

"He does that," Rufus dismissed, expressionless. "No need to be upset. It's nothing personal if he suddenly quits your company."

Fae had half a mind to open the shutters, if not simply for Rufus's unspoken implication. She reminded herself to be patient. "I wasn't upset. I was concerned. When he returned, he seemed troubled. I was hoping he might have said something to you last night."

Rufus shook his head. "I'm sorry, I got in very late. He was already asleep."

"Very well then." Fae motioned to go. "I will leave you to it."

"Wait." Rufus rose quickly, water streaming down his long body. He stepped out of the bath, and stood over Fae, his eyes searching her face. Fae was struck by how tall he was in the stout room. "You care about him," he murmured. "You really care."

Fae frowned, pushing herself back against the wall. "Yes," she whispered. Something about their proximity in the dark room required a kind of secrecy.

"Why?"

"I don't know. He's special."

Rufus gave her a soft smile, the almost childish beauty of his face broken by the stubble of dark, unshaven hair. Fae stared up at him, confusion rising through the pit of her stomach. She couldn't translate the strange look in his eyes.

"Why do *you* care about him?" she asked. "He seems to lead you into trouble at every chance."

Rufus's smile elongated, and he laughed breathily. "I ask myself the same question sometimes," he said. "No, Jionat is… He's good. Good hearted. Kind. Just. People like me, we seek out people like him."

Fae narrowed her eyes. "And what kind of person are you?"

"Nobody of importance."

For some reason this comment irritated Fae. "Ah, the innocent act of the lowly lord," she growled. "If you keep disguising yourself, Rufus, people will stop trusting you."

Rufus's eyebrows arched in surprise. "Disguising myself?"

Steam curled from his body, the unnatural heat of his skin drying him slowly. To the naked eye, this was the only peculiarity, but Fae could see beneath it. She could see the flow of magic, her senses built to look through glamour.

Power curled around Rufus's body, licking up and down his frail skin like flames. He wore it like a coat of armour, invisible to everyone around him, but Fae.

"You told us your magic, your skill with fire was inconsequential," Fae said. "I didn't argue then, because I didn't know you, but don't you think it's about time you stopped lying?"

Rufus eyes widened, and in that moment there was a great pulse in the magic around him. Fae's heart skipped a beat.

It had only been for a second, but the jolt of power had been close to blinding. Sweat prickled on her forehead. Almost instantly, the magic returned to its usual flow, but she could see now that it wasn't because that was its base level. No, something had pulled it back. Something was tethering it to Rufus, holding it down. Restraining it.

A cold, sick feeling rushed over Fae. This was beyond her. Beyond what she'd imagined. Beyond what she was trained to handle. All of that power bound up inside, thrashing to get out, and all Rufus had to do was lax his grip.

What kind of person are you? Her question hung in the air, unanswered, and Fae realised she had no idea what Rufus was capable of. She had no idea who he was.

"If you're asking now," Rufus said, "does that mean you finally trust me?"

"No," she snapped before she thought, still pressed against the wall.

Rufus nodded, his eyes downcast. Leaning over to a chair on the side, he picked up his clothes, his back ripping as he pulled his chemise over his head. "Then I don't have an answer for you," he said. "I'm sorry."

He dressed quickly, and left the room, leaving Fae behind.

In the darkness Fae quivered, filled with uncertainty. All at once, she could hear the words her brother Korrick had whispered into her ear a child, describing the explicit way men skinned her kind and wore their fur like a prize. She clutched her hands and brought them to her lips, wishing she'd been more guarded.

What was she doing here? Here in this bathroom, confronting a Magi like he was her friend, for the sake of a Prince she'd barely known a few weeks? Suddenly, the Rossignol house seemed alien to her, and Fae looked around with a strange, sad clarity.

It is time to come home.

Decided, she followed Rufus out and returned to her room, trying to ignore her heavy heart.

CHAPTER
32

"One apple!" Annabelle begged and Rufus raised his hands defensively, his back to the wall. Beside his sister, Rowan piped up with a similar chant, eyes gleaming. "One apple! Please, Uncle Rufus!"

"Etheus blind me—please tell me they're not begging you for apples," a voice called from behind him. Rufus turned to see Jionathan slouched in the doorway. His eyes were rimmed with dark lines, but his smile was sincere. "You've contaminated them with your obsession."

"Jionat!" Annabelle flung herself fearlessly at Jionathan and hugged his waist.

Jionathan petted her head, quite used to this behaviour by now.

"Jionat, tell Rufus to do the apple trick! Please!"

Jionathan tiled his head. "Apple trick?"

"Deconstruction," Rufus said. "It's a level five technique which allows you to break the bonds holding an object together—sometimes quite explosively."

"I recall." Jionathan peeled Annabelle off of him. "What does that have to do with apples?"

"In my younger days I was able to use a primal version of deconstruction to make apples...well, explode." Rufus laughed at Jionathan's look of incredulity, and added, "In my defence, the first time was entirely in self-preservation. I was protecting myself from a rotten projectile—I did it purely on instinct."

"A rotten projectile?" Jionathan's lips curled slightly. "Someone was throwing old fruit at you?"

"Not me—my father. And it was Michael. A drunken joke. Unfortunately, drunken was the operative word—he missed my father entirely," Rufus said. "Needless to say, having proven myself with soft, rotting fruit, the children of the town took to pelting me with slightly trickier things. The last thing was a pumpkin, I believe..." Rufus drew off dreamily, recalling the event in fine detail. "That was a very messy disaster. The village parents checked their troublesome children after that, and I've since been left in peace."

"Until now," Annabelle interrupted. "One apple! Please, Rowan hasn't seen it!"

Rufus sighed, and Jionathan frowned. "You can't, can you?" he realised. "Because of the cap?"

"A man must prioritise." Rufus gave him a strained smile. "I'm sorry, Annabelle, Rowan. Not today. Maybe...maybe next time."

Annabelle pouted grumpily. Before she was given the chance to complain however, Lily-Anne leant out of the window with a scowl. "Annabelle Nora Rossignol. I have just found your work book, and your studies are far from complete. Come inside now!"

Annabelle whined, but stomped into the house, Rowan following her like a faithful duckling. Jionathan came and joined Rufus out in the garden, the pair walking instinctively down into the orchard.

"Have you seen Fae today?" Jionathan asked as they walked. "She's usually one of the first to rise—along with you."

"Hm, yes. She came to speak to me this morning—or rather to torture me."

"Torture?"

Rufus quickly recounted the events in the washroom, with certain adaptations for Jionathan's sake. The Prince didn't need to know he'd been the topic of their conversation.

Jionathan laughed a little too long at the story, and Rufus rolled his eyes. "It's not funny, I was in agony." Jionathan only laughed harder, and Rufus's face softened.

Jionathan noticed him looking. "What?"

"It's good to see you laugh." They reached the wall at the edge of the garden and leant on it, looking out into the distant fields. "Last night, you disappeared very suddenly. Where did you go?"

"To the town wall, at the top of the hill," Jionathan said, but Rufus heard a slight hesitation in his voice. "I didn't realise anyone noticed I was gone."

"Fae did. She said you seemed out of sorts when you returned."

Jionathan shook his head, and rubbed his eyes tiredly. They were bloodshot and a little sunken. "I had to think," he said, almost defensively. "I wasn't feeling well...But I'm fine now."

"Jionat," Rufus said, "I'm not a child. And not so fragile either. The other day, with Mielane...I stumbled, I'll admit. But don't think that that means you can't unburden yourself with me again. If there's something troubling you, I'm strong enough to hear it."

Jionathan chewed over these words. "I'll remember that."

They watched a pair of birds take off from a nearby tree and dance through the air, twirling and soaring away over the hills. Jionathan rubbed his eyes again, pinching the bridge of his nose.

"Well," Rufus broke the peace, sensing a gloom, "if it cheers you in any way, I think I've thoroughly ruined any chance I had of starting a wild romance with Fae."

Jionathan snorted. "It's fortunate, then, that you held no such ambition."

"I should've liked to be friends though," Rufus sighed. "However, she shouldn't have confronted me whilst I was crapulous. I'm a merry enough drunk, but put me down with the Betheanian malady, and you'd better have woken up in bed with me."

"Rufus, I would rather not hear it," Jionathan bit, still rubbing his eyes, now a little aggressively. "Why would it cheer me, anyway?"

"Because in contrast, she truly cares for you. But then," Rufus cooed, "you must've already suspected something of the sort, seeing as she let you kiss her."

Jionathan went rigid. "How did you know about that?"

Rufus laughed, the sound growing from the pit of his stomach.

Jionathan opened and closed his mouth in dismay, and then gave a long growl. "You didn't know."

"No, but I thank you for the confirmation."

"You...you—I will end you!"

Jionathan struck his shoulder, and Rufus yelped, cowering dramatically. Jionathan folded his arms with a snarl, and Rufus sniggered.

"You had no right!"

"Come now, there's no reason to be put out. It's a perfectly natural thing. The pair of you have a strong affiliation for one another."

"No, you don't understand." Jionathan turned away, his hands over his eyes, fingers balled into fists. Rufus immediately stopped laughing. Jionathan's voice was high and tight. "It makes no sense. Within me I feel...I feel a great affection for her, for all we've been through. And yet the wonderment, the sense of adoration I felt when I first saw her...those are the feelings of another man. They're not mine—how can they be? I've only known her for a few weeks, but this affection is years old. I—I love her, but it's not me who loves her." Jionathan leant heavily on the wall, pressing his palms into the sockets, teeth gritted. "Athea, damn it," he growled.

"Jionat?"

"Damn it—they're back."

"Who is?"

"The colours."

"Colours?" Rufus frowned, and Jionathan groaned, covering his whole face.

"Not now," he pleaded, and sat down at the base of the wall, hunching around himself.

Rufus squatted anxiously beside him "A vision?" Rufus reached for him instinctively, steadying Jionathan as he swayed.

Jionathan nodded, kneading his palms desperately into his eye sockets, his breathing laboured. He gave a low moan and dropped his head back against the wall. Rufus leant across and cushioned Jionathan's skull in his palm looking anxiously around to make sure no one else could see them.

Jionathan twitched and shook, his hands falling so that his eyes could stare vacantly forward, bloodshot and unseeing. They darted this way and that, as if following an invisible battle, and all the colour drained from his face. He looked as if he'd just spotted a giant wolf lolling up toward the house, and Rufus's stomach knotted.

"Jionat?" he called gently. "What is it? What do you see?" Jionathan didn't respond. He'd stopped breathing, his face twisted in abject horror. Rufus's stomach plummeted.

"Jionat, what do you see?" he repeated with more urgency.

All at once, as if released from a stranglehold, Jionathan jolted forward, grabbing Rufus by the collar and gasping for air.

"Bandits," he choked. "Bandits in the town. They're here for Fae. Rufus, they're going to kill us all!"

∽≈∾

Rufus skidded down the road with Michael close on his heel, breaking into the town square.

"I'll get the guard," Michael said. "You find my Luca-girl!"

"Yes," Rufus agreed, and they charged off into opposite directions. "Luca!" Rufus pushed through the bubbling crowd.

"Luca! Where are you? Luca!"

"Rufus?" her voice responded, and he spun on the spot and saw her darting up the road, her skirts hitched up. "What is it?"

He swept her up into his arms in relief. "Thank the gods you're safe." He pressed his lips to her forehead and settled her down, dropping his voice. It wouldn't do to cause a panic now—Michael would see the town evacuated safely. A stampede would do no good. "Quick. You have to get to safety."

"What? Why?" Luca stammered.

"Bandits," Rufus hissed. "An army of them, They're approaching the town. We have to clear it."

"Bandits?" Luca's eyes widened, and she looked all around her, before leaning in. "How do you know? Are you sure?"

"Jionat saw them." Rufus took her by the arm and began to pull her away. "Hurry, I have to get you away—"

"Me? What about my family? And Jionat, and Fae?"

"Your family's safe. Uncle Michael's gone to warn the guard and begin the evacuation. I don't know about Fae, but Jionat's gone to look for her in the orchards. Now come on."

"And what about these people?"

"Uncle Michael will evacuate them!"

"Aren't you being a little optimistic about the time we have?" Luca drew herself away from Rufus and leapt up onto the fountain ledge, standing above the crowd. "People of Sarrin town!"

"Luca!" Rufus tried to draw her down, but she kicked him, standing firm.

"Please, listen to me! You're all in grave danger," she said firmly, her voice carrying over the square. Some people nearest turned around to listen, but most ignored her, content in their merriment. Luca spoke louder. "Please, if you'd just listen to me—this is important!" A few more glanced her way, but many still did not listen.

"Luca, leave it. Uncle Michael will evacuate them!" Rufus tugged at her arm, but Luca drew in a deep breath and, sticking both fingers in her mouth, gave a shrill, deafening whistle.

"I said listen to me, you merry-drunken rats—I am speaking to you!"

This time the chatter died down instantly, and the entire town turned to her, faces stunned.

"I am Luca Rossignol. You all know me well, and by Prospan's lactating teats, you're going listen to me like my word is gold! An army of bandits has been seen approaching our town—do not panic!" she added as a woman close by dropped her basket of wares with a cry of terror. "Right now, my father has gone to fetch the guard and begin the evacuation. Everything will be fine as long as you do precisely as I say, do you understand?" Her voice rang in the silence, and Rufus watched her with wonder. "Good!" she barked. "Leave your wares—they are not as important as your lives. Those who can, gather weapons and arm yourselves. Everybody gather at the town hall. Go quickly and remain calm. Waste no time on packing material possessions."

Even as she finished, people began to speak, some amongst themselves, some calling up to Luca. Terror rippled through the crowd. Luca shushed them with a wave of her hands.

"We don't have time to debate. Gather your loved ones, and do as I say. Now!"

The finality in her voice reminded Rufus of Michael, and he watched proudly as the townspeople responded, moving swiftly and working together. Rufus helped Luca down just as Michael came running up to them.

"Luca-lass, you're a dream. Hurry and get everyone up to the hall—we're compromised."

"The guard?"

"Those on patrol are dead." Michael shook his head. "The bandits must've sent scouts ahead. They're in the town. Keep watch." He moved back into the crowd. "Those who can fight, come with me!" he ordered, and a cheer passed through the people, men and women stepping forward with swords and spears.

"Luca, we need to get everyone else to safety," Rufus said. "You know the people better than anyone—"

"Rufus!" Luca gasped, grabbing at his shoulder. Rufus turned his head in time to see someone rapidly moving toward him from the crowd. He saw the glint of sword and his stomach plummeted. He whirled around, raising his hands, his mind going blank—

And then something shot past his head so quickly, Rufus almost lost his footing. He jumped.

The bandit named Jak stopped dead in his advance and stood, mouth agape beneath his broken nose. An arrow had lodged itself deep his chest, almost to the fletching. He stumbled back, blinking stupidly. His sword slipped from his hand, and he toppled to the ground.

"Lowly lord!" Fae's voice rang out. "Unless you wish to die, I suggest you move."

Rufus looked back to see Fae balanced on the head of the fountain above them. She was dressed for battle in her leather armour and had her usual arsenal. She nocked another arrow just as screams began to pierce the air.

"They're here! They're here!"

Fae leapt down from the fountain and landed a few feet in front of them. Another bandit moved out of the crowd, drawing his own weapon. Fae shot him, almost without looking, her bow snapping taut as she released the arrow. Luca gave a short scream.

"Swallow your good nature." Fae jabbed a finger at her. "These men are murderers and worse. Do not mourn their deaths."

Luca nodded shakily, stammering an apology. Rufus was faring little better, his breath short and uneven. He'd seen men die in his time, but never at such an intimate proximity.

"Those were the scouts," Fae said to Rufus. "The others are following close behind."

"My father and his men aren't ready," Luca said.

"I will buy them time. Hurry." Fae turned and ran toward the entrance of the town, where a dark mass of people were moving in from the woods—an entire army of bandits.

Rufus pushed Luca up toward the town hall. "Find Jionat. Tell him Fae's here and to stay away!"

"What about you?"

"Go, I'll be fine! Go!" he urged.

She kissed him firmly on the cheek and ran off with the fleeing crowd. Rufus watched her, looking out over the townspeople who still lingered.

"Hurry," he cried. "To the town hall, quick!" He sprinted after Fae, who was now speeding toward the invading bandits. "Fae!" he called, vaulting over the town wall. "Fae—stop! FAE!"

But she only moved faster, replacing her bow with her curved blades. With a ferocious battle cry, she leapt inhumanly high into the air, and descended upon the bandits, spinning. Rufus winced at the sickening sound of tearing flesh as shrieks of pain rose into the air. Fae tore through the ranks, the bandits turning in on themselves. Their advance halted.

"She's cornered herself on purpose," Rufus murmured, transfixed.

From within the mass of bodies, Fae roared, spinning and twisting at a dangerous speed. She could have been dancing, her movements were so graceful—yet despite this display, every strike hit its mark, huge arcs of blood spraying in the air. If she didn't tire, Rufus imagined with time, she could effortlessly cut through each man. There was no comparison in speed or skill.

"You're astounding," Rufus whispered.

"Yes, she is," an unfriendly voice agreed beside him.

Rufus threw himself back just as a sword swung dangerously close to his head, catching the tip of his fringe.

Bruatar cursed. "You're a quick one yourself, milord."

Rufus landed hard on his backside and scrabbled away. Bruatar smirked at him from where he sat astride his horse.

"No matter," the bandit said. Tucking away his sword, he drew a crossbow from his back, and pointed it—loaded—at Rufus's chest. "It's good to see you again. I came for the Sidhe, but if you're here, then so must the Delphi Prince be, and he is a much greater bounty."

"Bruatar," Rufus hissed, and the bandit's yellow eyes gleamed.

"You remembered my name?" He touched his chest. "I'm flattered. Ah-ah!" He warned as Rufus began to draw magic into him, ready to fight. "Look closer."

Rufus froze. He could sense it now. There was an invisible force surrounding the bandit. A magical shield—there must've been an alchemist in the vicinity, protecting Bruatar. Rufus realised with a sick twist that his magic was useless.

"There, now lay back and die easy for me, why don't you?"

Rufus eyed the crossbow bolt. It was made of a dark, glistening material—mica, no doubt—designed to shatter in his body. Not only would it stop him using magic to attack, but it would be impossible to heal himself. Bruatar had come completely prepared to face him.

"Wait, wait!" Rufus edged further away, until his back hit the wall behind him. "I can take you to him—I can take you to Jionathan."

Bruatar raised an eyebrow and then threw his head back and laughed. "You flat-nosed snake!" he cackled. "So quick to betray your charge at the slightest provocation." The crossbow tilted up, and it was all the chance Rufus needed. Gathering magic into him, he called upon Malak's power—air. His magic couldn't touch Bruatar, but Rufus recalled a trick technique Marcel Hathely had created a few years ago. Though Rufus had never tried it himself, he understood the theory. Bruatar, in his arrogance, had forgotten that magic was not simply a blunt tool, but could be used as a much finer instrument, given the correct calculations.

"What are you doing?" Bruatar asked as Rufus moved.

The changeling didn't have a chance to say any more. Rufus, completing the quick calculations in his head, began to manipulate the air pressure around Bruatar's shield. Immediately a vacuum formed behind him, outside his shield, creating a sharp current of wind. Bruatar, surprised, looked back as his clothes began to whip around him, and the bolt in his crossbow rattled. Rufus increased the power.

Before he knew what had happened, Bruatar was being dragged off his horse by the ferocious suction of air. In a flailing panic, he squeezed his crossbow, and the bolt shot past Rufus's shoulder, skimming the fabric of his shirt. The horse reared in panic as Bruatar landed in a heap on the ground.

Rufus rolled to his feet, caught the horse's reins and leapt up onto its back. "Magi, remember?" He planted his foot hard in Bruatar's face as the changeling tried to rise, and then spurred the horse away. "Fae!" he shouted. "Over here! Fall back! Fall back!"

From amongst the heave of outlaws Fae emerged, like the helm of a ship rising from a sea of black. Rufus turned the horse back toward the town, and Fae ran up beside him, easily keeping up.

"It's Bruatar, the changeling from the forest," Rufus told her.

She nodded and, falling behind a little, made an extraordinary leap and jumped up into the saddle behind Rufus, her back to his. She gripped the horse tightly with her thighs, and drew her bow. Rufus heard the soft hiss and thud as she began shooting down the enemies pursuing them.

"Where's Jionat?" Fae called over her shoulder.

"With my uncle, I hope. They should be assembling the men in the square."

"Are any of them soldiers?" Fae asked, and Rufus urged the horse on without response.

Fae shot another bandit down in silence, and then rested her head against Rufus's back, suddenly limp.

Rufus heart lurched. "Fae?"

At the sound of her name Fae straightened, as if breaking from a stupor. She looked around at him, their noses almost touching. "They followed me," she said. "Bruatar. He hunted me down, and I led him straight to Jionat." She drew an arrow and shot it angrily into another bandit who was following on horseback. "But I swear to you, I will end this."

"We will fight together." Rufus pushed the horse on, and then added very quietly, "I kicked him in the face, if it helps?"

He sensed Fae's smile as they broke into the square together.

CHAPTER 33

"You men take the left, you lot, the right! And you eight—with me!" Michael barked, as Jionathan observed the surroundings. The peaceful town of Sarrin had been turned into veritable barracks in a matter of minutes. Market stalls had been thrown on their sides and stacked high, to block the roads leading further into the town, people bringing out furniture from their homes to add to the piles.

"When those thieving bastards enter the square, we'll cut them off from behind and surround them!" Michael was shouting, a large broadsword already in his hand.

The efficiency and speed with which Michael had conducted this preparation had surprised Jionathan. Gone was the friendly merchant that Jionathan had dined with at breakfast, there was a steeliness to Michael's dark eyes now—the look of a hardened warrior. Jionathan knew knights in Harmatia who would've cowered before the mountain that was Michael Rossignol in that moment.

From the last open pathway into the square, the clatter of hooves drew Jionathan's eye. He twisted around, and his chest squeezed with relief as he spotted Rufus and Fae atop an unfamiliar horse.

"Where have you been? Are you mad?" he demanded as Rufus drew to a halt in front of him, the horse stamping its feet.

Fae leapt elegantly down as Rufus slid off the other side, throwing the reins to one of the townsfolk.

"Jionat, thank the gods you're safe." Fae ran to him and took his hands in her own. "You need to hide. The bandits are here for you."

"What?" Jionathan balked. "I can't cower in hiding whilst you all fight, don't be ridiculous—"

"Jionathan," Fae spoke over him. "Bruatar knows you're here. You are their point of attack. If they see you, they have purpose. You must hide."

"But—"

"Please." Fae's fingers tightened over his. Jionathan knew that with an effortless squeeze, she could have broken his hands, but her grip was gentle. Controlled. "They tracked me. I am responsible for leading them here. It is my duty to protect this town now, even if I die doing so."

"Nobody is dying today." Rufus pushed passed them, his voice high and irritable as he strode toward where the townspeople were making their final preparations. Fae watched him, a ghost of a smile on her lips.

"It is unlike him to optimistic," she said.

"Fae," Jionathan began, but she locked eyes with him once more. Her smile fell.

"Jionat, for my sake, please hide."

"The lady is right." Michael laid a vast hand on Jionathan's shoulder, making the Prince jump. He'd been so quiet, Jionathan had forgotten he was there. "Rufus!" Michael called. "Take Jionathan, and hide in the smithy. You'll be safest there."

Rufus looked over from where he now stood beside Luca, who was armed and ready for battle, dressed in in the same armour as the town guard.

"Uncle," Rufus objected, "they have an alchemist among them. I'm better off—"

"Rufus, do as I say!" Michael boomed, and Rufus snapped to attention, his back going rigid. "You have a duty, and it is the Prince. We'll hold the town—you do as you're supposed to."

Rufus and Jionathan exchanged a look, both pale. Then Rufus bowed his head and, stalking back across, seized Jionathan by the wrist. "Very well." He dragged Jionathan away.

"No, wait! Rufus—let go of me!"

"Be quiet and stay low." Rufus yanked him toward the blacksmith's forge and pushed him inside, stepping in afterwards so they could huddle behind the half-door. They both peered out, watching for the bandits. They didn't have to wait long.

The bandits approached in a tight, organised pack, weapons drawn. Fae faced them down, a lone figure in the centre square, her once loose hair now bound in a tight knot. She stood as firm as stone.

"Why are they all clumped together?" Jionathan asked. It was a military defence tactic, but such good form amongst bandits seemed strange.

"Alchemists," Rufus hissed. "Bruatar must've brought more than one. They're shielding the men against a magical attack." He swore beneath his breath. "Damn it, my magic is useless."

Jionathan scanned the crowd. "The shield doesn't stop physical attacks, does it? So they'll have hidden the alchemists in the centre of the crowd?"

"Most likely."

"We should warn Fae."

"I think she can hear us," Rufus murmured, and from where she was stood, several strides away Fae inclined her head ever so slightly. "Incredible."

Even from the distance, Jionathan saw the edge of Fae's mouth curl in a tiny smile. Almost immediately it was gone, and a tense silence fell across Jionathan and Rufus as they watched.

Fae observed the bandits, her eyes darting over them, as if looking for a break in their ranks. Nobody moved, Jionathan's blood thundering loudly though his ears and body.

Then, all at once, Fae turned and ran toward the fountain, and the bandits broke forward after her. She jumped up onto the statue and, spinning, drew her bow again and let loose an arrow. It landed amongst the crowd, and Rufus whistled.

"Her eyes are as good as her ears," he whispered, as Fae drew another arrow in the same second and let it loose. Her second target anticipated the attack and ducked beneath the bodies of his comrades. "She's already spotted them."

"Who?"

"The alchemists. She's picking them off before she attacks." Rufus frowned. "Jionat, what does she need?"

"Cover," Jionathan said. "She needs cover."

Again, Jionathan saw Fae give a fraction of a nod, though it was hard to tell with how fast she was now moving.

"Can you create mist?" Jionathan asked.

Rufus snorted. "Can I create mist?" He extended his hand, and concentrated his focus on the fountain. For a moment nothing happened, Rufus's fingers locked and tense, and then a vapour began to rise from the water, swirling like steam.

Fae's half-smiled returned, as the mist grew into great billows, floating out over the bandits. It swirled around them, until they couldn't be seen, and that's when Fae struck. Jionathan watched with an almost squeamish delight as, with the elegance of a hunting falcon, Fae descended down into the white mass from her vantage point. The mist marked the bandits all but blind, but with her heightened senses, it was be no hindrance to Fae.

There was a shriek of metal, and then the screams began. Sightless, and human, the bandits were nothing to the Cat Sidhe.

"No, stay in formation! Stay in formation!" Bruatar's voice broke above the cries of terror, but it was too late. His men divided into a confused gaggle and began to flee out of the mist.

Michael and the townspeople were ready for them as they did.

The battle commenced. The Sarrin folk beat the bandits back with such ferociousness, it was hard to believe these were the same people who had occupied the market earlier. The mist swirled around them, threatening to swallow the battle whole as townspeople drove the bandits back.

"Clear the mist," Jionathan ordered Rufus, and Rufus did so with a wave of his hand.

The air cleared instantly, and everything came into view. The chaos of the battle transforming the once beautiful scene of Sarrin's square. Blood spattered on the cobble stones as the fighting went on, tiny red rivers webbing out from beneath felled bodies. Rufus gave a low groan, and Jionathan tried not to look too hard at the fallen—he couldn't bear the idea he might recognise some of them.

Even amidst the confusing flurry, Michael was easy to spot, towering over most of the men with his monstrous broadsword. He brandished it with a fierce snarl as two of the bandits leapt at him, coming from either side. Jionathan's heart jumped into his throat, and Rufus inhaled sharply, but Michael dispatched both attackers in one fell swoop. He fought and moved effortlessly, a man well-versed in the steps of battle.

"Rufus," Jionathan choked, his mouth dry. "Where did you uncle learn to fight like a knight?"

"I have no idea." Rufus was slack-jawed himself.

"The Sidhe! *Get the Sidhe!*" Bruatar roared.

From somewhere in the fray Jionathan heard Fae laugh, and she appeared again, bursting out toward the fountain once more. A few foolish bandits followed after her, leaving the safety of the mass.

Fae reached the fountain, and pivoted around—a false retreat. With an exceptional jump, she spun up over the bandits' heads and landed on the other side of them, pinning them. The few closest to her, she killed with a several easy strokes, whilst the two bandits behind climbing foolishly back into the water to escape.

From beside Jionathan, Rufus gave a mischievous laugh and raised his hand once more. Jionathan watched gleefully as the water in the fountain grew pale and both bandits cried out, looking down at their legs with dismay. Rufus had frozen the entire thing solid. Jionathan stifled a whoop.

"I learnt that one from Zachary," Rufus laughed, and at Jionathan's sobered expression, changed the topic quickly. "Gods, Fae is terrifying."

Fae left the two struggling bandits to try and thaw their legs out, and planted a kick into the chest of another who was bearing down on one of the townspeople. The bandit hit the wall of a house with a rib-cracking crunch. Jionathan and Rufus both shuddered at this monstrous display of strength.

"*Luca!*" Michael's scream cut through the uproar, and Jionathan jolted with fear as he spotted Luca on the other side of the square, being thrown down by the enemy.

"No—" Rufus made to rise, his eyes wide, but before either he, or Jionathan could take action, Luca lashed out with her leg and caught her attacker in the groin. As he hunched over himself, face twisting, Luca rolled to her feet and swung her sword around, catching him across the face. The bandit howled and Luca brought the hilt of her sword over the bandit's head, felling him instantly.

"I'm fine!" she shouted.

"Well fought, Luca—" Fae laughed, but was cut off abruptly as a net fell over her head. She jumped back instantly, but was caught as another net came swinging down and snagged around her, tightening until her arms were bound to her side. She'd been so distracted by Luca's fight, she hadn't noticed the bandits swarming in behind her.

"Bring her down!" Bruatar cried with glee.

Fae struggled, but the nets only seemed to get tighter. The

bandits dragged her to the floor.

"*Fae!*" Jionathan tried to rise, but Rufus pulled him back, covering his mouth. Bruatar drew his blade and pushed his way through the crowd to make the final cut. Jionathan watched, his stomach summersaulting, vomit rising in his throat. He didn't want to watch this. He didn't want to see it. He needed to stop it!

Colours pulsated behind his eyes, and enveloped him.

"Go on," Bruatar goaded. "Transform for me. Save me the effort of skinning you like this, and having it reversed. Go on, Cat Sidhe, transform. For the pride of the Neve, try to take one last bite. Or, you can save yourself and tell me where the Prince is."

"For the pride of the Neve, you can boil in a pit of your own piss," Fae snarled. "Kill me as I am."

Bruatar shook his head. "Pity." He raised his sword. "What will your poor parents say when they hear that their only remaining daughter is dead?"

Fae stiffened, and it was the sign that Bruatar was waiting for. With a triumphant laugh he stabbed the sword down between the bindings, into the soft muscle of Fae's diaphragm.

The world seemed to freeze. Somewhere Luca was screaming, but Fae seemed deaf to it. Her eyes rolled upward and around, as if in surprise. Blood pooled out of her mouth, dribbling from the corner of her lips. She twitched, her mouth quivering as she blinked sluggishly, trying to form words. None came out, and as Bruatar dragged the sword out from her body, she collapsed back. Her blood ran freely down the streets of Sarrin, joining the red river as her eyes slowly lost their focus.

"No!" Jionathan broke from the vision, twisting this way and that until he was free of Rufus. "No! I won't let you! *NO!*"

"Jionat, stop!" Rufus grabbed for him again, but it was too late.

With a cry, Jionathan threw himself out into the square, toward Bruatar.

CHAPTER 34

"Oh for the love of—" Rufus cursed, running out after the Prince.

"*Bruatar!*" Jionathan boomed, his voice rising over the sound of battle. "Bruatar, you greasy-haired mongrel, here I am!"

Bruatar spun on the spot, excitement dancing in his yellow eyes. "Well, how is this for a treat?" he cackled. "You're not jumping out to save the Cat Sidhe, are you?"

"And if I am?" Jionathan's fists clenched at his sides. Rufus tried to pull him back to safety, but Jionathan ripped his arm free again. "Get out of my way, Rufus."

"Heavens above, you're more stupid than I remembered," Bruatar said, as Jionathan stalked toward him. The Prince growled.

That reckless fool, what's he doing? Rufus gritted his teeth. Jionathan was certainly skilled in a fight, but he'd never seen battle like this. And if Fae had been felled, what hope did the Prince have?

What was more, Bruatar was still shielded against magic, and Rufus doubted the bandit would fall for the same trick as before.

If only my magic wasn't capped, Rufus thought, frustration burning up through him. *I could overpower that alchemist easily!*

"So what now, little Prince? How do you propose we proceed?" Bruatar drawled.

Jionathan reached toward his side, as if to draw his sword. Bruatar tensed, and then blinked, incredulous, as Jionathan drew his dirk instead. Bruatar stared at the tiny knife, and broke out laughing. "D'you mean to fight me with that toothpick? I'm not sure if I'm supposed to be insulted, or amazed."

The bandits all joined in the chorus of laughter. The sound quickly died out as Jionathan raised the dirk and held it up to his own eyes. "I don't have to fight," he said.

Rufus went numb, and Bruatar stood to attention.

"What are you doing?" the bandit demanded.

"My eyes, my *Sight*--this is what you want, isn't it?" Jionathan twisted the blade, letting it gently kiss the skin around the socket. "Don't think I won't do it—cut them out. They have caused me more grief than joy. All they show me is blood. Perhaps I should return the favour."

"Please," Rufus half-whispered, perhaps to the gods, perhaps to Jionathan. "Please don't."

Bruatar seemed to consider Jionathan. "What do you want?"

"Step away from Fae. Tell your men to pull back," Jionathan ordered, and he looked so much like his Thestian in that moment, Rufus had to look again.

A hush fell over the square, and Rufus saw that the commotion had drawn an audience. The townspeople and bandits had ceased their fighting, a wall of bodies between them. They watched Jionathan and Bruatar as if they knew this was the pinnacle moment of the battle.

"Jionat, stop!" Fae pleaded, twisting in her binds.

"I'm sorry, Fae, but I can't." Jionathan fixed his eyes on Bruatar. "Cease this fighting, and I will come with you. No more killing."

Bruatar raised his hands and put away his blade, beckoning the men around him to stand down. They did so, stepping back.

"There, I've done as you asked, your Royal Highness. Now, why don't you lower that blade?" He motioned to Jionathan who took a few steps back, his knife still in place. "Prince Jionathan, *please,*" Bruatar repeated, his tone mocking.

Rufus saw Jionathan wince as his name spread through the townspeople. Slowly, he let the dirk drop.

"Rufus," he breathed, his mouth barely moving. "Get to Fae."

And then he bolted, the bandits immediately flocking after him.

"I never said I would come quietly!" Jionathan baited, with a haughty laugh and ran faster, leading them away. He was used to being chased, and by things which were much worse than mere bandits.

"Defend the Prince!" Fae bellowed to the townspeople, struggling to untangle herself as Luca skidded to her side. Michael gave a similar battle cry, and the fighting recommenced.

Rufus threw his hands into the air and did as he was commanded, darting through the heaving mass toward Fae. "Runs out like a half-wit hero," he ranted. "Throws himself onto the blade of danger, and then sets an army on himself! Oh yes, that's Jionat. Prince of impulse, brain the size a walnut."

He reached Fae, skidding across to her, and falling on his knees. Luca looked fearfully up at him as she tried to cut through the net. "It won't come loose, and it won't cut!" She tugged at the slim rings. "It's harder than metal!"

"They're enchanted." Fae lay still, perfectly ensnared. "These nets were made to withhold my strength and my magic. No sword or knife will cut through them."

"No, but my magic might. Hold still." Rufus placed his palm over the rings, trying to concentrate over the sound of battle flooding around him.

"It won't work!" Fae said. "Go and protect Jionat!"

"It will work. It has to work, because I can't protect Jionat—the only thing I'm good for is magic, and Bruatar's shielded! But you—you can fight them," Rufus hissed, drawing power into himself. He couldn't just use a blast of air, as Fae was wrapped too tightly within the nets, and it would cut clean through her too. Rufus's best bet was to use an adapted form of one of Zachary's techniques—the water whip. He could shape the whip into a knife-like form instead, make it thinner and combine it with more air to make it sharper.

"Hurry, Rufus," Luca urged him, and Rufus began to calculate. Too much and he'd cut through Fae, too little and the nets would hold.

"Alright, hold very still." He began the process, gathering water from the air around him and forming it into a sharp stiletto at the end of his index finger. He laid his other hand flat across Fae's stomach to steady her and slipped the tiny blade—no thicker than a needle—between the joints of the net. His arm throbbed with pain, the high concentration of magic building at the tip of his fingers, begging to be released in more than a mere trickle. It had been so long since Rufus attempted anything this delicate. And to think—this had once been his specialty. Taking a deep breath, the blade now in place, Rufus allowed some of the air to pass through and then, with a flick, he cut the net, creating a small tear.

"It worked," Luca breathed, and Fae gave a triumphant grunt and ripped her way free, the small cut breaking the enchantment.

Rufus sat back, releasing the magic and clinging to his arm.

"Go—the idiot's outnumbered twenty to one. Go," Rufus begged, and Fae didn't hesitate, drawing her weapons and charging.

Rufus smiled after her and then, with a small moan, toppled onto his side.

Luca caught him in a flurry of panic. "Rufus?"

"I'm fine." He closed his eyes. "Just exhausted. Gods, I'm out of practice."

"Perhaps this'll teach you to get back *into* practice then." Luca looked up at the disarray. With Fae released and the bandits no longer in any sort of formation, the battle was quickly turning in Sarrin's favour. Rufus imagined it would all be over in a matter of minutes, Fae and Jionathan cutting through the enemy side by side.

"They fight as if they shared blades," Luca noted, and Rufus watched as Jionathan dove beneath an attacker's swing and, veering in close, shouldered the bandit into another who was engaging Fae. They toppled over, Jionathan and Fae swapping sides, like they were walking through the familiar steps of a well-known dance. Jionathan was laughing.

"Magi!" a voice hissed close by, and Luca cried in alarm as Bruatar appeared above them, his face twisted, yellow eyes burning with venom. His sword was already drawn back, and Rufus watched with a caged terror as it arched down toward him.

Luca shoved Rufus off her lap, and grabbing her own sword, she raised it up and caught Bruatar's blade. He snarled at her.

"Move away, girl!"

"No." Luca pushed herself up from her knees, and with a sudden burst of strength, drove Bruatar back. "No—you get away!" she shrieked, and began a ferocious barrage, swinging wildly and hard. What she lacked in precise skill, she made up for with rage.

Bruatar stumbled back a few steps, but recovered himself and began to match her heavy strikes. They locked themselves in furious battle, and a red hue almost seemed to rise from Luca's body, her teeth bared as she hit at Bruatar again, and again. She was close to feral—like a bloodhound or a wolf. Beneath her hefty blows, cracks began to appear in Bruatar's sword.

"*Get out of my home!*" Luca screamed, and with a power that such a small body shouldn't have permitted, she struck Bruatar's sword so hard, it shattered. Rufus watched, flabbergasted, as Bruatar fell back, defeated.

Luca stood over him, heaving. One of the sword's shards had

nicked her leg and torn her trousers. Blood seeped out, but Luca didn't seem to notice it, pinning her sword against Bruatar's chest. Rufus had never seen such a heated bloodlust in his cousin's eyes. She looked possessed. Inhuman.

"You killed good men today." Her voice shook, but it wasn't in fear. "*My* men, *my* people. I'll take back what you stole, in blood!"

"Luca." Fae was there a moment later, and had hold of Luca's hands. "Luca," she eased, her voice soft but firm. "Enough now—enough."

"No, let me do this!" Luca didn't relinquish her grip on the sword. "Let me see the light fade from his eyes. You said it yourself—he's a murderer and worse! We won't mourn his death."

"No, but I would mourn the part of you that dies when you execute an unarmed, defenceless man." Fae squeezed Luca's hand. "Let me take that burden from you. That is *my* purpose, to be the weapon. Not you, sweet Luca."

The anger in Luca's eyes faded, and she looked up to see that the battle was over. The bandits were either dead or had surrendered, surrounded by the townspeople. A grey tone settled beneath Luca's dark skin, and she began to shake. Michael crossed over to her as, with stiff fingers, Luca relieved her sword to Fae and stepped back, turning into her father's arms.

"My brave girl, you fought well." Michael cradled her head to his chest.

Jionathan came to Rufus's side and pulled him to his feet. Neither of them said anything as Fae coaxed Bruatar up onto his knees, her own blades now trained at his neck.

"You think you've won?" he laughed, but it was a weak and breathy sound. "You haven't. It doesn't matter if I die today, you won't keep the peace. News'll spread. They'll discover *he's* here." Bruatar eyed Jionathan. "And then others'll come. Others like me—or worse, Magi. And how'll this town stand against them? I'd have been content to only take his eyes. Will they be as good-hearted? The *Night Patrol?*"

A shiver of fear passed through Rufus, but Fae remained calm despite the threat. "Let them come." Her voice didn't waver. "Sarrin town will not be taken, nor will Jionat."

"You think the world of yourself, don't you?" Bruatar spat, and Fae brought her blades up a little higher into his throat. "Think you're better than me."

"I am better than you. Yours is not a high standard to compete with. You have power, and even some skill, but you're greedy, and arrogant, and blood-thirsty and now you will reap the fruits of your failure, Bruatar."

"Oh Titania, spare me your blather." Bruatar swore, trying to feign nonchalance, though his voice was high and tight. "As if you didn't enjoy killing my men—as if you don't relish your victory. I know what you are, and you're no more a friend to these people than I am."

Fae's expression didn't change, but Rufus saw a stillness come over her, her eyes hard. Bruatar sensed it too, and gave a low laugh.

"You stand on your podium, with your sense of superiority, and you snub your nose at the ugly things. What am I? A faerie castaway, a changeling boy, not good enough for my faerie parents, not good enough for my human ones." Bruatar reared toward Fae, the blades biting into his neck. "But when we treat others as we've been treated, you call us the villains?" He shook his head, grinning manically. "Why? Because I sell slaves whilst your kind have spirited away humans for centuries? Or because I steal gold whilst the Sidhe take an extortionate tax and feed off the wealth of Bethean?" Bruatar's voice grew, ringing across the square. "You were pampered from birth, and I rose and scrabbled from the depths of nothing, and yet the only difference between you and me, Fae, is that *you're beautiful.*" He gnashed his teeth.

"No, Bruatar." Fae drew herself up. "The difference is that hatred has clouded your judgment, and I am willing to let love

369

change mine." And with a sharp flick of her wrists the blades glided through the thick muscle, and Bruatar's head rolled from his shoulders, yellow eyes still burning.

With the morning's adventure over, and magistrates sent for to escort the outlaws to the King's court, an odd stillness fell over Sarrin. The excitement and terror of the day had faded into the dejected acceptance of what had been lost. The dead—mostly bandits—were lined up along the wall, and Rufus was borrowed, along with two local priests, to bless the bodies before they were buried at the border of the wood. Jionathan found that, rather than be of any help, he only got in the way.

With the townspeople now all aware of who he was, they gawked and whispered around him, pointing and staring until Jionathan retreated to the Rossignol's house. The beautiful image of Sarrin had been tainted. He was sure that soon, when people had calmed, they would be out in force to bring cheer back to the streets. And yet, Jionathan couldn't help but feel his stomach turn when he thought of what Bruatar said. He knew Bruatar was right. If the soldiers came from Harmatia, the town would be devastated. What the bandits had possessed in force, they lacked in skill, but if Rufus struggled with one alchemist, what could a force of Magi do?

Jionathan knew that, even if the townspeople kept their silence, as Michael assured him they would, sooner or later he would be found. The spell was broken—the severity of his situation descended on him once more. If he remained in Sarrin town, he damned them all. But if he returned to Harmatia, he would die.

He lingered outside of the bedroom, his palms slick with sweat, skin clammy as he prepared himself for what he was about to do. It would be considered treason in Harmatia, for a Prince to leave the allied lands and turn his back on his own kingdom.

Worse than that, he and anyone who assisted him in this venture would face the death-sentence, if they ever tried to return.

A chill passed over him, but he gathered his resolve and knocked on the door. Fae beckoned him in, her voice tired and sad. He stepped into the room.

She sat on the bed, staring at the far wall. The shutters were closed to keep the room cool, and beams of light illuminated tiny columns of dancing dust that hung lazily in the air. Jionathan stood in the doorway, wrapping his arms around himself. Even in the heat of the day, he felt cold.

"You were going to leave, weren't you?" he said. "That's why you were dressed like that." He gestured to her trousers and leather armour. "You were going to leave us and return to the Neve."

"Yes." She didn't deny it.

"And now?" His eyes lingered over her. She hadn't changed since the battle.

"It wouldn't be right to stay." She stood, her posture stiff. "But you know that already. You, too, are dressed to travel."

Jionathan stared at her, searching for courage, for another answer, for a way to fix it all. He'd been so happy these last days, and now there was a vast emptiness that could never be filled. He'd never loved a place as he loved Sarrin. The beauty and pride of Harmatia was breath-taking, and Jionathan would have gladly dedicated his life to it, but Sarrin was kind. The people of Sarrin were kind. Rufus was kind.

Jionathan closed his eyes, his bottom lip trembling. His resolve almost slipped away, but he caught it and straightened his shoulders.

"Take me with you," he said.

"The bandits you seek are dead or captured," the Korrigan informed Zachary from where she stood, safely hidden in the shadows of the cave.

Zachary folded his arms. "Oh wonderful—a wasted journey." He glanced over to the distant figures of Marcel and Emeric, who were stood waiting on the other side of the lake. "Rumour has it they had a prisoner amongst them. Jionathan of the Delphi."

A dagger flew out from the gloom and landed close to his feet. Zachary considered it a while, and then picked it up, turning it in his hands. He recognised it—Jionathan's dirk. Or rather Sverrin's, before the Delphi brat claimed it as his own.

"Ah. Is he still alive?"

"He means to cross the road into Avalon in the company of a Cat Sidhe," the Korrigan said.

Zachary straightened, his heart skipping a beat. He smiled widely. "And here you had me thinking the day was lost." He tucked the knife into his belt. "Oh happy news, our Prince is found, and my orders are clear. Into Avalon you say? It seems fortune favours me at last."

"If you move swiftly, you may cut him off on the road."

"You *are* a useful creature, aren't you?" Zachary said.

The Korrigan bowed her head a little, though Zachary got the impression she was humouring him. Even at their politest, there had never been even a shred of true respect in any of the Korrigans' blood coloured eyes.

She turned to descend back into her darkness, but Zachary called to her

"One last thing then, before I go," he said. She stopped and turned back. "You said the Prince was with a Cat Sidhe. What about a Magi? My little brother should also be with him by now."

The Korrigan was silent a while. "You have no brother," she said, and Zachary gave her a grim smile.

"No, I suppose not," he agreed, and before he could say any more, she turned and was gone. Zachary stared into the deep, dark tunnel and resisted the urge to shiver. Even with his question unanswered, he didn't dare follow.

CHAPTER
35

Jionathan was showing the familiar signs. Rufus had known him long enough now to understand what it meant when Jionathan got jumpy, and unsociable. The Prince hadn't even been able to look Luca in the eye, when she'd caught him on his way up to the house. Jionathan had forced out a few terse, monosyllabic responses to her concerned questions, and then shaken her off and disappeared.

"He's very upset, isn't he?" Luca whispered to Rufus. "Doesn't he know? None of this was his fault."

Rufus didn't reply, but continued to watch Jionathan throughout the day, unease growing in the pit of his stomach. Finally, after hours of waiting for Jionathan to come to him, Rufus went and sought him out.

He found Jionathan in their bedroom, dressed for travel and with his bag packed.

"You're leaving." Rufus didn't bother to shape it as a question. He ran a hand through his hair, leaning heavily against the door. "We can stay, Jionat."

Jionathan heaved a sigh, his shoulders slumped. He kept his back to Rufus, unable to face him. "No, we can't."

"Jionat—"

"I cannot be responsible for any more deaths," Jionathan snapped, slapping his hand against the wall. "If the Magi attacked—"

"I could stop them," Rufus said. "I could fight them."

Jionathan threw Rufus a dubious look, his brows arched, and Rufus tried not to show how deeply that disbelief hurt him. Jionathan's reservations, as much as Rufus didn't want to admit it, were entirely justified.

"I *could* do it," Rufus said. "If it came down to it, then I could fight them. I could protect you. I'm more powerful than you think, and I'm clever, I—"

"Rufus, I'm not debating your skill or intelligence. But you're not a killer."

"I could be, if you needed me to," Rufus blurted, before he could think. Jionathan turned to stare at him, his silver eyes wide. Rufus's words caught up with him, and he swallowed. "I could," he said again, after a moment. "I could, if you needed me to."

Jionathan moved his mouth, stuttering over silent words, as if unsure what to say. Finally he swallowed, his eyes squeezed closed like he was in pain. He turned away, his breath audible, somewhere between a soft huff and tight laugh. "It's not a matter of need, Rufus." He rested his head against the wall and breathed out slowly, his shoulders rigid. "Don't say things like that—it doesn't sound right coming from you."

"Jionat," Rufus said, "you haven't been this happy, this relaxed, in two years. Sarrin's good for you."

"It is," Jionathan conceded wearily. "It's wonderful. I could spend the rest of my life here. But that's not my fate. I'm a Prince." He raised his head and knocked it lightly against the wall. "I'm a Prince."

Rufus saw the depression forming over Jionathan again like condensation on a washroom window. He saw the boy he'd known in Harmatia, grey-faced and tired. "Where do we go?"

he asked.

Jionathan seemed to wilt further, and gave a half-laugh. "Are you going to follow me again, Rufus."

"Always."

"Even if it means death?"

"Especially if you *think* it means death."

The words hung heavily in the air, and Jionathan seemed to consider them a long while. Finally he nodded.

"Réne. We could catch a boat, hide in the far-east." Jionathan turned back and drew out his drinking pouch, giving it a quick swig. He wiped his mouth with the back of his hand, his gaze thoughtful, and offered the pouch to Rufus. Rufus declined, but Jionathan shook it more insistently.

"Have you poisoned it with opium?"

Jionathan rolled his eyes and smiled, a fleeting moment of sincerity. Rufus relented and took a swig. The water was sweet and cool, despite the heat of the day.

"Réne's good, but we have no connections there, no place to hide."

"I'm not looking for luxury." Jionathan folded his arms, leaning back against the wall. "I could find work, make a living."

"Starting a life somewhere new, with no connections isn't as simple as that, especially if you're hiding," Rufus said grimly, rubbing his eyes. The heat and work of the day was starting to take its toll on his body, and he felt tired. "There's also the problem of our skin."

"Our skin?"

"We're both too pale. I can put on a fair Betheanian accent if I need to, but you'll be recognised as Harmatian instantly. What's more, even if East Réne are a democratic state, there are still wealthy families out there who have a connection with the Harmatian court. It wouldn't...it wouldn't be long...be long before the Queen found us," Rufus said, his words dragging a little. His mouth didn't seem to be obeying him properly.

"You're right," Jionathan replied evenly. "No place in the allied lands is safe. No matter where I go, they will find me."

Rufus touched a hand to his head. The sleepy heaviness was getting worse, and he was starting to feel dizzy. He glanced down to the pouch and then up to Jionathan. "What…what have you done?"

"I used something a little stronger this time." Jionathan dove forward and caught Rufus as the Magi's legs gave way. He lowered him carefully onto the nearest bed, Rufus seizing Jionathan by the front of his leather armour. "I'm sorry, Rufus."

"No…" Rufus slurred, trying to fight the nauseating sleepiness that was coming over him. "No, Jionat, don't do this, don't…"

"It's because you always follow me." Jionathan almost seemed tearful, but Rufus's vision was now so blurred he couldn't be sure. "But this time, if they caught you following me, at best you'd never practise magic again. At worst…"

Rufus heard Jionathan gulp, and his own mind, tired and muffled as it was, conjured up a powerful picture. He knew exactly what would happen to him if he was caught trying to sneak Jionathan out of the allied lands. He'd be broken on the wheel, put on display as his limbs were cracked and pummelled, bones splintering until either the pain killed him, or someone took pity, and aimed for his head.

And yet, even with that knowledge, Rufus clung to Jionathan, unwilling to let him go. Jionathan gripped his hand.

"Rufus, thank you for Sarrin," he said. "Thank you for being a friend to me when I had none. You are the best and greatest man I know, so please, *please*, don't follow me. Where I'm going, I can never return."

Rufus's fingers grew lax, and he tried to concentrate, tried to keep hold of Jionathan before he too slipped away.

"You'll sleep, and when you wake, I'll be gone. Forgive me, Rufus." Jionathan pried Rufus's hand off his armour, still gripping it. "One more time. Please, forgive me."

"Stop fretting."

The words broke through the glum silence, and Jionathan looked up, his lip swollen and red from where he'd been chewing it with his teeth. Fae gave a small sigh and walked back toward him. Jionathan hadn't realised he'd stopped walking and looked pointedly to the floor.

"I'm not fretting. We left Rufus in Luca's care. The Rossignols will keep watch over him. He'll be fine, eventually," he said.

"And yet, despite your words, you worry." Fae looked pointedly at his abused lip, and then flicked her eyes back up to his.

Jionathan groaned. "He's going to try and do something stupid, I know it."

"Yes, that does rather seem to be his nature."

"You have no idea." Jionathan looked over his shoulder, half-expected to see Rufus galloping up behind them, clouds of dust in his wake.

"That potion we gave him was the strongest I have. He won't wake for a whole day, and when he does, he will be too exhausted for another two to come after us. By the time he recovers, we will be in the Neve, and without flight he won't be able to follow us." Fae must have seen the disappointment on Jionathan's face, for she reached up and squeezed his hand. "Jionat, he couldn't have come with us. A Magi in the Neve? They would execute him immediately."

Jionathan gave a forlorn nod, clutching his stomach. He felt sick. "I know, I know. But this is wrong. This is all wrong."

"Jionat."

"I can't do this," he said, the sick feeling rising. His face began to flush. "I can't do this, Fae."

"Jionat, it's done." Fae pulled him into an embrace before he could say any more. She held him tightly, brushing her fingers through his hair.

"If I return to Harmatia," he breathed, "I'll be killed. I saw it. A boy…an assassin named Joshua. He'll kill me."

Fae didn't react, but Jionathan knew he'd surprised her. She moved her hands down to his face, stroking her thumb over his cheek. Her fingers were cool against his burning skin. "Then that's decided. You can't return to Harmatia. You must forge another path." She pursed her lips, brushing his fringe out of his eyes. "I will help you. I swear it."

Relief flowed through him like a warm, golden light, even as he was struck by a desperate pang of homesickness. He wasn't even sure if it was for Sarrin, or Harmatia.

"Thank you," he said. "I'm not sure I would have found the strength without you."

"You would have found it," Fae said, and taking Jionathan's hand she guided him onward, the pair walking together. Jionathan forced the thought of Rufus from his mind and tried to distract himself. Fae was his anchor, her fingers entwined with his.

"Do you have a big family in the Neve?"

Fae snorted softly. "Big? Yes. My parents both saw the last century, and have had many children in their time, some of whom have married and started families of their own. The Ó Murchadha clan is a large one."

"I wonder what they'll think of me."

"My father will like you, and Korrick too, though he'll pretend he doesn't. And Reilly…" Fae drew off. "I really ought to tell you about Reilly."

"Another brother?"

Fae winced. "Not quite, he's—" she broke off and looked around sharply, her demeanour that of a startled cat.

"What is it?"

"Someone's coming," she whispered. "Quick, this way." She ushered him off the road and into the trees, signalling for Jionathan to be quiet as they lay down against the cold earth.

After a minute, Jionathan, too, heard the sound of footsteps—loud, lazy, and careless. Leaves and twigs snapped underfoot as Marcel Hathely came out from the forest, his face clean of expression, bored and blank. Stepping out onto the road, he looked either side of him, and Jionathan shrank back.

Despite his apathetic appearance, Marcel's golden eyes were as sharp as always, hawk-like in their countenance as they scanned the path. Jionathan held his breath, waiting to be spotted, but the Magi's eyes passed right over them, unseeing.

Marcel looked up and down the road once more, and then gave a despondent grunt, blowing his blond hair out from his eyes. Quietly, he removed his pipe from his belt, stuffed it with leaf, and lit it. Fae wrinkled her nose at the heavy, stale smell as Marcel began to smoke. Across the other side of the wood another figure emerged.

This one was younger, sweet-faced, with curls and doey brown eyes—Emeric Fold, Marcel's apprentice. Jionathan's stomach twisted. The two were frequently seen shadowing Zachary, and it couldn't be a coincidence they were in the forest now.

"Anything?" Emeric called across to Marcel, who gave him a once over and a discouraging shrug. Emeric walked across to him, picking leaves out of his hair. "This is madness," he huffed. "We've been patrolling for hours now. How does he even know they'll come this way?" he kicked a stray rock. "I hate this damn forest."

"On that, we agree." Marcel blew a ring of smoke and stopped to admire it. Emeric gave a tense look over his shoulder and spoke again, his voice hushed.

"Marcel…" He caught his lip between his teeth. "Marcel, are we doing the right thing?"

Marcel gave him a stern look, his eyes narrowed slightly.

Emeric dropped his gaze. "I'll follow him to the death—you know I will. I'm loyal him, to both of you, but…I hope that loyalty isn't doing more harm than good. Does loyalty justify what we're doing? Are we doing this for the right reasons?"

Marcel considered these words with his usual reserved severity. "There is no lesser evil on this path," he eventually said. "We made our choice. That is all we can do."

Emeric gave a reluctant nod and turned on his heel. "We'd best get back to it then."

Marcel inclined his head and the pair moved off separately, Emeric padding almost silently whilst Marcel made no great attempt to conceal his presence, his long robes making an orchestra of the leaves underfoot.

Fae waited another minute before turning to Jionathan, who'd covered his mouth with both hands, afraid to betray himself. "We must go quickly," she urged. "Those were powerful men."

"How did you know?"

"Elemental Magic smells like blood, and those two have the scent of a slaughterhouse. It's overpowering. Hurry, there's an open field this way—we'll take to the sky." She pulled him after her, darting seamlessly though the foliage as he struggled to keep up. Together they ran, Fae soundlessly, Jionathan struggling to keep his footfall light, holding his cloak around him so it didn't flap behind. He could feel his heartbeat in his ears and throat, the colours dancing warningly in the corners of his eyes. The trees began to grow sparse, the green hue of the forest lightening as they neared the open expanse.

Breaking through into the clearing, Fae skidded to such a sharp halt Jionathan almost collided with her. Her shoulders went rigid and Jionathan glanced around her to see why.

A familiar, menacing figure leant against a tree ahead of them, his arms folded. He straightened, and tipped his head. "Many happy returns from the day, young rambler. Welcome to the road to Avalon."

"Zachary…" Jionathan shrank back, his fingers curling around Fae's shoulder. Zachary swept into an intricate bow.

"At your service, Your Highness."

380

CHAPTER 36

Jionathan forgot how to breathe. He and Fae stood, paralysed as Zachary approached, his hands behind his back, gait long and leisurely. It was like a nightmare, and for a moment Jionathan's mind went blank, despair and fear flooding through him. And then he found his voice, and with it came his anger.

"You son of a whore," he snapped, stepping up to Zachary, who raised his eyebrows. "What are you doing here?"

"Now that's a greeting!" Zachary gave a mock gasp just as Marcel and Emeric emerged from the woods behind Fae and Jionathan, effectively surrounding them.

Fae lowered her stance, but didn't speak, studying each of their new foes with a calculated look. Jionathan felt his anger rise, as Zachary's smile widened, his hazel-green eyes glinting in sick self-satisfaction.

"We came all this way to meet you, and this is the abuse we get? Typical," Zachary tutted. "Though speaking of people to abuse, where's Merle? Shouldn't he have caught up to you by now?" He looked up to Marcel. "See, as you are my witness, you can tell my master I at least asked."

Marcel rolled his eyes, and Emeric looked worriedly between

Fae and Jionathan, refusing to meet their gazes. Jionathan trembled, resisting the urge to lunge at Zachary. Zachary was stronger and faster than him—a formidable opponent even without his magic, and not one to be taken lightly.

"Why should it matter to you where Rufus is?" Jionathan snapped.

Zachary stilled, his expression darkening. "If you've killed him, Sire, I might take issue with that."

Jionathan stared. What was so badly twisted in Zachary, that his first assumption was Jionathan had killed Rufus to get rid of him?

Still, Jionathan thought, *as long he thinks Rufus is a victim, he won't suspect his involvement.*

Jionathan squared his shoulders, and gave, what he hoped, was a nonchalant shrug. "Why? Were you hoping to get to him first?"

Zachary frowned, which only emphasises the severe line of his brow, darkening his face. "Merle is a Magi. We are brothers. If we happen to disagree, we can settle it as men, equally. Brothers fight, we even kill. But against a common foe we will unite."

"Am I that common foe?" Jionathan narrowed his eyes.

"That rather depends." Zachary's demeanour seemed to cool even further, his voice icy. "Where's Merle?"

Jionathan stepped back, trying to hide the shudder that ran through him. "I haven't seen him since I left Harmatia," he lied.

"Oh, good." Almost instantly Zachary's expression brightened. "In that case, we can get to business. Your Highness," he bowed again, "we are here to bring you home. Resistance is encouraged, as it gives me a reason to break your arms."

Jionathan could feel his breath shortening, the colours dancing around the corners of his eyes. His skin became clammy, a cold sweat dewing across his face as the severity of the situation pressed over him. Marcel and Emeric abandoned their vantage point with a leisurely ease and came to stand either side of

Zachary. They were confident Fae and Jionathan wouldn't outrun them.

"Your Highness?" Zachary repeated, his smile sickening as he held out his hand, ushering Jionathan over.

"No," Jionathan tried to force authority into his voice. "No, I cannot return. Not yet."

"Perhaps you thought my threat was in jest." Zachary's tone remained light. "Allow me to reiterate—you don't have a choice. Or do you despise your kingdom so badly that you'd let me mangle you for the pleasure of a minute more away? Come now." Zachary stepped closer, his hand still outstretched.

Immediately Fae drew her bow, aiming an arrow at his head. "Not a step closer."

Zachary stared down the arrow without a flicker of fear. "Such hostility. Is there really any need for it? We're all friends here—"

"You're no friend of ours. Step away or die," Fae bit back coldly.

Zachary considered this, looking over his shoulder at Marcel and Emeric before shrugging. "Alright then, Cat Sidhe," he said. "Shoot."

Fae tried to keep her surprise from her face, but her eyes narrowed a fraction, and Zachary's inane smile widened.

"Oh yes," he whispered. "I know what you are. And I know you want to kill me. So shoot, if you will…But answer me this first." He tilted his head to one side. "How fast would you have to draw the next two arrows before one of my friends burnt you to ash?"

Fae didn't move, as Zachary tapped his chin, letting the question hang in the air. No one spoke, the tension high, and then Zachary barked a laugh that made Jionathan jump.

"Its times like these we need Merle, isn't it?" Zachary said. "He could probably tell you exactly how quick you'd have to be. He would calculate it—estimate your chances of survival. Alas, my own grasp of numbers isn't as good as his, but my guess is that you would have to be very, very fast. So would you like to try?" He cocked an eyebrow, as if challenging Fae, as if his own life was worth the price of finding out.

"Fae," Jionathan choked, and he took her elbow. "Fae, put it down. Put it down."

Fae snarled and lowered her weapon, though she didn't remove the arrow from the bow. Zachary seemed contented and spread his arms in a welcoming gesture.

"Progress! I am almost giddy with delight. Well then, come along, Sire. Harmatia awaits."

Jionathan's knees grew week. "Please, I can't. I can't return. My father understands, I know he does. Please, let me stay a while longer—just a while."

"Stay?" Emeric interrupted, his face furrowed. "Your Highness, you were about to cross the border into Avalon. That's high treason. You're lucky we caught you here. Any further, and the Queen would have had the right to disown you and order your incarceration."

"But don't you see?" Jionathan's voice quavered. "If I return, she'll kill me."

This seemed to give the three Magi pause, and they looked between each other.

Zachary collected himself first. "That's a strong accusation. Do you truly think the Queen would leave the throne without an heir at such a time?"

"My unborn sibling would work as well," Jionathan replied. "She has no issue with them."

"I rather fear the Queen's issues extend to all of the Delphi actually, not just you." Zachary's voice was gravelly, and Jionathan saw a sudden, keen hatred boiling in his eyes. Jionathan understood—Zachary blamed him for Sverrin's death, in the same, perhaps irrational way Jionathan blamed Zachary.

"Please," Jionathan said, squashing down his shame. He would beg for his life, if that's what it took. "Let me go. I..." He swallowed. "I won't return."

Any pretence Zachary had maintained of joviality fell, and that same, cold sternness grew up from his centre, as if he were turning to stone. "You would abandon your kingdom," he said coolly, "just for fear of your life?"

Jionathan was stunned, and then a great humiliation crashed over him. No. No, he wouldn't abandon his kingdom. Not to men like Zachary, who would gladly terrorise Harmatia on the whims of a Kathrak Queen.

Zachary nodded. "If it's the Queen you fear, then we will deliver you to my master. He'll keep you safe," Zachary offered. "He's a good man. A better one than I, certainly. Now come along—the light is fading, and so is my patience."

Jionathan didn't move, his feet rooted to the ground.

"Alternatively, if you continue to defy me, perhaps I will deliver you to the Queen straight?" Zachary said.

Beside him, Marcel exhaled. "Arlen," he warned, eyeing Fae, whose fingers were twitching to draw back her bow. "Put down your weapon, Sidhe. You are powerless."

Fae glowered, but Jionathan placed a gentle hand on her shoulder before she could raise the bow in sheer defiance. "It's alright, Fae."

"Return, Jionat, and you die. That's what you told me. You *saw* it. Trust your Sight."

"I do, and I know the consequences. But if I go to the Neve with you, I could never return. I thought I was ready to face that, but I can't abandon Harmatia. Not to the likes of him." Jionathan spat toward Zachary.

"She's safer in my hands than she ever was in yours, Delphi," Zachary retorted.

"Jionat, it's not safe for you," Fae insisted, her voice hitching a little. "Please, don't do this."

"Oh Hexias give me strength," Zachary groaned. "Have I not already made it abundantly clear this isn't a choice?" He threw his hands into the air. "Fine, if it helps, I will make it even simpler for you. Come with us now, Sire, or I am going to kill the Sidhe and wear her skin."

Quick as lightening Fae drew her bow and fired at Zachary's face.

The arrow never met its mark. A sudden blast of air knocked it out of its path, and it skimmed past Zachary's ear instead, hitting the tree behind him. Marcel lowered his hand, returning to his pipe. Zachary didn't even blink, his face set.

"That's settled then," he murmured.

Jionathan put himself between the Magi and Fae, throwing up his arms. Rufus had once told Jionathan that Zachary's bark was worse than his bite—up until he bit. As long as Zachary was theatrical, his threats were as colourful and empty as a paper lantern. But when the words died to nothing, the hound would attack.

Fae gave a sharp cry of pain, her back arching, as her body grew unnaturally taut, hands curling into fists. Jionathan looked back at her in horror as her eyes rolled, her teeth clenched. Zachary reached out to her, almost as if he intended to help.

"What are you doing to her?" Jionathan demanded.

"Do you feel that, Sidhe?" Zachary said. "That's me reaching out to every drop of water in your body. You would be surprised how much there is. And all I have to do is draw it out," he twitched a finger, and Fae whimpered, "and you would die. But that's not all I can do. I can raise the temperature, bring you to boil."

"No, stop! *Stop it!*" Jionathan screamed, trying to throw himself at Zachary. Zachary's eyes locked with his, and a second later, pain seared through Jionathan's body and he went rigid, hanging in the air.

"You have water in your body too, Delphi," Zachary said, his other hand now raised toward Jionathan. "Would you like me to bring you to boil as well? Is that what it's going to take? Or is it enough, to watch her suffer?"

Jionathan gasped, swivelling his eyes over to Fae. She had

begun to sweat, her eyes watering as she choked on each breath, struggling. Her face grew red. Zachary curled his fingers a little more, and Fae made a desperate keening noise, squeezing her eyes closed in agony.

"Of course," Zachary said, "from boiling, I can then bring you to freezing in a matter of seconds." He flicked his hand the other way.

Fae gave a strangled, almost delirious moan, her chest heaving, and then screamed as the colour drained from her face, the skin turning a faint blue.

"Please, please, let her go!" Jionathan begged, his voice strangled, mouth barely able to move. "I'll come with you! I'll come with you, but let her go! Please! *Please!*" he tried to fight against the grip Zachary had over him, but it was too strong. "She's my friend. Please," he sobbed. "She's my friend. Please, Zachary, please! *PLEASE!*"

Something rippled overhead, a sharp bolt of hot air, shooting straight toward Zachary. Zachary dropped his hands and threw up a shield, crossing his arms in defence. The strike hit the mental shield and dissipated, and Jionathan and Fae collapsed to their knees, Fae shaking, but alive. She heaved in several ragged breaths, coughing and spluttering as Jionathan dragged himself toward and pulled her close.

Zachary looked over their shoulders to the newcomer, and his face broke into a masquerade smile. "Oh, well this completes our little gathering tidily. Our final member has arrived, at last. You're late, Merle."

"I can't be held entirely accountable for that," was the curt, cold reply, and Jionathan looked up in disbelief. His heart soared as he took in the strict, looming figure of Rufus—face of thunder and eyes blazing like thief fire on a stormy night.

"You're here now, that's what matters." Zachary bowed his head. "It's good to see you, Merle."

"And you," Rufus said grimly. "Zachary."

CHAPTER
37

"Rufus," Jionathan sobbed in relief. "Oh gods, Rufus, thank you. I'm so sorry. Oh gods, thank you. I thought—the drug—it was a mistake—"

"We'll talk about this later," Rufus replied, his words seeming to curl in the air. Jionathan went quiet, and Rufus turned back to Zachary. "There was a time, Arlen, when the *sight* of someone raising a hand to a woman, would have put you on the war path."

"She's not an innocent, she's a warrior," Zachary said stiffly. "And she shot at me first. Man or woman, when you raise a blade, you do so with the acknowledgement you might die. I treated her accordingly."

"She's my *friend*," Rufus said. "And I'm not going to let you hurt her, or take Jionat."

"Keep the Cat Sidhe then, if you like, but the Delphi brat is not up for debate."

"I'm not debating, Zachary. I'm telling you—turn back. The King assigned me with finding and protecting the Prince. He's *my* charge, and you're not going to lay a finger on him."

"Merle," Zachary laughed, "this isn't a matter of responsibilities and pride any more. Or did the King relay some private order that you and the Prince were to go gallivanting off into Avalon together?"

"I was doing no such thing," Rufus said tonelessly. "Truly."

"It's an act of *treason* for him to steal away into the unallied lands, and your part in letting him go would land you on the gallows at best. Do you honestly think I'm going to let you do that?" Zachary glared. "Even Master Odin couldn't save you if you crossed that line."

"I don't think you're in the right standing to be throwing accusations of treason, Zachary." Rufus stepped forward, moving carefully around Jionathan, his hand lightly brushing Fae's shoulder to ensure she was alright.

Zachary's eyes darkened. "Oh?" he said softly.

"Did you think I wouldn't find out?" Rufus asked. "About your dealings with the Korrigans?"

Jionathan sat up straight, his arms draped around Fae, who shivered still, her face set fiercely.

"You mean *he's* the conspirator?" Jionathan breathed. It shouldn't have been a surprise, on reflection.

Zachary watched Rufus evenly. "How did you find out?"

"We had a run-in with them. Pleasant sort, your comrades."

"We don't like them any more than you do, Rufus," Emeric said.

Rufus snapped his gaze at the smaller Magi, his mouth tightening in dismay. "Fold, not you too. Why would you get involved with something like this?"

Emeric drew himself up. "I did as my captain required of me, and I would do it again."

Rufus turned on Zachary, venom in his voice. "You have used and corrupted a good man, Zachary."

Zachary sniffed. "What I do, Merle, I do because I must. You wouldn't hold that against me. You're not so cruel."

"I am infinitely so."

"Wait, how long have you known?" Jionathan found his voice, rising up onto his knees. "How long have you known it was Zachary?"

Rufus exhaled impatiently. "The Korrigan who tortured me—"

"Tortured?" Emeric mouthed in dismay.

"—said something I recognised. I tried to recall where I'd heard it before, and then I remembered your words in the library, Zachary. 'Everything changes, all you can do is change it back.' That's what you said that to me."

"Alas," Zachary cried dramatically. "I was betrayed by my poetry?"

"You know what you're doing is wrong," Rufus said. "You wouldn't have said it otherwise. There's still a good man locked beneath your anger and bloodthirst, and I know he can hear me. Please—go back, Arlen. The Prince won't cross into Avalon, I swear it on my life."

"That doesn't bring me comfort," Zachary said. "I don't trust your ability to keep him in check, and I don't trust him not to toss you aside when you've outlived your usefulness."

"I would never do anything to Rufus—he's my friend!" Jionathan shouted, and Rufus grunted, rolling his eyes. Jionathan prickled at the unspoken message. "I left you behind to protect you, you idiot. I didn't want this to happen."

"Oh no, you'd rather Zachary killed Fae and broke your arms instead?" Rufus's voice broke from its steady pitch. "You don't make decisions on my behalf, Jionat—do you understand me? Never again! Now, we're returning to Bethean and *you*," he pointed at Zachary, sweeping his finger across to Emeric and Marcel, "you can go back to Harmatia."

Zachary's expression went blank. "No," he said. "Not this time. No. I have had enough of waiting. The King is dying, and either you're going to bring the Delphi home now or, Merle...I will kill you, too." There was soft sincerity to his words, and Jionathan

390

didn't doubt them.

Rufus rose to his full height. "You can try."

Zachary rolled his eyes. "Must we do this?"

"Apparently so."

"Rufus," Zachary sighed. "You *cannot* win. You *know* that."

"You have no idea what I'm capable of."

"You are each as stubborn as the other," Marcel cut in impatiently. "If you mean to fight, get on with it."

"Marcel!" Emeric turned on his master. "No, surely there's a way around this. Come, now. This is ridiculous."

"No, Fold." Zachary widened his stance a little, in preparation for a fight. "Merle has made his mind up, and so have I."

"You're brothers, for Athea's sake. You're not going to kill each other!" Emeric looked worriedly across at Marcel again. "They wouldn't kill each other, would they?"

Marcel shrugged, rolling his head up to look at the sky. "Sunset approaches. You are running out of time, Zachary."

Rufus gave Marcel a peculiar look, his brow furrowed, and Marcel stared blankly back and replaced the pipe in his mouth, tipping his head slightly. Jionathan couldn't pretend to understand this silent exchange, but Rufus's thoughtful expression hardened with resolve.

The first blow came without warning—another blast of air, which Rufus swept up and around toward Zachary's side. It deflected over his mental shield, which rippled, humming slightly. Zachary summoned a water-whip to each hand, streams of water tightening into delicate ropes that he snapped out toward Rufus.

Rufus threw up his hands, and summoned his own shield, the whips curling harmlessly around him, hissing and spitting through the air like snakes.

"We're wasting our time, Merle, hitting at each other's shields. Eventually you'll have to let yours down, and when you do—"

Rufus brought his hands around sharply, and something strange happened around Zachary's barrier. The air seemed to shift from the side of him, as if it was folding in on itself. Jionathan watched, amazed, as great, hurling wind sucked through with exceptional force, enough to send a man spinning. Zachary sensed the attack in the last second and dove out of the way, rolling deftly across the grass. He rose to his knees and grinned at Rufus, his hair sticking up, as Marcel pulled his pipe out of his mouth, and Emeric gaped.

"Did you just create a vacuum of air outside my shield? That's Hathely's technique!" Zachary laughed. "When did you learn that?"

Rufus paused. "This afternoon," he confessed between gasps for air. He already looked haggard from the concentration. Zachary gave a genuine laugh, clapping his hands as he mounted to his feet.

"You never cease to amaze me," he said. "But now you've rather shown your hand."

"You don't know the half of it yet." Rufus attacked again, air twisting as he created another vacuum around Zachary. But Zachary anticipated him this time, and ducked, throwing out his own attack. Two jets of air skimmed out toward Rufus, like arrow shafts. They bounced on Rufus's barrier and flung off in opposite directions, tearing through the trees behind in an explosion of wood and leaves.

Jionathan covered Fae, as Rufus directed his magic into the ground. The earth around Zachary's feet reared up, like hands bursting out of the ground, and grabbed him by the ankles. They sank him down to the knee, Zachary flailing his arms to stay upright.

"When you attack, you drop your barrier," Rufus said, as Zachary laughed again, trying to pull his legs free.

"And that was Fold's technique—Merle, you've been studying us! But again, you haven't quite mastered it." Zachary rested his hands against the ground, and it trembled and then cracked, turning to sand. He pulled his legs free, shaking away the dirt.

392

"Jionat." Fae clutched Jionathan's arm tightly, her voice barely above a whisper. "Jionat you need to run. These men...that man, he's toying with Rufus—humouring him. Rufus may indeed be a genius, but this is a display of children's tricks."

Even though he didn't want to believe it, Jionathan knew it was true. Rufus's instinctual understanding of magic gave him a natural ability to create, or mimic techniques that others had slaved over for years. Even so, as far as Jionathan knew, Rufus possessed no experience in combat and had no training. His role in the Magi was one of a theorist, and whilst he had genius on his side, Zachary was a soldier, and so were his men.

What was more, Jionathan had seen Zachary fight. Even without his magic, his skill with the sword was almost a match to Fae's. It would be no great task for Zachary to draw a weapon on Rufus and cut him down—that he hadn't was a display of good humour, not luck.

"What now?" Zachary's voice grew more menacing. "Shall I simply cease my attacks?" Zachary extended his shield, and it rippled as it met Rufus's, two barriers pressing against each other so that they almost sparked. "Do you think you can push my shield back? Overcome it perhaps, and set the Cat Sidhe on me? Without magic I would no doubt fall to her. Is that your plan?"

"It's an option." Rufus's jaw and neck were so taut Jionathan could see the pulse running down the side of his throat.

Zachary gestured to the two men either side of him, and both raised their own shields, Emeric with a doleful expression.

"And what about all three of us?" Zachary asked, and Rufus's shield shivered and shrank beneath the pressure of the other two. "Ah."

"You're not alone in this fight, Rufus." Fae struggled to her feet, her breath still short.

"No, Fae," Rufus hissed between his teeth. "If you step out of this barrier, they'll burn you alive."

Fae gave a low growl and cast her eyes down. Rufus's shield

shuddered again and grew even smaller, his breath quickening.

"You know, I saw a man's mental shield get shattered once," Zachary drawled. "Do you know what happened to him, Merle?"

Rufus didn't reply, but gave a small groan, his hands shaking as he tried to hold up the steadily shrinking shield around them.

"No, I don't suppose you do. It was rather grim." Zachary moved slowly forward as his own shield grew, pushing Rufus's back. "If it were only us, perhaps you might've held me off, but three against one? What are you trying to achieve?"

"Who knows?" Rufus said breathlessly. "And you? Dealing with the Korrigans? Spells that cheat death? Immortality? What are *you* trying to achieve, Zachary?"

Zachary shrugged. "Who knows?" he mimicked.

Rufus's shield shrank even more, barely circling the three of them. The Magi advanced, swarming in. They were preparing to attack, the thin layer of magic was all that separated them now.

And then it was all over. With a strangled cry, Rufus's shield failed, and the Magi swamped them. Marcel covered Fae, whilst Emeric went for Jionathan, standing above him.

Rufus grunted and threw a clumsy punch at Zachary, who caught the fist easily and twisted Rufus around and down, dropping him to his knees. Zachary drew his sword, bared it across Rufus's throat, and held him up straight. Above them, the sky was rapidly turning orange, Notameer sinking into the horizon as the night began to rise, the clouds glowing a vivacious blood red. Neither Jionathan nor Fae dared to move, their hands reluctantly raised in surrender.

Rufus caught Jionathan's eyes, and in an instant they blazed with a terrible fear. Zachary let his blade skim the delicate skin of Rufus's throat, scratching along the fine stubble.

"No," Jionathan begged as Rufus grew still, his breath misting up the blade of the sword. "Don't kill him! Please don't kill him!"

Zachary ignored the desperate plea, leaning down to Rufus.

"You're a prodigy, Merle," he breathed into his ear. "But as you are, each of us alone is more powerful. You should have known you couldn't defeat us. Surrender now, and I won't kill you."

"I won't let you take him." Rufus's voice was small and unsteady.

"Rufus," Zachary groaned, the sword flashing as it moved gently up. "Your natural understanding and ability with magic is unmatched, but you're *capped*. There's no way to stop us. You're a man of reason. Be reasonable."

Rufus closed his eyes, his throat bobbing as he swallowed. "You're right," he finally said, and Jionathan was caught between relief, and disappointment. For a moment he'd hoped, hoped that maybe Rufus could save them. Hoped that maybe Rufus would be enough…

But Rufus wasn't finished speaking. "As I am, I'm no match for you," he said. "The truth is I've been hiding all this time. All this time, trying to quell it down, trying to starve it out and be smaller and lesser until I extinguished it. But enough now. If I'm going to die…if I'm going to die…"

Rufus drew in a sharp breath, and flames exploded around him.

Zachary cried out, throwing himself clear. He threw up a shield, scrabbling away as a wave of intense heat flared into the air.

Rufus clambered to his feet, the flames rising from his skin harmlessly as they ate away his robes and shirt. Emeric and Marcel stepped away cautiously, drawing up their shields. Rufus advanced toward them.

"You asked me why I bothered challenging you? I was biding my time, but the sun's setting now. That's all I needed. I can't face you capped, you're right." The flames flickered and died down, and Rufus placed a hand up to his forehead, his mouth drawn into a thin line. "This is all I can do."

Zachary drew himself into a crouch, and his eyes flew wide. "Merle—no. What are you doing?"

Rufus's fingers tightened as around his temples. His expression was grim, lips drawn down, like he was in pain.

"He means to break the cap," Marcel said with hushed intensity, and Jionathan choked.

"Merle, stop. Have you gone mad—you'll *kill* yourself! *Rufus, stop!*" Zachary scrambled up just as a wave of power pulsated from Rufus's hand into his forehead. Rufus's breath hitched, his body going rigid, and then a scream tore through his throat, and his legs gave way. He crumbled to the ground, gasping in pain.

"Rufus!" Jionathan darted out, but Emeric caught him by the wrist and dragged him back, heat still rising from Rufus's scalding body, enough to make the grass around him curl brown. Even from where he stood, Jionathan could feel it searing against his skin. If any of them got close, they would burn.

"Healing Septus, Merle," Emeric panted, holding Jionathan firmly back. "What have you done? Oh Septus, what do we do? Oh gods. Oh gods…"

Rufus dropped his head against the ground, prostrated like he was in prayer. His breathing was laboured, and he hugged his arms around himself, curling forward as he twitched in pain.

"There is nothing we can do," Marcel whispered grimly. "He has sealed his fate."

"No, if you get him back to Edwin—if you get to Harmatia— you could save him," Jionathan begged, and in an instant the Magi around him were no longer enemies. Zachary edged forward, despite the glare of heat which rose from Rufus's twitching body.

From between his arms, his face pressed against the earth, Rufus's voice came out, muffled and gravelly. "Nobody's returning to Harmatia today."

"Merle?" Zachary breathed, reaching for him, and Rufus straightened, looking up.

The whites of his eyes had burst red, weeping blood, which streamed from his ears and nose. Smoke curled from his bare shoulders as the flames appeared once more. They danced along his skin, licking it greedily until it covered his arms, chest, and torso like a coat of armour. Jionathan had never seen anything like it, and amidst his apprehension, his heart soared. Rufus staggered to his feet, his arms swinging loosely as he straightened, finding his balance. He planted his feet firmly in the ground and rose to his full height.

"All of you…" He loomed over them, taller than ever—like a mountain looking down. "All of you underestimated me for the *strength* I showed in controlling myself. No more. See me for what I am." The fire along his skin began to mark it. At first they looked like burns, and then Jionathan saw patterns begin to appear—swirling knots and designs, which glowed in the burning light.

Zachary shrank back, raising his hands as the fire grew, burning inside and out, light dancing behind Rufus's once blue eyes, like the flames were in him. It was like staring into a blazing hearth, and that hope in Jionathan suddenly grew cold.

Gone was Rufus's steady control, gone was the comforting assurance of his presence. A wild, hungry power flickered in its place.

"No, that's…that's not possible. You can't be…" Zachary shook his head. "You can't be!"

"What's he talking about? Rufus?" Jionathan looked between Zachary and the man he barely recognised as Rufus now, enclosed in flames.

"I am a child of Aramathea," Rufus's voice boomed like thunder, the sky darkening overhead. "I am born of Athea. And If I am going to die," he pointed down at Zachary, "I am going to *burn* the world first."

CHAPTER
38

❧

Power raged through him, burning unchecked, and Rufus wondered why he'd never reached out to it before. He wondered why he'd been so frightened.

It didn't matter anymore—he embraced it now like a long-lost lover. Like Mielane.

I will embrace her too, soon.

The heat made the blood on his face dry and crack, like war-paint. The raging current of magic had stemmed the flow of the bleeding, but even so Rufus knew the damage was too great. This was to be his final act, and in his anger and his excitement he welcomed the consequences. If it meant being granted this one sip of freedom in his earthly body, then Rufus didn't mind dying.

The fire rose around him in a column, bursting over their heads and doming over them until they were all caged in flames. And yet still more power bubbled out of him, like a dam had been broken, unleashing the force of the sea. Rufus was dying, and yet he felt as if he were breathing for the first time.

He looked down at his enemies and smiled. "Shall we begin?"

Summoning a ball of light to his hands, he released a flaming projectile at Zachary. The burst of fire—an arrowhead—morphed in the air, springing wings and growing until it was a gargantuan bird, circling their heads. Its eyes glowed like embers. Rufus felt a part of himself in the creature, felt as if he were flying with it, wings of flame sparking and crackling, leaving trails of smoke in their wake. At his command it swooped down.

Zachary threw himself out of the way, raising a shield. Rufus let him—he knew Zachary's limitations, and knew he wouldn't be able to withstand this barrage for long. He would be getting tired by now. Rufus turned his eyes on Marcel and Emeric.

The bird attacked, driving the two Magi away from their hostages. Jionathan and Fae huddled together, away from the rising flames.

Zachary lashed at the bird with a water-whip, whilst Emeric built a cover, making a wall around Jionathan and Fae to protect them from the blaze. Rufus focused his attention on Marcel.

"*Marcel!*" Emeric screamed as the bird swooped in toward his master.

Marcel threw up his own shield, but the glaring heat alone was enough to make him stumble back, unable to stop it. The bird was no longer a personification of magic—it was alive and wild and more powerful than any of them.

One of Zachary's whips shot through the air, and cut the bird in two, splitting it before it could reach Marcel. Zachary was given one moment of triumph, and then the two flaming halves morphed into separate birds and began to circle once more. They looped around playfully, growing in size as their wings skimmed the ring of fire enclosing them.

As his enemies gawked, transfixed by their amazement and terror, Rufus took the opportunity to summon a ball of air and toss it between them. Emeric ducked beneath his wall immediately, pulling Jionathan and Fae's heads down with him. Neither Marcel nor Zachary were as fortunate.

The ball exploding, blasting them both back several strides. They landed hard, Zachary rolling precariously close to the wall of flames. It reared out to meet him, and he scrambled back with a cry. There was a panic in his voice now that Rufus had never heard before. It was almost child-like.

Marcel stumbled to his own feet, his breathing laboured. Rufus watched him, cocking his head to one side, a primal feeling coming over him. He'd bruised a few of Marcel's ribs, and the blast had winded him. Marcel blinked, disorientated, and one of the birds spun down toward him, preparing to strike the final blow.

"NO!" Emeric threw himself out from hiding and dove straight into Marcel, throwing him down. Marcel grunted in surprise, his wounded ribs aggravated by the fall. Rufus could almost see the pain, like a red glow on his body. The bird swooped up again, missing its target, and Emeric turned to Rufus, tears in his eyes, his face and clothes already smoke-stained. He had the audacity to look betrayed, and Rufus fought hard not to laugh. As if Emeric, Marcel and Zachary hadn't been the first to attack. As if they hadn't threatened Fae and Jionathan, and terrorised Harmatia for two years. As if they hadn't aligned themselves with the Korrigans.

Rufus summoned the two birds and set them flying toward Emeric and Marcel.

"MERLE!" Zachary threw himself between his men and Rufus's rage, his arms wide, trying to block as much of Emeric and Marcel as he could. His shield was gone, soot and dirt clinging to his face and body. "*Enough, please!*" he shouted over the howl of the flames, the skies above livid with black, billowing clouds. "You've done enough!"

"Zachary, run! *Arlen!*" Marcel cried.

"That's not Rufus!" Emeric echoed, his arms still wrapped around Marcel. "Get out! Get out!"

Zachary didn't move, his arms spread, feet set in the ground like he was made of stone. He pretended not to be afraid, but Rufus could see right through him, as if looking straight into his heart. Every year that Zachary had lived, every hardship, was visible to Rufus.

Just as with Marcel, Zachary's pain was a visible red hue, cracks and cuts glowing like cinders. Rufus could count the number of broken bones, healed now, but forever marked, a tally of abuse that dated back to childhood. Scars ran like rivers up Zachary's body, and collided along his back, stitched together like a fleshy patchwork. Rufus had once thought Zachary as incapable of feeling fear as he was of feeling pain. Now he knew better.

With these eyes, Rufus could see that Zachary had taken his splintered bones, his torn flesh, his anger and fear, and he'd gathered it around himself, like a cloak, until it solidified into armour. He hid in a shell of his own pain, hardened and experienced, but beneath it all, he was as vulnerable as the rest of them.

"Tremble, Arlen Zachary," Rufus said, and though it was his voice, he was but one strand in the current that flowed through him. A single stone in a brick wall, one of a million souls combined. He was Athea. "You have dabbled in something that condemns you to darkness."

"Then lay your judgment," Zachary said, his chest heaving. "But my men—your friends—leave them! They were only following orders! Please, Merle—let them go."

Something of the gleeful expression on Rufus's—no, *Athea's*—face must have reminded Zachary that, moments ago, Jionathan had made the same desperate plea.

Zachary grimaced. "I made them do it. They were following my orders—I threatened them! Fold was trying to protect you, for Notameer's sake—"

"Do not dare call upon my brother now," Athea said. "You are in my domain."

Zachary didn't move. "You can't do this."

Rage coursed through Athea's body. "I can do as I please! This is my ruling time!" He threw his arms up, and suddenly the two

401

circling birds were replaced with a flock, spiralling around and around, hundreds and then thousands spilling into the sky. The men before him cowered, and he felt powerful.

"Merle...Rufus...have mercy," Zachary choked, and Athea laughed.

"The man you call for is gone. You killed him." He moved toward Zachary who stood petrified and small. "I heard your slight, Arlen Zachary, that I am unfair. Death is not fair. But it is the only companion you have to life, and without it your human morality is groundless. Do not plead to me of justice and mercy. Those are not my qualities. I am chaos. I am passion. I am the road after death and the guide to the lost. I am your emotions and your darkest thoughts. I am your love and I am your war." The fire gathered into his hand as the earth jutted up from beneath him. He touched the rock, drawing the elements in together as the earth twisted and shrieked, becoming a terrible blade of molten rock. Rufus's voice boomed out with a thousand others as he raised the sword to take Zachary's head. "I am the one you call *Athea*."

"RUFUS!" Jionathan voice pierced through the thundering bloodlust, and struck the small part of Rufus that swirled within it.

It was like being flicked. Sharp, slightly irritated consciousness blossomed through Rufus. He could feel Athea in and around him, foreign intention and rage pulsating through him. What was he doing? This wasn't him. Rufus pushed against himself, pushed against the sense of Athea that had made him a meagre passenger in his own body. Athea pushed back—the rage was not yet quailed, the job not yet done. But Rufus had had enough. He struggled with himself, grappling to quell his anger, to find his peace. He had surmounted so much anger over the years—now that it was unleashed, there seemed no end to it.

Jionathan climbed out from behind the wall, trembling from head to foot, face pale and sweat-sodden.

"Rufus," he repeated, silver eyes darting over Rufus's face, as if trying to find him. It was all Rufus need. A burst of fierce love for this foolish boy cut through the madness, and the part of him that was Athea ebbed away without resistance, relinquishing its hold.

Rufus looked back at Zachary, who'd fallen to his knees, a willing sacrifice, his eyes on the molten sword that Rufus had drawn back, ready to strike. But where once the thought of sliding the blade through his neck had filled Rufus with a righteous delight, it turned his stomach now.

"And I am Rufus…" he murmured, and let the sword drop. It melted back into the earth.

The flaming birds disappeared, swirling into nothing as the clouds dissipated. Where once the air was heavy with heat and smoke, it grew clear and peaceful. And in its wake it left the desecration it had reaped—a circle of burnt, dried grass, blackened earth, and the smell of fear and fire.

Rufus looked down at his steaming hands, and he let the heat leave him before reaching forward. With shaking fists, he pulled Zachary up.

"Go." It was his own voice, only his, hoarse but firm. "And don't send any others…if you return, I'll kill you." He released Zachary's collar.

Zachary rose to his feet, barely able to stand, and gestured to Marcel and Emeric behind him. They scrambled to their own feet and fled, still holding each other. Zachary remained between Rufus and his men until they were hidden beyond the trees, and then he, too, bolted, stopping only once at the treeline to look back at Rufus before he disappeared.

Rufus stared into the trees, and then looked down at his hands. The ancient swirls and patterns that had covered his skin were fading away, and with them, his energy drained. He felt weightless and altogether heavy at the same time, as if he were on the cusp of sleep. A low, blinking pain began to resound in his head.

Slowly, he turned on Jionathan and Fae, who were still watching him in horrified wonder. Everything felt slow, and lethargic after that burst of power, and Rufus struggled to find any energy through his growing grogginess. There was no anger left in him, no excitement at their victory. He felt bitter, and hollow.

"It's sickening really," Rufus said. "How little faith the pair of you have in me."

"Rufus, we…" Jionathan began, but his voice died in his throat.

"Six years. *Six years*, Jionathan! And for what?" Rufus stepped toward them, trying to ignore the way they both shrank back. "Insulted, abused—am I a plaything to you?" His chest felt like it was caving in, his throat tight. "You cast me away, you treat me like a child—you think I don't understand the consequences of my actions? You think I didn't know exactly what I was agreeing to, when I chose to come after you? I have my *own* mind, and I made it! The pair of you…the pair of you! I've lived more than you *ever* have!" His legs gave way and he stumbled, falling to his knees. He dropped back and sat, overcome.

Jionathan stood on the edge of the burnt circle, Fae lingering fearfully behind. Rufus covered his mouth and bowed his head—exhausted and grieving. He felt alone, his vision darkening in the corners. The steady thumping in his head grew to a sharp sting.

"Why?" Jionathan's voice was soft and strangely derelict. "Why do you follow? After everything? Why? Why do you *always* follow?" He choked on the words, his bottom lip quivering.

Rufus stared at him, and through the mounting pain in his head, his expression softened. He opened his mouth to tell Jionathan, to berate and reassure him, but the pain spiked and he cried out instead.

"Rufus?" Jionathan gasped, as Rufus doubled over himself, clinging to his face. It felt like someone had thrust needles in through his eyes sockets. An eruption of blood burst from his nose, and eyes, and spilled between his fingers onto the floor. His vision blackened, the pain taking over, and with a soft moan, Rufus collapsed, Jionathan and Fae screaming his name.

～⚬～

Jionathan thought the worst had passed when Rufus's unconscious body finally stopped seizing. Blood dripped from beneath his half-lidded eyes, his breathing stuttered and broken, lips parted. Yes, Jionathan had thought the worst had passed...

And then Rufus stopped breathing.

For half a second Jionathan went entirely numb, the air rushing his lungs. And then Fae threw herself down beside them and placed an ear against Rufus's chest.

"He's not dead," she assured breathlessly. "Not yet, but his breathing is shallow, and his heart slow. We need to get him help, fast."

"Can you fly?"

Fae nodded, though she was still pale and couldn't disguise how laboured her movements were. In the tree line, Jionathan could hear the sound of agitated nickering, and he spotted his bay tied up close. Rufus had clearly taken the horse and ridden after them. Fae transformed, and together they managed to manoeuvre Rufus onto her back. Without another word, she took to the sky, bearing her precious cargo away. Jionathan mounted the bay and spurred it hard, turning it back onto the path.

The road to Sarrin seemed to stretch on for far too long, and by the time Jionathan spotted the familiar walls, he was sick with fear. Fae flew above him, a tiny speck in the sky.

Tearing through the town, Jionathan could scarcely believe that they were still clearing away the rubble from the bandits' attack. It seemed so long ago now—a vague memory.

Luca was waiting for them at the entrance of the house, sat on the wall. Jionathan wondered if, when Rufus had gone after them, Luca had chosen to remain outside until they returned. She jumped down as she spotted him, beaming widely, and shouted back up toward the house. Her expression fell as Jionathan rode up beside her, his face dripping with sweat, and bloodless.

"A physician!" he rasped, as Luca dove forward to grab the horse's reins, the bay throwing its head wildly. "You have to get a physician! Rufus—Rufus is hurt!"

From the house, Lily-Anne appeared, and she reached for Jionathan as he all but dropped from the saddle, staggering on weak legs.

"Jionat, what happened?" Luca demanded.

"Attacked. Magi. Rufus fought. He's hurt. He needs a physician, now!" Jionathan forced out.

Lily-Anne shot Luca an alarmed look, and grabbed the reins from her. With a single bound, she threw herself up onto the horse's back, and wrenched it around, back toward the town. The bay reared and tried to shake her off, but she grappled with it, and with a hard kick, set it galloping back down the road, her skirts flying behind her.

Jionathan collapsed against the wall, light-headed and bleary eyed. He was breathing too fast, he knew, but he couldn't stop. Luca clung to his arm.

Are you hurt?" she asked, her voice shrill.

He shook his head, his hearing muffled.

"Where's Rufus?"

"With Fae. Fae has him," Jionathan said hunching over and clutching his stomach. He felt like he'd run the whole way. Luca laid a trembling hand on his back.

"I…" She stammered, "I have to get my father. Hold on. Hold on!"

She turned and ran back to the house, screaming for Michael. Jionathan rested his back against the wall and looked up at the darkening sky. Fae had begun her descent, flying as carefully and smoothly as she could.

What if Rufus hadn't survived the journey? The uncomfortable thought settled in Jionathan's mind as he watched Fae fly down. What if those pitiful heartbeats that Jionathan had clung to had been the last in Rufus's body? What if the last thing Jionathan had done for him, was betray Rufus?

Fae landed heavily, with a low groan that sounded like a tree being felled.

"Is he—" Jionathan began.

"Still alive," Fae said, and Jionathan almost cried.

"Are you—"

"Fine." She began to walk toward the house, her wings curled protectively around Rufus. Jionathan jogged at her side.

"Where is he? What's happened?" Michael's came tearing out through the door, Luca behind him. He skidded to a halt at the sight of them, and went rigid. "Rufus," he breathed. "Oh Healing Septus..."

"We need to get him into the house," Fae said.

Michael didn't move, petrified to the spot, his dark red eyes wide.

"*Michael*," Fae said with more urgency. "I can't fit through the door like this. Help me get him inside."

Michael blinked, and then nodded dumbly, hurrying down the steps toward them. Fae lay low to the ground, and allowed Michael to reach up, lifting Rufus from her back. Rufus didn't even stir, as Michael heaved him over his shoulder, and carried him up into the house. Jionathan made to follow, but faltered as Luca made a quiet exclamation.

"Fae?"

Jionathan looked back to see Fae had transformed. She tried to rise but her legs folded under her, and she sprawled to her hands and knees, breathing heavily.

"It's alright," she said between laboured breaths. "I just need a moment. Go on ahead—stay with Rufus."

Jionathan hovered in the doorway, unwilling to leave her, but

Luca ducked down, and pulled Fae's arm around her shoulder, lifting her up.

"Go," Luca said. "I have her. Go on. We'll follow in a minute."

Jionathan nodded, and ran after Michael, who carried Rufus into a small bedroom on the ground floor, beside the washroom.

This bedroom, Luca had told Jionathan, was the room Mielane and Rufus had once shared together. It had remained unoccupied and empty since her death, and as Michael laid Rufus on the large wooden bed inside, Jionathan wished they could have brought him upstairs instead.

Mielane Rossignol had died in that bed. Seeing Rufus placed so tenderly on the same pillows felt like a dreadful omen.

Michael began to wash Rufus's face, cleaning it of blood as he tapped his cheeks, trying to rouse him. Rufus didn't wake, his jaw slack, skin turning grey.

It was a few minutes before Luca and Fae joined them, and a few more before Lily-Anne came rushing in, a brisk, middle-aged man shadowing her. The physician.

"Wounds from the bandit attack?" he asked, taking a look at Rufus's bare chest, stained in blood and smelling of smoke.

"No, he was attacked on the road." Fae settled in a chair nearby, her eyes sunken with exhaustion.

"Was it a blow to the head?" The physician examined Rufus critically, taking his pulse and watching his breath. Jionathan described what happened, omitting only that Rufus was a Child of Aramathea.

The physician grew still, his hand pressed to Rufus's forehead. "Has he woken since?"

"No."

The physician pried open one of Rufus's bloodshot eyes. His expression became grim, and he let it fall closed again. "This is beyond me," he said. "I have learnt some elemental healing techniques, but what you have described—the trauma is too extensive."

408

It was like he'd been knocked in the chest. Jionathan stood, mouth agape, the room void of sound. No one moved. No one spoke.

"No." Fae shattered the silence, rising from her chair. "There must be something you can do."

"I'm sorry—he's bleeding into his brain." The physician moved away from the bed. "It's only a matter of time, I'm afraid. You should prepare yourselves."

He reached for his bag to close it, but Jionathan grabbed him by the front of his shirt.

"No!" He wrenched the physician toward him. "No! He's *not* going to die. You cannot leave him die!"

"My dear boy—" the physician began.

"Please," Luca begged. "Please, don't give up on him. Please." Tears spilled, hot and heavy down her face, her lip wobbling.

"I can't lose another child in this room," Michael said in a voice barely above a whisper.

The physician looked between them all, and wilted. He nodded his head. "I will try everything I can to save him," he said. "But please forgive me, for try is all I can do."

CHAPTER 39

The hours crept by like a solemn funeral procession, but sleep evaded Fae. She sat in her chair, keeping vigil, despite her exhaustion. The physician, after doing all he could, had returned home for the night, and Fae had offered to keep watch over Rufus until morning. He'd had two more nose-bleeds since, and another seizure, but was calm now.

In the opposite room, Fae could hear Michael and Lily-Anne, both still awake, despite the hour. Lily-Anne was crying, the sound muffled by Michael's embrace. They'd sent an urgent letter to Rufus's parents, but feared it wouldn't arrive in time.

Fae didn't give into that pessimism. "They don't know what you are," she said to Rufus, who lay as still as stone. "They don't know what you're capable of. Child of Aramathea…I should have realised from the start."

The once roaring power that usually swirled around Rufus had died away to a trickle, like a flame on the cusp of being snuffed. But so long as it burnt, Fae wouldn't give up hope.

"He should have told us." The door opened, and Jionathan slipped into the room. Fae had heard him upstairs, pacing restlessly. No doubt Rufus's empty bed had done little to ease Jionathan's anxiety. Shutting the door softly, Jionathan approached Rufus, avoiding Fae's gaze.

"Would either of us have understood?" Fae leant forward, brushing Rufus's fringe out of his eyes. When Rufus had broken his cap, he'd untethered the magic he'd been supressing, and as terrible and great as it was, Fae had lost her fear of it. Somehow, seeing Rufus wield that power had assured her in a way words couldn't.

All that magic at his fingertips, all that destructive capability, and Rufus was still kind. Not evil, not born of darkness, or malice, but deeply loving, and full of pain.

"You know," Fae said, "I was so concerned with being suspicious of him, I never thought to question why he chose to be so secretive. He wanted to be seen for who he was, not what." She withdrew her hand and cradled it. Her body still ached from the Magi attack, but she was alive. Saved twice in one day, first by Jionathan, and then by Rufus. "I couldn't do anything," she breathed. "Faced with battle—my specialty, my purpose...and I was useless."

"We both were." Jionathan came and sat heavily beside her. "All of this, it's my fault," he said. "I should have never left."

"Sarrin or Harmatia?"

Jionathan buried his face in his hands with a long groan. He ran his fingers up into his hair and tugged on it hard, a gesture reminiscent of Rufus.

"I was so selfish." His voice wavered. "I thought it was about protecting him, but really I didn't want the guilt on my hands... and now..."

"Jionat," Fae ran her hand down his back, "those Magi would have come for you either way. Our only mistake was making Rufus's choice for him."

"He was right," Jionathan mumbled into his wrists, his face hidden. "He's lived more than either of us."

"Yes," Fae said faintly, shame filling her as she rested the side

411

of her head on Jionathan's own. She could feel his grief, and she kissed his temple lightly, trying to combat her own.

Through the hush, Jionathan mouthed an apology to Rufus over and over and Fae pretended not to hear.

"I'm sorry Rufus," Jionathan said. "I've killed you. I'm so sorry."

～∞～

It was just after the sixth hour, dawn on the horizon, when the sharp knocking came from outside. Torin thought perhaps the Lemra'n had returned for more twine, but then reasoned the assassin wouldn't have the courtesy to knock first. He would have just let himself in again.

Climbing from the bed, Torin assured Nora he'd see to it and descended into the shop. The knocking continued, insistent.

"Yes, yes, hold on." He unbolted the door and drew it open, squinting in the pre-morning light. Arlen Zachary stood outside, looking both ways up the street, his shoulder set stiffly. "Lord Zachary?"

"Torin Merle," Zachary said briskly, locking eyes with Torin. "Your son has been badly injured. You know where he's hiding. I suggest you hasten to him as soon as possible. You heard nothing from me."

He turned and marched away down the street, leaving Torin, horrified, in the doorway.

～∞～

As the second and third day passed, the nose-bleeds and seizures lessened, and Rufus slipped further into sleep, until he lay like a corpse, with barely a murmur of breath.

A solemn gloom fell over the house. The children, who didn't understand Rufus's condition, sensed the darkness. Rowan cried and spent much of his time pressing his face into the skirts of whichever woman was nearest, but Annabelle tried her utmost

412

to create cheer. She told jokes, laughed, and tried to drag her family to play. Once, Jionathan caught her kneeling beside Rufus, whispering into his ear. He wasn't sure what she said, but it seemed to be something between an order for him to wake soon, and a veiled threat. Jionathan almost admired her for that.

Michael had taken to his study and wouldn't be seen for hours at a time, though there was often mead or something stronger missing from the cellar. Luca too was scarce and quiet and spent her days in the orchard working, or sitting silently by Rufus's side, mopping his brow and feeding him sips of water.

Amidst all the despair, it was Lily-Anne who proved to be the axle of the house. She made her children continue their studies, saw to the meals, took Michael to bed when he was too drunk to walk himself, and when she caught Jionathan skulking outside the bedroom, pale and sick with worry, she drew him into a silent embrace. She never spoke, but Jionathan knew she didn't blame him for Rufus's condition. Indeed, everyone seemed of the mind that Rufus's fate was the fault of no one but Arlen Zachary and the Magi. Everyone, except Jionathan.

He spent his nights in Rufus's company, praying until he fell asleep in his chair, or until Fae came to sit with him. Jionathan couldn't remember a time he'd been so devout.

When he wasn't with Rufus, Jionathan preferred to spend his time outside. He avoided the others, choosing to walk up through the fields, busy with his own thoughts. He couldn't abide the Rossignols' unspoken forgiveness.

On the eve of the third day, Jionathan was just slipping out of the house before the meal when he almost collided with a tall man running in. Both of them leapt back in surprise, and Jionathan's heart seized.

With the same boyish black hair, sharp face, and dark stubble, Torin Merle looked so much like his son, Jionathan was almost fooled.

They stood back and studied each other, Torin's pale green

413

eyes darting over Jionathan's face. Jionathan braced himself. Surely, even if the Rossignols had forgiven him, Rufus's father could not.

Torin drew in a sharp breath, reached forward and seized Jionathan's hand, shaking it fervently.

"Your Highness." He gave a hasty bow. "Sire, *thank you*. Thank you for taking care of him, thank you for protecting him. Bless you."

Jionathan stuttered, taken aback by the raw gratitude. "I…"

From behind, he heard Michael descend into the hall, his footsteps clumsy.

"Torin?" Michael called in surprise, and Torin looked over at him with wide eyes. "How…how did you get word so quickly?

"Michael," he said. "It doesn't matter. Where is he?"

Without hesitation, Michael gestured for Torin to follow, Jionathan stepping out of the way and then following, as if led by a leash.

Fae greeted them at Rufus's door, having heard the commotion, and again Torin stopped, though there was an impatient fretfulness to the set of his shoulders.

"You must be Fae," he said. "My Rufus-lad spoke about you a great deal in his letters, and about everything you did for him."

"I am sure he neglected to say all did for us." Fae stepped back, and opened the door for him, letting Torin through.

As Torin laid his eyes on Rufus, it was hard to read all the emotions at once—relief, fear, anger, sadness, guilt—his face contorting. Slowly, he moved forward, seeming to age as he dragged his feet. He sat on the side of the bed, stroking Rufus's brow and kissing him on the forehead. "I'm here. I'm here now, my boy. Don't be frightened. I'm here."

With Torin's arrival, Jionathan was forced to change his routine. The Rossignol women fretted over Torin, who insisted on remaining with Rufus at all times, sleeping in the chair and taking meals in the room. When asked after his wife, and whether she was coming, Torin explained that she'd stayed in Harmatia.

"If we both left together, we would've aroused suspicion. We didn't want the Queen's men to know you were in Sarrin, so Nora agreed to stay…I don't think she'll ever forgive me for being the one who came, whilst she stayed behind."

The words had been like a dagger to the gut. That Jionathan could be responsible, however indirectly, for separating a mother and her son at this time, made him sick to his stomach.

He avoided Torin after that, even though it meant he couldn't sit by Rufus any more. It didn't seem right for Jionathan to be there, when Nora couldn't be.

Fae, in contrast, spent even more time in the room. She would keep watch of Rufus whenever she insisted Torin sleep a few hours, and would sit with him until he'd eaten. She even managed to get Torin out of the room for a half-hour one afternoon when she stated in no uncertain terms that he stank, and needed to bathe.

"My wife would like you," was all Torin said, a small smile on his increasingly gaunt face.

By the sixth day Rufus was dehydrated, despite the sips of water they'd slipped into his mouth. Jionathan found it hard to breathe unless he was out of the house, and would stay out as long as possible. He had stopping having nightmares during the sparse times he slept, but only because the worst seemed to be when he was awake, and he was awake a lot of the time.

This night was no different. After hours of tossing and turning in bed, Jionathan finally got up and decided to take a walk. Stealing downstairs, he paused at the sound of muted chatter nearby. Fae and Torin were with Rufus, talking together.

Feeling as if his feet were not his own, Jionathan crept down the corridor and stood outside the door listening.

"You need to eat," Fae said.

"I will. Just, not yet. Not yet."

"Torin, you barely touched the last meal. Starving yourself won't help him."

Torin was quiet for a moment, and when he spoke his voice was husky. "Then what will?" he breathed. "Oh gods. I could never cope when he was ill, even when it was just the result of too much drink. I *doted* on him. He didn't fall sick often, he was strong. He's always been strong in his own way."

"Yes, I imagine so."

"I tried to raise him right. I was too strict sometimes, and other times…I should've taught him to fight. I should've taught him, but I always thought if it came down to it, he'd find the strength. Fine temper he's got, my lad," Torin said, almost proudly. His voice fell again. "I was taught to fight when I was just a lad. The streets of Harmatia weren't as safe as they are now, so my father saw to it I was ready for the worst. I'd have done the same for Rufus, but by time he was the right age, he was so involved in his magic I put away any ambition of teaching him the sword. He was just so *clever*," Torin huffed. "I lived each day just to see the light in his eyes when I gave him a new book. Like I'd given him the world. He would just devour them."

Jionathan closed his eyes, and imagined Rufus in his youth—small and bright-eyed, curled up on the floor in a fort of books. It was easy to picture, not least because that was the position the guards had found Rufus in when he'd broken into the royal archives.

Torin gave low chuckle. "First time I saw him pick up one of my books on magic, I gave him such a tanning, the little git. I didn't know he could actually *read* the sodding thing! I thought he was just playing with it. I never realised he understood—not only the words, but their meaning. Theories that grown men've laboured over for years, and he read them like he wrote them." There was another long pause. "First time he did magic, he came into the house clutching something so carefully in his hands

Nora and I thought he'd brought a stray kitten in from the street. We ordered him to show us, and he was holding a tiny flame in the palms of his hands, nursing it like it was a new-born babe. He used it to light the cooking fire—told us it came from his heart. He was only five. My boy," Torin's voice broke. "My boy…"

"Torin," Fae eased, "when those Magi attacked, all our courage and skill in battle meant nothing. It was your son's magic that saved us. His magic and his kindness. So don't fret about the past, because you truly nurtured the best part of him."

Jionathan heard Torin sigh—but in relief or exhaustion, he didn't know.

"You're a good woman, Fae," Torin said. "It doesn't surprise me that he fought for you and the Prince."

"Yes, even when the sensible thing would have been to run, or give in…He was very stubborn."

"Hah. That's my son. Gets it from his mother—stubborn ass."

They laughed, and then fell into contemplative silence. Once again, Fae tried to urge him to eat. "A little, please?"

"I will," Torin promised. "But now…I just need to be by him."

"Rufus wouldn't want you to starve on his account."

"Aye, as if the wordy little bugger has any right to lecture me on that, when he's nothing but skin and bones himself. No, I'll eat. But for now…it's ridiculous, I know, but I feel that if I love him, I shouldn't."

"Why?"

"I'm not sure. Maybe…" Torin hesitated. "Maybe if I died instead, the gods would let my son live?"

Jionathan fled before he could hear any more, sprinting for the door. He wrenched it open and dove out into the night. He ran until his throat was dry, his breath short and his limbs sore and aching, and then still he ran. Onward into the nothing of the next field, and then further still until Sarrin was a small speck in the night, and he collapsed to his knees and screamed into the earth.

Because there was no justice, no fairness, or integrity in a man wishing he could take his son's place in death, wishing as if it were his responsibility. Jionathan recalled Athea's words, spoken through Rufus's mouth and looking up at the sky he found her star.

"You may not be justice, but you know love! *He's one of yours!*" he howled. "If you want to take anybody, if you *have* to take somebody, then let it be me! Not Rufus—he doesn't deserve this! Please—*take me!*" He bowed his head to the ground. "Please," he sobbed. "Just take me."

∼∞∽

Everywhere he looked Sverrin's reflection stared back, until eventually Jionathan wondered if he was Sverrin. Yet the images beyond the glass changed, flittering and disappearing, whereas he didn't move.

In front of him stood Rufus, arms loose at his side, his head tilted slightly to one side in curiosity. Jionathan stared back at him, ignoring Sverrin's presence in the mirrored walls. He was glad to see Rufus.

Rufus blinked sluggishly, his tousled hair sticking up at the fringe, as if he'd been running his hands through it. Neither of them spoke. Someone once told Jionathan that the dead couldn't speak.

It was a peaceful silence. Around them there seemed to be turmoil, a sickening spinning, the blinding, skull-splitting headache of the outside world, but here they were safe. Jionathan felt a fierce gratitude well up within him, and he grinned at Rufus, who grinned back, almost laughing.

And then Rufus was moving, walking past him, so that Jionathan was left staring in the abyss ahead, suspended in darkness in the mirrored room. He felt Rufus at his back, as if they had paused on the crossroads, looking in opposite directions. Then Rufus departed, moving on to somewhere Jionathan couldn't follow. Jionathan wished he'd had the chance to say farewell.

Without a breath of sound, he closed his eyes and reached forward. He touched the reflection of Sverrin beyond the glass wall, and quietly accepted his fate.

CHAPTER
40

She was daydreaming again. He could tell, because although her hands were busy with their work, there was a softness about her eyes that said she was far away.

He admired her in the mellow glow of the evening, golden light bathing her dark skin and hair. When she blinked, her eyelashes brushed the tops of her cheeks.

"There you are."

He roused himself from his own daydreaming, surprised, and realised she'd spotted him. Her eyes sparkled.

"I didn't mean to disturb you," he said.

"You didn't." She set down the basket she'd been filing with apples, and reached for him. He stepped into her, letting her run her hands down his arms until she reached his fingers. She held them lightly. "I was waiting for you."

The wind blew her skirt against his legs, and he closed his eyes, cherishing the warmth on his face. He could smell her skin, the scent of home.

"You have to go," she said.

He opened his eyes, and then sighed, nodding solemnly.

She smiled and, leaning forward, pressed a kiss to the side of his mouth. "My fiancé, Magi of Harmatia, is called to more important things."

"Don't say it like that."

"But you are. I understand." She got up on her tiptoes, and pressed her forehead against his, their noses brushing lightly. "Take care." She kissed him. "Be safe."

"I will." He embraced her, wishing he could carry her away with him, her arms around his waist, head pressed into his chest. "Mielane?"

"Yes?"

"I love you."

"I love you, too, Rufus."

Everything hurt. Someone had sandpapered the inside of his mouth and throat, and then banged his head against a wall for good measure. Rufus lay, his eyes too heavy to open, and vowed he would never drink again.

He balanced on the cusp of unconsciousness, too exhausted to move, but roused by his own discomfort. He realised he was incredibly thirsty.

With a bleary effort, he opened his eyes. The room was filled with light, and it made his head thunder like a river was passing through it. He closed his eyes again with a low grunt, and then forced them open. Everything was blurry, and he had to blink away the sleep, before his vision started to focus.

He was in the downstairs guest room of the Rossignol house, though he had no recollection of getting there.

Did I get so drunk last night I stumbled to the wrong bed?

He turned his head. On the bedside table, there was a cup, and his thirst spiked. He could piece together the mystery afterwards—for now, he desperately needed some water.

Reaching for the cup, however, proved to be more difficult than he'd anticipated. His arms were dead weights at his side, sore and stiff, like he hadn't moved in days. He swallowed dryly and tried to shift, his shoulder arching as he finally lifted the offending arm. His hand brushed the cup, and he hooked two fingers over the rim, dragging it toward him. He tipped it to see inside, and realised it was empty.

"Urh..." He released the cup with a low groan, his dry throat searing with pain. If he wanted a drink, he was going to have to get up.

His body objected to each movement, as Rufus tried to heave himself upright. He felt like a corpse trying to move itself, and after several attempts to sit up, he considered just closing his eyes and going back to sleep. He'd been having such a pleasant dream after all.

No, his thirst was too great. With the feebleness of an old man, he finally managed to sit upright. His wrists felt brittle, like old bone, and he shook from the exertion as he reached for the cup again. Holding it up, Rufus closed his eyes and drew on the elemental magic around him, summoning Notameer's power. Water appeared from the air, and spilled like a spring into the cup. Rufus drank greedily, refilling several times until he couldn't gulp down any more. It was the sweetest taste in the whole world.

Hydrated and feeling a little more alert, Rufus looked around the room. Small recollections were starting to come to him. Fae confronting him in the washroom, then a bandit attack, and then—

It came back to him in a great wave—the fight, the pain. Rufus's hands flew up to his face, half expecting to find blood still pouring from his nose and eyes. They were clean, his stubble long and scratchy beneath his fingers.

He was alive. Jionathan and Fae must have brought him back to Sarrin. Which begged only one question.

Where were they now?

It was incentive enough. Preparing all his strength, he swung his legs out of the bed and stood. A moment later, he found himself face to the ground, sprawled across the tiles. His legs had no strength.

"Athea, damn it..." he huffed, dragging himself onto his hands and knees. He crawled toward the dresser, and used it to pull himself to his feet. It shook precariously, but bore his weight enough to get him standing.

Vertical, and determined not to slump back into the bed, Rufus took several unsteady steps toward the door, feeling like a new-born child learning to walk. He dragged in more elemental magic as he moved, running it through his body. It revitalised him, easing some of the aches and pains.

He went out into the sunlit corridor. It was late morning, by the feel of it, and the house was quiet around him. Someone was in the washroom next door, but the instinctual tug that always led Rufus to Jionathan was directing him outside.

He set off, each step a little surer than the last, and left the house, going out into the front garden.

It was a beautiful day. The sky was bright blue, with only a few tiny wisps of long, lazy clouds that glided overhead like barges on a river, offering occasional respites from the sun. The garden was alive with the hum of insects and birds, bees and butterflies dancing between clumps of lavender, and the carpet of thyme that covered some of the garden.

On the lawn ahead, Lily-Anne had put some clothes out to dry, and they blew in the gentle breeze, chemises and skirts flapping slightly. Rufus, realising that his chest was bare, stopped at the clothes line to look for a shirt. Finding his, he carefully unpegged it and pulled it over his head, enjoying the feel of the fresh linen against his skin.

"Good morning," a voice said behind him, and he jumped in surprise. "It's good to see you outside, Torin. Some fresh air will do you—"

"Torin? My father's here?" Rufus whirled around excitedly and beamed at Fae who leapt back, startled.

"Rufus!" she cried, and before he knew what was happening, she had thrown her arms around his neck and was embracing him. "Oh Titania, Rufus—you're alive!"

"Was I dead?" Rufus asked, flustered.

Fae drew away. "All but. We all thought—that is to say—*good gods*, and here you are walking about!" She gripped his face tightly, turning it this way and that and looked out across the orchards. "Jionat!" she shouted. "Jionathan!"

Rufus sagged in relief at the sound of the boy's name. From the gate he saw Jionathan come running, roused by the shouts. When the Prince saw Rufus, his face drained of all colour, and then they both lunged, grabbing each other by the arms.

"You're still here!" Rufus said.

"You're alive!" Jionathan retorted, wide-eyed.

Rufus gave a hearty laugh, and yanked Jionathan into an embrace, before he had a chance to think. He released him a moment later, remembering himself, but Jionathan didn't seem to care. A wide smile had replaced his slacked mouth, and he kept a firm grip on Rufus's arms.

"It's you. It's really you." He grinned furiously. "Damn you, Rufus, you really scared us."

A sharp scream behind them drew their attention to Luca, who had come around from the orchards. Her basket of apples dropped, and she flung herself at Rufus, trapping Jionathan between them, and sending them all cascading to the floor. Fae dove forward and caught Rufus's head before it hit the ground.

"Are you trying to kill him again?" she snapped. "Be careful."

Luca cried, Jionathan and Rufus laughing giddily in their heap.

"Oh, Rufus, Rufus, oh sweet Rufus," Luca sobbed into his shoulder, and Rufus kissed what he could reach of her face, his arms around them both as Jionathan continued to laugh.

"What in Prospan's name is going on?" Lily-Anne bustled out of the house, her voice strangely shrill. She looked down at the bundle of bodies and went still. Rufus smiled up to her, waving as best he could beneath Jionathan and Luca.

"It's only us, Aunt."

Lily-Anne drew her hand up to her face, stumbling back into the doorframe before running into the house, shouting at the top of her voice. "Torin! Torin—come quick!"

"My father *is* here?" Rufus tipped his face back to ask Fae, who still had hold of his head, cushioning it.

"Of course he's here—Rufus, you were dying!" Luca sat up a little, relieving some of the weight from his chest.

"It can't have been that bad." Rufus felt far too revived to have been on the cusp of death.

Luca shot him a dangerous look, her face still wet with tears. "I'm going to hit you so hard."

Torin ran out the house, his hair wet and chemise clinging to his skin. Lily-Anne and Michael followed, standing back as Torin tore down to his son. He slowed on the approach and stopping, staring in wonder. Luca and Jionathan relieved their hold of Rufus, rolling away, and Torin gave a small gasp as his son came into full view.

"Father—" Rufus began, but Torin had already dropped to his knees, and dragged Rufus up into his arms.

Rufus sank into the embrace, feeling small and assured, like a child who'd been woken from a nightmare. Neither of them spoke, and Rufus's dry throat well up, overcome with gratitude and love. It was good to have his father with him.

After a minute or so, the two men pulled away, studying each other's faces. Both tried to speak at once, cutting each other off, and laughed. They embraced again.

"Never again," Torin said fiercely. "D'you hear? Never again."

"I'm sorry. I won't. I'm sorry," Rufus apologised into his father's collar, and Torin reluctantly released him, rising to his feet and pulled Rufus up after. Rufus wobbled precariously on his long legs, but Jionathan put a hand out and steadied him with a warm smile.

Lily-Anne and Michael then took their turns embracing Rufus, Michael so tightly Rufus felt his spine crack. The love in those arms was kind and dizzying, so by the time Annabelle and Rowan had run up to his feet, demanding their own, Rufus felt lightheaded from the affection.

"I just can't believe it—this must be a dream," Jionathan gabbled, excitement crackling through the air. "You were asleep a whole week."

"A week?" Rufus whistled. "That long?"

"The physician said you would never wake again."

"Oh," Rufus mumbled, bashful of the attention. "I suppose I enjoy proving people wrong."

"How do you feel?" Fae asked.

Rufus considered this. "Hungry," he said. "Ravenous actually, like I haven't eaten in…well."

Running to her fallen basket, Luca returned and presented him with an apple. Rufus took it gratefully and bit into it, enjoying the explosion of taste in his mouth. He savoured it, and then paused in his chewing.

The apple was fresh—sweet and sour all at once, and yet, though he knew it was in part because of his starvation, the flavour still seemed to possess an impossible vivacity. He glanced down at the apple and wondered why. Why did it taste so exceptional? Why did the air feel so clear and clean? Why was the sun so deliciously warm, and the earth beneath him so welcoming?

And then he realised why—he was feeling it with his every, uncapped sense. And suddenly he recalled what he'd done when facing Zachary. He recalled his reckless behaviour, and he breathed in the exquisite taste of true freedom for the first time in three years.

Before anyone could stop him, he threw the apple up into the air as high as he could. Mapping its descent he stretched out his senses and, reaching into its core, he released a burst of energy. With an abrupt clap, the apple exploded into tiny pieces, showering them in juice. Annabelle and Rowan squealed in delight. Rufus was barely able to catch his breath for his own excitement.

"Your cap," Jionathan breathed. "Of course, you destroyed it. Which means—"

"I'm free," Rufus choked, and Luca hit his arm. "Ow!"

"You were supposed to eat it, not blow it up," she said, and the crowd laughed.

Rufus apologised sheepishly, and looked up to the sky. His capacity was open to its fullest now, magic flowing through him on uncalled instinct. As joy welled in his stomach, Rufus decided that never again would he confine himself in such a way.

With Rufus well again, Torin decided to return to Harmatia and relay the good news to Nora. They were all sorry to see him go, but it was agreed it was for the best.

Michael immediately began to busy himself with things in the town, and there was suddenly a lot of movement, and preparations being made that were a total contrast the solemn hush that had plagued the Rossignol house for a week.

Decorations began to appear along the streets of Sarrin—arrangements of flowers, streams of ribbon, stalls and stages being set up in the square.

"It's for the Summer Festival in a few days," Luca explained, as she and Jionathan walked down into the town, together. "We do it every year. Really, we should have been preparing from last week, but with Rufus as he was, it didn't seem right. Now, it feels as if we have even more reason to celebrate."

"What exactly is the Summer Festival?"

"Really, it's just an excuse for a party," Luca admitted. She walked with a light step these days, like she was constantly on the cusp of dancing. She'd scarcely stopped smiling since

Rufus had woken. "It's a tradition that dates back from before the Betheanians adopted the True Gods. We welcome in each season. Autumn is the time of harvest, winter the time of rest, spring the new beginning, and summer is the season of life. We celebrate them all."

"I can't believe summer's already upon us," Jionathan said, but it was hard to deny. The days had grown impossibly hot, and were bright and clear. In Harmatia, the market would be getting bigger, as traders came in from further to sell their wares, taking advantage of the good weather to travel.

"I reserve a dance with you, of course, at the festival," Luca said, and Jionathan laughed at her boldness. He'd truly grown to admire that carefree trait.

"I would be honoured, though I fear I might shame you."

"You can't be any worse than Rufus," Luca said. "Last time someone made him dance, he accidentally set the tent on fire, and then we had several weeks of howling rain afterwards and general poor fortune. He's the harbinger of bad luck."

"Gracious, something Rufus can't do? In which case, I'll try to keep up with you," Jionathan promised lightly, and Luca giggled.

The sun was warm on their heads as they reached the square, and Jionathan realised that he hadn't had a single nightmare or vision in days.

CHAPTER
41

Rufus was trying hard not to laugh. Jionathan turned to face him, his face flushed with humiliation.

"Well?"

"Yes…it's good. You look good," Rufus managed, before breaking down into peals of laughter.

Jionathan growled.

"I'm sorry," Rufus finally managed to compose himself. "I'm sorry, but Sweet Haylix, you're so *small*."

"No. You're too tall!" Jionathan retorted furiously, gesturing down to the ill-fitted clothes. The jerkin went almost to his knee. "You're freakish."

"I am not," Rufus said. "There are plenty of people who are taller than me."

Jionathan snorted. "List three."

Rufus paused. "My uncle—" he began slowly.

"Is a giant."

"Regardless, he's taller," Rufus continued, casting his mind back. "And there are plenty of others, too."

"You can't name any."

"You wouldn't know them," Rufus said matter-of-factly.

Jionathan's reply was interrupted by a knock on the door.

Fae peered into the room. "Arguing again?" She spotted Jionathan, and snorted loudly.

"They're the smallest clothes I own!" Rufus said as Fae walked into the room, her arms crossed.

"Well they look ridiculous on you, Jionat. Luckily, Lily-Anne anticipated your needs. She says you might find something more appropriate in the stock they've just acquired."

"Oh Haylix be praised," Jionathan sighed in obvious relief, darting out of the room to find Lily-Anne downstairs. Rufus sniggered, Fae closing the door.

"You know, you might've warned him yesterday we needed to wear formal clothing. He could have bought something in the market."

"It's a festival, I thought he'd know."

"He's not been to a Betheanian festival before."

Rufus grunted, sitting down on the bed, his arms rested on his knees.

"How are you feeling?" Fae asked.

"Better than I have in a long time."

"You seem brighter."

"You seem as if you have a question." Rufus gestured for her to take a seat opposite him. She remained standing, but moved closer.

"It's been troubling me a while, but the potion we drugged you with…" She chose her words carefully. "I wanted to know how you overcame it. It was the most powerful of the stock my physician gave me."

"Ah, that…well I can't answer you for sure." Rufus hesitated. His memories of the event seemed clouded still, but he recalled drinking the poison. "If you must know, I woke up just after you left. With Luca's help I managed to retch up all I'd drunk, and even then it took me some time to recover enough to saddle Jionat's horse and come after you. It was a real struggle, but I fought against it with all my might. Perhaps my being a Child of Aramathea enabled me to battle the magical components of the potion? Or it was my natural tolerance against drugs and alcohol. I can't tell you for sure."

"You're a unique man."

"I try."

"Yes, you are very trying." Fae deliberated a moment, and then came and sat on the bed opposite him. "I wanted to apologise," she said, and raised her hand to stop him before he could speak. "I didn't trust you, Rufus. I judged you and made assumptions about you, and it was all through my own conceit. I apologise for that, and I apologise for thinking of you as anything less than a true and honest friend. I don't expect your forgiveness, but—"

"You have it," he said without hesitation. "Always. Because *I* should have been more candid, I should have trusted you... trusted you both."

Fae struggled to hold back a smile and leaning forward she poked his arm. "Never die like that again," she ordered, and he laughed and promised he'd certainly try not to.

The door opened again, and Jionathan stepped back into the room in a new set of well-fitted clothes. Fae stood and examined him. "Much better," she decreed, and Rufus had to agree. Wearing a handsome, dark green summer doublet with gold trimmings, the Prince looked suitably regal, though his hair had grown longer and was tousled boyishly, like a crown of curls.

"What shall I do with these?" he asked, holding up Rufus's clothes.

"I'll wear them," Rufus said, "since they're clearly not good enough for you."

"You're the only one they'd fit," Jionathan said, throwing them over.

"I had better get ready." Fae excused herself, catching Jionathan's hand quickly as she passed. They exchanged a secretive smile.

Rufus dressed quickly, pulling on the jerkin over a fresh chemise. It was made of a dark material, and cut similar to his Magi uniform. The collar, however, was less strict, and the body of the fabric was embroidered with faint patterns. Luca had jibed that it almost looked like a corset, bound tight around Rufus's body, but cut loose around the hips, to allow for easy movement.

"It's because you have such a womanly figure, and such a pretty face, too," she had mocked, and Rufus decided to forgo ever being clean-shaven again.

"Are you ready yet?" Jionathan whined.

"Yes, yes, hold on," Rufus grunted, securing his belt before following Jionathan out. Going downstairs they met Michael and Luca, who were waiting at the bottom. Luca wore a shoulderless white chemise with puffed sleeves and embroidered cuffs, all below a wine-red laced corset and gathered crimson skirt. Her usually bound hair was loose, and curled around her face, framing her cheeks and bright eyes. In her ears a set of garnet and pearl earrings glimmered, and around her throat a string of the same pearls gathered around the centrepiece of an impressive ruby. She gave them both a provocative smile.

Jionathan's cheeks tinted with red as Rufus descended toward them with a whistle.

"You look absolutely stunning." He kissed her cheeks lightly. "Uncle, are you sure it's wise to let her out looking so well? She'll be swept away by the crowd."

"They're welcome to try." his uncle sniffed. "I've seen better men than you flee at my daughter's temper. She's quite safe from any complimenting fool, have my word on."

Michael, in comparison to Luca's bright clothing, wore a dark golden doublet with a cream tunic and brown breeches. His hair had been smoothed back, and his beard groomed and brushed immaculately.

"The pair of you look wonderful." Luca gestured to them both. "Perhaps it's you who's in danger of being swept away."

"That is a happy risk, indeed," Rufus said. "Where are the others?"

"Mother's gone ahead with Annabelle and Rowan. They were putting up a fuss. Apparently we were taking too long."

"They know not the troubles of adulthood, and the pains of proper grooming," Michael said theatrically.

"What about Fae?" Jionathan asked.

"Here I am," a voice announced from the top of the stairs, and Fae descended toward them. She looked exquisite, and the crowd below grew still in appreciation as she stepped into the light.

Her outer dress was made of a dainty, floating material, which covered a simple, white silk body. It was a peculiar cut, Avalonian in style without a corset, the fabric gathered tightly just below the breast before falling loose like cascades of water. The sleeves, too, tumbled freely and flared wide at the end. She wore her hair loose, tiny braids within the curls glittering with star-shaped hairpins. She looked like she'd been born of moonlight. Rufus could already imagine what a pair she and Luca would make, walking together into town.

"Fae, you look beautiful," Luca said. Beside her, Jionathan made a small appreciative sound of agreement.

"The four of you make a most excellent troop." Michael clapped his hands together. "But you'd all best watch yourselves. I've heard some Gancanagh have come to join the merriment tonight, so be on your guard. They're more likely to target a finer party. Don't wander away with any beautiful men, the lot of you."

"I won't," Jionathan said quickly, and Luca giggled.

"No, but I know someone who might," Fae said to Luca in a loud whisper, shooting Rufus a glance.

Rufus huffed, folding his arms. "The pair of you are far too comfortable in each other's company. Uncle, I implore you, separate them before it's too late."

"Not on my life," Michael said. "Even if I escaped punishment from the good Lady Fae, I know it's well within my daughter's ability to bitch me to my deathbed. As such, they may have their fun, and I shall shoulder full responsibility for whatever ensues. Now get along—in pairs, if you please." He brushed them out the door.

Luca took Fae's arm. "Come, Fae, let's go find ourselves suitable dancing partners for the night," she said, and the pair set off down the path together, Luca almost skipping.

Jionathan and Rufus walked after them at a steadier pace.

"If there are Gancanagh," Jionathan said, "do you think Reagon will be amongst them?"

"For his sake, I hope not. Fae would rip her dress strangling him."

Both of them shuddered at the image, and then grew still as they entered Sarrin's square, pausing to take in the sight.

The place was transformed. Filled with people, the buildings were all decorated with banners, ribbons and bunting. Fabric tents dotted the square, and colourful paper lanterns hung overheard, music spilling out into the air, which was heavy with the scent of food. Children ran in an endless game between their parents' legs, and the town was alive with the sound of laughter and merriment.

A stage was set at the far end of the square, and upon it men and woman of all ages danced, dresses swirling.

"Michael really spared no expense." Jionathan whistled, sniffing the air hungrily.

"He rarely does."

"I shall have a good time tonight," Jionathan decided, and darted out into the heaving crowd like an excited child.

Rufus chuckled, admiring the sight before—drawn by the sound of languid laughter—he spotted a group of endearing youths sat together around the fountain ledge, surrounded by gushing men and women. So the rumours were true—some Gancanagh *had* come to join the merriment, and were being much too easily obliged. Rufus craned his neck to take a better

434

look, and saw that, thankfully, Embarr Reagon wasn't among them. Rufus deliberated, and then decided not to approach—he had no need for a faerie love tonight.

Pushing his way through the crowd, he located Jionathan, who was stood beside one of the gambling stalls, in the middle of a game.

"Don't waste your money," he warned, slipping in beside Jionathan.

Jionathan bit into some sweet he'd bought and threw the ball in his hand, hitting his target on the other side of the stall. There was a great cheer, and Jionathan received his payment back and another sweet. He grinned at Rufus self-assuredly. "It's not wasted."

Rufus shook his head, ruffling Jionathan's hair. "Behave yourself," he said, before stalking up to the next stall. At the corner of the booth he was met by a band of young children led by Annabelle. Spotting him, they gave chase as he ran in the opposite direction, fleeing with a cackle. He led them around the stalls and through the crowd, never running fast enough to lose them entirely. Finally they caught him, leaping like a pack of wolves, and tackling him to the ground. Rufus gave a forlorn cry and toppled, letting them clamber over him.

"Gods, I have been felled!" He threw his arm over his eyes, and then huffed as Rowan jumped on his stomach, giggling. Up above him, Fae peered over, her eyebrows raised.

"Oh look," she said dryly. "A lunatic."

Rufus gasped a laugh. "Is that all you can say in my hour of peril?"

"Apples! Apples! Apples!" Annabelle and the others chanted, and Rufus struggled to sit up, brushing himself down.

"Apples?" he sighed. "Is that all you have for me? You lack originality. Come, we can do better. Go and find me a pumpkin, and I'll show you a real explosion!" He sent them off, screaming with excitement, and allowed Fae to help him back onto his feet.

"A pumpkin?"

"Yes. Just because the apples grow almost all year round here, doesn't mean everything does. I'll give it about twenty minutes before they realise pumpkins aren't in season, and come back for me."

"And what will you do with those minutes?"

"Enjoy your company, of course."

They walked together, toward the dancing. As they passed the group of Gancanagh, each of the faeries bowed their heads immediately, seeming to straighten from their seductive sprawl.

"You have a reputation," Rufus noted, and Fae glowered at the faeries forebodingly, a silent warning to behave.

"I like to think so," she said as they moved on, her innocent smile returning. Rufus sniggered.

"You're wicked."

They reached the dancing stage, the sound of the steps almost deafening on the wood.

"Will you—" Fae offered.

"Dance?" Rufus shook his head. "Not unless you want me to kill someone."

"Are you so sorely out of practice?"

"I've never been *in* practice. Bad things happen when I dance, Fae," Rufus said sagely.

"Of what nature?"

"Oh—famine, flood, plagues…the usual sorts."

"You're just making excuses."

"If I was, do you think Luca would have spared me?" Rufus pointed to the far corner of the stage, where people were gathered, waiting to join in. "There's a fetching young man without a partner there who I think would do you well. Provided he can keep up, that is."

An almost feral look came over Fae's face. "He'll do." She climbed onto the stage and crossed to the young lad, whose eyes bulged at the sight of her. He'd been watching Luca's graceful figure until that moment.

The dancing went on a while, Luca slipping out for just one of the dances to come and kiss Rufus on the cheek. A band of admirers watched jealously as she chattered to Rufus, her arms around his neck.

"Where's Jionat?" she asked.

"He'll find his way here soon enough," Rufus promised, and Luca returned to her sport, choosing from the stock of men and women who flocked around her and Fae, the favoured partners of the night. Two dances later and, as Rufus predicted, Jionathan appeared by his side, finishing off a mouthful of something.

"Are you just going to eat all night?" Rufus teased.

Jionathan licked his fingers lazily. "If I can get away with it, yes."

Rufus knocked his elbow. "Will you dance?"

Jionathan raised his eyebrows, looking Rufus up and down with a slight smile. "As much as I now respect your obvious inclination Rufus, I don't think—"

Rufus cuffed him across the head. "Not with me, you imbecile."

Jionathan grinned, before looking back over the dancers. "Probably not," he said. "I've never seen this dance before. It looks horrendous—the footwork that is," he added hastily. "It's very impressive. Luca does it beautifully, and Fae...Fae looks perfect." He drew off, and Rufus bowed his head.

"She does," he agreed. "But as for dancing, Jionat, I don't think you really have a choice."

"What do you mean?" Jionathan asked.

Fae leapt out in front of them, seized Jionathan's hand, and dragged him up onto the stage. Rufus waved encouragingly as Jionathan was forced into a dance. Despite all his objections he seemed to fall easily into step with Fae, his face pinched in concentration at first and then slowly relaxing as he and Fae glided through the crowd. Rufus clapped as the partners swapped, Luca swooping in and taking her chance with Jionathan, the pair spinning and moving faster as the music picked up. Rufus envied Jionathan for his ability to make it look so easy.

Finally, after a few people started pestering him for a dance, Rufus retreated back into the stalls, happy to lose himself for an hour amongst the friendly Sarrin folk. Catching up with a few friends, Rufus found his uncle outside the tavern, which had set up benches and tables in the square.

"So what do you think, Rufus-lad? As festivals go, is it passable?" Michael threw a large arm around his shoulder, guiding him to a table.

"Uncle, you've outdone yourself." Rufus took a seat at a table of Michael's friends, most of them already deep into their third tankards. "The evening's a great success."

"It'll be more of a success if we manage to get a Magi drunk," one of the men at the table said, and the others all cackled with agreement.

Rufus peered into their tankards. "You'll need something stronger than that."

Michael called for the strongest liquor of the house. A clap on Rufus's shoulder signalled Jionathan and Fae's arrival, the pair slipping onto the bench beside him. Jionathan's face was red from dancing.

"Michael, your daughter is insatiable," he said.

"Aye, her husband will have to be a strong-stomached sort." Michael received his own tankard, sliding Rufus's drink across the table to him.

"What makes you think she'll take one?" Fae asked primly, though she was suppressing a smile.

"What indeed?" Michael said. "She might take two."

"What're you drinking?" Jionathan nudged Rufus as he took a sip from his cup.

The liquor was foul, and Rufus almost choked and spat it back into the cup. He swallowed instead and grimaced, his throat feeling like it had shrunk. "Something used to light funeral pyres,

I think."

"What's the matter, boy?" Michael boomed. "Taste too strong for your delicate constitution?"

"It's not a taste, if it makes your mouth numb." Rufus cleared his throat.

Up on the dancing stage a bell began to toll, rousing everyone from their chatter. Luca stood on the cleared platform, a fiddle in her hands, which she raised up to the cheering crowds.

Michael stood. "The duels are about to begin!"

"Duels?" Jionathan whispered to Rufus as they, too, stood, going with the others toward the stage.

"Music duels," Fae said. "Normally played between flutes or fiddles. Two instruments battle together over a steadily more complex melody until the player with less skill can no longer play." Her voice was light with excitement. "Has Luca challenged somebody?"

"No, they challenge her. She's the champion of these parts," Rufus said with a fierce pride.

On the stage, the first contestant arrived, a weedy-looking man with greying hair. He eyed Luca with scrutiny, his gaze lavishing over her breasts. Luca let him, her focus on the instrument she put to her shoulder. She caught Rufus's eye in the crowd and he winked at her.

"The challenger may choose the piece," Luca invited.

"Balgair," the contestant said, and Luca accepted.

As the champion, she began, caressing the bow over the violin with the delicate precision of a master. She moved as if she were dancing, and as the fiddle hummed, the night air grew alive.

Behind them the band began to play along, setting the beat as the contestant joined in, slow and steady to begin with.

"How does it work?" Jionathan whispered, conscious of the concentrated silence that had come over the rest of the crowd.

"The challenger chooses a piece to play, which the champion may or may not accept," Rufus said. "The pieces are especially designed and consist of two parts, which mimic each other but leave room for embellishments and improvisation. As the piece goes on, it grows more complex, faster, and harder. The loser is the contestant who fails to finish the piece, makes the most errors, or provides a duller performance."

"Who judges?"

"In Luca's case, it's often fairly obvious."

They turned back to the duel, which had grown more intense, the crowd now happy to whoop and cheer as the music grew. Finally the speed rendered a winner, and Luca graciously stopped as her opponent made several grave errors at once, his fiddle screeching hideously. He stormed off the stage, red-faced with embarrassment.

Almost immediately another took his place—a younger contestant, who ambitiously requested 'Fear-siubhail'. Once again, Luca accepted without complaint, and the duelling recommenced.

Luca performed with an enviable ease, skipping over the notes like she were singing them, long and sweeping and then short, growing faster. The contestant, daunted by Luca's skill, gave in quickly, and so it went on, the queue of combatants growing thinner until Luca had run through them all, still the firm winner.

"I've never seen anybody play like that," Fae marvelled, her hands clutched tightly together, wringing with excitement. She looked like she was barely holding in the desire to burst into dance. "None of them could even reach the end of the song. She's superb."

"I rather think you're in love," Rufus jibed.

"Oh, I am," Fae said.

Rufus leaned across to Jionathan in false worry. "I think we need to warn Michael. His daughter is on the verge of being spirited away by a Sidhe."

"If Fae succeeds, it would only be because Luca wanted to go,"

Jionathan said. On that, Rufus couldn't fault him.

"Is there nobody else?" Luca called into the crowd. "Nobody who will do me the honour of performing on this stage in our ancient tradition?"

She was met with silence, and Rufus became suddenly very aware that Luca was searching for his face in the crowd. He bent his knees until he was at head level with everyone else, and then lower, edging away slowly. Hopefully, his uncle would be too drunk on his daughter's success to think of making a fool of him, and the evening would continue without incident.

"Rufus will!" Michael volunteered, and Rufus groaned, dropping to his hands and knees and attempting to scrabble away. He didn't get very far. Jionathan and Fae grabbed him by each arm and dragged him up to his feet. Rufus wriggled childishly.

"Why?" he whined. "Why do you conspire to humiliate me?"

"Primarily, a huge, gratifying sense of amusement," Jionathan said. "Secondly...No—it's just for the amusement."

Together, they forced Rufus up onto the stage. Rufus stood, frozen in terror under the eyes of the crowd, his clothes suddenly tight around his chest.

"I...I don't have a fiddle," he tried, but even as he spoke one was passed up to him by Lily-Anne. His aunt gave him an encouraging smile, and Rufus whimpered. "Why?" He turned to Luca. "Why would you pit a student against their master?"

"To enforce the fact that I am player supreme," Luca said. "And it's hardly my fault you've neglected your fiddle these last three years, though I insisted you keep to your practise."

"I practised. I did. But I had to wait until my parents were out of the house," Rufus said. "Luca, don't you remember what happened last time you made me do this?"

"Yes, I do." Luca fluttered her eyelashes prettily. "It's precisely why I've called you up here again today. Now put that fiddle to your shoulder, Rufus, before I force you to play something truly dreadful with me."

441

Rufus obeyed, his fingers shaking as he smoothed his hands over the neck of the instrument.

"I propose we play Rach 'na lasair," Luca said. "Do you accept?"

"How could I refuse?" Rufus gulped. "Please. Tell me."

Luca winked at him. "Enjoy it," she said, and began to play.

The crowd whistled in excitement, the piece renowned for its tricky melody. Rufus let the music wash over him, closing his eyes to the audience and concentrating on the sound of Luca's fiddle. He reminded himself that the crowd were under no illusion that he might best her. They expected nothing, and with that he was able to relax a little more. Why worry about the impossible, when instead he could relish the chance to perform with such a musician.

Luca started slowly—a low, mellow tone, which Rufus mimicked, adding a slight twist at the end. The sound of his violin wasn't as clear as Luca's, but it wasn't unpleasant, and he surprised himself with his own skill, falling back into the habit with a satisfying ease. Slowly the music grew, rising from its mellow origins to something excitable until, despite his earlier objections, Rufus found himself lost in his enjoyment. His breath was quick, his fingers flying up the fret board, eyes narrowed in concentration as he tried to match Luca's pace.

And suddenly Luca was dancing, tapping and twirling as she played to the crowd, who cheered and applauded. Rufus couldn't believe it—his own feet rooted solidly to the ground, fearful that even the slightest movement would throw him off course. He was barely keeping pace with Luca as it was.

The faster and more complicated the music grew, the easier it seemed to be for Luca. Their parts twirled and clashed in surprising harmony, twisting and trilling around each other until Rufus was giddy and his eyes were blurred.

Finally, when it looked as if they had reached the peak of complexity, Rufus broke off to allow Luca her final solo. He listened carefully, knowing he would have to mimic her, and yet after the first bar he was lost. Luca was no longer playing, she was truly dancing, her fingers darting at impossible speeds. The bow weaved in and out so fast it seemed impossible for so much sound and music to be coming from one body. She finished with a flourish and turned to him expectantly. The crowd watching with bated breath. Rufus gazed, dumbstruck.

"I can't play that!" he said, horrified. "Are you mad?"

"Oh, just try it," Luca dismissed, as if she had done an easy thing.

"Not on my life!" Rufus choked. "I'll lose a finger." He pulled the violin from his shoulder. "No, no, I surrender! You have bested me, cousin. I am a humbled student still." He bowed to her, and the crowd cheered and roared in appreciation as Luca graciously accepted their praise, curtseying.

But amidst the joy and celebration, a strange, sinister feeling suddenly took over Rufus, like a touch of cold air. His head shot up, eyes snapping to a figure sat on horseback on the outskirts of the gathered crowd.

Below him, at the foot of the platform, Jionathan turned as well, the pair of them drawn by the presence of the figure.

The rider wilted in the saddle, her hood tumbling down to reveal a pale, distraught face.

"Lady Éliane?" Rufus took a step forward, eyes wide as he saw the dark stain across the Lady's front.

"Mother!" Jionathan shouted.

His sharp voice distracted the townspeople from their chatter and they turned to see the spectacle. Éliane stared forward, her gaze almost unseeing as her lips parted.

"King Thestian is dead," she breathed, eyes set wide in shock and Rufus's insides constricted. She blinked, her face contorting with sudden, terrible anguish. "The King is dead!" She clutched her belly and gave a sudden wail. "*Harmatia is damned!*" she screamed, and then tumbled from her horse in a dead faint.

CHAPTER
42

Jionathan stumbled up the path, his stomach twisting as Michael carried Éliane to the house. He felt sick, and breathless, and had to stop by the stairs to hunch over and vomit.

Fae came to his side, cool hands steadying him as he heaved. He regretted eating so much as the festival now.

"Come on," Fae coaxed him up when he'd finished emptying his stomach. "I have you, it's alright."

She eased him up the stairs and into the house, guiding him to the guest room on the ground floor, where Michael had carried Éliane. Jionathan decided he *hated* that room.

Rufus was already attending to Éliane, when Jionathan came in, leaning over her and administering what care he could. Luca arrived a minute later with the physician in tow.

"This is a house of bad fortune," the man muttered as he took Rufus's place beside Éliane, and began to examine her. She was bleeding sluggishly from a wound across her belly, which had been hastily bound with strips of cloth. The physician peeled away these sparse bandages, and Jionathan groaned.

"It's a stab wound," said the physician. "A spear, I think. We have to repair the damage as quickly as possible."

"She was—" Jionathan choked, struggling not to be sick again. "She was with child. Is the baby…?"

"It seems she's already given birth." The physician rolled up his sleeves. "We are going to have to operate to close the wound."

"She's lost too much blood already. If you operate, she'll lose more," Rufus said, but there was no strength in his words. The inevitable had already reared its ugly head.

Jionathan could scarcely breathe. "Is there nothing else you can do?" he whispered.

The physician shook his head, and Jionathan turned to Rufus, half-hoping that the Magi would have another solution. Rufus didn't look at him, his expression wooden, eyes cast down. He was stealing himself, which could only mean one thing. Jionathan bowed his head.

"I'll need clean towels, hot water, and strong alcohol," the physician said.

Nodding, Michael turned and left the room, Luca following after him.

"Let me help," Rufus said to the physician.

"My boy, I hardly think—"

"My ability to heal is meagre, but I'm trained. I can ease her pain, help her stay strong," Rufus insisted.

The physician relented with a weary sigh, and Rufus stepped closer, laying his hands gently on Éliane's stomach.

Jionathan stumbled backward into the wall and slipped to the floor. Around him, they bustled and moved, talking urgently, but Jionathan felt separated from them all.

His father was dead.

His wise, gracious, powerful father, the *King*, was dead.

A harrowing emptiness settled in Jionathan, and he could almost see the event. The slow, whisper-like way his father had passed from the world, tucked beneath the blankets of his bed, Éliane curled at his side, comforting him as his breathing grew more laboured, and then eased to nothing.

His father was dead, and suddenly the world was cold.

"Lady Éliane, can you hear me?" Rufus spoke, and Jionathan jerked his head up to see his mother's eyes roll open, darting anxiously around the room.

"Rufus?" she murmured seeing him, and then broke into a soft smile. "It is you, Rufus. My Rufus. Where's Jionathan?"

"I'm here, Mother." Jionathan mounted to his feet, trying to summon the strength to hold himself steady. Éliane reached for him, and he took her hand.

"Jionathan, thank the gods you're safe." She kissed his fingers, her own shaking. "Queen Reine has run mad! She's taken over Harmatia. She...she killed my baby." Éliane's voice hitched, and Jionathan felt like someone had plunged a dagger into his chest. Rufus turned away, his hand to his mouth.

"They killed—" Jionathan cut himself off, unable to finish.

"I went into labour, provoked by the shock of your father's death," Éliane said. "But the Queen's men stormed the room, and they took my baby. They tore him from my arms!" She gasped, gripping his hand tightly, as if trying to hold onto the child she'd lost. "I tried to fight. He wasn't even an hour old. But they killed him. *My baby boy...they killed him!*" She gave a soft wail, and Jionathan pressed his face to her trembling hand.

He would kill them. He would kill *every last one of them* for this.

"I managed to escape," Éliane composed herself and continued, "but they followed me, and caught me at the edge of Anaes's Fortress. One of them stabbed me with a spear, but I lost them in the forest...oh gods, Harmatia is damned. Harmatia is damned!"

"Peace, Mother, please. You'll hurt yourself." Jionathan fought back his own tears, trying to find courage in himself. Now wasn't the time for grief or anger—he needed to comfort her. "You're safe now, that's all that matters. I promise to make them pay for what they've done, but for now you need to rest."

"My sweet boy." Éliane's lips trembled. "My sweet sons. If only you could have known your brother. My sweet sons…"

Rufus rested his hand on Jionathan's arm and pulled him gently away. "We have to begin the procedure. There isn't much time. You should wait outside."

Jionathan nodded numbly, as Luca came into the room, and guided him out. "They're going to take care of you," he told his mother. "I'm going to take care of you."

Éliane gave him a faded smile, and the door shut behind him. Jionathan slammed into the corridor wall and slid again to the floor, his fists against the stone. Luca sat beside him, holding his head so he didn't crack it against the tiles too.

They remained like this until his breathing had evened. And then, from within the room, came a loud moan of pain and a broken sob. It was all Jionathan could bear.

He snatched himself from Luca's arms, and left the house, striding away into the fields on a route that was increasingly familiar to him. There wasn't enough air in the world for him to breathe as he bared his anger and grief to the skies, his face burning.

Thestian was dead. Reine had control of the capital. His little brother had been born and murdered in the same hour, and now his mother lay bleeding.

Jionathan slumped against a nearby tree beside the river. He rested his head against the bark and dug his hands into the roots, trying to anchor himself. He wanted desperately to cry, but he felt too separated from the tragedy. It felt like nothing more than a nightmare. Any moment he would wake up. Wake up to his father, well again, restored to his rightful seat on the throne, Éliane at his side with her new born baby clasped in her arms.

They killed the baby… They killed a baby!

Jionathan clenched his teeth together, ripping at the roots of the tree as he tried to hold in the searing fury that jolted through him. He would burn the city to the ground for this, tell Rufus to unleash Athea's fire, and cleanse the capital once and for all.

Something moved in the corner of his eye, and Jionathan snapped his gaze around, snarling, half-expecting to see the Royal Guard coming toward him through the trees. A small part of Jionathan hoped it was, his hand flying to the dirk he kept at his side.

Instead, he was met by the cold, dead image of the Bean Nighe, knelt down beside the stream, her head bent so that the tips of her hair dipped into the water. Jionathan grew stony, not daring to move, as he watched her scrub quietly, her face poised. It was too dark to see, but Jionathan knew streaks of blood were soaking into the stream from whatever she washed.

Carefully, she lifted the clothing up to inspect the bloodstain, and Jionathan leapt to his feet. She was holding his mother's dress.

Silently, the Bean Nighe replaced the garment into the water and Jionathan's rage returned to him like a roaring fire, blinding him to reason.

"Stop that!" He leapt down into the ravine. "Stop! Stop it! You're wrong!"

The Bean Nighe didn't hear him, continuing her washing as though he wasn't there at all.

"You're wrong, you hear me! She's not going to die. You're a liar—*a liar!*" He strode into the water, the current pushing against his legs. "Stop doing that! *STOP IT!*" he screamed, and lunging forward, he grabbed her by her shoulders.

Her dress dropped into the water, and icy hands snapped up and clamped hard around his wrists, like shackles. Jionathan's burning anger instantly turned to fear, as the Bean Nighe reared her head. Her eyes were impossibly black and depthless, and Jionathan felt himself falling through them. He knew then, he should have never touched this dead thing.

The veil parted within him, and he tipped his head back and screamed.

Rufus quickened his pace, pushing through the long grass as he scanned the area for Jionathan. He'd been walking for some time now, but suspected he was getting close. The instinct that usually guided Rufus to Jionathan was tainted by a hue of rage and despair, like the heavy scent of blood. Wherever he was, the last thing Jionathan needed was to be alone now.

Passing through a cluster of trees toward the stream, Rufus finally spotted Jionathan down on the opposite bank. He had his back to Rufus, and was muttering to himself, his head rocking from side to side in agitation, hands ringing.

"Jionat?" Rufus jumped down and crossed the stream. "Jionathan, are you alright?"

Jionathan ignored him, whispering frantically to himself. Frowning, Rufus moved around, and peered into Jionathan's face. His stomach plummeted.

Jionathan's eyes had turned the colour of moonlight and were glowing with magic. He held them wide, his pupils shrunken to pinpoints, his gaze directed beyond Rufus, and the mortal world around them. He didn't look human at all in that moment. He looked faerie.

"Jionat?" Rufus shook Jionathan's shoulder, his voice rising. "Jionat? *Jionat!*" He grabbed Jionathan's chin, waving his hand in front of his eyes.

Still Jionathan didn't respond, lost to his muttering, his breath short and rapid. His skin was bitterly cold to the touch.

"Is this a vision?" Rufus asked desperately. "Are you having a vision? Jionat, please, talk to me."

Jionathan didn't reply, but his muttering started to grow. At first, only the odd word was intelligible, and then full sentences, Jionathan's voice rising. Rufus tried to make sense of what he was saying, but it was garbled mess. Jionathan spoke in odd phrases, broken and put together awkwardly, as if he were relaying strips of conversation from a crowded room where everyone was speaking at once.

"I should have never gone—What will Alice think? —Why am I here? —They knew, they knew! —Oh Athea have mercy, oh Athea I'm dead—Mother! Father! I'm here, look at me!" His voice jumped from tone to tone, expression never changing. "Don't leave me here, please don't leave me here!—Athea forgive my soul, I stole only to survive—I loved him and you took him from me—this is hell. I am in hell!—it hurts, please it hurts—Mother?—I thought we were friends, I thought we were friends—forgive me. Oh Notameer, forgive me!—Let me out! Help me, please!—She promised me, she promised to never love again, that treacherous little *bitch!*"

"Jionat!" Rufus slapped him across the face and Jionathan jolted and grew quiet, his lips parted in surprise. Then, very slowly, he reached up and hooked his fingers into Rufus's sleeves, tugging them. He looked up, his face broken in anguish.

"Rufus," he whispered. "I'm sorry, Rufus, please forgive me. I am so sorry." He shut his eyes and slumped, resting the top of his head against Rufus's chest.

Rufus held him upright, unsure what to do. He ran a soothing hand down Jionathan's back, trying to calm him. Somehow he sensed that the apology hadn't come from Jionathan.

When Jionathan at last lifted his head his eyes had returned to normal, and he looked more himself.

Rufus didn't relent his grip. "What did you see?"

"Not a vision," Jionathan mumbled. "Something else."

"What happened?"

"I had a dispute with a Bean Nighe." Jionathan dropped his gaze.

Rufus drew in a sharp breath. "Was it…?" He couldn't say her name.

Jionathan only nodded.

"And the clothes. Did you recognise—"

"She's wrong," Jionathan said stiffly, and Rufus gritted his teeth. He had a dark suspicion he knew whose clothes Mielane had been washing.

"My mother?" Jionathan asked, in a small, terrified voice.

"Is recovering. We closed the wound. Jionat," Rufus ducked down so he was eye-level with the Prince, "I think you ought to sit a minute, you look very unwell."

"Please, Rufus."

Rufus bit his bottom lip, raking his fingers through his hair and tugging at his fringe. "Then you can come and see her. She's very weak though, and she's lost a great deal of blood. Perhaps too much. Do you understand, Jionat?"

Jionathan nodded weakly, his gaze still set resolutely to the floor. Rufus released him, and Jionathan turned and began to march back toward the house. Rufus stalked silently after him.

"Jionat," he said, as they came to the door.

"Yes?"

"Be gentle with her."

Jionathan finally caught Rufus's eye, and gave him a weak, but appreciative, smile. "I will," he said and let himself into the room.

As Jionathan turned away, a terrible, bone-crushing foreboding overcame Rufus. He almost reached after Jionathan on instinct, but caught himself, his heart beating hard in his chest. It felt like Jionathan was walking away down a road from which he couldn't be recovered.

I'm just tired, Rufus thought, trying to console himself even as an odd, stinging sense of loss settled in his stomach. *It's nothing. I'm just tired.*

He forced down the strange feeling, and followed Jionathan into the room.

Éliane lay in a deep slumber, finally peaceful after the turmoil of the operation. Carefully, Jionathan placed himself at her side. Rufus, unwilling to leave, stood in the corner, trying to make himself as invisible as possible. Jionathan didn't seem to mind his presence.

"How does it always come to this?" Jionathan broke the silence. "Me, waiting at the bedside of the people I love, watching them die."

"Your mother isn't dead."

"No. And neither are you." Again, Jionathan gave that weak smile, and it made Rufus's heart ache. "But my father..."

"I'm so sorry, Jionat."

"And my brother...to lose *another* brother after Sverrin." Jionathan's voice broke. "How could this have happened?"

"For now, you must concentrate your energies on your mother," Rufus said. "And also on yourself."

"It's hard."

"I know."

Jionathan bowed his head, rubbing his eyes furiously. "Thank you, Rufus."

A small, tired voice interrupted them. "It's nice to see the pair of you finally getting along again." Éliane blinked tiredly and gave them a smile. "Small blessings."

"Mother." Jionathan leant forward, forcing his expression into something more cheerful. Éliane would see through it, but Rufus knew it wasn't Jionathan's nature to simply not try. "How do you feel?"

"Comfortable. Rufus has eased my pain."

"I'm sorry I couldn't do more," Rufus said.

"You've done enough—much more than I deserved." Éliane squeezed Jionathan's hand, and like her son she put on a façade of cheer. "And who are these people I have intruded upon? I must thank them as well."

"The Rossignols," Jionathan responded. "They're friends, Mother, good friends. Rufus's family."

"They are most gracious. And the young Sidhe with them?" Éliane's smile seemed to be all knowing.

"Fae," both of them responded at once.

The Lady looked between them with that same smile, and Rufus found himself avoiding her clever gaze, staring hard at the ground.

"I shall leave you in peace," he said. "If there's anything you need, please don't hesitate to call for me." He turned to leave, but Éliane's voice called after him.

"Rufus," she started, sounding almost mournful. She paused over her words, trying to gather them. "Thank you," she finally said.

It was the single most emotive thing she'd ever said to him, even in its simplicity. And in her eyes was a great blessing—a love and kindness that was raw and unshackled. Rufus swallowed and bowed his head, his throat constricting.

"You're welcome," he managed to whisper in return.

CHAPTER 43

"Are you cold?"

Éliane shook her head, as Jionathan put his hands in hers, interlocking their fingers. "Look at you," she said, "I dare say you're a thumb taller since I last saw you."

"It's the hair."

"Is that so?"

Jionathan chuckled weakly, resting his chin in his hand as he leant over the bed, allowing her to stroke the offending mane, her hands frail.

"You get your curls from your father," she sighed. "You look so much like him."

Jionathan kissed her shaking hands, struggling to contain himself as his grief welled through him. Éliane squeezed his fingers, and then frowned, looking at the inside of his wrist. The ghost of the Bean Nighe's grip still marked his skin. Éliane reached up.

"Where did you get these bruises?" she asked. "Did you get into trouble?"

Jionathan stared, stunned by the question, and then he began to laugh, long and hard until there were tears in his eyes. Because there wasn't enough energy in the world for him to recount his story to her now—to tell her about saving Princess Aurora and infiltrating the Korrigans' nest. About how he'd been captured by bandits, and met Fae. About the Bean Nighe and Embarr Reagon.

How could he tell her that he'd accepted his powers of the Sight? Or explain the dreamy wonder that was his time in the Rossignols' home? And what of the sad discovery of Mielane's death, and then the bandits' attack on Sarrin? And then the Magi conspirators and Rufus's power, and consequently his near death. It all made Jionathan dizzy.

"Oh gods, I wish things could be simple again," he rasped, his throat raw from the unhappy laughter. "That Sverrin had never died, that Queen Reine had never turned on us, that I never became the heir. How much easier life would be if I'd never been born at all."

"No, Jionathan, please, never say that." Éliane's voice wavered. "You are the light of my life, and if that's all you ever wish to be, that is enough."

Jionathan rested his face against her hands, comforted by her smell. "What do I do now? If I return to Harmatia, they will kill me."

"You will find a way. I know you will. You are your father's son," she said. "Trust your friends, Jionathan. They will guide you through these trials."

Jionathan looked up at her. She was as weak as a lamb, but she would get better, he knew it. She would grow strong and help claim the throne that was rightfully his. He had only to wait until she recovered—to plan and gather his allies. With his mother at his side, he found courage in his path.

"I'm glad you're with me," he whispered into her fingers. "Sleep now, you're tired. I'll watch over you." He leant forward and kissed her goodnight. "You'll feel better in the morning. And when you're well enough, we'll light a beacon to honour father, and my brother."

She stroked her thumb down his cheek and gave a slow, deliberate nod.

Grief, Jionathan thought, *she is grieving, too.* She'd lost both a husband and child in one fatal swoop, and for that Jionathan would rain fiery retribution on the Queen.

He kissed his mother's forehead again.

"Sleep," he said. "Things will be better in the morning."

"The mystery of the stolen Saphar book," Sverrin said, and Jionathan leapt, startled by his sudden appearance. "And it's another boring end, I see. Here I was hoping some ghost from the dungeon had moved it, but it's only you. Brat."

Jionathan bristled, clutching the book closer to him in childlike anger. "I'm not a brat," he said. "And I didn't steal the book, I borrowed it."

"Again?" Sverrin ducked down and sat beside Jionathan. "You've taken this one three times already. Can't you steal another from my collection?"

"No," Jionathan said stubbornly. "This is the best." He held up the book and showed his brother the page he'd been reading. It was the chapter where the King of Pensia—hero of the story—and his trusted childhood friend, Douglas, found themselves grievously outnumbered in battle. They fought valiantly, eventually finding victory, but not before brave Douglas sacrificed himself for his King. "This is the best," Jionathan repeated fervently.

"Yes, yes, until you read the next." Sverrin sighed, and peered over his brother's shoulder. "You like Douglas the best, don't you?"

"Of course, he's the cleverest," Jionathan said. "And he fights like a lion, the King says so."

"And yet he dies." Sverrin sniffed dismissively. "A true warrior would never let himself be felled from such a simple blow."

"It was a sacrifice. He did it for loyalty of the King," Jionathan said, rolling his eyes at his brother's simplicity. "For the King,

Douglas said he would take a hundred arrows."

"A grand statement, but I don't think there's enough room on the human body," Sverrin said dryly. At Jionathan's irritated expression, he added, "Though perhaps he didn't mean it literally. Yes, you're right, Douglas is an honourable character, the best kind of man."

"Exactly." Jionathan nodded. "Of course he sacrificed himself for his King—it's his duty. If I were Douglas, I would be proud to lay my life down."

Sverrin raised his eyebrows. "I'll be king one day. Would you die for me, Jionathan?" His eyes were strangely old. "Would you give your life for mine, so that I might rule?"

Jionathan blinked, puzzled by the severity in his brother's tone. Then he broke into a bright smile. "Of course. You know I would."

Jionathan woke slowly, blinking in the early morning light. His back was sore from sleeping upright in the chair, and he groaned, stretching with a yawn. Across the room, yellow strips of light stained the floor, and in the fireplace the embers glowed a dark red. The room was warm, and comfortable. Éliane was already awake, staring peacefully up to the ceiling, her face bathed in light.

Jionathan rubbed his arm lazily over his eyes as he drove the sleep out, rolling his shoulders. "Good morning Mother, how do you feel?"

She didn't respond, staring serenely up at the ceiling, a slight smile on her lips.

"Mother?" He gently touched her arm. Her skin was cool beneath his fingers. She wasn't breathing.

Jionathan's stomach plummeted.

"Mother?" He shook her. "Mother, wake up." He reached for her face, cupping her chin. Her eyes were frozen, her jaw slack. "Answer me," he implored. "Answer me, *please*." His voice dipped into a whisper. "*Mother.*"

But Éliane continued to stare unseeingly, her lips parted, cheeks pale and lifeless.

Rufus knocked before entering, pushing the door open as quietly as possible. He knew it was early, but there was little else for him to do. Sleep hadn't come to him that night, and his thoughts, like a flock of restless birds, had fluttered in his mind until he found an excuse to rise.

Stepping into the chamber, he was surprised to find Jionathan awake, standing at his mother's bedside, his back to Rufus.

"Jionat?"

Jionathan whirled around. His face was paper white, and he seemed unsteady on his feet, staggering slightly. He opened and closed his mouth in silent declaration, and then covered it with the back of his hand.

"Rufus," he managed to whine. "Rufus, she…Mother…she—" He broke off with a gasp. "*Help her.*"

Rufus pushed past him and hurried to the Lady's side. He pressed his hands against each side of her face, searching for any signs of life. His fingers met cold skin, and Éliane's gaze was blank and veiled. No spark of magic or energy hummed within her, and Rufus let his hands drop. He tried to find words, tried to give the body a blessing, but no sound came out.

"Do something!" Jionathan demanded.

Rufus couldn't bear to face him. "She's gone."

"No!"

"She's gone Jionat."

"*No!*" Jionathan shook his head, his mane of curls flying around his face. "No, you're a Child of Aramathea—you're born of Athea. *Do* something!"

"Jionat…"

"DO SOMETHING!" He threw himself at Rufus, who turned

458

and caught him. They struggled for a moment, Jionathan's hands closed into fists. He lashed out, striking Rufus wherever he could reach, and then, with great sob, slipped to his knees.

Rufus dragged Jionathan close, turning him away from his mother as the Prince broke to pieces.

"Not her. Not her…oh gods, please no! Please no! Please! *Please!*"

Rufus pressed his forehead against Jionathan's shuddering back, holding him tightly, Jionathan curled around himself, bent over Rufus's arm, his head against his chest.

"She's gone," Rufus said, through his own tears. "She's gone, Jionat."

Jionathan's chest expanded, and Rufus braced himself. But nothing could prepare him for the heart-shattering howl that ripped from Jionathan's mouth. It was the sound of a tortured man, the anguish of an orphaned child, and Rufus could only clasp him tighter, rocking Jionathan back and forth feverishly as he continued to stutter broken words into his chest.

"Please," Jionathan cried. "Please. Please give her back. Don't let her go. Not her too. Please."

"I'm sorry," Rufus said, over and over. "I'm so sorry. She's gone. I'm sorry. She's gone."

Jionathan twitched, his voice fading into incoherent sobs, rising and falling with each breath. Rufus struggled to find any words of comfort, knowing there was nothing he could truly say that would help. His mind blank, he settled on a passage he'd memorised as a child.

"And great men fall, like birds with broken wings," he recited, his face wet with tears. "And death welcomes them at her door. For death is the hand that embraces the world, and in her palm we are of the same dust: ash and earth. And I say unto you there is no dignity in fear, and say unto you there is no honour in war. But courage is born of terror, and love is the rope that binds us to our feet. And that is why we fight—not for dignity, nor for honour, but for the pride of that humanity. That we might find even the barest light in this dark place."

Rufus held Jionathan tightly as the Prince began to shudder and seize in a silent fit, losing himself to a vision. His eyes rolled backwards and his head twitched from side to side in Rufus's arms.

"And if I fall, let me fall," Rufus said. "Let me rest amongst the stars. I will bear your weight and be the bridge that carries you to victory. For when my darkness came, yours was the light that raised me high, and if death's toll is the only price, then let it be me to die."

The colours relented, the vision passing, and afterwards Jionathan lay very still, his breathing long and deep. Rufus cradled him protectively and Jionathan was so weak he couldn't have pushed him away if he wanted to.

He felt as if, should he try to move, he'd fall away into tiny pieces and slip between the cracks in the tiles. Such was the power of all he now knew. His future in its frightening entirety had come to him in flashes. Like waves over a drowning body he saw it all—every face, every moment, every sunrise and sunset until his last breath.

Rufus shifted and looked down at Jionathan who stared up into his bright, sky-blue eyes. They were the final assurance he needed, and with a cold understanding, Jionathan of the Delphi understood exactly what he had to do.

CHAPTER
44

~≈~

They placed Éliane in an ivory dress and long red cloak—
the colours of the innocent, and the martyr. Her feet were left
bare, her jewellery removed, a wreath of lily-of-the-valley placed
around her head.

She looked pure—a sovereign of a sort, the loose folds of
her clothes arranged purposefully around her in the casket, her
hands clasped together in paused prayer.

When sunset fell, they came with candles and carried her
body out to the fields. Jionathan walked quietly behind, first
in the procession, Rufus to his right, Luca and Fae on his left.
The pyre they had prepared was tall, and adorned with flowers
and sweet-smelling woods, so that as the fire was lit, it masked
the smell of cremation. And Éliane burned, spirals of embers
reaching the heavens.

They faced east for the service—the direction of sunrise
and salvation—but the wind blew out to the north that night,
as if even the gods were paying their respects and carrying her
ashes back to Harmatia, to her husband. The townspeople sang,
clutching their candles like sanctified ghosts, voices carrying
through the night.

In the glow of the fire, Jionathan held both Rufus and Fae's hands, but never uttered a sound—his lips sealed, eyes dry as he watched his mother burn. He couldn't say he felt at peace, but a comforting emptiness had settled inside him and he found strength in the grip of his friends. Neither of them tried to talk to him—they were like rocks anchoring him down.

They stayed until the pyre was reduced to nothing but cinders, and then finally returned to the house. The moon, like a lone watchman's lantern, lit the dark path home for them.

In the days following Éliane's death, Jionathan did nothing, paralysed by his fear. A part of him was tempted to abandon his kingdom and live out his days free of duty. But the dreams came vividly each night, and time scratched at his aching heart, raking him with guilt until he couldn't bear it any longer.

After the five, customary days of mourning were done, Jionathan finally took action.

He gathered his things and dressed for travel, ignoring the discomfort in his stomach. The door opened behind him, and Rufus—ever-faithful Rufus—came in.

"Where are you going?" Rufus asked.

"To the capital of Bethean," Jionathan said.

Rufus lowered his brow. "You haven't mentioned anything about this. What do you mean to do there?"

"I must speak with the King, if I can. Harmatia won't wait any longer."

"Jionat," Rufus murmured, "you don't need to do this yet. You're still recovering from a terrible shock. Go in a few days."

"My parents are dead, Rufus," Jionathan said. "I'll be recovering for the rest of my life."

"Jionat—"

"I've mourned for five days. I've taken the luxury to do so. But their spirits are free now, and I can't delay the inevitable any longer. I would rather make it a clean cut. Rufus, please understand…if I don't go now, I will never go."

Rufus made a small sound of discomfort, but nodded, defeated. "Alright, I'll fetch the horses."

"No," Jionathan said, a little quickly. "You stay here."

"Jionat, you don't know the way."

"Michael has offered to guide me there, I won't be alone." Jionathan hesitated. "Please, it's something I need to do, Rufus. I wish you could come with me, but you need to stay."

"Why?"

Jionathan gave him a forced smile. "I need someone to pack my bags for me."

Rufus laughed, bowing his head. Jionathan allowed himself to be pulled into a tight embrace. He could feel how tense and anxious Rufus was.

"Why is it I feel like I'm about to lose you?" Rufus said.

"The feeling will pass," Jionathan said quietly. "When the sense of loss has numbed and I have a crown on my head." He pulled back. "You'll see what a good King a Delphi brat can make."

"I already know it." Rufus's smile was forced and apprehensive. "Gods, boy, but you've aged years in several days."

"Well, I can't afford to be a boy anymore." Jionathan avoided the hateful look of pity in Rufus's eyes.

Rufus winced. "I suppose not."

"If it makes you more comfortable, I can revert to my bratty ways and abuse you?"

"I'd be obliged if you didn't." Rufus relaxed, the pair expelling the uneasy tension with the weak humour. "Insufferable shite."

"Arrogant bastard."

"Brat."

"Pestilence."

"Hah. Get gone, or you won't be there before nightfall." Rufus said, but he kept his hands on Jionathan's shoulders, holding him in place. "Be careful."

"Only cowards are careful."

"Because cowards are wise."

"Yes, and they miss all of the best adventures because of it." Pushing Rufus back, Jionathan threw his cloak over his shoulders and secured it. "Now, I could stand and insult you all day, but I've got better things to do. Be ready to leave by morning. We're returning to Harmatia."

"Yes, Your Highness, I'll do that." Rufus gave him a mock bow.

Jionathan turned away before he could really see the saddened look in his friend's eyes. He couldn't bear it. How was Rufus to understand? This was a responsibility Jionathan should have taken years ago. How could he possibly know how much Jionathan had already delayed his obligation? How long he'd run from it?

Jionathan didn't deserve pity now. He was only facing what he'd postponed. Everything would all become clear when they returned to Harmatia. Jionathan had just to tie one last loose end.

Rufus walked down the orchard, toward his favourite tree. Fae was already sat there, nestled among the roots, her legs folded up to her chest and her chin rested on her knees. Rufus considered her for a moment, and then went to join her, settling himself at her side. She didn't look at him. There was an unnatural rigidity about her shoulders—not her usual, strange stillness, but something tight and forced.

"You're returning to Harmatia," she said. It wasn't a question. "I, too, will return home."

"To Avalon?"

"I am long overdue. My father is expecting me." Her eyes shone their faerie green, bright and magical, and very mournful.

"Pity," Rufus whispered. It seemed a crime to break the hush of the orchard. "I'm sure Jionat would have liked you to come with us."

"He would never propose such a thing. He's not a fool."

"I never said he'd proposed it, but he'd like it."

She gave a dismissive wave of her hand. Her actions seemed jerky, like her joints were stiff. "You shouldn't make claims on the behalf of others. How can you be certain of his true feelings?"

"I am certain. Besides, I'd have liked you to come to Harmatia, too," Rufus said. "You could see the beauties of the city, meet my mother, maybe scare a few Magi—the regular attractions of a holiday."

Fae chuckled faintly, and Rufus was glad to hear her laugh.

"You're right of course though," he said. "As it is now, we couldn't welcome you…but soon enough. Perhaps you can come see Jionathan's coronation? You can help fend off those throne-coveting cousins of his?"

"As amusing as that sounds, I think you can manage on your own."

"Me?"

"Of course." Fae smiled deviously. It didn't quite reach her eyes. "What with that explosive power of yours, you could scare them all away. Burn a few alive and the rest will learn quickly enough."

Rufus barked a laugh. "Athea have mercy—you're positively tyrannical. Yes, Harmatia could easily welcome you for that quality alone."

Fae laughed again and there was an edge to her voice that jarred Rufus. "Thank you for the courteous invitation. But for now I will stay away. Harmatia is a country torn from the inside. What place do I have there, as a faerie? I would only cause trouble, and you both have enough of that already." She exhaled heavily. "No, it's best I go home. That's where I belong."

They lapsed into an almost uncomfortable silence. Rufus shifted a little closer to her. "Everything happened very fast, didn't it?"

"Death has a habit of doing that," Fae said, her voice quiet and dulled. "As children in the Neve we are taught of the legend of Death and Betrayal. Twin snakes, both as likely as the other to bite. In the myth they could transform into humans. Betrayal would entice young men to fall obsessively in-love with her, and would then turn her back on them, and leave them penniless, homeless, and on the wrong side of the law.

"Her cruelty was matched only by her brother, who took pleasure in bringing people together, uniting them in friendship or love and then, when the unsuspecting victims were at their happiest, killing only one of them, and leaving the other to mourn."

"That's a horrible story."

"Yes. The snakes were representative of humanity."

"Humanity?"

Fae nodded. A muscle in her jaw twitched. "A human will always betray you eventually, and if they don't, it's because they died before they could."

"You can't possibly believe that."

"Yes I do," Fae said, stiffly. "I wish I had never met you at all."

"Fae, that's a miserable thing to say."

"Miserable?" Fae turned to him. She was smiling, but it was unnatural, and ugly, her eyes wide and a little manic. "Do you know how long I will live? Do you know how fragile humans are? You will fly through my life. You will be gone as quickly as you came." She spread her hands out, as if wringing the neck of some unseen foe. "Dying is easy." Her voice jumped a tone, and cracked a little. "It is the *living* who must remember. It is the living who must suffer."

"So you'd rather hide?" Rufus asked softly.

Fae went silent, her hands dropping.

"Fae, I know—please trust me, *I know*. We're the same, you and I. Magi can live double, triple the life of an ordinary man." He stopped, gazing down to his hands. "When Mielane died, I thought about living for over two hundred years, and the idea tore me apart. Two hundred years without her? I felt like dying after the first month. And what if I fell in love again? My mother and father would be dead before I reached a hundred. My friends would age and wither. I was so scared, I barely did any magic at all, limiting it. I was trying to kill myself, slowly." He flexed his fingers, drawing fire to them, so that flames erupted, and then flickered over his palm. "But the truth is magic is natural to me, and with my capacity recovered I know I'll live long. I know that I'll lose people I love, that I'll have to watch them pass away. But that does nothing to the quality of the time I spend with them now, *today*. They are worth the pain that will come later." He curled his hands into fists, extinguishing the flames. "I let my fear rule me, and it corroded me from the inside. Don't make the same mistake. Don't hide from us Fae. You'll only ever regret it."

Fae didn't speak, but her wide eyes grew heavier, and she peered into Rufus's face with an almost surprised curiosity, like she was seeing him for the first time. Rufus looked back, and realised that there were tiny flecks of gold in her green eyes—like sunlight peeking through the roof of a tree. The usual faerie glow heightened for a moment, and then dimmed, her eyes narrowing, though not in suspicion. She bowed her head, shoulders hunched almost around her ears now, her mouth curled up unhappily. The first tremor was all but invisible, and the sobs that followed almost inaudible, but Rufus felt them.

"I am sad," she finally whispered, and the statement was so stark and truthful it had a purity in itself. "It hurts." She cried gently, pressing her face into her knees. Rufus put an arm around her, and she leant into his embrace. She shook beneath him, her sobs stifled, but raw. "I love this life, the life you lead here. I don't want it to end—not like this." She sobbed again. "Not now that every moment of joy we shared has become fuel for my grief." She pushed her head against Rufus's chest, tears spilling out. "I should have known this would be the price. I should have known that these happy memories would betray me. I loved it *so* much."

She gripped Rufus's shirt between her fingers. "It's your fault—inviting me to stay when I should have left. I should have never let myself be drawn in. You made me believe that the story was wrong, and it wasn't. *It wasn't.*"

Rufus ran a gentle hand up and down her arm, his other cradling the back of her head. They stayed like this a while, until Fae ceased to shake, her tears drying. When she spoke again, her voice was tired, but clear, and she sounded more like herself.

"You're right," she said. "I don't regret it, not really. Even if this is the price, I would do it all again. I would betray myself every time." She sniffed and pulled back, staring out to the orchard, her eyes red-rimmed but her face calmer. "You have forced me out of hiding and now I will never forget Sarrin. It will stay with me for as long as I live and it will haunt me. And for that, Rufus Merle," she smiled, wiping her eyes, "I will never forgive you."

The capital of Bethean was built on the top of a hillside, and was protected by a wide moat that surrounded the entire city, making it look the whole thing was floating. When Jionathan remarked on the peculiar, but strategic layout, Michael made an off-hand comment that the patrolling guards on the wall were nothing to what lay in wait, in the water below.

Reaching the drawbridge, Michael shouted to the watchmen above to let them pass. Jionathan waved two pieces of gold to catch their interest. The watchmen lowered the drawbridge with a grumble, demanding an unreasonable—according to Michael—fee to pass. Jionathan paid without question.

"How do you intend to seek an audience with the King?" Michael asked, as the pair trotted though the streets.

"I have a contact in the court who can help me. But I need to go alone. May I leave the horses with you?"

"Of course. Where shall I meet you after?"

"I'll find you." Jionathan jumped off the bay's back, passing

Michael the reins.

"As you wish, Your Highness." Michael bowed his head. "I pray your business is a success."

"It will be." Jionathan gave a lifeless smile and moved off into the city alone. It was much smaller than the Harmatian capital, the streets lively, people still celebrating the first days of summer. With his dull expression and dark cloak, Jionathan slipped through the crowd, unnoticed as a shadow.

At the head of the capital, in the richer districts outside the castle, a finer crowd were gathered and mingling. Upon a podium beyond a wall of guards, Jionathan spotted the King and the Prince. But he didn't move for them, choosing instead to stalk toward a crowd of women. He made it almost all the way before being noticed, the guards drawing on him as he approached the gaggle.

"Stand back!" they ordered.

Jionathan raised his hands, happy to cause a commotion.

"State your name!"

"I am Jionathan of the Delphi, Prince of Harmatia," he replied clearly, and from within the group of women he heard a gasp. Aurora emerged, and ran to him, her red hair blazing in the late afternoon light.

"Lay down your weapons," she ordered. "Let him through."

The guards did as they were instructed, and Aurora hurried forward, Jionathan bending his knee as she approached, his head dropped in a bow.

"Prince Jionathan," she said. "It is you! I am so happy."

"Princess Aurora." Jionathan raised his head. "You look well. I hope you have recovered from your ordeal. I'm sorry I haven't come to see you sooner."

"I am more than recovered, thank you." She gestured for him to rise, and follow her back toward the crowd. "It's so good to see you. After you went back to the Korrigans' nest, I thought for sure you would be lost forever. Did you save him, your Magi?"

"Rufus? Yes, I reclaimed him." It seemed so long ago now. "And then I nearly lost him again a few weeks later. I'm not sure if you heard of the events that came to pass in Sarrin town, but we were attacked by bandits there."

"You leap from one heroic deed to another."

"I fear it's more that I attract disaster." Jionathan reached for her hand. "Aurora," he began, "Princess, I need your help. I'm coming to you in a desperate time, and I have need of friends."

"Then you have come to the right place. For all you have done, Bethean will ever be your friend, and so will I." Aurora gripped his fingers tightly. "We heard about what happened—your father...Please accept my condolences."

"It's not just my father." Jionathan swallowed. "Queen Reine has taken control of the kingdom. She murdered my mother, and my little brother."

Aurora clamped her free hand to her mouth. "Athea have mercy," she breathed. "Jionathan, I am so sorry."

"Please, call me Jionat. You don't need to be formal with me." Jionathan gave her a watery smile, trying to maintain his composure. The pain and fear was resurfacing in dreadful waves and he had to force it down before it won over him.

"Jionat," Aurora repeated. "Tell me what I can do to help you. Tell me what you need."

"I need to speak to your father," Jionathan said. "I need to warn him that war is coming."

Markus Anthemn, King of Bethean, was a man who exuded a sense of trustworthiness. Thestian had always described him as a man of honour and good judgment and Jionathan was strangely relieved by the stark similarities Markus shared with his daughter, Aurora.

With the same mane of red hair, the King was tall and square in shape, with pale eyes and a neat beard, like many of the men in his court. For all the Harmatian chatter of Bethean's weakness, the King before him was not the wistful, awkward character he'd been made out to be.

"My daughter claims you are the Prince of Harmatia, and that you rescued her from the Korrigans." His accent was full, like his daughter's. "Is this true?"

"It is," Jionathan said. "Though I can offer no formal evidence."

"No need." Markus seemed to appreciate Jionathan's candid response. "I know your mother and your father very well. I see them in your every step."

"You knew them," Jionathan corrected. "They're both gone."

Markus sobered, his eyes narrowing slightly at the sombre topic. "Your mother, too?"

"The Queen killed her, and the child she carried." Jionathan felt his own eyes grow heavy with the weight of fatigue.

Markus's mouth drew tight. "This crime cannot be forgiven."

"Nor will it be," Jionathan said. "I swear to you, the Queen will regret her actions."

"If it's reinforcements you desire, Jionathan," Markus said, "then in your father's name I will provide them. You are the rightful heir to the throne, the rightful King."

Jionathan felt as if someone had taken his legs out from beneath him. The thought of being 'King Jionathan' rattled through him and he drew in a deep breath, letting the title weigh on his shoulders like chainmail.

"No," he finally managed to say. "That's not what I need. Not yet."

"Not yet?"

"No." Jionathan held the King's gaze. "Forgive my evasiveness, King Markus, but for the safety of all concerned, I must speak in this broken way."

Markus's temper seemed to rise. "My daughter told me war was upon us. If it is not reinforcements you seek, then is this a declaration?"

"You may consider it so, yes." Jionathan said. "But not from me."

"Then from whom?"

"Kathra."

"Kathra?" King Markus barked. "The Kathraks spit on us, and we on them, but we've no cause to fight unless Harmatia turns on us. Why should Kathra declare war on Bethean?"

"Not now," Jionathan said, "but soon. And when they do, they will rain hell upon your kingdom and tear it apart."

The King stared at Jionathan, who gave a weary sigh, knotting his fingers together.

"Explain then. I am listening," Markus said eventually, his voice hushed in conspiracy.

"When I return to Harmatia, many things will change. For a few years there will be peace, but then a revolution will begin. Alchemists will scour the kingdom. The Magi will be outnumbered, and the balance of power will tip in Kathra's favour." He drew in a deep breath. "I beg you, don't ask how I know this—know only it is accurate. In thirteen years, a boy will come to you, and ask for an army. I cannot demand that you adhere to his wishes, but war is coming, and it is inevitable. If you give him an army," Jionathan said, "Bethean will be saved."

"Then why do you look so pale at the prospect?" Markus was more observant that Jionathan would have liked. He swallowed.

"Because that boy," he said, "will march into Harmatia and he will be the death of me."

CHAPTER
45

He watched her work silently, leaning against the wall. Once, she'd struck him with fear, but now the Bean Nighe was a sad and sorry friend.

"I thought you were haunting me, but it was Rufus you wanted to speak to," Jionathan said, though she made no sign that she could hear him. "You and I are the same. Bearers of bad news. I can't blame you for my mother's death, or my father's. You simply foretold what would happen, in the only way you could. But you're free now. Rufus thought it was him keeping you here, but it was you all along. You didn't need to apologise to him—he already knew. He loves you very much. You said what you needed to say, Mielane, you don't need to linger anymore." His gaze dropped to the armour she was washing. "But you came to warn me anyway."

"Jionat?" a voice called from the distance.

Jionathan turned and spotted Rufus leading their horses behind him. Giving Mielane one final smile, Jionathan left the river-side and walked back toward him.

"Ready?" Rufus asked when he was close enough, and Jionathan gave a quick nod.

Behind Rufus, the Rossignols had gathered. Luca and Fae embraced in farewell, and Annabelle stood clutching Lily-Anne's skirts, bleary-eyed.

"Then it's time."

"Your Highness, it's been an honour having you with us," Michael said, before Jionathan could muster any words of farewell.

Jionathan chuckled, ducking his head. "It is I who was honoured," he said earnestly. "You have been the kindest, most gracious hosts I could have ever hoped for. You are true friends, and I will never forget that. Thank you." He shook Michael's hand, tousled the children's hair, kissed Lily-Anne on both cheeks, and was engulfed in a deep hug by Luca.

"Come back to us soon," she whispered, and his breath hitched.

"I will," he said, knowing he would never honour her invitation.

Turning back to the horses, he checked the girth of his bay, pressing his head against his stallion's stomach.

"I, too, had best say my farewell now." Fae lingered with Luca, who embraced her again, tears now gathering in her eyes.

"You, too," Luca said. "Come back through this way soon."

"Nothing could keep me away," Fae assured. "Be well, dear Luca."

Fae turned to Rufus, who smiled at her, extending his arms. Jionathan was surprised when Fae stepped forward and, without hesitation, embraced him warmly.

"I think I may actually miss you a little in the next months, lowly lord."

Rufus laughed, kissing the top of her head. "And I will miss you. Tremendously."

Fae pulled away. "How surprising," she said. "I think I just heard a heartbeat."

"I'm glad to hear that."

Fae smiled. "An astonishing discovery. I will have to tell my people in the Neve—I found a Magi who wasn't heartless."

Rufus barked another laugh. "They'll tell you I'm a fake."

"You must be," she retorted, before leaning up and kissing him on both cheeks, her eyes bright. "Stay safe."

"I'm riding with the Prince of Harmatia. My chances of that are vastly improbable."

"I am here, may I remind you?" Jionathan snipped, irritably.

As Rufus took his chance to say goodbye to his cousins, Fae approached Jionathan.

"Jionat." She took his hands. "We didn't spend as much time together as I would have liked. Now I fear it will be some time before we have the chance again."

"Sadly, yes," Jionathan replied, forcing his voice out. He'd never seen Fae look so beautiful then in the hour of their departure. He never wanted to let go of her. "Fae..." He pulled her away from the others, dropping his voice. "There's something I must ask of you, before you leave. Something which won't make any sense now, but that I need you to remember."

Fae blinked, and then narrowed her eyes, her expression growing tense. "What is it?"

"If history ever repeats itself," Jionathan said, "and you find two idiots lost in a forest again, please take care of them. Just as you took care of me."

Fae searched his face. "And who are these idiots that I may have to rescue?"

"You'll know them when you see them."

"Do they not have names?"

Jionathan drew his mouth into a line and Fae huffed faintly.

"I see," she said. "The curse of foresight."

"The more you see, the less you can say." Jionathan echoed her words from the forest. He truly appreciated them now. "I'm sorry."

Fae leant forward and rested her forehead against his,

brushing her hand up his neck and into his hair. "Can you at least tell me that *you* will be alright?"

"Yes. I'm going to be fine." He closed his eyes and, tipping his head back a little, he pressed his lips to hers in a feather-light kiss. "Goodbye, Fae."

"Goodbye, Jionat."

She released him and, taking one last look at the Rossignols, transformed. With black mist billowing around her, Fae sprang forward and leapt into the air, her powerful wings beating as she soared away toward Avalon.

"No matter how many times I see it, I'm still impressed." Rufus came and stood beside Jionathan, his hands on his hips as they watched Fae disappear into the sky. "Shall we?"

"Yes." Jionathan turned back to his horse, and leaping up into the saddle, he kicked the bay forward.

"I'll write when I reach home," Rufus called to the Rossignols. "See you soon!"

"Travel safely," Luca called back, waving her arm over her head.

Jionathan waved in turn and then looked back toward the river where he could still see Mielane, ushering her last warning, invisible to the rest of them. He lingered for a moment, watching her as she raised her work from the river to inspect it.

"Jionat?" Rufus said. "Is something wrong?"

"No, just a passing thought." Jionathan turned his back on her, and urged his horse on. "Let's go."

"Yes." Rufus spurred Moyna in turn, and the pair moved off toward the main road.

From the river, Mielane gently placed Jionathan's armour back into the water, and scrubbed with all her might. The blood did not wash away.

476

The streets were empty when they reached Harmatia. Around them, the doors and shutters were closed, as if curfew had been set in the middle of the day. The horses' hoof-beats were loud in the hush and Jionathan was conscious of eyes peering through cracks in the windows, watching them as they passed.

The wind howled through the city, hard at their backs as they made it through the forum and into the castle grounds. There were no guards, or Magi, but again Jionathan felt eyes watching them from unseen places. They were certainly not alone.

Reaching the stables at last, they both dismounted, hunched against the silence. As Rufus went in to see if he could find a stable boy, Jionathan removed the book of dreams from his pack and placed it amongst Rufus's things. His visions would be safer in Rufus's hands for now.

"There's nobody," Rufus called from inside, coming back out into the sun. "We'll have to leave them tethered here for now. It seems the Queen has shut down the entire city. We're lucky we managed to get in at all. I imagine they've been expecting us."

"Yes. The Queen doesn't want the people to rally to my side, so she's locked them in their homes." Jionathan kept his back to Rufus, drawing a letter out from his bag. "I forgot to give this to the Rossignols on my departure. It's a formal letter of thanks. Do you think you could forward it to them for me, when you send your own letter?"

"Certainly, though they don't need such a thing."

"All the same."

"I shall." Rufus took the letter and tucked it in his inside pocket. "Are you ready?"

"Yes," Jionathan said. He had discussed his plan with Rufus on the road to Harmatia but repeated it anyway, if only to cool his nerves. "The Queen will be holding counsel in the throne room now. When I go in and make my claim, the loyalty in the room will be divided. You need to go to Lord Odin's chambers and fetch him. He is the only one who can sway courtiers in my favour and earn me the support I need."

"Then I'll go—" Rufus turned.

Before Jionathan could stop himself, he'd grabbed Rufus by the elbow, anchoring him back. Rufus looked around, surprised.

Let him go, Jionathan thought to himself, staring angrily at the hand that had betrayed him. *Let him go. This needs to be done.*

"Are you frightened?" Rufus asked, and Jionathan felt his heart jump. Was his fear written so clearly in his face? Sweat prickled in his palm, and he slowly released Rufus's elbow.

"What if—" he began, and then swallowed. He could feel his blood draining from his face. "What if I made a mistake? What if I interpreted this all wrong? What if—"

"Jionat," Rufus said, "you returned today for a reason. Trust yourself, trust your instincts. Everything will be fine, and if it isn't, then I will come and get you out."

Jionathan nodded jerkily. "Thank you, Rufus," he forced out, his voice wobbling. "Thank you."

Rufus smiled gently, ruffled Jionathan's hair, and then set off at a run toward the Magi Towers.

Jionathan watched him, his chest heavy. "Thank you," he repeated. "Goodbye."

~⁂~

Rufus sprinted down the empty corridors, his footsteps ringing loudly—a declaration of his return. *Let them know I'm here,* he thought. *Let them know Jionathan had come for his throne.*

Skidding to a stop outside his master's chambers, he almost lost his footing and collided with the door. Straightening himself, he knocked and then, unable to wait, burst into the room.

"Master, I apologise for the intrusion but—"

He stopped, his eyes falling on the empty room.

"Master?" he called, his shoes scuffing loud as he stepped in. A familiar uneasiness welled up inside of him but Rufus pushed it down. Belphegore wasn't at his desk, but it was possible he was in the store-room at the back, looking for something or arranging his books. He often didn't hear people, when he was in there.

Rufus moved toward it, straining his ears for signs of life—the shuffle of feet, the soft hum of someone deep in thought, the thump of books being placed in large piles. There was nothing.

He reached the door and pushed it open.

His master wasn't there, but what Rufus saw made his blood run cold.

The intricate design, the points within the circle, curved faerie writing painted elegantly through the twisted abomination. Rufus stumbled back. The Korrigans' array.

"No..." he choked.

"You survived." A voice rang out clearly behind him and Rufus whirled around. Zachary stood in the doorway, his arms folded. He looked like he'd had the life sucked out of him—his eyes hollowed out and skin an odd shade of grey. "You won't believe me, but I am glad."

"Zachary," Rufus hissed, throwing up his mental shield in preparation for a fight.

But Zachary didn't attack. He simply stared at the array behind Rufus, as if transfixed. "It's horrible, isn't it?" he said, tracing the lines with his eyes. "I can imagine it, Merle, seeing it for the first time from your eyes. I would be terrified." He frowned, emphasising the dark lines under his eyes. "To me, it's the single most beautiful thing in this cursed world. Salvation if you will."

"What's going on? Where's Master Odin?"

"With the Prince," Zachary replied. "He went to greet him personally. He didn't want the Queen's men to arrive first."

Rufus lowered his defence a little. There was something off about Zachary. More than just his unusual pallor, he was tense. His bearing was feral, shoulders hunched like an animal, listening out for prey, or predator—Rufus wasn't sure which—

and he moved jerkily, like he was nervous. Excited.

"And where was he when the Queen's men came for Lady Éliane? Where were you all when they executed her and her baby?"

"I never wanted that," Zachary said sharply, his arms dropping as he drew himself up. "We *never* wanted that. The Queen acted without our knowledge. Do you think I would have stood by and let it happen, if I had known?"

Rufus didn't reply. Zachary's breath had grown short and loud, his eyes bulging a little. Rufus's accusation had snagged something in his conscious, the small part of him that was still human and decent.

"Lady Éliane," Zachary said, and hesitated. "So she's…She's also—"

"Dead."

Zachary's throat moved as he swallowed, and he closed his eyes. "I am sorry," he rasped, and again there was a sudden nervousness about the way he stood, as if he'd been spooked by something. "She wasn't supposed to die. No innocents were supposed to die."

"You've been killing innocents all along."

"I killed criminals, Merle!" His eyes flashed open, and he snarled. "There's a difference. The curfew was laid out to stop mayhem falling over this city—to catch the bastards who killed our Prince! My orders were not kind, but they were necessary."

Rufus gave a long, harsh laugh. "Listen to you—all sanctified. As if you never enjoyed it. As if you didn't revel in the murders you committed."

"I like the power, Merle," Zachary admitted plainly. "And if you had ever felt powerless in the same way, so would you."

Silence fell between them. Rufus flicked his eyes across the room. Zachary blocked the only exit and it was clear he had no intention of letting Rufus pass.

"Tell me where Jionat is."

"He went freely," Zachary said. "He knows everything, he came to us willingly. He sent you here so you couldn't object. That boy's more intelligent than I gave him credit for."

Rufus felt cold, anxious thoughts rising through him as he searched the room for an escape. "What's happening?"

Zachary was silent for a long time. Finally he sighed. "Do you know that after Sverrin was killed, Kathra threatened war?"

Rufus's surprise must have shown in his face, because Zachary chuckled darkly.

"Oh yes," he said. "Harmatia assassinated its own Prince and the Kathrak King took the loss of his grandson rather personally. He expected the Delphi to be punished, not given the throne." Zachary laughed again, the sound cruel and cheerless. "You, who locked yourself away in the archives, how could you understand? You never felt the tension that rose in the court, you never saw, or cared what was happening." Zachary sucked in a deep breath. "Queen Reine was the only one keeping Kathra at bay. They wouldn't abide a Delphi on the throne, so she promised to produce another heir...Promised, even though she was barren. Now tell me, did the Delphi brat ever even consider that threat, when Sverrin was killed? Did he consider the consequences of his actions at all?"

"Jionathan loved Sverrin," Rufus said tightly. "He had nothing to do with his death!"

"*He could have prevented it!*" Zachary roared, making Rufus jump. "All he had to do was give the order! All he had to do was tell the Knights to stop and none of this would've happened. Loved him? The day Sverrin died was the single longest day of my life!" He seemed to lose momentum, leaning against the doorframe. When he spoke again, his voice was cool and collected. "For two years we lived every day just waiting for the Delphi to take the throne and Kathra to attack. And all that...All that because one boy did magic. All that because of one harmless mistake, that anyone could have made."

And in a flash Rufus understood. He looked at Zachary and saw himself—saw the depth of his love, and his guilt and his regret. And it all made sense. "It was you," he murmured. "You gave Sverrin those books on magic."

Zachary's mouth spread into an ugly grin, his teeth bared in an almost obscene display. "Oh, well done," he said. "You figured it out. Yes. I gave him the books. He asked me for them and I couldn't deny him."

"Sverrin's death was an act of evil," Rufus said, his throat tight. "He should've never been killed in that way. But he's *dead*, Zachary. And now we have Jionat and I promise you, he'll be a better King than you know."

"He could never be what Sverrin was."

"You're wrong. I've seen what Jionathan can do. He'll raise Harmatia from the ashes." Rufus took a step toward Zachary, pleading with him. "He'll push Kathra back, I know it. They will fall at our strength. At our King."

"Harmatia will never take Jionathan of the Delphi as its King."

"It already has—he's the last of the sons of Thestian. He's the heir, Zachary."

"Not for long." Zachary gestured to the array. "Look at it, Merle. *Read it*. Look at what you were afraid to see."

"I don't understand. I don't know faerie magic."

Zachary pointed at Rufus accusingly, as if he were a liar. "One life for another—one life, Rufus! And one chance." He slammed his fist into the wall. "The gods be damned, natural order be damned, because we are defying it. It took years, Merle, *years*. But the Korrigans were prepared to oblige us, were prepared to give us a spell that would save us, unite Kathra and Harmatia's strength again…and all it costs is that Delphi brat's life."

Rufus felt his heart stop, the world slowing—and then panic and rage overcame him, and he lurched forward without fear, seizing Zachary by the front of his robe.

"That's *regicide!*" he gasped, and Zachary grappled with him, shaking Rufus by the shoulders.

"No, Merle—we're not killing a King," he snarled. "We're *making* one."

"Get out of my way!" Rufus screamed.

Zachary threw him to the floor, straightening his robe. "I am sorry, Merle, but I can't do that." His eyes hardened. "Sverrin will rise again and your Prince is the price."

CHAPTER
46

Jionathan watched Belphegore closely and Belphegore let him, his expression grim and tired. Jionathan knew the leader of the Magi was still mourning Thestian's death. He also knew that Belphegore was bound by his duty, regardless of what that entailed.

When the soldiers tried to detain Jionathan, Belphegore ordered them away. He granted Jionathan some decency, and they walked side by side into the castle dungeons.

"You did well to hide this from Rufus," Jionathan said as they descended down into the crypts.

Belphegore heaved a sigh. "Yes, he is a perceptive boy. I was always wary he might discover the truth, which is why I left so much of the footwork to Arlen and his men. I am sorry that you and Rufus became so attached. It will make it harder on you both…I tried to discourage him, make him more distant."

"I'm glad you failed." Jionathan said. "Rufus is very important to me…but," he eyed Belphegore, "I don't need to tell you that. You *know*."

"I do," Belphegore said solemnly and something of the way he looked at Jionathan changed. They were both aware of each-other now, in a way they had not been before. There were secrets that Jionathan knew. "I confess," Belphegore said, "I underestimated the strength of your foresight, Prince Jionathan."

"I had an encounter with something that…widened it." Jionathan could still feel the ghost of Mielane's grip around his wrists. Whatever had happened in that moment, it had pulled back a veil inside of Jionathan. Now, his visions were clear and loud. "And it's Jionat," he added. "Just Jionat."

"That is hardly befitting a Prince."

"This is hardly the way you treat a Prince."

"No." Belphegore smiled humourlessly. "You are quite right. But you came to us of your own volition. You have seen the future and are sacrificing yourself for it. Therefore you *are* still a Prince—an honourable one, who puts his people before himself."

"Thank you." Jionathan felt cold and drained. His hands were shaking and he felt close to being sick, but everything else was dampened down.

"How much of the future did you see?"

"Everything," Jionathan said, his voice trembling a little. "I saw everything to my last breath. I saw hope."

"Incredible. To be so powerful so young."

"It was brought on by my mother's death."

Belphegore grimaced. "Your mother…I had hoped she might have escaped. Her death, the death of her child, it was never my intention—"

"I know what you've done," Jionathan cut him off. "And I know who you allied yourself with. I know what you *bartered* in exchange for this spell. The Delphi have never been your friends. You don't need to say any more."

Belphegore eyed him warily, and Jionathan moved on down the tunnels, following the Magi and soldiers up ahead.

The final chamber was larger than he remembered in his vision. At the back, he saw Queen Reine, adorned in great finery. She squinted at him and smiled, like a cat about to feast.

Closest to the doorway were Marcel Hathely and Emeric Fold, turned in toward one another as if whispering secrets. Jionathan caught their gaze and they watched him descend into the room. There was no malice in their eyes.

A hush fell over the few who were gathered and Jionathan approached the centre. There were two large altars stood there, the bodies made of a dark marble, with a thick slab of labradorite on the top. The one to the left was empty, but the other...

They'd preserved Sverrin perfectly. He looked like he was sleeping, rather than two years dead. It surprised Jionathan, stirring up childish feelings of hope. As if a part of him expected Sverrin to sit up, to grin at him and tell Jionathan that it was all fine. That he didn't have to do anything—that his sacrifice wasn't necessary.

But Sverrin didn't move. Lord Edwin stood at the side, fidgeting fretfully. When Jionathan caught his eye, he saw the feverish excitement and the nauseous unease of a man who'd achieved his dream, but knew he was about to do something abhorrent. Jionathan couldn't imagine what it must have been for Sverrin—two years without his spirit released, trapped in the darkness and never passing on. Now, he'd return to the light. And Jionathan...

A sudden terrible fear came over him—fear such as he'd never felt in his life, the terror of death beating in his chest. No, not death—inability. Inability to speak, to act upon his will, to reach out and touch beyond the reflection in the frame—and it filled him with horror. He looked weakly back at the door. He would never make it, if he tried to run. What was more, Rufus wasn't coming for him either. He was being stalled by Zachary on the other side of the castle. Jionathan was alone.

"Will it hurt?" he asked, his voice breaking.

"They assured me it would be peaceful, but you are the one who has seen it." Belphegore remained at his side. "*Will* it hurt?"

"No." Jionathan looked around. "I'll sleep, trapped within

that between-world until the day Sverrin dies. But it won't hurt. I won't feel any pain. I won't feel anything." He touched Sverrin's arm. "I promised I would die for you, you see? It wasn't right to ask me for such a thing when I was a child. But fair's fair, Sverrin." He turned to the congregation. "You cannot run from you fears because they will always find you. All you can do is face them."

"Wise words from the Runaway Prince," Reine mocked. "It seems he has learnt his lesson at last."

"Yes, I have. And now it's your turn," he said. "Because you are all going regret this day—make no mistake. There is a price for raising the dead and you will pay it ten times over." He straightened and looked back at Belphegore. "Tell Rufus..." he began, and then shook his head. "No, tell Rufus the truth. He deserves it, for once."

༄

"*Let me pass!*" Rufus bellowed. "Let me pass, or I'll kill you— *I'll kill you, Zachary!*"

Zachary wouldn't be moved, raising a shield around himself. Rufus threw out his own, striking Zachary's so hard it shrank back. Zachary couldn't hide his surprise—the difference in power was noticeable. But he stood his ground.

Rufus growled. Even if he was stronger now, panic muffled his mind. He couldn't formulate a plan and he didn't have time to defeat Zachary. Every second Jionathan was drawn closer to danger and Rufus had to reach him before the unspeakable could be done.

"*Move*" he screamed.

"I won't—"

"*NOW!*" Rufus lurched forward and snatched a book from Belphegore's desk. He launched it at Zachary's face. Zachary stumbled, taken aback, but he still had the advantage of training. As Rufus ran at him, Zachary grabbed him by the collar and swung him around into the wall. He pushed his full weight against Rufus, pinning him.

"Enough, Merle!" he snapped. "You have to accept it."

"Could you?" Rufus choked and Zachary stiffened, his eyes wide.

It took only a second. Zachary's grip loosened a fraction and Rufus brought his leg up and kneed him hard in the stomach, driving him away. Zachary doubled over with a grunt and it was all Rufus needed. Slipping past, he ran as hard as he could, casting out his senses for Jionathan, searching the castle.

He caught his trail and followed it, bolting down the servants' stairwell and then down into the abandoned dungeons and tunnels below the city. Of course they could assemble such a spell down there, where there was no sunlight to expose them and let them see the evil they constructed.

"I won't let them bury you here." Rufus skidded, almost falling down the crumbling stone steps. He could see red in the corner of his eyes and with it he heard Jionathan's voice. His laughter, his anger, his jibing and tears—every day that had passed, every minute that they had grown closer, everything that had happened in Sarrin. It couldn't just be for nothing—living through all that to die like this? Surely even the gods couldn't be so cruel?

He heard the cries before he reached the door and by then he knew the truth. The applause—like rain—hammered down through the walls. He broke through into the chamber with his heart already weak and sick with terror.

Sverrin sat upon a stone altar, looking out at the group of hailing Magi. They called his name in formation, as if it were rehearsed, chorusing with joy. He surveyed them all silently from over his mother's shoulder as she held him, weeping. Sverrin looked strangely fascinated by the crowd, by the taste of new life.

Rufus stared at the new Kathrak King of Harmatia, and began to shake, his eyes not daring to stray to the other altar at the side, where another figure lay like a stone effigy.

Belphegore, who was attending Sverrin, caught Rufus's eyes,

his own widening in pity as Rufus felt his stomach lurch. From the side, Marcel Hathely hurried toward him, face solemn. Rufus knew he didn't have time, but still he couldn't force his eyes across to the other altar. Fear chained him. He didn't want to see.

Not Jionathan, with his boyish grin and crown of curls. Not the boy who was so easily angered and so effortlessly heroic at once. Not the naïve brat who didn't know how to haggle and liked to draw, and still blushed at the sight of Luca's bare legs—*not him*.

But it was Jionathan, lying so peacefully he could have been asleep, his expression serene, untroubled, as if he truly had lain down willingly. His lips curved softly, as if he'd even smiled as he did it. There were no marks of shackles on his wrists, no redness where he might have been handled. No, there were no signs of struggle at all. Jionathan had walked himself to the altar, climbed onto the cold, lonely stone and lain down to die.

"Jionat," Rufus croaked, his head reeling as a pair of arms grabbed him from behind.

"Come away, Rufus," Zachary said. "Don't look."

But it was too late, Rufus had already seen. Zachary dragged him back as he kicked and screamed.

"Jionat!!" he howled. "No, Jionat! Jionat, please! Wake up! *Jionathan, please, wake up!*" The world tipped, spinning sharply on its axis as a darkness rushed toward him, ready to consume him whole. "*JIONAT!*"

"Fetch some water, he's going to faint," Zachary ordered Marcel urgently, Rufus's vision tunnelling. His screams died into a defeated whimper as Zachary pulled him away from his charge—away from his best friend. And still, even as his vision darkened, he could see it—see Jionathan lying there, gone forever.

And the world was black.

489

CHAPTER
47

Rufus felt cold—cold inside. He'd been confined to a room in the castle, a comfortable chamber with a large bed, a desk and shelves of books to keep him occupied. Yet the locked door and the mica-lined walls told Rufus enough to know this was nothing but a glorified cell.

He settled himself in a chair, and waited. A night passed, and servants came in to bring him food, and fresh clothes. He ignored them, his eyes cast to the floor, as the light from the bolted windows changed again from morning to dusk in a few, slow blinks.

He heard the cries and celebrations from the streets far below, as the curfew was lifted and the people flocked to see their new King. Still Rufus didn't move to go and look. His body was hollow. He wished he was dead.

As the moon finally began to rise on the second night, the door of the room opened and a small crowd came in. Emeric, Marcel, Zachary and Belphegore—his esteemed master and betrayer. Rufus didn't greet them. He kept his eyes on the floor. On the table, a tray of untouched food was sat exactly where it had been left and Emeric approached it hesitantly, looking down at the cold meal. Rufus hadn't moved or eaten anything in over twenty-four hours and for those who weren't used to his stints of self-abuse, it was unnerving.

"Merle, you must eat." Marcel broke the silence, his voice calm and collected. He waited for a response and, when he got none, gave an exasperated sigh.

"At least drink something." Emeric came forward, his eyebrows pinched together in concern. He lifted the glass of water and held it out to Rufus. "Please, Rufus—you look awful."

Rufus strayed a glance at the man. "Unless that's straight gin, Fold, get it out of my face."

"Oh for the gods' sake, Merle!" Zachary seized him by his front and lifted him clean off the chair. Rufus's back arched and he tipped his head up. Their eyes met. Rufus stared into Zachary without restraint, projecting every ounce of the hatred and steely anger that churned like ice-water in his veins. Zachary's grip tightened a fraction, and then he dropped Rufus and stalked away. "Do what you want with him, Master, he's a lost cause!" he barked and exited the room, followed shortly by Marcel and a crestfallen Emeric. Rufus couldn't say he was sorry to see them leave, but there was no space within him to be glad.

Silence plagued the room. Rufus restored himself in his chair and Belphegore sat down opposite him at the table.

"What did you tell the people?" Rufus asked dully.

"The truth," Belphegore replied. "Prince Sverrin was revived from the dead, by sacrificing—"

"Murdering," Rufus corrected. "By *murdering* Jionat."

Belphegore frowned. "The Prince is not dead, Rufus, not truly."

"Really?" Rufus tittered sickly. "An unresponsive vessel who'll never rise, speak or smile again. You call that living?"

"Rufus, listen—"

"No, *you* listen!" Rufus leapt up, slapping his hands flat on the table. "I did everything you ever told me to. I followed your word like it was gold! And all along you were conspiring to kill what I loved. Was I a spy for you, Master? Have you been using me all this time?"

"Enough Rufus, you're upset."

"*Am I?*" Rufus's voice grew hysterical. "Upset? Now why would you say that?"

"*Rufus!*"

The name silenced him like a blow to the stomach, but he didn't retreat back into his chair or drop his gaze. Belphegore stared his apprentice down and then sighed, slumping back. He looked exhausted. Rufus didn't care.

"Prince Jionathan told me to tell you the truth. He gave me the task because he trusted me to be faithful to my affection for you. Rufus you are my protégé. I did none of this with the intention of hurting you and the fact that I have is detestable to me." He sat up, resting his arms on the table, and clasping his hands together. "I promised Jionathan I would tell you everything and so I will. Please Rufus, if not for me, then for Jionathan, listen to what I have to say."

Rufus considered this request and then slowly sat down. Belphegore took this as an invitation to speak.

"When the Delphi Knights killed Sverrin, Queen Reine came to me and demanded I use my knowledge to bring him back to life. Kathra was on the brink of invading us and the Queen could not conceive another child.

"Being an apprentice to Lord Horatio of the Delphi in my youth, I learnt through him many secrets of the world of faeries. Despite the dangers, Arlen insisted on helping and so then did his men. It was through their efforts we were able to make contact with the Korrigans. What do you know of Jionathan's power, Rufus?"

"He has—he *had* the Sight."

"No, his ability went far beyond that," Belphegore said. "I am one of a few in Harmatia who knows, from first-hand, what the

Delphi truly are and why their powers are so strong. It is not only because they are the decedents of Niamh and the Tuatha de Danaan, but because they born of both worlds."

Rufus narrowed his eyes. "Both worlds?"

"This one—and the land below the sea. Have you heard of it?"

Rufus had. Myth said it was another world that lay beneath the oceans of Avalon. "That's only a story."

"No, it is quite true. I know that for sure. The Delphi were born of a Sidhe from Avalon and a human from the other world. Their innate magic therefore connects them to the power of time itself, to the land of the living and realm of the dead. This is what gives the Delphi their unique powers—the ability to see into the future, natural empathy, manipulation…all of these stem from that origin. And it was through that origin that this spell was possible."

Rufus processed this information slowly, taking it all in. What would Jionathan have thought, if he'd heard this? What would he have had said if he'd discovered the source of his power was something so ancient and strange? What would he have said if he'd discovered that that very same power was the reason he was dead?

Belphegore gestured around the room, oblivious to Rufus's thoughts. "Everything in this world," he said, "is born of something. These chairs were once trees, these books were once ink and paper. Everything we create requires a sacrifice of time, energy, and above all, substance. So too does restoring a human life. It was possible to preserve Sverrin's body using magic, it was possible to keep him breathing, but he was vacant. He lacked the main substance that would make him whole—a human soul. In death, it had been parted from his body and existed now beyond our reach in another realm. Do you understand, Rufus? A carpenter may use as many tools and nails and polish as he wishes, but without the wood, the chair cannot exist. Without the soul, a human cannot be reborn."

Rufus nodded. Belphegore went on.

"The only way to liberate Sverrin's soul and return it, was to offer another in its place. That would usually be impossible but Prince Jionathan is connected, through his power, to these other realms. He is a doorway, one might say. What was more, his blood-relationship to Sverrin, his similar age, their connection, made the exchange easier. That's why it had to be him, and no one else. That's why we were able to pull Sverrin back, at the cost of Jionathan."

Rufus sat, stony. "Are you trying to comfort me by saying Jionat didn't give up his life, only his soul?"

"Rufus, Jionathan willingly sacrificed himself for the love of his brother and his people…and for you. He thought of you until the last minute."

Rufus insides twisted and squeezed. "No, he didn't. If he'd thought of me, he would have told me what he was planning. He wouldn't have…not like this…"

"He knew you would stop him. Now the spell is done, it cannot be reversed. The pair of them are bound forever."

"So if I kill Sverrin, Jionat will also die?" Rufus said.

Belphegore's frown deepened "That is treason. You are mad with grief so I will let it slide, but don't let a comment like that cross your lips again, Rufus, or it will be the end of you."

"Will you sell me out, Master?"

"If I have to."

"You loyal dog." Rufus put his head in his hands, raking his fingers through his fringe. "Tell me one thing, Master. Does this make you happy?"

"It has nothing to do with happiness, Rufus. Everything I have done was in the name of restoring order and justice."

"Justice?"

"Yes, Rufus. Archaic as it may sound, when the Delphi Knights murdered Sverrin, they tipped the scale and unleashed chaos. This was the only way to balance it again peacefully—a

494

life for a life." Belphegore cast his eyes down. "And no," he said. "Seeing how badly it has hurt you does not make me happy."

Rufus huffed cheerlessly, pressing his palms against his eyes.

Belphegore made a small, sad noise in his throat. "You do not have to hide your tears from me, Rufus."

"I'm not crying," Rufus said. "To cry one needs a seat of relief, but I feel as if I'm endlessly falling. There's no relief. You've made me hollow."

"You need to rest and recover. The feeling will pass."

"I hope not. I'm afraid to hit the end—the bottom of the chasm. I don't think I'll survive the impact." He paused, suddenly remembering something. The letter tucked in his pocket. Jionathan had given it to him, saying it was for the Rossignols, but Rufus realised it must have been for him. Jionathan had left him his final words.

"Am I free to go, or do you mean to keep me here?"

"No, you should go home," Belphegore said. "I have sent word to your parents. They are expecting you. Rufus, take care. This grief will pass, I promise you. But until then, please, be mindful of your body's needs—food, drink, *sleep.*"

Rufus stumbled to his feet. "Yes," he murmured, distracted. "I may take a little time to myself…"

"Do." Belphegore nodded. Rufus turned and started toward the door. "Rufus?"

Rufus halted. "Yes?"

"Arlen told me how you destroyed your cap in order to fight him. You are very fortunate to still be alive."

"That's debatable."

Belphegore gave a sad smile, his gaze diverted. "It must have been painful."

"It was excruciating."

"I can only imagine." Belphegore kept his eyes on the far wall. "When you have recovered, do come back and see me. I will put another cap in for you."

Rufus stared, frozen in the doorway, and then nodded. "Thank you, Master," he said, and left.

Dear Rufus,

By the time you read this, I will be gone. I know Odin will have kept his promise and told you everything, at least so far as suits him, but I also know you won't be satisfied until I have confirmed it. That I did this all of my own volition.

It's strange, Rufus, addressing the future as if it were the past. I have seen everything of these last few hours—I even saw you reading this letter, you drunkard. You didn't need to be so scared of my last words. I know you're in pain, but Sverrin will rule well enough and hold back Kathra until a new ruler can appear. You mustn't forget, the Delphi were destined to rule. Someday, somewhere, someone will carry that bloodline to the throne, and you will live to see it.

Rufus, I know it's difficult for you, I know that my actions cannot be forgiven—lying to you has been especially hard. But I had to, because you have always been stronger than me, and I knew that if I told you the truth you would scare me away from the right path. You have allowed me to be selfish too many times.

You cannot know how valuable our time together was. Your friendship, our adventures—you made me into a better man and my sacrifice will not be in vain.

Do you know 'The Righteous King' by Saphar? I'm sure you've read it, the amount of time you spend in the library. It was one of my favourites as a child. I always liked the character of Douglas the best. At the end of the book he lays down his life to save the King. I always thought his loyalty was born of duty, but now I know the true meaning of Douglas's sacrifice. It wasn't about the loyalty to a King, but to a friend.

I saw a future where I ran, Rufus. I saw it in my dreams, and we were hunted. War broke out. Many were killed, you amongst them. I could not afford that, not when it could be prevented so easily and at so small a cost.

Rufus, there are so many things I wish I could tell you, but by doing so I would alter your future. I cannot risk the plans I have laid out. You have a heavy responsibility on you now, and it will stay with you for a long time. I am sorry to have burdened you again, but I have no choice—you are my most trusted and truest friend. Now put that bottle away, and go home. Your parents are worried.

Rufus's hands were shaking too badly for him to read the rest. The letters crumbled into a single black mass.

⁓

The darkness that greeted him was a blessing as he entered the front of the shop, the familiar scent of linen lingering in the air. He swayed and walked forward, fingers curled around the neck of the bottle.

"Who is it?" A deep voice called from upstairs. Rufus slipped past the serving desk and continued toward the kitchen.

"It's me." His voice was gravelly from drink. He heard footsteps hurrying down the stairs.

"Rufus?" Torin called.

"In here," he replied, putting the bottle on the table, his back to his father.

"Where in Athea's name have you been?" Torin demanded.

Rufus didn't reply.

"Rufus!"

Rufus stared at the table, his fingers dropping around the neck of the bottle. Very slowly he turned to look at his father. The sight of him must've shocked Torin because he went pale, almost shrinking back. Rufus took in the image of his father, the comforting familiarity of his face. His knees went weak.

"Father…" The world blurred around him, and his legs gave way for the second time in so many hours.

Torin caught him as Rufus collapsed, his expression finally breaking from its cold mask as grief raked through him. And at last, tears came.

Rufus held his father tightly and sobbed. He gasped as Torin hunched over him, kneeling on the floor and rocking Rufus as he came undone. After hours of falling, Rufus had reached the bottom of the depression within him, and rather than kill him, it left him broken. Death would have been better—anything would have been better.

And suddenly he couldn't restrain the howls, his muscles clenching as he bit down on his own arm, trying to muffle the screams with the pain of teeth against skin.

"Damn you, Jionat, damn you!" He grabbed fistfuls of Torin's clothes. "Dying's *easy*, you bastard—you had no right to take the easy road! It's not fair! *It's not fair!* Why do they always leave me behind?" Rufus wailed. "For once, let it be me. *Please, Athea, let me die too!*"

CHAPTER 48

He sat in silence, head resting in his father's shoulder as the last, quiet stray tears trailed down his face. He wasn't sure how long he'd cried but his energy was spent. He could have almost succumbed to sleep, his head was so heavy.

A sudden muffled cry startled him and he lifted his gaze to the entrance of the kitchen. His mother stood there, staring at him sorrowfully. In her arms a tiny baby wriggled amongst blankets—the cause of the noise. Rufus shifted, staring at Nora and the infant.

"Mother?"

"My darling." She came forward, offering him a watery smile.

"Who is that?" Rufus's voice was rasped, his throat sore.

"Piglet," Nora replied with a weak giggle, kneeling down carefully to show the child to Rufus. "He's not been named yet." She bit her bottom lip. "His official title would be Prince now, I believe. The Delphi Prince."

Rufus felt a jolt pass through him. He jerked back, staring at his mother, aghast. Torin shifted and stood.

"What?" Rufus whispered.

"Sit down, Rufus. We have a great deal to tell you." Torin

hoisted Rufus to his feet and forced him back into a chair, fetching him a cup of water as Nora took the child and sat by the fire. Rufus felt faint again, his head spinning.

"What's going on?" he asked—almost begged. "Is this some joke? A dream? What—"

"Calm down, Rufus. Drink." Torin forced the cup into Rufus's hand and refused to say any more until he'd drank it. Rufus downed the water, and Torin sat opposite him. "What I'm about to tell you is going to make you very angry, but I beg you'll let me speak. You've had enough shocks these past days but I'm afraid that this can't wait anymore."

"Secrets?" Rufus rasped. "*More*? Etheus blind me." He buried his face in his hands, weak and dizzy.

Torin hesitated before speaking. "I'll begin, Rufus, by telling you plainly that you've one reason to rejoice. The child your mother's holding is the son of Lady Éliane and King Thestian."

"The son of…?" Rufus looked between his mother and father. "But that's not possible. Lady Éliane told us herself the child was killed. She said they took the baby."

"They did," Nora remarked. "He'd barely had his cord cut when the guards burst in. They took the baby, threw me from the room, and dragged Lady Éliane down to the dungeons to be executed as a traitor. Unbeknownst to them, I went to raise the alarm. Your father rescued the Lady from the guards, and I went after the child. By the time I retrieved him, the Lady had already taken flight and we couldn't tell her that we had her child." Nora looked down at the baby in her arms, which suckled sleepily on her finger, his eyes half blinked open. "Queen Reine ordered for the child to be killed in front of her. We replaced the guard, bribed the executioner—one of our own—and replaced the Prince with a piglet. The Queen overlooked from a distance, but her eyes have never been strong. She heard frightened cries, saw pink skin, and smelled blood. The deed was as good as done. Your father and I then smuggled the Prince out of the castle and brought him here to safety."

Rufus stared at his parents, and then threw his head back, laughing. "Lords, but you're drunkards," he cackled. "Completely raving mad. Either that or I've been drugged again and I'm dreaming."

"Rufus it's true."

"I'm drunk." Rufus slapped his hands to his face, his eyes rolling to the ceiling a little madly. "Totally drunk."

"Rufus, listen—this is the Delphi Prince. If you love us, then believe us. We wouldn't lie to you about this," Torin said, his tone intense, and Rufus looked down at him. There was such sincerity in both his and Nora's faces that Rufus's heart clenched hopefully, his teeth chattering.

"It's true?" He didn't dare believe it. "Really? *Truly?*"

"Yes, Rufus."

"But—" He looked back to the child and sank into his chair. "How? Why?"

"I'll tell you everything," Torin said.

Rufus squeezed his eyes shut, trying to banish the confused burst of colours that shone there.

"You know about the origins of the Delphi family—that they came from Avalon and brought with them a group of Knights who swore utter fealty and allegiance to the family."

"Yes. What of it?"

"Many believed that the Delphi Knight disbanded after... certain incidents in the family. But we remain, working in secret throughout Bethean and Harmatia."

"*We?*" Rufus interrupted, sitting up sharply.

"Your grandfather—" Torin began, and Rufus lowered his head into his hands again.

"Oh Notameer, no. You're one of them," he moaned. "You're a Knight of the Delphi."

It all made sense. The strange snips of chatter Rufus had occasionally heard as a child, the fact that his father—a tailor—

had training in combat, the mysterious people who stepped in and out of their lives that Rufus was always encouraged never to speak of.

"Knights of the Delphi." Rufus shook his head. "That's why you saved the baby, you're Knights of the Delphi..." He laughed, ripping at his fringe. "Why? Why didn't you tell me? All these years, you could have told me any time. Why?"

"Because I didn't want this life for you, Rufus. Only those who pledge themselves can know the secret, but with you being a Magi, I didn't want to put you in a position where you might have divided loyalties...Rufus?" Torin murmured as his son shuddered, covering his ears.

"It was you." Rufus's voice broke. "You killed Prince Sverrin. It was you."

"Not personally, but yes, I gave the order." Torin looked weary. Rufus covered his face. "You bastard."

"Rufus—" Nora scolded, but Rufus spoke over her.

"You started all of this," he growled. "This entire chain of pain and madness—you started it!"

"Prince Sverrin broke the law. If we hadn't taken action, it would have been the end of the Delphi legacy. We were all but wiped out. The Kathraks—"

"The Kathraks? *The Kathraks?*" Rufus pulled his hands away from his ears and sat erect, staring. "Enough! People are pinning all of their actions on the Kathraks, pinning all the blame on Kathra. Kathra didn't force our hands, they simply did what they've always done—been a threat. You killed Sverrin because Kathra threatened. He was brought back to life because Kathra threatened. Do you see a pattern? None of you are making any sense! It was *us*, we Harmatians, who created this madness!" Rufus shouted, before wilting forward across the table, his forehead against the wood. He was too exhausted. "You began all of this," he repeated.

"I continued it, Rufus. But that doesn't absolve me of blame,

502

I know." Torin pulled his hands up through his own hair. "Don't think ill of us, lad. We did what we thought we had to. We had no way to predict what would happen, that the Queen would go so far. We didn't expect it."

"Nobody did. Least of all me." Rufus raised his head, and then dropped it lightly against the table again, with a thump. "I hate this," he whispered. "I hate this—every part of it. And there's more." He looked up with narrowed eyes. "I can see, I can see it in your face—more bad news to torture me with. More secrets kept by those I trusted." He stared accusingly at Torin, who stared straight back. Rufus felt his anger ebb away again. He dropped his head back onto the table, his hand reaching for the bottle beside him. "Tell me."

"My parents were born in this city and worked under Lord Vincent of the Delphi, the last remaining heir of the Delphi family," Torin said, choosing his words carefully. "It was his duty to maintain his line, but following a terrible accident he lost motion below his stomach and was left with only one daughter: Éliane.

"At that time that I was travelling frequently to Bethean, learning to be a Knight myself. During my time spent in Brexiam, a village on the border, I met a fellow trainee and the son of my father's closest friend. That was Michael, of course, of the Rossignol family."

Rufus snorted, his whole body juddering. "The Rossignols are also Delphi Knights? I shouldn't be surprised."

"Michael and I devised a system of communication from Bethean to Harmatia by using trade. Michael set up his merchant business in Sarrin and I bought this shop. One month when I went down to visit, I met Michael's cousin—your mother, Nora. We travelled back to Harmatia together, as you know, and she agreed to come and work in the shop.

"Queen Reine was pregnant with Prince Sverrin at that time. The Kathrak presence in the city grew, and Lord Vincent was wary of the attention on his daughter, Éliane. She was young and beautiful, and a powerful Kathrak family could've used a Delphi connection to make claims on Harmatia. As such, he sent her away to their home in the country and I travelled with her as a personal guard. During that time, I grew very fond of her." He stopped a moment. "Éliane didn't have many companions and so we were close. In the months we spent together, I became increasingly enamoured. And then, one night we shared a bed together."

Rufus's entire body tensed, and he sat bolt upright. "You…"

"She became pregnant. Lord Vincent was enraged. Éliane was the last hope for the Delphi line. She couldn't afford to have a bastard child."

"No…"

"Your mother was sent to the house and Éliane was confined there under the pretence of some illness, until she gave birth."

"No." Rufus shook his head desperately.

"The child was born just as the sun was setting."

"No, please, no."

"Lady Éliane returned to the court shortly after and attracted the attention of the King."

"No. No, no, no, no—please, *no*."

Torin stared at his son, his eyes filled with unshed tears. "And I took *my* son home and I named you Rufus."

Rufus refused to look at his father, his hands clamped over his mouth as he rocked, trying not to vomit. He felt as if his stomach had been wrung out, and someone was pounding against his chest. He stood and went to the kitchen counter, laying his hands flat against it, his shoulders rising and falling under the strain. Each breath was a struggle.

"I spoke too suddenly," Torin murmured. "You're upset."

The words set Rufus on edge and his hands curled into fists, hot flares coursing through his blood. "Everybody keeps saying that to me." His voice quivering with undiluted rage. "That I'm upset...I'm *upset*?" He spun on the spot, and swept his arm across the counter, throwing the plates and crockery onto the floor at his father's feet. "*Of course I'm upset!*" he screamed. "Not only have you *lied* to me my entire life about who you were, and who I was, but now you're telling me that my mother was that woman? And that the boy—my best friend—who I've lost forever...that Jionat was my brother!" He broke down and stumbled back into the counter. "My *brother?*"

The worst part was that, secretly, he'd always known. Deep within him the truth had been clear. Their blood was connected from the start—it was how Rufus was always able to find Jionathan, and why he'd felt such an unreasonable attachment to Éliane. He'd known all along, but had only realised when it was too late. Worse than that, Jionathan must've known, too. He must've seen it—the tone of his letter said as much. Rufus swept another stack of plates to the floor with a bellow but he was cut short by a shrill cry.

Within Nora's arms, the baby began to kick and wail, frightened by the sudden outrage. Rufus stared in horror and the anger within him dissolved to nothing in an instant. In his rage, he'd almost forgotten about the baby, and a terrible guilt filled him.

Slowly, and with limbs like a new-born lamb, he crossed the kitchen and reached for the child, taking him from Nora.

"Don't cry. Please don't cry." He rocked the baby gently, cradling him in his arms as he lowered himself into a chair. He let the child suckle on his finger, stroking his cheeks. A pair of stunning blue eyes stared back up at Rufus—the same as Éliane's, the same as his own.

"I'm here," Rufus said, and he whispered soothing words until the baby fell asleep in his arms.

Nobody spoke in the kitchen for a long time, and when Rufus

finally looked up, it was to find his parents both watching him tearfully.

He sniffed. "I'm sorry. I didn't mean to shout. I shouldn't have said what I said."

"No, Rufus." Torin's voice was hoarse. "*We're* sorry. You had every right to be angry. We should've never kept the truth from you. We have made terrible mistakes."

Rufus sniffed again and looked back at the boy in his arms. "He can't stay here. Harmatia's not safe for the Delphi anymore."

"Yes. We've organized for some trusted friends to take him to Bethean. He'll be cared for there and—"

"No." Rufus cut across. "I'll take him."

Torin raised his eyebrows. "Rufus…"

"I've got nothing left in Harmatia, I can't stay here. This child is the last essence of everything I believed in. I'll take him away, I'll raise him and teach him all he needs to know. And one day, we'll return, and we'll take back this kingdom."

"We thought you might say that." Nora came forward and put an arm around Rufus. "He is your brother, after all."

"Yes." Torin reached down and stroked the baby's head. "And nameless, too, unless you want to keep calling him Piglet."

"I hardly think that's appropriate." Rufus smiled weakly, gazing down at the infant in his arms. "We'll have to name him."

"Why not call him after his father? Thestian? Or perhaps Vincent?" Nora suggested, but Rufus shook his head, his eyes never leaving the child's face.

"No," he said. "No, I know exactly what to call him."

"Go on." Torin crouched down beside Rufus, who brushed his thumb over the baby's cheek.

"Joshua," he said. "His name is Joshua. The true Prince of Harmatia."

EPILOGUE

In the hush of the night Rufus pulled Joshua in closer and faced his parents, his face hidden beneath his dark travelling hood. The cart he'd bundled himself into was crowded with people, but they were all blind to Rufus and his precious cargo, as the driver negotiated his pay with one of the last riders.

"Do you know where you're going first?" Torin asked.

Rufus nodded slowly. "To the Knights on the eastern border, I know, Father." He glanced down at the sleeping baby in his arms. "I'll try and stay there for as long as possible."

"Be inconspicuous lad, the Magi will come looking for you sooner or later."

"They won't find me," Rufus said. "I've become quite adept at disappearing."

"I'm sure." Nora leaned up and kissed her son. "Take care and write when you can."

"Expect my letter to be folded in the next delivery," Rufus said. The driver climbed to the front of the cart and prepared to pass through the gates. "Goodbye, Mother, Father. I love you both."

"We love you, too. Be careful." Torin looked a little bleary-eyed as Rufus nodded again, his own gaze wandering up to the tall towers of the castle far off in the distance. Below them somewhere lay Jionathan, imprisoned until death, his mind stolen and life being leeched away. Joshua, akin with Rufus's thoughts, squirmed a little, and Rufus's expression darkened at the sight of his once beloved city.

"I promise you, Jionat," he said faintly, and his eyes glowed blue as he stared at the black shape of the castle, "for this, there will be blood."

GLOSSARY of NAMES & TITLES

COUNTRIES & PLACES

MAG MELL (mag-Mel) The main continent, comprised of Kathra, Harmatia, Bethean & Avalon.

HARMATIA (her-Marsh-ee-ah) Capital and kingdom of the central lands, stood between Kathra and Bethean. Founder of human magic, and home of the Magi.

- **ANAES'S FORTRESS** (a-Nee-us) A fortress on the edge of the Myrithian forest.

BETHEAN (beh-THeen.) Capital and Kingdom of the south-eastern lands. Divided from Harmatia by the **MYRITHIAN** (mer-Rith-ee-un) forest.

- **THE JAWS** A steep cliff that runs through the eastern part of the Myrithian forest.

- **SARRIN** (Sa-rin) A northern province in Bethean, with a town of the same name.

KATHRA (Kath-rah) Kingdom of the far north.

- **ISNYDEA** (is-nah-dee) Land of the Damned, Northern most providence in Kathra.

AVALON (ah-vah-lon) Land of the Sidhe, stood to the far east, between the sea and Bethean.

RÉNE (rhen-Ay) Country across the sea to the south of Mag Mell, known as the "Country of the Sun."

～⁂～

HARMATIANS

KING THESTIAN (Thest-ee-un) King of Harmatia

QUEEN REINE DuBLANCHE (Ren doo-Blon-shuh) daughter of King BOZIDAR of Kathra. Thestian's first wife.

- **PRINCE SVERRIN DuBLANCHE** (suh-Ver-rin) Deceased. Known as the Warrior Prince.

LADY ÉLIANE of the DELPHI (eh-lee-Ann of the Del-fee) Daughter of Lord VINCENT. Thestian's second wife.

- **JIONATHAN (JIONAT) of the DELPHI** (Yo-nat-an [Yo-nat]), heir to throne. Known as the Delphi Prince.

BELPHEGORE ODIN (Bel-fa-gore Oh-din) Leader of the Magi, successor and apprentice of HORATIO of the DELPHI.

- **ARLEN ZACHARY** (Ar-len Zack-uh-ree) son of RIVALEN ZACHARY & ELIZABETH DuMORNE. Leader of the Night Patrol.

- **RUFUS MERLE**, (roo-Fus Murl) son of TORIN MERLE & NORA MERLE (nee ROSSIGNOL.)

MORGO EDWIN (more-go ed-win) Leader of the Healing Sect.

MARCEL HATHELY (mar-Sell hath-a-lee) Second in command of the Night Patrol.

- **EMERIC FOLD** (em-Ah-rick fold) Marcel's apprentice and lover. Member of the Night Patrol.

PHEOLUS PATRUDE (fee-yo-lus pa-true-d) Harmatian lord.

SAPHAR (sa-far) A famous Harmatian writer & novelist from the last century.

- **CIARÁN** (Keer-awn) A Gancanagh from *The Lover's Sin* by Saphar.

- **SOPHIA** (so-Fee-ah) Ciarán's lover from *The Lover's Sin* by Saphar.

- **DELLATANIA** (del-ah-Tan-ya) A Knight from *The*

Barrel Men by Saphar.

- **ARDIOS** (Ar-dee-yos) A Knight from *The Barrel Men* by Saphar.

- **VESPUS** (Ves-pus) A Knight from *The Barrel Men* by Saphar.

- **JOSHUA** (Joh-shew-ah) The forgotten prince from *The Barrel Men* by Saphar.

- **DOUGLAS** (dug-Lus) A Knight from *The Righteous King* by Saphar.

- **PENSIA** (Pen-see-ur) A fictious land from *The Righteous King* by Saphar.

BETHEANIANS

KING MARKUS (Mar-kas) King of Bethean.

- **PRINCE HAMISH** (Hay-mish)
- **PRINCESS AURORA** (ah-Roar-rah)

MICHAEL ROSSIGNOL (My-kal ross-in-Yol) Patron of Sarrin town, first cousin to Nora Merle.

- **LILY-ANNE** (li-lee-An) Michael's wife.
- **MIELANE** (mee-Len) Deceased. Eldest daughter.
- **LUCA** (Loo-ka) Daughter.
- **ANNABELLE** (a-na-Bell) Daughter.
- **ROWAN** (row-en) Son.

FAERIES

FAE Ó MURCHADH of the NEVE (fay oh Mur-ra of the neh-Vay) Courier of the **CAT SIDHE** (cat-shee), a mercenary Sidhe.

EMBARR REAGON (em-Bar Ray-gun) A **GANCANAGH** (gan-can-nah) a Faerie Incubi.

BRUATAR (broo-Tar) A Changeling from the Myrithian forest.

NIAMH (neev) One of the Tuatha de Danaan, Fae's Grandmother and an ancestor of the Delphi.

TITANIA (te-Tah-nee-ah) Queen of the Seelie Court.

KORRIGAN (Koh-re-gen) Priestesses of the Sidhe Goddess **MORRIGAN** (Moh-reh-gen)

BEAN NIGHE (ben-nee-yah) Foretellers of death.

RED CAP (red-cap) A ghoulish creature that haunts ruins and abandoned castles.

TUATHA DE DANAAN (too-Ah-tha deh Da-nan) Descendants of Danu.

FOMORII (fah-Moor-ree) Descendants of Domnu. Also known as 'Elves'.

KELPIE (Kel-pee) A water-horse.

CHANGELING (change-ling) A faerie baby that has been swapped for a human child, or vice-versa.

THE TRUE GODS

ARAMATHEA (ah-rah-mah-Tay-ah) Mother of the Gods, Daughter of Danu.

MALAK (Ma-lack) Goddess of Wisdom, Travel & Merchants, Daughter of Wind.

ETHEUS (Ee-thee-us) God of Swiftness, Cunning & Thieves, Son of Wind.

PROSPAN (pro-Span) Goddess of Nurture, Parenthood & Farmers, Daughter of Earth.

HAYLIX (hay-Licks) Goddess of Arts, Elegance & Children, Daughter of Water.

PENTHAR (Pen-thar) God of Pride, Courage & Warriors, Son of Earth.

HEXIAS (Hex-ee-us) God of Will, Strength & Forging, Son of Fire.

SEPTUS (Sep-tus) God of Healing, Science & Medicine, Son of Earth.

OCTANIA (oc-Tay-nee-ah) Goddess of Creativity, Intelligence & Scholars, Daughter of Fire.

NOTAMEER (Not-ah-meer) God of Justice, Logic & Life, Ruler of the Day and Giver of Light. Son of Water. Notameer's star is the sun.

ATHEA (Ah-tee-ah) Goddess of Emotion, Battle & Death, Ruler of the Night, Guide to the Lost and Giver of Dreams. Daughter of Fire. Athea's star is known as the 'Red Star'.

ACKNOWLEDGEMENTS

I first wrote *The Sons of Thestian* when I was seventeen, whilst studying for my exams. In the years between then and now, a great many people have had a hand in seeing me, and the book through. I therefore have a lot of people to thank.

To my family—We Persevere. That is our motto. And throughout it all, I have tried to live by that. It wasn't always easy, but your collective encouragement, your love and your support have allowed this book to happen, and for that I am ever thankful. I know that Maman would be proud us.

To Séan—you lit up my life in a way I never thought possible and taught me that, for all my scepticism, there is such a thing as love at first sight. You have set me back on my feet after every complication, disappointment, or hiccup and you have done it all with a smile. Thank you for your—frankly—saintly patience and your love, both of which were needed in abundance during the completion of the editing.

To my Dissecting Dragons co-host, J.A. Ironside—I can no longer imagine my writing journey without you. Your friendship has meant everything to me during some of the most difficult periods in my life. You continue to inspire, inform and genuinely make my world a warmer, brighter place.

Thanks must go to my editors—Danielle Romero and T. Denise Clary who edited the first edition of this book, and to the wonderful Amelia Mackenzie who edited this latest edition, and whose ardent and unwavering support and friendship has gotten me through many a rough patch, and set me on the right path.

Thanks also to Stef Tastan, the wonderful artist who has

brought this edition to life with a stunning cover that is just beautiful in every way.

To the rest of my friends—Alex, Adele, Kari, Moe, Katie, Lizzie, Charlotte, Kathryn, Sasha, Gareth, Bryony, Rebecca, Tom, Jo, Hamish, Liam, Max, and more—you all supported me from the start, and I will never forget that. Thank you also to my work colleagues and friends at the University of Winchester, Enigmatic Studios and my Karate family at the Honbu. Without you, none of this would have been possible.

There are many more people who I haven't named here—friends, family and teachers who have rooted, pushed, and cheered for me. Know that you are not forgotten, and that I appreciate all that you have done to set me on this path. And thank you to whomever has picked up this book, for taking the time to read my little story. I can only hope you've enjoyed, or are enjoying it.

Lastly, there is one final thanks to give.

Maman, I was hoping you'd be around to see this day, but the cancer took you mere months before the book came out. I know, despite this, that before anyone else (even before me) you knew that it would happen. You were my inspiration in life—your warmth, your vivacity, and your courage are a mark of the truly remarkable person you were. Your unwavering faith in me made a dream become reality and I will forever be thankful for that. I miss you so much, but I know that you are here in the pages of this book, as you are in every day of my life.

ABOUT THE AUTHOR

Madeleine E. Vaughan is an Anglo-French author from the United Kingdom. Head writer and founding member of the Hampshire-based gaming studio Enigmatic Studios, she lectures in Creative Writing at the University of Winchester, where she is currently undertaking further studies.

A keen lover of mythology, Madeleine's nomadic upbringing has brought her in contact with a wide collection of cultures and folklore, which have strongly influenced her music, art and writing. Her particular interest in faeries was incited by her mother who, one day, unwittingly implored Madeleine to 'write something nice for a change, with faeries'. This request birthed the first draft of *The Sons of Thestian*, and the subsequent start of Madeleine's career. Faeries, as it turned out—to Madeleine's delight—are utterly horrible.

When Madeleine isn't writing or teaching, she enjoys composing music, drawing, and practising Washinkai Karate, for which she is a 1st Dan Black Belt. She currently splits her time between Winchester and her family's home in Horsham, where she lives in the middle of a dragon forest.

Find out more at:

www.madeleinevaughan.com
www.harmatiacycle.com

The story continues...

BLOOD
OF THE
DELPHI

*"Praise Harmatia, it is a city of gold and light. Praise it until it
crumbles to dust."*

Rufus Merle is a wanted man. After twelve years on the run—
raising the infant Prince Joshua in secret—the last of the Delphi
line now stands in grave peril. Sick, friendless and out of places
to hide, Rufus and Joshua are hunted by dangerous alchemists,
a deranged assassin, and a powerful faerie goddess, who will do
everything in her power to turn Rufus into a living weapon.

With the net closing around them, and the sparks of unrest
and rebellion igniting across the Kingdom, Arlen Zachary is
forced to question his own allegiance between the Crown, and
the people he swore to protect. As the gods play their hands and
the ancient Sidhe prepare to settle a century old feud, Harmatia
trembles under the tyrannical rule of a King whose only
commitment is to the dead.

M.E. VAUGHAN